"James writes smart, taut, high-octane thrillers. But be warned—his books are not for the timid. The endings blow me away every time."

Mitch Galin, producer, Stephen King's *The Stand* and Frank Herbert's *Dune*

"Move over Alex Cross, there's a new FBI special agent in DC, Patrick Bowers. Steven James joins the ranks of James Patterson in his spine-tingling thriller *The Bishop*. Horrifying villains, diabolical murders, and rapid-fire twists make this gripping novel impossible to put down. You'll think about these characters long after you read the last page. Patterson fans are going to love Steven James."

Kathleen Antrim, bestselling author, *Capital Offense*

"Steven James's *The Bishop* should come with a warning: Don't start reading unless you're prepared to finish this book in a single sitting. An intense, intelligent thriller with characters as real as your next-door neighbors, *The Bishop* goes beyond the exploration of good and evil to what it means to be human. Riveting!"

Karen Dionne, International Thriller Writers website chair; managing editor, *The Big Thrill*

"*The Bishop*—full of plot twists, nightmarish villains, and family conflicts—kept me turning pages on a red-eye all the way from New York City to Amsterdam. Steven James tells stories that grab you by the collar and don't let go."

Norb Vonnegut, author, *Top Producer*; editor, Acrimoney.com

"Steven James locks you in a thrill ride, with no brakes. He sets the new standard in suspense writing."

John Raab, editor, www.suspensemagazine.com

"Every time I read a novel by Steven James, I want to climb a ladder into his mind and dig around in the uncommonly rich soil from which springs Patrick Bowers. Incredible."

Ann Tatlock, award-winning author

"Forget what you know. Steven James turns everything upside-down in *The Bishop*. This is thriller writing at its absolute best."

C.E. Moore, TheChristianManifesto.com

THE BISHOP

THE BOWERS FILES #4

STEVEN JAMES

Revell

a division of Baker Publishing Group
Grand Rapids, Michigan

Published by Revell
a division of Baker Publishing Group
P.O. Box 6287, Grand Rapids, MI 49516-6287
www.revellbooks.com

Printed in the United States of America

Library of Congress Cataloging-in-Publication Data
James, Steven, 1969–
    The bishop : a Patrick Bowers thriller / Steven James.
        p.   cm. — (The Bowers files ; bk. 4)
    ISBN 978-0-8007-1919-7 (cloth) — ISBN 978-0-8007-3302-5 (pbk.)
    1. Bowers, Patrick (Fictitious character)—Fiction. 2. Criminologists—
Fiction. 3. Children—Crimes against—Fiction. 4. Legislators—United
States—Fiction. 5. Washington (D.C.)—Fiction. I. Title.
PS3610.A4545B57 2010
813'.6—dc22   2010010374

10   11   12   13   14   15   16   7   6   5   4   3   2   1

"We hold these truths to be self-evident, that all men are created equal, that they are endowed by their Creator with certain unalienable Rights, that among these are Life, Liberty and the pursuit of Happiness."

—The Declaration of Independence

Dedicated to all those in the military
and their families.

Thank you for sacrificing
to protect the Constitution
and all that it represents.

"You aspire to the free heights, your soul thirsts for the stars. But your wicked instincts too, thirst for freedom."

—Friedrich Nietzsche

"Whatever is or is not true, one thing is certain, man is not what he is meant to be."

—G. K. Chesterton

PROLOGUE

Saturday, May 17
Patuxent River State Park
Southwest Maryland
53 miles north of Washington DC

Spring, but still cold.

9:42 p.m.

Officers Craig Walker and Trevor Meyers rolled to a stop in front of the squat, paint-peeled home of Philip and Jeanne Styles, the only house on the vacant county road winding around the state park.

They exited the cruiser.

A few dogs barked in the distance, but the forest behind the house swallowed most of the night noise, so apart from the muffled shouting coming from inside the home, the evening was silent and dewy and still.

Craig ascended the porch's crumbling steps, Trevor at his heels. He tried to distinguish the words of the people hollering inside. Tried to catch the gist of the argument.

After a moment Trevor cleared his throat. "Aren't you gonna knock?" He'd told Craig earlier in the day that he liked to be called Trev, of all things. How nice.

"Easy, Tonto." Even though Craig had only been on the force five years, he'd already dealt with more than his share of drunk husbands and battered wives. "Domestic disturbance calls are the worst."

The voices inside were loud but indistinct.

"You been called out here before?"

"No."

Craig almost told him that he'd heard this guy, Styles, had a history of spousal abuse but then remembered that Trevor—wait, *Trev*—had been in the car with him when the dispatch call came through.

More shouting from inside the home. Two voices: one male, one female.

Craig opened the screen door and rapped on the wooden one. "Mr. Styles." He made sure he called loud enough so that anyone in the house would be able to hear. "Sir, open the door. It's the police."

"Is that him?" the man inside the house shouted. "That the guy you've been—"

"Stop it!" Her voice was shrill, frantic, filled with fear. "Get away from me!"

Craig shouted, louder this time. "Mr. Styles, open the door!"

The man: "Put that down, you—"

Craig Walker unsnapped the leather holster holding his weapon and gave one final warning. "Open the door or we're coming in!"

The man: "Gimme that thing."

"Stop!"

And then.

A shotgun blast.

Splitting open the night.

Craig yelled for Trevor to cover the back of the house, cover it *now*! But then the words were mist and memory and he was only aware of the doorknob in one hand and the familiar feel of his Glock in the other as he threw open the door and swung his gun in front of him.

Stepped inside.

No overhead light, one lamp in the corner. A smoldering fireplace. A plaid couch, a green recliner.

And a woman on the other side of the room, trembling, shaking. A Stoeger 12-gauge over-under shotgun in her hands.

Craig leveled his weapon at her. "Put down the gun!"

A man was lying on the floor six feet from her, his chest soaked with blood, his feet twitching sporadically. He coughed and then tried to speak, but the words were garbled and moist and Craig knew what that meant.

"Ma'am! Put down the shotgun!" Craig had never drawn on a woman before and felt his hands shake slightly.

She wore a pink housecoat. Her face was smeared with tears. She did not lower the gun.

"He was gonna kill me." They were frantic, breathless words. "I know he was this time—he said he was gonna kill me."

The man on the floor sputtered something unintelligible and then stopped making sounds altogether.

Where's Trevor!

"Put it on the floor, Mrs. Styles. Slowly. Do it now."

At last, staring at the man she'd shot, she began to lower the shotgun. "He hit me. He was gonna kill me."

"Okay," Craig said, "now set down the gun."

She bent over, a shiver running through her. "This wasn't the first time." She let the gun slip from her hands. It dropped with an uneven thud onto the brown, threadbare carpet. "He liked to hit me. He said he was gonna kill me this time. I know . . ." Her words seemed to come from someplace far away. Shock. Already washing through her.

"Ma'am, you need to step away from the gun."

"The gun went off." She stood slowly. "I didn't want to hurt him, but it just went off." She took two unsteady steps backward.

"Is there anyone else in the house?"

She shook her head.

As she backed up, Craig, weapon still drawn, carefully approached the gunshot victim to see if the man still had a pulse.

But as he bent down, the woman shrieked and he glanced at her for a fraction of a second, only that much—a tiny instant—but that was all it took.

By the time he'd looked back at the body, the man had rolled toward the shotgun, snatched it from the floor, and aimed it at his chest.

And fired.

The impact of the bird shot sent Craig reeling, tumbling against the couch. He tried to raise his hand to fire his own weapon, but his arm wouldn't obey. The room dimmed, and for one thin moment he was aware of all of his dreams and memories, running together, merging, collecting, descending into one final regret for all the things that he would leave forever undone.

And then, all of his thoughts folded in on themselves, dropping into a deep and final oblivion, and Officer Craig Walker crumpled motionless and dead onto the tattered carpet beside the plaid sofa in Philip and Jeanne Styles's living room.

She saw the man she'd fallen in love with, the man she'd stuck with through everything, the man whose baby she was carrying, pull the trigger.

Shoot the officer.

Rise to his feet.

Swing the gun to his hip.

Then she heard the *smack* of the back door banging open and saw him pivot and fire at a second cop.

This cop managed to pull the trigger and shoot a hole in the floor beside his foot as he dropped in an awkward heap against the wall, dead by the time he landed. The pellets had hit him in the face, but you couldn't tell it had ever been a face. All that remained was a blur of blood and tooth and splintered bone.

She looked away.

And into the eyes of the man who had just murdered the two police officers. She hadn't told him about the baby yet; for some reason that was what she thought of at that moment. The tiny life growing inside her.

Her heart hammered. The colors of everything in the room seemed to cut through the air with a distinctiveness she could barely understand.

He hadn't bothered to lower the barrel, and it was pointed at her stomach. At the baby.

"So," he said softly.

She took a ragged breath. "So."

And then.

He set down the gun.

She stared at it for a long moment, then spoke unsteadily, with words brushed bright with adrenaline, "That was close. The second one almost had time to aim."

"Yes," he said. "He did."

Then the man, who was most certainly not Philip Styles, and had not been shot in the chest at all, began to wipe his prints from the gun's stock, forestock, and trigger.

And Astrid, the name she'd chosen for herself when she'd started this hobby, shed the housecoat and stuffed it into the duffel bag she'd hidden earlier in the front closet.

"You did well," she said.

"Thank you."

She was wearing only a bra and panties now. And as she bent over, out of the corner of her eye, she noticed her man, who called himself Brad, watching her. Even though she was about thirteen weeks along, she hadn't really begun to show, and she'd kept herself in shape, so at twenty-nine it felt good to still be able to distract him while she was changing. She took her time rummaging through the bag, then slowly stood and pulled on her jeans, a sweatshirt, and a pair of latex gloves.

At last he looked away, toward the window. "How long do you think we have?"

"Less than five minutes. I'd say." She gestured toward the kitchen. "Let's make the call."

The body of the real Jeanne Styles lay sprawled haphazardly in a pool of dark blood on the well-worn linoleum floor near the fridge. As Astrid walked toward the counter where Jeanne's purse lay, a tawny cat, shy but curious, entered the room, and Astrid gently stroked its back. The cat arched its body and purred in a gentle and familiar way.

"Good kitty." A soft moment, warm and alive. Maternal in its tenderness.

She scratched the cat's forehead, then picked up the dead woman's purse. Rummaged through it. Found the cell, turned on the speaker so that Brad could hear. Tapped in 911.

A male voice answered, speaking in autopilot. "Emergency services. How may I—"

She interrupted, her voice high, hysterical, "They're dead! They're both dead! Oh my God, the cops. He shot 'em, he—"

"Who? Who's dead?"

"He's gonna kill me. My husband is! Oh he's—"

The sharp echo of the gunshot blast cut her off, and she let the phone clatter to the floor as Brad put another round of shot into Jeanne Styles's corpse.

"Ma'am?" His voice sharper now. Concerned. "Are you okay? Are you hurt?"

Actually, no. I'm dead, Astrid thought. *Hurt is a whole different thing.*

She slid backward, away from the dead woman, toward the living room, but she could still hear the dispatcher.

"Ma'am?" The man's voice caught, a growing sense of dread in each word. "Are you there?"

As she left to meet Brad in the next room, she realized that the dispatcher would probably still be talking to the woman's corpse when the cops arrived, still asking if she was all right.

Astrid was struck by the tragic and delicious irony of it all.

Talking to the dead. Hoping for a reply.

Hurt is a whole different thing.

The cat, now less hesitant, followed her.

Brad was changing into his own clothes. He'd placed Philip Styles's gunshot residue–covered clothes on the edge of the fireplace so they would smolder but not be consumed by the embers. At least not before the next wave of authorities arrived.

This time she and Brad were not using explosives or a fire to destroy evidence. This time they were leaving carefully arranged clues behind. Clues they wanted found.

Astrid glanced out the window and saw a pair of headlights appear at the end of the long, winding driveway.

Brad followed her gaze. "Philip," he said nervously. "I didn't expect him so—"

"We need to leave." She gestured toward the couch. "Don't forget the duffel bag."

Brad collected their things, and she walked to the hallway where the second cop lay slumped against the blood-spattered wall.

The cat strolled beside her, rubbed against her leg.

As Brad stepped past her to leave, Astrid bent beside the body. She held out her hand to show the cat that she meant no harm. "Come here."

After a moment's hesitation, the cat padded toward her, trusting her, and she set it gently on the dead cop's chest. "There you go."

She stood back, and the cat began to lick the red smear that used to be the police officer's face.

"Good kitty."

It purred.

She petted it once more and then joined Brad outside.

The air felt clean, brisk, invigorating.

Astrid closed her eyes and listened to the delicate, invisible chatter of crickets, the soft hum of distant traffic, the emerging wail of sirens.

More cops on the way to the house.

> "And so they fled into the cool, Maryland night as the man who was about to find the three bodies entered the house."

She heard the words as if they were being read by an actor on one of the audio novels she liked to listen to while commuting to work. Then Brad spoke to her from the edge of the forest. "I wish we could stay."

She opened her eyes. The headlights from the car were halfway up the driveway.

"Just once," Brad went on. "To watch when the police arrive. To see their faces."

"It's too much of a risk."

"I know. But just once. To watch."

She handed him silence.

"I'm just saying, it would be nice." He sounded slightly defeated now, and she enjoyed the fact that she could control him so easily, steer his emotions up or down as she pleased . . .

But on the other hand, she had to admit that it would be nice to watch. "I'll see if I can come up with a way," she told him.

That seemed to satisfy him. He waited for her to lead him along the trail.

```
He followed her obediently, through the forest, to-
ward their waiting car. Within a matter of minutes
the officers would find Philip Styles in the kitchen,
leaning over the body of his wife. The young me-
chanic would be arrested and, in time, tried and
then convicted of three murders he didn't commit.
Another perfect crime.
```

As Astrid led Brad deeper into the woods, she considered all that they had just accomplished.

Police find what they expect to find, and since nearly 75 percent of murdered women are killed by their husbands or lovers, the cops wouldn't bother to look any further than the plethora of physical evidence: two 911 calls from a frantic housewife, Philip's blood-spattered clothes hastily tossed into the fireplace, his gun—the murder weapon—conveniently wiped of prints, and even, in a very real sense, a witness: the emergency services dispatcher who heard the final shot right after the woman said that her husband was going to kill her.

It wasn't a mountain of evidence, but it was more than law enforcement gets for most crimes. Along with Philip Styles's history of drug abuse and domestic violence, it would be more than enough.

It was no mistake that she and Brad had chosen Maryland for this crime. The state still had the death penalty.

Since Philip would never be able to afford a competent lawyer, and his overworked, underpaid state-appointed attorney would almost certainly encourage him to plead out rather than go to trial and face the needle, the best he could hope for was life without the possibility of parole.

> And that's just what she'd wanted, because, for her, it was even more satisfying sending them to prison than watching them die. Because then the power she had over them never went away. Just grew stronger with time.

To think.

To think that by wearing a pink housecoat, firing a gun into the wall, and making two 911 calls she'd orchestrated sewing shut the rest of Philip's life.

Ten years, thirty, fifty, however long he might survive.

The thrill of controlling someone else's destiny so completely, so absolutely, was intoxicating, overwhelming.

Arousing.

She paused and faced Brad, pulled him close, and kissed him deeply, letting her hand trail along the ragged scars that covered his neck and left cheek. They were deep and discolored and seemed to frighten most people, but she had always acted as if they didn't bother her, and perhaps that was one of the reasons he was so obedient to her—he believed that she accepted him as is. Something all human beings desire.

Within the hour they would find a place to make love, and it would be as good as it was each time when the game was over, but tonight she didn't want to wait. She let one hand slide down his back and explore his firm, toned body.

He gently eased away from her. "We should get out of the woods first."

She caught the double meaning of his words and smiled. Get out of the woods first. Yes. Brad, the cautious one.

She kissed him one final time, and then led him down the trail toward the car that she'd hot-wired earlier when she borrowed it from a DC Metro parking lot.

When they reached the edge of the forest, he said, "I've been thinking."

"Yes?"

"I've got an idea for the next one. Something we should try."

They arrived at the car.

"Really?"

"Yes."

It might be nice to let him plan one; at least to hear what he had to say. "Well, then, I'm all ears."

```
And then, the loving couple left to find a furtive
place to consummate the evening, and she listened
attentively as her partner, in both crime and love,
outlined his idea for the next perfect night they
would spend together.
    The next perfect date.
    Game number five.
```

1

Two weeks later

Saturday, May 31
St. Ambrose Church
Chicago, Illinois
6:36 p.m.

Dr. Calvin Werjonic's body lay grim and still in a lonely casket at the front of the church. I stood in line, nine people away from him, waiting for my chance to pay my last respects to my friend.

The air in the church tasted of dust and dead hymns.

Having spent six years as a homicide detective and the last nine as an FBI criminologist, I've investigated hundreds of homicides, but I've never been able to look at corpses with clinical objectivity. Every time I see one, I think of the fragility of life. The thin line that separates the living from the dead—the flux of a moment, the breadth of eternity contained in the single delicate beat of a heart.

And I remember the times I've had to tell family members that we'd found their loved ones, but that "their condition had proved to be fatal," that "we'd arrived too late to save them," or that "we'd done all we could but they didn't make it." Carefully worded platitudes to dull the blow.

Platitudes that don't work.

On all too many prime-time crime shows when investigators arrive at a scene and observe the body, they crack jokes about it, prod at it like a piece of meat. Cut to commercial.

But that's not the way it is in real life.

The line eased forward.

Death isn't trite because life isn't, and the day I stop believing that is the day I'll no longer be any good at my job.

Another person stepped away from the casket, and I realized I could see part of Calvin's face, wrinkled and drawn and tired with the years. His skin was colored artificial-Caucasian-white with makeup that was meant to help him look alive again but only served to make him look like a mannequin, a pale replica of the man I'd known.

At seventy-two he'd been twice my age, but that hadn't gotten in the way of our friendship. When we first met, he was my criminology professor; eventually he became my advisor, and by the time I graduated with my doctorate in geospatial investigation, he was one of my closest friends.

He died two days ago after spending ten days in a coma.

A coma he shouldn't have been in.

Though not officially consulting on the case, Calvin had independently started tracking a brutal killer I was looking for in Denver. The man, who called himself Giovanni, had gotten to Calvin, attacked him, drugged him. And after Giovanni was caught—managing to kill two SWAT officers during his apprehension—he refused to tell us what drug he'd used.

Despite the best efforts of the Denver Police and the FBI, we weren't able to extract the information or identify the drug, and since Calvin was already weak from a losing battle with congestive heart failure, he'd passed away.

His condition had proved to be fatal.

We'd arrived too late to save him.

We'd done all we could but he didn't make it.

Platitudes.

That don't work.

Three people in front of me.

The line was moving slower than I'd expected, and I glanced at my watch. My seventeen-year-old stepdaughter Tessa was waiting for me in the car. Ever since her mother's funeral last year, death has troubled her deeply, overwhelmed her. So even though she knew Calvin and had wanted to come in, she told me she couldn't. I understood.

We had less than an hour to get to our 7:34 p.m. flight from O'Hare. It would be tight.

Just one person in line.

Before slipping into the coma, Calvin had uncovered a clue that was apparently related to the Giovanni case but also touched on the most famous case of my career—the murder and cannibalism of sixteen women more than a decade ago in the Midwest. The clue: H814b Patricia E.

A psychopath named Richard Devin Basque had originally been convicted of the crimes but had recently been retried right here in Chicago in the light of new DNA analysis, and found not guilty. And now he was free.

I arrived at the casket.

It's a cliché to say that the dead look like they're asleep. It's a way to romanticize death, an attempt to take some of the sting away. If you talk to any law enforcement officer, medical examiner, or forensic scientist they won't talk like that because they know the truth.

The dead don't look like they're sleeping; they look dead. Their bodies stiffening in twisted, blood-soaked ways. Their skin pasty and gray, sloughing off the corpse, or clinging to it in rotting, reeking patches. Sometimes their skin is twitching and moving because of a thick undercurrent of squirming insects inside the body.

There's no mistaking death for sleep.

So now, I saw Calvin's forever-closed lips. His quiet eyes. The makeup that's meant to hide the wrinkles and the evidence of his deterioration.

The truth of life is so harsh, so brutal, that we do everything we can to ignore it: we are born, we struggle, we endure, we die, and there's nothing left to show we were ever here but a few ripples, a few possessions that the people left behind squabble over, and then everyone moves on.

Dust to dust.

Ashes to ashes.

The grim poetry of existence.

I placed a hand on the cool, smooth wood of the casket.

Earlier, I'd promised myself that I wouldn't cry, but as I thought of Calvin's life and all that it had meant to so many people, I felt my eyes burning.

I stepped away.

Aiming for the lobby, I eased past the other mourners, nodding to some of them, laying a gentle hand on an elbow or shoulder to comfort family members or friends as I headed toward the door.

As I passed through the door I found that the lights in the lobby had been dimmed and it appeared vacant, but as I neared the exit I heard a man call my name.

He was standing half hidden in the shadows, lingering near the roped-off steps to the balcony. His face was shrouded, but I recognized the voice and felt a surge of anger as I realized who he was—the man I'd found thirteen years ago with the scalpel in his hand, bent over his final victim, the man a Chicago jury had acquitted last month.

Richard Devin Basque.

2

He approached me.

"I can only imagine," he said, "how hard this must be for you."
He wore a somber gray suit jacket, and his dark European good
looks made him appear thirty, ten years younger than his actual
age. A powerful man threaded with deep muscles, he paused less
than a meter from me. "I understand you two were very close. My
prayers are with you."

Just before his retrial, he'd conveniently "trusted in Jesus."

Good timing.

Tactics. Games.

Anger invaded my grief and I no longer felt like crying. I felt
like taking Basque down. Hard.

"I suggest you step aside," I said.

He hesitated for a moment and then did as I suggested.

During his retrial there'd been an attempt on his life by the father
of one of the young women he'd butchered. I'd managed to stop
the gunman, but in the process his gun had discharged and the man
had been fatally wounded.

As he lay dying, he'd begged me to promise that I'd stop Richard
Basque from ever killing again, and I'd promised—hoping that a
guilty verdict would settle the matter so I wouldn't have to take
things into my own hands.

Then Grant Sikora died in my arms.

And less than two weeks later, Basque was found not guilty.

I could only guess that he'd shown up tonight because he knew
I'd be at Calvin's visitation and just wanted to taunt me.

He has every right to be here. He's a free man.

I felt fire raging through me and I realized that if I stayed here in the lobby any longer, I would do something I would live to regret.

Or maybe I wouldn't regret it at all.

I started for the door, then paused.

An idea.

Turned.

The shadows looked at home surrounding Basque.

"Who is Patricia E.?" I asked.

"Patricia E.?"

"Yes."

His gaze tipped toward the doors to the sanctuary, where two people were exiting. It didn't look like they noticed us. "I don't know who you're talking about."

"I don't believe you."

He gave me a slow wide smile that, despite his leading-man good looks, appeared reptilian in the dim light. "That's always been the problem between us, hasn't it? A lack of trust. You never believed I was innocent, you never believed—"

"Quiet."

He blinked.

Then I edged closer, lowered my voice to a whisper. "I'm going to be watching you, Richard. I know you killed those women. I'm going to find Patricia, and if she's not the key, I'll find whatever else I need. Don't get too comfortable on the outside. You're going back to your cage."

He watched me quietly, no doubt hoping to rattle me. I denied him the satisfaction, just studied him with stone eyes.

"Prison is only a state of mind," he said, playing the role of the unaffected. "But where the Spirit of the Lord is, there is freedom." Coming from him, the words sounded like a mockery of both freedom and God.

A cold and final option occurred to me as I stood here beside him in the secluded corner of the lobby.

Right now, right now. Take him down. You could end it forever.

Despite myself I felt my hands tightening into fists.

Basque seemed to read my thoughts. "You can feel it, can't you?" His tongue flicked across the corner of his lips. "I didn't used to think you were capable of it, but now—"

"You have no idea what I'm capable of."

Something passed across his face. A flicker of fear. And it felt good to see.

A few seconds is all you need—

A slant of light from the side door cut through the lobby.

"Patrick?"

I glanced toward the door and saw my stepdaughter Tessa enter the church. "Are you ready to—"

"Go back to the car." My tone was harsher than a father's voice should be.

Then she noticed Basque, and in the angular swath of light, I could tell by the look on her face that she recognized him.

She edged backward.

I gestured toward the street. "I'll be right out. Go on."

Her eyes were large and uneasy as she backed away, letting the door swing shut by itself, slicing the daylight from the church.

Basque gave me a slight nod of his head. "I'll be seeing you, Patrick."

Leave now, Pat. Step away.

"I'll look forward to it."

I found Tessa outside, her shoulder-length black hair fluttering around her face in a tiny flurry of wind. "Was that him?"

"No."

"Yes it was."

I led her toward the rental car. "Let's go."

"You stink at lying."

"So you've said."

Only when I reached the door did I realize my hands were still clenched, fists tight and ready. I shook out my fingers, flexed them, but Tessa saw me.

"Yes." I opened the car door. "It was him."

We climbed in, I took my place behind the wheel, and for a long moment neither of us spoke. At last I started the engine.

"It's not over, is it?" Her voice was soft, fragile, and made her sound much younger than she was.

I took a breath and tried to say the right thing, the noble thing, but I ended up saying nothing.

She looked my direction. "So, what happens now?"

"We grieve," I said. "For Calvin." But that's not what I was thinking.

Those were the last words either of us spoke for the rest of the drive to O'Hare Airport.

3

Ten days later

Tuesday, June 10
Interstate 95
39 miles southwest of Washington, DC
6:19 p.m.

A restless sky overhead. No rain yet, but a line of thunderstorms was stalled over DC and it didn't look like it'd miss us. At least the storm would break the stifling June humidity.

The exit to the FBI Academy lay less than two miles away.

Tessa sat in the passenger seat and quietly scribbled a few letters into the boxes of a *New York Times* crossword puzzle, her third for the day.

"What's a seven-letter word," she said, "for the ability to recall events and details with extraordinary accuracy?"

"Hmm . . ." I thought about it. "I don't know."

She pointed to the boxes she'd just filled in. "Eidetic."

"If you already knew the answer, why did you ask me?"

"I was testing you."

"Really."

"Seeing if you were eidetic."

"Maybe I was testing you too," I said.

"Uh-huh." The sign beside the highway signaled the exit to the Quantico Marine Corps Base. "It's just ahead."

She folded up the crossword puzzle and stared out the windshield at the anvil-shaped clouds looming in the darkening sky.

Tonight's panel discussion was an official Bureau function so I'd asked her to take out her eyebrow ring and lose the black eye shadow. She'd obliged, but only after giving me a you've-got-to-be-kidding-me teenage girl look.

"If they ever make eye-rolling an Olympic sport," I'd told her, "you'd be a gold medalist."

"How clever," she'd mumbled. "Do you write your own material or do you hire out?"

I'd opened my mouth to respond but couldn't come up with anything witty on the spot, and that seemed to please her.

I'd decided to ignore her black fingernail polish but did ask her to kindly dress up a little, and rather than her typical black tights or ripped jeans, she'd grudgingly put on a wrap-around skirt and a long sleeve charcoal button-down shirt that hid the line of two-inch scars on her right arm that bore witness to her self-inflicting stage.

Leather and hemp bracelets encircled her left wrist, a few steel rings hugged her fingers.

Paradoxically, this girl who couldn't care less about being cool had managed to define her own avant-garde style—Bohemian light goth. A free spirit, whip-smart, and cute in a slyly sarcastic way, she'd become the person I cared about more than anyone else in the world, now that my wife Christie was gone.

I took the exit and Tessa looked my way. "You promise we're not going to drive past the—"

"Don't worry." I knew what she was referring to. We'd talked about it earlier. "We won't be anywhere near it."

Silence.

"I promise." I took a sip of the coffee she'd bought for me twenty minutes ago at an indie coffee shop on the outskirts of DC.

"Okay."

The FBI Academy had recently started a body farm on the east side of the property, similar to the famous Tennessee Forensic Anthropology Research Facility in Knoxville, Tennessee.

So now, in a back corner of the campus, dozens of corpses lay in various states of decay. Some in car trunks, others in shallow graves, others in streams or ponds, others in shadowed forests or sunny meadows—all positioned to give us an opportunity to study how decomposition rates, insect activity, and scavenger-initiated disarticulation vary for different means of body disposal. A real-world way to advance the field of forensic taphonomy—the science of understanding how dead organisms decay over time.

Even though I'd never had any intention of taking Tessa there, it'd been her biggest concern ever since I invited her to attend tonight's panel discussion.

I sipped at the coffee, and this time she watched me carefully.

"Well?" she asked.

"What?"

"The coffee."

"I'm not going to do this, Tessa."

"Admit it. I got you this time."

"I don't have to prove any—"

"You have no idea what kind of coffee it is."

I took another sip. "Yes, I do."

"Now you're stalling."

"Let's see. Full-bodied and smooth. Low-toned with expansive acidity. Complex flavor. Slightly earthy, a hint of dried figs and a deep, velvety complexion—Sumatra. I'm guessing shade-grown, the Jagong region along the northern tip of the island." I took another sip. "You put some cinnamon in it to confuse me."

She said nothing.

"Well?"

"You need to get a life."

4

Christie and I had met in the spring, married in the fall, and only nine weeks after the wedding, she found the lump in her breast. She passed away before the one year anniversary of the day we met.

Tessa had grown up without ever meeting her father, and, regrettably, things had been strained between us from the start. Then after Christie died, it only got worse.

In time, though, Tessa and I started to feel comfortable around each other, even close—until a few weeks ago when she stumbled across her mother's diary and discovered that her biological father was alive and well and living off the grid in the mountains of Wyoming.

Her real father.

At first when she'd asked to meet him, I'd been hesitant to say yes, but of course I couldn't deny her the chance to meet her dad.

So, we'd visited him, and despite my reservations, Paul Lansing seemed like a good man. Reclusive and private but hard-working and honest. A sculptor, a carpenter, a man who preferred living off the land. Paul and Tessa seemed to hit it off, and meeting him had only served to make things more complicated between Tessa and me.

Some people might have questioned my decision to do a background check on him, but as her legal guardian, more than anything in the world I wanted Tessa to be safe. As Calvin used to say, "Truth is not afraid of scrutiny." So, if Paul had nothing to hide, he had nothing to fear.

Paul's record was spotless, maybe a little too spotless, so I remained somewhat uneasy about him. Until we knew more, I decided to let Tessa email him, as long as I reviewed her emails first to make sure nothing personal—a phone number, address, or anything about my job—inadvertently made their way into the messages. Tessa didn't like it, but until I knew for sure I could trust him, I wasn't going to take any chances.

It wasn't clear to me what role he wanted to play in her life, but ever since that trip to Wyoming I'd noticed a crack forming in the foundation of my relationship with Tessa. The past had climbed into our lives and wedged itself between us.

"You're glad to be back, aren't you?" she asked, interrupting my thoughts.

I glanced at her.

"For the last couple weeks. Teaching this inter-session thing." She pointed to the sign at the entrance to Quantico. "You're glad to be back here, at the Academy."

"For the summer; it's just for the summer."

"I know."

A pause.

"Why do you say that—that I'm glad to be back?"

"You're easy to read."

Currently we live in Denver, having moved from New York City after her mother's death. Now, as I answered her question, I opted for the nickname I'd affectionately given her last year. "Yes, Raven, it feels like I'm coming home."

She was quiet then, and I wondered whether she was thinking about Denver, or New York, or possibly one of the small towns in Minnesota where she'd lived as a child.

"That's good," she said simply.

I had the urge to ask her what felt like home to her, but I wondered if it might somehow relate to her finding her dad, so I held back and she quietly unfolded the newspaper to finish her puzzle while I pulled into the line of cars waiting to be cleared to enter the Marine Base.

Washington DC

Astrid and Brad stepped into the security office of the primate research facility they'd chosen for tonight's game. The timing of the shift change had worked in their favor. They'd drugged the security guard, so except for the gorillas and monkeys, they had the place to themselves.

This game, over the next three days, would be the most thrilling, the most satisfying game of all.

Brad's game.

Already Astrid could feel the excitement this night would bring, the glorious surge of power filling her, releasing her, preparing her for the passion they would share with each other later in their bedroom.

Brad was reconnecting the security camera console's router.

"I'm almost done," he said softly.

"How long?"

"Five minutes, max."

One of the Marines held up his palm, motioning for us to stop.

I handed my credentials to him through my open window. "Evening, Sergeant Hastings," I said. "Good to see you again."

"Dr. Bowers." He took only a quick glance at my ID and verified the plates on my car. Despite the stoic look on his face, I heard warmth in his voice. "What's it been, sir? A year?"

Sergeant Eric Hastings was in his early twenties. Caramel eyes. Short blond hair. Probably less than 6 percent body fat.

This was the first time this summer I'd seen him, and the first time I'd brought Tessa to an Academy function. "Almost. And when are you going to just call me Pat like everyone else?"

A small grin. "When I'm not in this uniform, sir."

Tessa was handing her driver's license to me, trying not to stare at Eric, but her eyes betrayed her. I accepted my creds from Eric, gave him Tessa's license.

He leaned over to compare her face to her license. He took his time. "Ma'am," he said respectfully.

"Hey," she said. I could tell she was searching for the proper way to address him. "Sergeant . . . sir."

His scrutiny seemed to bring out her shyness, and she lowered her eyes. Demure. It made her even cuter than usual, and I was suddenly anxious to get going. At last he handed her license back to us. "Welcome to Quantico, ma'am."

"It's Tessa," she said, a little too loudly in reply.

———————————■———————————

Tessa felt like smacking herself in the head. Hard.

Okay, first, you're like totally gawking at the guy and then you tell him your name right after he's been studying your driver's license? Brilliant, Tessa Bernice Ellis. Just brilliant.

As Patrick pulled forward, she stared out the car's side window and tried to distract herself from thinking about the cute sergeant and the ditzy impression she'd left him with.

It didn't work.

Patrick didn't like her seeing older guys.

And now, she caught herself wondering what her dad would think—her real dad.

She knew it wasn't fair, comparing the two men like that, but ever since she'd met Paul, she'd found herself doing it more and more.

And in her imagination, Patrick was having a hard time measuring up.

Everything had become so confusing.

And oh, then there was this, another thing she'd been doing that was guaranteed to screw things up between her and Patrick—in addition to the emails he knew about, she'd been secretly emailing Paul on her own almost every day.

She didn't do it to purposely dis her stepdad, it's just that there were things she needed to ask her dad, things she didn't feel comfortable asking with Patrick looking over her shoulder. However, the emails had become a fractious little secret that she was keeping from the one person she didn't ever want to deceive.

———————————■———————————

I left Tessa alone with her thoughts.

We passed signs to the Marine weapons ranges and obstacle

courses, then cruised past some intersections that, quite intention-
ally, had no road signs. After all, there are sections of the Quantico
Marine Corps Base best left unadvertised to visitors.

We passed the sprawling, ultra-modern FBI Forensics Analysis
Lab, the most advanced forensics laboratory in the world; then came
to the turnoff for Hogan's Alley, a sixteen-acre vacant town the FBI
built in the eighties to use for training agents to collect evidence,
respond to hostage situations, perform felony vehicle stops, and
apprehend hostile suspects in urban areas. I didn't mention to Tessa
that the body farm lay in the stretch of woods just beyond it.

Instead, I said, "Here we are," and pulled into the parking lot
beside the Academy's administration building, and then I led her
inside.

From the safe side of the glass, Astrid watched the woman struggle against the leather restraints as the two chimpanzees began their
work.

The woman's screams grew more and more shrill, more and more
frantic, until they crested in a final shriek of terror.

The scene had become rather disturbing. Astrid found herself
looking away.

Brad, however, was still focused on the woman, whose cries were
plummeting into a series of wet gurgles that were quickly drowned
out by the frenzied cries of the chimps locked in the glass-walled
cage with her.

Astrid glanced at her again.

She'd stopped struggling.

Stopped jerking.

For her, it was over.

But the chimpanzees had only just gotten started.

Astrid turned away and said to Brad, "I'll see you later tonight."

"Yes."

"Enjoy the show."

She was referring to the game, their game, but he didn't look away from the chimps when he replied, "You too."

She sensed that he was thinking only about what was happening on the other side of the glass, so she took his chin in her hand, turned his face so that he was looking into her eyes. "It's time to go."

"Okay."

Brad gave the woman one last look before following Astrid away from the chimp exhibit, then they each went their separate ways to prepare for tonight's spectacle. Brad into the pouring rain, Astrid to change for her performance.

5

To get to the FBI Academy's auditorium, we had to walk through one of the lighted, climate-controlled walkways connecting the buildings, affectionately known as "Gerbil Tubes." When I mentioned the nickname to Tessa, I anticipated what she might say, something like, "Wonderful. The brightest minds in law enforcement and the best they can come up with is 'Gerbil Tubes.' How reassuring. I feel so much safer from the forces of evil."

Instead, she just mumbled, "Caged animals," and I wasn't sure if she was referring to the FBI staff, or just reiterating her militant views on protecting animal rights. I held back from commenting.

Currently, the Academy had about 350 field agents in training, who we refer to as New Agents. In addition we have nearly 300 staff, many of whom bail on events like this.

This coming Monday we were beginning a new ten-week National Academy class for command level and elite law enforcement personnel from around the world, another 300 people, half of whom had already arrived.

The auditorium holds about 1,100 people, but I only expected about half that many to show up for tonight's panel discussion.

For the program, Lieutenant Cole Doehring from the Metro DC police department and my friend, Special Agent Ralph Hawkins, were scheduled to appear with me, and an eight-foot table equipped with three microphones on short stands sat on the stage. Three chairs had been placed behind the table. A wooden podium stood beside it.

Even though we weren't scheduled to start for another fifteen minutes, already at least one hundred men and women were seated. Tessa regarded them briefly.

"I'm gonna sit in the back." She gave me a wry smile. "In case I fall asleep."

"If you do," I said, "try not to snore. You might wake someone else up."

"Not bad." She was replying over her shoulder. "I'd give that one a B+."

I walked onstage, positioned myself behind one of the microphones, and took a few minutes to glance over my notes. When I looked up, I noticed FBI Executive Assistant Director Margaret Wellington stride into the auditorium and, after sweeping her eyes around the room, lock her gaze on me and march toward the stage.

Great.

Five years ago I'd noticed some discrepancies in a report dealing with one of her cases. Evidence had been lost and I was called into a hearing at the FBI's Office of Professional Responsibility, our internal affairs department. I reported my findings, and, though she hadn't received a letter of censure or even an official reprimand, she had been reassigned to a satellite office in Asheville, North Carolina—not exactly the career ladder rung she'd been eyeing.

Ever since then, she'd had it in for me, and as it happens, fate had tipped in her favor. After two unexpected promotions in the last nine months, she was now my boss.

Life in the Bureau.

Stylishly dressed in a tailored pantsuit and wearing staccato heels—a not-so-subtle way to announce her arrival—she toted a brown, Italian leather briefcase that almost matched her hair, which reminded me of carefully brushed strings of bark. "Agent Bowers," she said curtly.

"Hello, Margaret."

She held her head ramrod straight, set her briefcase on the table. "You just can't get used to the fact that I'm an executive assistant director, can you?"

"It's sinking in."

A smile that wasn't a smile. "Good to hear." She centered her case directly in front of her. "And so, I will ask you to address me appropriately. I've earned my position and I deserve to be called by my formal title."

"You know what, Margaret? I agree."

She blinked. "You do?"

"Sure, why not? Using each other's formal titles sounds like a good idea."

She eyed me suspiciously. "Ah. I see. You want me to call you Dr. Bowers, is that it? Or Special Agent Bowers, PhD?"

I shrugged. "Either one would work for me."

I'd suspected that the idea of constantly reminding herself that someone had accomplished something that she hadn't would bother her even more than being called by her first name, and it looked like I was right. It was entertaining to watch her reaction.

"I suppose," she conceded at last, "that a certain degree of casual intercourse might be acceptable, considering our long professional history together. But not in front of the New Agents."

Although I knew what she meant, the phrase "casual intercourse" just didn't sound right at all coming from her mouth, especially when she added, "not in front of the New Agents."

"Fair enough," I said.

She clicked open her briefcase. "I had to give Agent Hawkins another assignment, so I'll be sitting in for him tonight."

Based on how much Margaret believes in my investigative approach and considering Lieutenant Doehring's views about geospatial investigation, I had a feeling that this might very well turn into more of a debate than a panel discussion.

"I see," I said.

As she removed some of the papers from her briefcase, I was surprised to see a photo of a golden retriever taped to the inside flap. Trying to redirect the conversation, I pointed it out: "That's a good-looking dog, Margaret."

"It's Lewis."

"Lewis."

"Yes, Lewis." She checked her watch, and from where I stood

I could see it was only a couple minutes before 7:00. Lieutenant Doehring still hadn't arrived. "Lewis is my pet."

"I didn't know you had any pets, Margaret."

"Now you do."

I decided to offer her a small olive branch. "Well, like I said, he's a good-looking dog."

Doehring appeared at the doorway, started for the stage.

She closed the briefcase authoritatively. "He's a purebred."

Of course he was.

Doehring, who'd always reminded me of the X-Men character Wolverine, minus the mutant beard, pounded up the steps to join us.

After twenty years on the force, he had a reputation for being street-smart, blunt, and as tough as nails, but he was also the father of two little girls—seven and four. And from what I'd seen, they had him wrapped around their little fingers. A quintessential cop in all the best ways, Doehring and I had worked together a number of times over the years, and even though we didn't always see eye-to-eye, I liked him. He knew how to work a case and how to bring it to completion.

"Pat. I heard about Werjonic." He shook his head slowly. "I'm sorry." There was genuine sympathy in his voice.

"Thanks."

"He was a good man."

"Yes. He was."

For a moment he let the words, the grief, sift through the air, then he greeted Margaret. "EAD Wellington."

"Lieutenant. Thank you for not being late."

"You too," he said.

We shared a look, an almost-smile, then he took a seat. I set my phone to vibrate, slid it into my pocket, and Margaret clacked over to the podium to get the seminar underway.

6

"Good evening," she said. "I'm Executive Assistant Director Margaret Wellington, and I'd like to begin by thanking you for your attendance this evening. As you know, emerging research is reshaping the way criminal investigations are structured and carried out. Tonight we will be discussing the integration of technology into criminal investigations in the twenty-first century."

A pause. "We are honored to have Washington DC Metro Police Lieutenant Doehring with us." She gave him a nod. "And Patrick Bowers, one of the Bureau's most experienced criminologists. I'm sure you'll find his insights scintillating."

Her comment about my scintillating insights was completely devoid of sarcasm, which in itself seemed to be a new and novel form of sarcasm.

"Tonight promises to be an engaging and thought-provoking discussion." She added a few more opening comments and announcements, then gave Lieutenant Doehring the floor.

Doehring took the podium and began describing ways in which the Washington DC law enforcement community was implementing the use of cell phones equipped with touch screens that also scanned fingerprints so that suspects' prints can be run through AFIS within seconds of apprehension.

Currently, the National Geospatial-Intelligence Agency, a little-known branch of the defense department that I consult with on behalf of the FBI, had given me the prototype of a new phone, still in development, that included the function Doehring had just mentioned, as well as defense satellite mapping capabilities and a 3-D hologram projector for mapping and analyzing crime scene locations. Amazing stuff.

Doehring listed advancements in using microwave emitters for non-lethal crowd dispersal, Israeli-developed guns that can shoot around corners, ways to x-ray crowds to determine if armed assailants are present, three-dimensional orthodigital photographs to help with bite-mark analysis, and so on—all devices we'd been using at the Bureau for the last several years.

"However," he said, "you can have all the high-tech gadgets in the world, but unless you stick to time-tested, proven investigative procedures, you'll come up short every time. Good investigations always focus on uncovering the perp's motive, means, and opportunity."

And this is where our views began to diverge.

I don't look for any of the above.

And I definitely do not use the word *perp*.

Doehring went on to detail a few cases that had "gotten bogged down in technology" until "good old-fashioned gut instincts" broke the case wide open. I sensed his tone shifting, becoming slightly antagonistic. From where I sat on the stage, I could see the attendees' faces, and most of the people appeared to agree with him that the classic approach was best.

Great. That would make my job so much easier.

Twenty minutes passed, Margaret encouraging Lieutenant Doehring, occasionally asking for my input, never questioning his assertions. I was careful to keep my comments focused on the valid points Doehring was making. No sense diminishing his authority in the eyes of the attendees.

At last he finished, and Margaret turned to me and said simply, "Agent Bowers."

My turn to use the podium. "Well." The mic squealed and I backed away from it, tried again. "Recent advances in technology have allowed us to utilize geospatial intelligence, or GEOINT, from the defense department's satellite array and apply it to law enforcement. By analyzing the locations related to serial offenses and studying the timing, location, and progression of the crimes, we can work backward to find the most likely location of the offender's home base, a geographic region we typically refer to as the hot zone."

"A geoprofile," Margaret interjected, possibly with a slight note of derision, it was hard to tell.

"That's right." Before I moved into the technical aspects and algorithms, or demonstrated my cell phone's geospatial hologram capabilities, I needed to lay out some theoretical groundwork. "Geospatial investigation builds on research in environmental criminology, sociology, routine activity theory, crime scene analysis, and environmental psychology, and is based on four basic principles concerning criminal behavior."

Blank faces in the audience.

Fantastic opening there, Pat. You've got 'em in the palm of your hand.

I took a breath. "First, even though it seems self-evident, all crimes occur in a specific place at a specific time; nearly all are committed in locations with which the offender is familiar, or along the pathways between these areas. Understanding those geospatial and temporal aspects of the crime leads us to a better understanding of the offender's travel patterns and cognitive map of his surroundings."

Even though she was near the back, I noticed Tessa yawn.

It might have been a subtle joke. I couldn't tell.

"Essentially, the distribution and timing of the crimes show us how the criminal understands and interacts with his environment," I explained. "Secondly, despite conventional wisdom that many crimes occur randomly, most of the current research supports the conclusion that people commit crimes only after a series of rational decisions shaped by environmental cues."

I paused, and Margaret asked me, cordially enough, to clarify the decision-making process I was referring to.

"Well, an offender's past, familiarity with the region, desire for seclusion during the abduction or attack, awareness of and availability of exit routes, and a lack of visible law enforcement presence all affect his choices regarding the commission of his crime.

Offenders choose the time and location of their crimes in order to avoid apprehension."

"In other words," Margaret interjected, "their motive is to get away with it?"

Oh.

That was clever.

With one tiny comment she'd found a way to agree with me while bringing up my biggest pet peeve—motive. I glanced at her. She was smiling in a Margarety way.

"Yes." *Follow up on that later, just get through the four points for now.* "Thirdly, offenders attempt to save time and money, put in the least amount of effort for the most possible benefit. This affects the routes they take to and from—"

One of the eight doors on the right side of the auditorium edged open. Even though most of the attendees didn't seem to notice, the movement caught my attention. A woman entered. Naturally beautiful face. Frizzily curled red hair. Coy smile. Wearing a dark green National Academy polo shirt.

I did a double take.

It couldn't possibly be her.

But it was.

Detective Cheyenne Warren from Denver.

A National Academy shirt? That doesn't make sense. She's—

Cheyenne gave me a slightly embarrassed look for interrupting, then held up her palms in a small sign of surrender, mouthed the word "Sorry," and headed for the nearest seat.

Margaret cleared her throat slightly, jarring me back to the discussion. "Agent Bowers? You were saying? Motives?"

Motives? Was I . . . ?

I struggled to regain my train of thought, but Cheyenne's smile had at least momentarily derailed it.

Over the last year I'd served on a joint violent crimes task force with the Denver PD, and Cheyenne and I had worked seven cases together. From the start, we'd both been attracted to each other, no question about that, but first my grief over Christie's death and then my relationship with one of the profilers here at Quantico had kept us from dating.

Then last month, when Lien-hua and I broke up, Cheyenne hadn't been shy in letting me know how she felt about me. However, at the time I realized that seeing her would have been, at least initially, a way of dealing with the breakup, and I couldn't stand the thought of using her, so I'd pulled away even though I knew it had hurt her.

But that was more than three weeks ago.

And now here she was.

Back to the discussion, Pat.

"Yes. I . . ."

Something about offenders . . . space and time . . .

Ah yes.

I wasn't sure if it was my exact point, but it was close enough: "So, while offenders might act, and in many cases, think, in aberrant or deviant ways, they're not fundamentally different from the rest of us. They're not monsters. They're human beings who understand and interact with their environments in the same ways all human beings do. So . . ."

Cheyenne had taken a seat in the fifth row and was now watching me attentively, pen in hand. I found it hard not to stare at her.

"Fourthly—"

My cell phone vibrated in my pocket. There'd been enough interruptions already, so I ignored it, but noticed that both Margaret and Lieutenant Doehring were glancing down, Margaret at the phone that sat on the table beside her legal pad, Doehring at his belt.

The fact that all three of us were being paged simultaneously could not possibly be a good sign. Doehring pulled out his phone while Margaret discreetly tapped the screen of hers. I eased mine from my pocket, but I kept my eyes on the audience. "As I was saying, the fourth premise is—"

"Excuse me, Agent Bowers." Margaret abruptly set her phone down and bent toward her mic. "I'm very sorry about this, everyone, but I'm afraid we're going to have to end our discussion prematurely tonight."

I read the text message on my phone: a body had been found in a primate research facility in DC. The message included an address on South Capital Street but no other specifics.

But what caught my attention was the sender's name: FBI Director Rodale, a man who didn't get involved in cases unless they were related to national security or involved a nationwide manhunt or unusually high media coverage.

After her terse announcement, Margaret promptly rose and headed toward the hallway.

Since she was the executive assistant director, I wondered if her text had contained more details than mine had. Before I left for the scene I wanted as much information as possible, so I quickly gathered my things and went to find her before she slipped away.

7

I caught up with Margaret just down the hall, near the entrance to the Gerbil Tube that led to the admin building.

"Margaret," I called. She kept walking.

"Wait."

She didn't turn.

"Executive Assistant Director Wellington."

She stopped. Looked over her shoulder. Eyed me.

"A primate research lab?" As I joined her, I noticed Tessa at the far end of the hallway, picking her way toward me through the already forming crowd. "Why are we getting involved in this? Is it on federal property?"

"No, Agent Bowers, it is not." I waited for her to elaborate, and at last she said, "A body was found."

"I know that much, Margaret. But why would Rodale—"

"Because"—her voice was both hushed and laced with urgency—"the victim is Congressman Fischer's daughter."

"What?" Now she had my attention.

"House minority leader. From Virginia. Democrat. First District."

"I know who he is." I was processing the implications. Quantico is located in Congressman Fischer's district, and he'd been outspoken lately on shrinking the size of the FBI by up to 20 percent because of what he called "bureaucratic redundancy." He favored "a more progressive approach to curbing criminal behavior," although he'd never specified exactly what he meant by that.

Congress's budget debates had been going on all week on Capitol Hill, and since Fischer's brother had been the vice president during the last administration, the congressman had clout and connections, and the last I heard he was gaining support for slashing the Bureau's funding. Needless to say, he was not the most popular political figure around the Academy at the moment.

She looked at her watch. "I have two calls to make. Director Rodale reassigned Agent Hawkins to this case, so he'll meet you at the scene. I'll come as soon as I can."

Normally, Margaret would work the strings on something like this from behind her desk, but with the inevitable media firestorm, I had a feeling she might see this as a chance to gain some political or administrative clout by being present at the scene near those television cameras.

She turned on her heels, strode away, and a moment later Tessa arrived by my side.

Obviously, I couldn't take her with me to the crime scene, but the house where we were staying for the summer was in the opposite direction, so I didn't have time to take her back there either.

I decided I could drop her off at a coffee shop or mall on the way. Not ideal, since I could be wrapped up for hours, but at the moment no better options popped to mind.

"C'mon." I placed my hand gently on her shoulder and guided her toward a side door to the parking lot. "It's time to go."

"It's bad, isn't it?"

There was no sense trying to hide it. "It's not good."

It looked like she was going to ask more questions, but she remained silent. We'd nearly made it to the exit when I heard footsteps behind me. The sound of someone running.

I turned.

"Pat." Cheyenne jogged toward us. "Is there anything I can do?"

"I wish," I said, and I meant it. She was one of the best detectives I'd ever met. For a moment I thought of the Bureau's Joint Op program of involving National Academy students in ongoing cases—both to train them and learn from them—but a pile of paperwork that would take hours to fill out stood in the way.

I wanted to ask her how she'd managed to wrangle her way into the National Academy, which typically involves a six-month application process, but that conversation could wait. I did, however, add, "I'm surprised to see you here."

"I'm surprised to be here," she replied ambiguously. The three of us reached the door. I pushed it open as Cheyenne nodded to Tessa and said warmly, "Ms. Ellis."

"Detective Warren." A hint of confusion. "Aren't you supposed to be in Denver?"

"I had some personal leave coming, and they had a last-minute opening in the National Academy."

The explanation was thin, making me even more curious.

The three of us stepped into the cloud-darkened evening.

Large round raindrops were plunking onto the pavement. Thunder rumbled overhead. The storm had arrived.

"Tessa," I said. "Let me talk to Detective Warren for a second." I tossed her the car keys. "I'll be right there."

After a glance at Cheyenne and then at me, Tessa went on ahead.

"Listen," I said. "Things are—"

"I know you need to go." Cheyenne cut me off. "I'll explain everything later."

I accepted that. "This looks like it might be messy."

"Yeah, no kidding. Fischer's daughter."

"How did you—?"

Using her body to shield her phone from the rain, she held it up so I could see the screen. A video of a newscaster doing a remote in downtown DC was playing. Beside the reporter was the photo of an attractive woman in her early twenties. The name beneath it read: Mollie Fischer. "CNN, FOX, and CNS News are already there. Live feed on the Internet."

"Wonderful."

Lightning slithered and crackled across the sky, and Cheyenne's eyes flicked toward it. "She was only twenty-two." Her voice was soft and sad and I didn't know how to respond. After a small moment she gestured toward Tessa, who was climbing into the car to get out of the intensifying rain. "You're not taking her with you, are you?"

"I'll drop her off somewhere on the way."

Cheyenne and I started toward my car. "I can take her back to your place for you."

"No, it's okay. We'll—"

"Pat." Cheyenne laid her hand on my forearm. "You read too much into things. I just want to help. Just as a friend. Honestly."

She was right; I was seeing ulterior motives in her offer and it bugged me that she'd nailed it. I felt a little embarrassed and yet slightly flattered that she could read me so easily.

Cheyenne removed her hand, waited for my reply.

Just let her help.

"Honestly, if you could take her home, that would be great."

"Great."

We jogged toward the car, and I opened the passenger-side door. "Raven, Detective Warren is going to give you a ride back to the house."

With Tessa's insatiable curiosity I expected her to ask to come along to the crime scene, which she did. "You know I can't do that," I countered. "Besides, there's a dead body there and you might see—"

She swung her legs out of the car. "Yeah, I get it."

Cheyenne started toward the south end of the parking lot. "My car's over here."

"I'll see you at the house, Tessa," I said.

"Okay."

The two of them were hurrying toward Cheyenne's car. "Hey, thanks again," I called to Cheyenne.

"No problem," she hollered back with a wave of her hand.

I got into my car. Flipped on the radio to listen for any breaking news.

And headed to the scene of Mollie Fischer's murder.

8

Brad stood anonymously in the crowd of people watching the television screens.

Despite the storm, fifteen people had gathered outside Williamson's Electronics Store on Connecticut Avenue near Union Station in the heart of downtown DC.

The high-end television showroom featured Sony, LG, Samsung, and Bang & Olufsen's next generation of organic light-emitting diode televisions. Razor-thin screens, sixty-five inch, seventy inch, and larger. The world's most expensive home theater systems on display and facing the street.

From observing the store over the last few weeks, Brad knew it wasn't unusual to find half a dozen people pausing by the window, coveting the TVs. In fact, the store's popularity was one of the reasons he'd chosen it.

Now, the grainy images carried on each screen looked like a movie in the tradition of *Blair Witch* or *Cloverfield*, but each television contained six different camera angles, and the time marker at the bottom of each screen made it clear that the feed was live.

The videos showed the interior of an expansive building, a walkway between walled-in glass enclosures at least twenty feet tall. Speakers located beneath the storefront's overhang projected the sound of the chattering monkeys, baboons, gorillas, and other primates as they swung from thick ropes and clambered over the stout limbs of artificial trees, obviously constructed to hold the apes' immense weight.

A flurry of FBI agents and DC police, easily identifiable by the letters emblazoned on their jackets, moved into and out of the picture.

Because of the indistinct shadows and the glare off the glass, it was difficult to tell how many bodies lay inside the farthest primate cage on the left. At least one. Maybe as many as three.

No one else knew this, but the footage was only being transmitted to this one location.

Brad listened quietly as those around him tried to figure out what was going on: "It's some kind of gorilla zoo or something," somebody said.

"Is this live?" a man in a gray Valentino suit asked. "This is live, isn't it?"

"They were talking about this on the news," the woman beside him said. "I think it's a senator's kid who was killed."

"Killed?"

"That's the security cameras from inside the building."

"No, it was a congressman," someone said.

"Fischer's daughter. That's what I heard."

Brad had snugged a Washington Nationals baseball cap over his head to shield his eyes from view and wore a fake, scraggly beard. Actually, disguises were one of his specialties.

He'd turned his collar up against the weather and was dressed in the reeking, tattered clothes he'd stolen from a homeless man he'd beaten senseless half an hour ago. Dressed as he was, Brad looked just like any other nameless, faceless vagrant.

Invisible.

In plain sight.

He wished he could stand here and watch for hours, but it was time to go.

He had a busy night—one more murder to commit, C-4 to pack into the metal tubes, a detonation sequence to set up.

And a few other chores.

He walked four blocks to the handicapped accessible van that he and Astrid were using; the van where he'd left the next two victims tied and gagged. Personally, he would have preferred leaving them unconscious, had planned to, but Astrid had told him it would be more fun if they were awake, anticipating what was to come.

Since they knew each other, if they hadn't been blindfolded, they would have been comforted. As it was, in the end, the impact would be so much greater this way.

One would die tonight.

The other would spend the night with him and Astrid at the house.

9

The Gunderson Foundation Primate Research
  Center
1311 South Capital Street
Washington DC
8:26 p.m.

Raindrops slashed against the windshield. Tiny dark knives in the deepening twilight.

Yellow police tape surrounded the facility and twisted and snapped in the sharp wind. Fifteen patrol cars sat angled to the curb, lights still on. Colors lancing the rain.

The facility's underground parking garage had been cordoned off, so I parked on the street behind one of the police cruisers. Already, half a dozen cable and network news crews were lining the neighboring streets.

Just what we needed.

Despite the media presence, the news coverage on the radio had been sketchy. The reporters couldn't seem to agree on whether there was one body or two or maybe three, whether or not the police had a suspect in custody, and whether or not Congressman Fischer was actually in the city or overseas meeting with soldiers in Afghanistan.

Clusters of FBI agents, Metro Police officers (who have jurisdiction over the city), Capitol police officers (who protect Capitol Hill), and even US Marshals stood around the entrance to the building.

American law enforcement is set up like a plate of spaghetti, and the individual noodles overlap, wind together, and get entangled all the time. Depending on the type of crime and where it's committed, you might have eight or nine state and federal law enforcement entities, intelligence agencies, military units, defense organizations, and justice department agencies all trying to investigate it.

And most likely not sharing information all that efficiently as they do.

Each of the armed forces has their own division of criminal forensic investigators; add in a helping of the ATF, DEA, CIA, FBI, NSA, the Defense Criminal Investigative Service, the US Marshals Service and Federal Air Marshals, the Secret Service, US Customs and Border Protection, the Bureau of Diplomatic Security, even the Office of Inspector General for the United States Postal Service—as well as regional and state law enforcement, sheriff's departments, and the six classified investigative agencies that don't appear on any government books—

It's mind-boggling.

All too often, conducting an investigation is like sticking your fork into the mess and twirling. Sometimes I'm amazed any crime gets solved or any terrorist attack gets thwarted.

Now, as I looked around at the variety of agencies already on-site, I could feel it happening again: The spaghetti was beginning to spill off the plate.

It struck me that Congressman Fischer might be right about wanting to cut down on bureaucratic redundancy.

A Metro police officer was approaching my car.

I picked up a pair of latex gloves from the crime scene kit I keep in the glove compartment, made sure I had my lock-pick set, my Mini MagLite, my 3-D hologram projection phone, then grabbed my FBI windbreaker and stepped into the storm.

The officer held up his hand. "Excuse me, sir, but—"

I already had my creds out. "Patrick Bowers. I'm with the FBI." I slipped the windbreaker on.

Rain boiled across the pavement, black grease frying in a dark, concrete pan.

He shifted his gaze from me to the facility. "The others are already inside." The wind tried to swallow his words, and he raised his voice. "Did you hear? The perp, he set the chimpanzees on her—they chewed off her face."

The news sickened me.

I pocketed my wallet.

Approached the building.

Stepped inside.

An expansive viewing area wound between eighteen enormous glass-enclosed areas, nine on each side. All of them were at least six meters high.

I shook off the rain, brushing my hand for a moment against the holster of my .357 SIG P229. Most of the Bureau has switched to Glock 23s to make it easier for the gunsmiths and for interchange-ability of ammunition in the field, but some of the senior agents had been allowed to keep their SIGs. I loved that gun, so I was thankful I was one of them.

Most of the law enforcement officers were clustered at the far end of the cavernous room, and I began walking toward them, taking in as much as I could along the way.

Three exit doors, including a stairwell that presumably led to the parking garage.

An elevator just to the left of the stairs.

Six video cameras, all non-panning, tucked into the shadowy nooks and crannies of the ceiling high above me. A few moments ago as I'd entered the building, I'd noticed two additional cameras covering the entrance to the parking garage, and I expected that there would be coverage above the emergency exits as well.

And of course, on both sides of me, behind the glass, the pri-mates.

It didn't seem like "cages" was the right word to describe the structures holding them. Habitats, maybe. Glass-enclosed habitats.

Each was nearly as wide and long as it was tall, and could be accessed through a door at the back of the ape-sized steel sliding doors that connected the habitats.

The constant chatter and shrieks of the primates filled the air.

Each habitat had a unique combination of rope swings and large canvas hammocks for the animals to lounge in. Some had tire swings or bars to hang from, others had blankets to hide beneath. All were lined with straw.

Agents Ralph Hawkins and Lien-hua Jiang stood conferring near a hallway that led to another wing of the center. Ralph's densely muscled bulk stood in stark contrast to Lien-hua's slim, willowy figure.

So.

The last I'd heard, she was working a case in Miami, and I hadn't expected to see her here tonight.

Ralph saw me. "Pat." His voice was low and gravelly, more of a growl than anything else. "Over here."

Lien-hua and I hadn't run into each other since our breakup. We gave each other a somewhat strained nod of greeting, then she averted her eyes to a nearby habitat. It appeared to be the one that contained Mollie's body, but my view was obstructed by the Crime Scene Investigative Unit officers inside.

Even though Lien-hua wore jeans and had on a T-shirt and windbreaker, she looked as orientally elegant as ever. Thoughtful. Beautiful. Intelligent. Two strands of sable hair framed her face.

It wasn't easy, but I shifted my gaze to Ralph. "Talk to me." I slipped on the latex gloves. "What do we know?"

"One victim: Mollie Fischer, Caucasian, twenty-two. Attacked by two chimps. The keeper who found her put 'em both down." His voice was steeped with thick anger. "The killer strapped the girl's wrists to the tree limb. She didn't have a chance. Still unclear why the crime occurred here. Mollie doesn't have any ties to this place. That we know of."

Lien-hua said, "The animals were injected with 1-phenyl-2-aminopropane." There was anger in her voice too, but tempered with deep sympathy. "Basically, they were drugged to make them as aggressive as possible."

"All right," I said, bracing myself. "Let's have a look."

10

We entered the maze of hallways that meandered behind the habitats and past a series of glass-walled research rooms equipped with wire mesh partitions to keep the researchers safely separated from the primates. The back door in each habitat opened to one of the rooms.

Lien-hua walked beside me. Graceful. A gazelle.

I could feel the weight of the unsaid stretching between us, and I tried to think of a way to clear the air, but before I could land on the right words, she broke the silence. "Pat, our past needs to stay in the past." She spoke softly, her voice rich with her Asian heritage, and though she tried to sound objective and detached, I could tell the topic was difficult for her to bring up. "This case, this is where we are. This is where we need to be."

She was right, of course, but that wasn't going to make things any easier.

"We can't pretend that nothing happened between us," I said, more for my sake than for hers. "That we weren't . . ."

In love, I thought.

"Close," I said.

A small pause. "I'm not suggesting we pretend, just saying we need to move on." A thin thread of pain ran through every word, but I couldn't help recall that she was the one who'd ended things, not me. "People do that, you know," she said. "People see each other, they break up, they find a way to work together again."

Yes. You're right. People do that.

She looked my way. "We need to do that too."

"I know," I replied.

"Okay." She took a breath, then added, "I'm glad you're back in town, though."

"It's good to see you too."

Lien-hua.

Cheyenne.

This was going to be a hard summer.

As we passed through the hallway, I noticed computerized testing stations, fMRI and CAT scan machines in the adjoining rooms. From a case I'd worked in San Diego last winter, I even recognized two MEG, or magnetoencephalography, machines used to study the magnetic fields that are caused by neurological activity.

There was definitely some big money behind this facility.

Lien-hua noticed me surveying the rooms. "We had a briefing before you got here." Her tone was professional, that of a co-worker, and it hurt to hear her use it on me. "Mostly the research here focuses on primate cognition, but in this wing, they're also studying primate aggression. The keeper arrived at 7:00 to check on the animals, found the security guard drugged, Mollie dead, and the chimps mutilating her body. She called it in. That's about all we know. Metro police are interviewing her now."

"Any indication she might be involved?" I guessed that Lien-hua would want me to mirror her cool, detached tone, and I tried to but failed pitifully.

"Not so far."

"How was the drug identified so quickly?"

"They use it in their research."

After a few more steps she said, "A personal question. Is that all right?"

"Sure."

"How are you and Tessa doing?"

Although I hadn't told Lien-hua about Paul Lansing, she was aware of my struggles connecting with my stepdaughter. At the moment I avoided the whole topic of Tessa's father. "She's good. Thanks for asking. Actually, she mentioned she was looking forward to seeing you this summer. Wants to talk to you about something called *Nāgas*."

A small moment. "Yes. That would be nice."

I kept my curiosity to myself.

We arrived at the doorway to the ape habitat where Mollie had been killed. The door was wide, but low, and at six-foot-three I had to crouch to get through.

As I entered, I was struck by the stark smell of straw and feces and the rusty scent of blood.

Death in the air.

To get to Mollie, I had to walk past the two dead chimpanzees.

Both had blood-stained teeth and streaks of blood smeared across their faces and hands. The larger of the two had a single gunshot wound to the chest. The other had been shot two or three times, it was hard to tell, and lay closer to the door. An officer was interviewing a distraught-looking female civilian, possibly the keeper, but I tried to avoid making assumptions.

Ralph was having a word with the three CSIU officers beside Mollie's body. By the time Lien-hua and I arrived, they had stepped aside.

And so, Mollie.

Lying at my feet.

I knew that chimpanzees are many times stronger than humans and can turn violent, but I had no idea they could be this vicious. Most of Mollie's face was missing, the deep, bloody bite marks trailing down what was left of her cheeks and gouging deeply into her neck.

With so much skin and meat missing from her face, her jaw jutted out grotesquely toward me. One of her eyes was pulverized, the other missing.

I felt myself grow both sickened and enraged.

She had a single piercing and earring in what was left of each ear and wore a silver chain necklace that was tucked beneath her Georgetown sweatshirt. Once light gray, the sweatshirt was now darkened with splattered blood. Using a gloved hand, I eased out the necklace and found a locket with two engraved initials: R.M.

Mollie had a small build, weighed perhaps 110 pounds, wore blue jeans and black pumps and had blonde hair, now matted with blood and several thin, grisly strips of flesh that had been torn from her face. Her right leg was obviously broken, the foot turned sideways, perpendicular to the rest of the leg.

A savage and brutal and terrible death.

The contents of her purse lay scattered around me in the straw.

Apart from the blood on her sweatshirt, her clothes were dry.

The leather straps the killer had used were still snugged tightly around each wrist, and the skin surrounding the straps was red and raw from what must have been her desperate attempts to get free. I noticed that two of her fingernails were chipped, and caught on the corner of one of them were several threads of blue cloth.

From the killer's clothing?

Carpeting?

Bedsheets? A blanket?

The guys at the lab would find out.

I mentioned the fibers to the CSIU, and they told me they'd already taken note of them. I glanced up and saw two strips of leather hanging from the branch of the tree she'd been secured to. I assumed the responding officers had needed to slit the straps to lower her to the ground. "When was she last seen alive?"

"We're not sure," Ralph answered. "Someone saw her at the Clarendon Metro stop at about 4:00 this afternoon. That's the last we know of."

I considered that.

4:00 p.m.

It was now 8:31.

I looked at the black soles of her shoes. Scuffed.

Felt the cuff of her jeans.

Dry.

I ran through the seven steps law enforcement officers take: secure the scene, secure the subject, assist the injured, call for responders, detain witnesses, identify the body, pursue all leads.

"Who made the ID?"

Ralph indicated toward Mollie's purse. "The keeper found her driver's license, called it in. They got the congressman over here right away. He IDed her. Yeah, I know it's unusual to do it on-site," he went on, "but there was concern this might be a politically motivated crime, that his life might be in danger, so the Capitol police brought him in. Took him to a secure location when he was done."

With the extent of her disfiguring injuries, I wondered how he'd identified her. A birthmark maybe. A tattoo.

He's her father, Pat. A dad knows his daughter. Even in death.

I scrutinized the blood-spattered straw surrounding Mollie's body. A frenzy of violence. "Other family members?"

"She's an only child. Her mom is in Australia for a relative's wedding." The CSIU officers eyed me quietly. I had the sense they were not happy I was on their turf.

I stood up, appraised the area, taking it in. "Anything else like this? Any similar crimes that we know of? Links to other homicides?"

"We checked ViCAP," Ralph said. "People have been fed to Dobermans, pigs, gators—but never primates. At least not that we know of."

I could look into that more in-depth later.

The crime scene technicians would be scouring the room for physical evidence. I wasn't here for that. My job was to notice the pieces of the puzzle other people miss.

I mentally ran down what I knew.

The Metro stop.

The rain.

The congressman's high profile position as house minority leader.

Timing. Location. Patterns. Routes.

Lien-hua was studying the position of the chimps' bodies. Ralph knelt beside Mollie, inspecting her injuries. The three CSIU officers were still watching me.

"Time of death?" I asked them.

"Not long ago," one of them replied. He was slim with blue eyes, blond hair, and had a nervous habit of rubbing his left thumb and forefinger together. The cloth name tag sewn onto his uniform read Officer Roger Tielman. "Body temp and lividity suggest one to three hours ago. Probably sometime around 6:00. Maybe closer to 7:00."

Not specific enough to help me narrow things down.

"Last call on her cell phone?" I asked. "Any texts?"

"We already followed up on the last ten calls—all from preprogrammed numbers. Eight female, two male."

"Any from an R.M.?"

A quizzical look.

"Were any of the calls from someone with the initials R.M.?"

He sent one of the officers beside him to find out.

"She's got hundreds of text messages from the last month," Ralph added. "The ERT guys are tackling that." The Evidence Response Team, or ERT, is the FBI's forensics unit.

I pulled out my cell. Tapped in a few numbers on the flat screen's touchpad.

"What about the facility's security cameras?" I asked Tielman. "Anything?"

"Yeah. We checked." He sounded almost insulted by the question. "The footage from 5:00 to 7:00 was deleted."

On my phone I surfed to the Federal Digital Database and logged into the National Oceanic and Atmospheric Administration's site. They might not record detailed data from every city in the US, but I was counting on the fact that they would track meteorological changes here in our country's capital. I punched in my federal ID number then looked through the glass to one of the cameras above the central walkway. "Were the cameras on when you arrived?"

"Yeah."

"And are they directed in the same position now as they were before the footage was lost?"

He looked a little confused. "The same position?"

I was getting frustrated by Tielman's repeated need for clarification. "The cameras are all stationary; non-panning. I want to know if someone has reviewed the footage prior to 5:00 and confirmed that the angles at which the cameras are currently positioned are the same as they were before the footage was deleted."

He let his eyes wander from me to his partner, a slim Hispanic woman, then back to me. "I would imagine they are."

"Don't imagine," I said. "Find out."

"Why would that matter?"

"Everything matters."

"Go," Ralph said, ending the discussion.

Tielman spoke to his partner, sent her to find out about the camera angles. He stayed behind as she passed out the door.

The NOAA precipitation data appeared on my screen in a series of condensed scrolling columns of numbers, organized by longitude and latitude coordinates.

A few more taps at my screen and I'd pulled up the defense satellite's imagery of the city.

I went to a corner of the habitat, pushed a little straw aside to make room for my phone, laid it on the concrete, and opened the hologram program.

A moment later, the phone was projecting a 3-D hologram of downtown DC. It hovered a meter off the ground, half a meter in width and length.

Glimmering buildings, shimmering roads.

With this phone I had the capability to rotate the hologram, zoom in and out, and overlay data to highlight specific locations and travel routes. Although I wasn't sure my idea would work, I transferred the precipitation stats and coordinates onto the city, overlaying them against the hologram's 3-D imagery, just as I do with the travel routes of victims when I'm doing a geoprofile.

The precip levels were marked in layered, darkening shades of blue corresponding to the precipitation level recorded by NOAA's satellites. Although it was difficult to discern the subtle changes in color, when I studied it closely I could just barely make out the differences. I began reviewing the levels at fifteen minute intervals starting at 4:00, when Mollie was last seen.

"It's not a spectator sport," Ralph growled. His words caught my attention, and when I glanced up, I saw that everyone in the habitat, except for Ralph and Lien-hua, was staring at the hologram.

"Get back to work." When Ralph speaks, people obey. Within moments they'd all turned away from me.

Lien-hua leaned down, brushed at a small pile of blood-spattered straw.

I continued to scroll through the time markers until I came to 7:00 and saw what I was looking for.

"I need to see the parking garage," I said.

"What is it?" Ralph asked.

I closed the program, the hologram disappeared. I pocketed the phone. "Shift change and the Metro station. It fits." I started for the exit, but before I could leave, I met two members of the Bureau's ERT crawling through the door.

First, Agent Tanner Cassidy, an old friend of mine, emerged. Medium build, brown hair. Soft spoken, meticulous, and dedicated. He introduced me to the attractive agent who, only a moment later, stood beside him. "This is Natasha Farraday. Transferred in from St. Louis."

I introduced myself. "Pat Bowers."

She shook my hand by squeezing my fingers lightly rather than by gripping my palm. "Good to meet you." With a disarming smile and wide, shy eyes, she made me think of a twenty-five-year-old Christina Ricci.

"You too."

"Agent Cassidy," Lien-hua called, her voice grim. "Over here."

"I've read your books, Dr. Bowers," Natasha said to me.

I was studying the deep concern on Lien-hua's face. "Okay."

Cassidy and Tielman joined her. Knelt beside her. Cassidy called for a photographer and an evidence bag. "We've got Mollie's eye here."

A sweep of nausea.

"Excuse me," I said to Natasha, indicating toward the door, but then realized I could probably use her help. "Wait. Can you join me in the parking garage?"

"Of course."

I asked Ralph if he could come along, and he followed me, barely squeezing his massive shoulders through the doorway.

"Good thing it's built for gorillas," I said.

"Watch it."

We took the stairs to the garage. If I was right, the killer's car would still be here.

11

I was scanning the vehicles.

"Mollie's car isn't here," Ralph said, somewhat impatiently. "We already checked."

"I'm not looking for her car." I'd expected only a handful of cars, but there were more than thirty here. "There was just a skeleton crew on hand here tonight; why all the vehicles?"

"I already went through this with the security guard." He sounded annoyed; maybe at me, maybe at the conversation he'd had with the guard. "Since the facility provides free parking for its employees, lots of the staff leave their cars here and take the Metro around the city. Beats having to pay for a spot near their apartments."

City life. Perks.

So these are only cars from employees . . . Good. That narrows it down.

Natasha stood beside me, waiting for instructions.

Ralph said, "Whose vehicle are you looking for?"

"The video would have caught the car leaving the parking garage. I was assuming that the killer was aware of that."

"I thought you didn't assume?"

A van would have been ideal for transporting an abducted woman. And, while I didn't see any vans, I did see six minivans, but right away I could tell they hadn't been used to transport Mollie. "Let's call it an initial hypothesis."

I let my eyes pass through the garage . . . eliminating possibilities . . . eliminating . . . "Look for cars that have trunks that are—"

Then I saw it.

"There." I started jogging toward it, a sky blue '09 Volvo sedan.

"How do you know?" Natasha called. I heard her and Ralph hurrying after me.

"Water." I pointed. "Under the wheel wells."

I arrived, used my MagLite to scan the wet concrete beneath the car, continued my explanation, "It started raining in DC at 5:06 p.m. and hasn't stopped. Mollie is wearing cotton clothes that would absorb water, but they're dry, so the killer had to have unloaded her inside here. Only three cars out of the thirty-two have water beneath them—two have monthly access stickers on them—one would be the security guard's, the other the keeper's. This one doesn't have a sticker. It doesn't belong."

I still had on the latex gloves. I tried the doors. Locked.

Then the trunk.

Locked.

"Couldn't it be someone else's car?" Natasha asked.

Maybe . . .

I pointed at the car's blue carpeting. "She had blue fibers caught on a broken fingernail."

I pulled out my lock-pick set and peered into the car windows but couldn't see anything unusual.

Beside me, Ralph had his phone out, already running the Virginia plates: 134-UU7.

"Why would the killer leave the vehicle here?" Natasha asked.

It was a good question, the obvious question.

Maybe to avoid being caught on camera . . . ?

But even if he didn't drive out, the cameras would have caught him walking out. Besides, the footage was deleted . . .

"I have no idea." I started working on the lock to the trunk, then I caught sight of movement and saw Lieutenant Doehring approaching with a stocky, mustached officer I didn't know swaggering beside him.

Ralph slipped his phone into the case on his belt. "Car's registered to Rusty Mahan."

"R.M.," I said.

"Mahan?" It was Doehring. "I just got off the horn with

Congressman Fischer. A guy named Rusty Mahan is Mollie's boyfriend. Twenty years old. Lives on campus at Georgetown."

"*Was* her boyfriend," the other officer responded. "Until yesterday. Big fight at her daddy's mansion. Fischer said the Mahan kid took it hard."

I was working on the trunk's lock. "We need to find him."

"Campus security's already on it," Doehring replied. "But you'll love this: he's a grad student in evolutionary biology. Worked here as an intern last semester."

"So he could have gotten access to the building," the burly officer said. I glanced at his badge: Lee Anderson. He continued, "The car places him at the scene, and if he just broke up with the vic, we've got motive." He sounded like he'd just solved the case.

"Well, then." I was still working on the lock. "As long as we've got that settled."

"Don't get him started," Doehring said to Anderson.

"On what?"

"Motive," he answered. "And don't say vics, doers, perps. You'll regret it."

Definitely not the time to have this conversation.

"We're looking for clues," I said. "Motive isn't a clue. At best it's circumstantial evidence, and even that's debatable."

"What do you mean, motive isn't a clue?" Anderson asked skeptically.

"Here we go," Ralph grumbled.

The lock was giving me trouble, and that annoyed me.

I was not in the mood for this. "There's no way to prove a person had any specific motive at any specific time, and there's no reason to even try—our justice system doesn't require showing motive to get a conviction for any crime on the books. Jurors like it, but it's misleading because trying to figure out motive is a guessing game you can never be sure you've won. Investigators should deal with facts, not conjecture."

There.

The lock clicked.

I popped open the trunk.

All three men and Natasha leaned close to peer inside.

Blue carpeting.

And a series of black smeared dints on the metal body on the passenger side. "She was conscious when they transported her." I didn't realize I'd said the words aloud until I saw Natasha looking at me curiously. I pointed to the marks. "Same color as the soles of her shoes. She kicked. Hard."

"She was in here awhile." Doehring was staring at them. "Struggled a lot."

Timing, location.

Timing.

I pulled out my cell and speed-dialed Lien-hua. "Any word on the security cameras?"

"Same angles, Pat," she said. "Whoever deleted the footage didn't redirect them. Why did you want that checked anyway?"

"The killer deleted footage—so he obviously knew the system—but then he would have had to leave the building after doing so, and the cameras would have been on when he left. I wanted to see if he redirected the angle of one of them so he could exit undetected. If he had, it would have told us which door he used to leave the scene, or if he used the parking garage."

A moment of reflection passed as she processed what I'd said. "Good call. Another thing: someone using a cell phone captured footage of an electronics store that's been airing a live feed from the security cameras here inside the research facility. They sent the clip to CNS News. We're all over the airwaves."

Oh, bad.

She told me the name and location of the store.

"We need to cross-reference a list of store employees with people who might work at the research facility. Also check credit card receipts, find the most recent, most frequent customers."

These weren't Lien-hua's duties, she knew that, I knew that, but she understood the way I work and she would make sure they got done. There'd never been any professional jealousy between us. No rivalry. We complemented each other.

Or at least we used to.

I leaned away from the phone. "Doehring, see if Mahan had any connections with Williamson's Electronics Store over on Connecticut."

Doehring nodded, went for his walkie-talkie.

I returned to my phone conversation with Lien-hua. "Come down here as soon as you can. We need to talk."

After hanging up I noticed that Natasha had called for two additional ERT agents and the three of them had started processing the car. When Doehring ended his transmission, Ralph began to bring him up to speed on what we knew so far, and I stepped to the entrance of the parking garage and stared into the night to sort through my thoughts and wait for Lien-hua.

If Mahan was the killer, why go to all the trouble of bringing her in here? Why leave your car at the scene? Why leave her purse and its contents in the habitat . . .

Rain spattered on the roof. A thin, constant drumbeat of water.

The nearby Nationals Park rose like a great black beast blotting out the skyline.

At the end of the block, traffic lights moved through their slow, methodical three-step dance from green to yellow to red.

Slashing rain. Curling lights from emergency vehicles. Dark DC streets.

Time of death—between 6:00 and 7:00.

Green.

She was last seen at the Clarendon Metro stop . . .

At least it gave us a location to work with. To try and follow her movement patterns.

Yellow.

Lien-hua arrived, and I caught the gentle scent of her presence. So familiar to me, but also, now, so much more distant than it had been a month ago.

Red.

"Pat. I'm here."

I took a moment to tell her about the car and Rusty Mahan, then said, "I know you don't like doing this on the spot. But can you give me the preliminary profile? Just whatever your first impressions are."

"I don't trust first impressions, you know that. I trust critical assessment."

"Yes, I know," I said. "So do I."

"The way you feel about profiling, Pat. I'm surprised you'd ask me to—"

"Please." It wasn't just the gruesome nature of this crime; I couldn't seem to wrap my mind around the context of what we had here. "What are you thinking?"

At last Lien-hua closed her eyes. Entered the profiler's world of empathy and understanding, the world I've never really understood, never stepped into. Using one careful finger, she traced her thoughts through the air as she spoke.

"The abduction, the sophistication of rerouting the video feed, drugging the guard, using the chimps, along with the ability to get in here, tells me he's experienced, highly educated, organized. Early to mid-thirties. Computer programming background. Hacker maybe. Demographics and Mollie's race suggest a Caucasian offender."

So far I agreed with her.

"However, it would have been difficult for someone working alone to abduct a woman undetected, subdue her, access the building, drug the chimps and the guard, transport her into the chimps' cage—"

"He had help."

A nod. "Considering Congressman Fischer's position, it might have been an attempt to hurt him, some kind of political statement."

I disagreed. "The political angle seems weak to me. There's no note, no threat, no demands. And a team of killers who could pull off a crime this elaborate could certainly go after the congressman if they wanted to. Why not just kill him?"

She opened her eyes. "This sends a stronger message."

When I thought about it I had to agree, although I had no idea what that message might be. "But," she added, "you're right; we need more information."

A moment later Doehring joined us.

"It's not the boyfriend," Lien-hua went on. "His age doesn't work for this, and the crime is too involved to put together in twenty-four hours. Besides, Mollie didn't break up with him. They might have argued, but that's all."

"How do you know that?" he asked her.

"Mollie was still wearing the locket with Rusty's initials on it. If she broke things off, she wouldn't be wearing it." Lien-hua averted her eyes from me, looked toward Doehring. "I'm a girl. Believe me. She would have taken it off."

Her words made sense, but I caught myself wondering if she still had any of the gifts I'd given her. It was painful to picture her throwing or giving them all away.

I buried the thought.

"Also, the sadistic nature of the crime points to a different—and I don't care if you don't like the term, Pat—but a motive other than jealousy or anger over a breakup."

She might have been right about that too, probably was—but that's the problem with psychoanalyzing someone: you can never be sure.

She finished, "We need to find Mahan and talk with him not as a possible suspect but for information about who else might have wanted to harm Mollie or her family."

"Why would someone send a video feed to a television store?" Doehring asked.

"Just like the killers who return to a scene to watch," she replied, "it was his, or their, way of being present, but also of being safe."

"They knew procedure—that we photograph those who gather at the scene."

Or the killers could have learned that by watching just about any episode of CSI *or* Law and Order.

I noticed that the rain was finally letting up. A small tilt in the weather.

"Do we know if there are any security cameras at the store?" I asked Doehring. "Focused on the street? The crowd outside?"

"They're checking."

Traffic lights.

Red.

Green.

I let the facts flip though my mind. Tried to lock them in place, but I found myself threading things together with unsupported assumptions rather than evidence.

Yellow.

I slid my speculation aside and went back upstairs to have another look at Mollie Fischer's body.

12

I spent two more hours at the scene, and by the time I was ready to leave, neither Georgetown's campus security nor the Metro PD had been able to locate Rusty Mahan.

We discovered that the security cameras at the electronics store had been disabled, making the job of tracking down whoever might have been present all the more difficult: all we had to work from was the brief CNS News video from the cell phone—which showed no faces—and the earliest the FBI Lab would be able to analyze the video was tomorrow morning.

The Evidence Response Team at the primate center had identified dozens of prints on the facility's doors and Mahan's car, but none of them matched anyone in AFIS.

A series of dead-ends.

All the circumstantial evidence pointed to Mahan, but when all the evidence points one way, it's usually a good idea to start looking in another; otherwise you all too often end up inadvertently confirming your assumptions rather than vigorously trying to refute them.

Margaret had arrived ten minutes ago, much later than I would have expected, especially considering what she'd told me at the Academy about having to make two quick phone calls before coming. I listened in as Ralph and Lien-hua briefed her on what we knew.

Margaret directed them to have reports on her desk by 9:00 sharp, then she turned to me. "Go home, Agent Bowers. I do not want the quality of our class offerings to be negatively affected because you didn't get enough sleep. We'll work things from this end and fill you in tomorrow on what we find."

It wasn't concern for the students that I heard in her voice but rather a subtle dismissal, as if she felt I'd fulfilled my role and she was now excusing me.

"Come here for a second." I motioned toward a corner of the parking garage behind a nearby SUV. "I need to ask you a couple questions."

When we were alone, her hands went to her hips. "Yes?"

"First, why am I on this case? From all indications, this is an isolated homicide. My specialty is analyzing linked serial offenses not—"

"Director Rodale made the assignment, not me. And I'm only guessing here, but I would imagine it's because of your field experience working cases with high media exposure rather than your area of expertise." Then, "Next?"

"All right. Detective Warren from Denver. There's a six-month application process to get into the National Academy. How did she get accepted if she just applied?"

"She is well qualified." I caught something in her tone. Slyness. "You should know that from working with her."

"Of course I know that, but you can't just discover you have vacation time coming and sign up for an NA class. Someone had to pull strings to get her in, and that someone would be—"

"Me."

"Yes."

"The chief in Denver was concerned about the emotional toll of the Giovanni case. He wanted to give her some distance from the city." A smirk. "I would have thought you'd be glad to see her. From what I understand, you two have a close working relationship."

I eyed her.

"Don't keep secrets from me, Margaret."

"And don't question my decisions, Patrick. I'll have Agent Hawkins brief you at 11:30 a.m. tomorrow. That should give you enough time to get to NCAVC after your class is done." The National Center for the Analysis of Violent Crime is a section of the FBI that Ralph, Lien-hua, and I work for. The building is a twelve-minute drive from the Academy at Quantico. "Good night."

She took a step.

"Wait," I said.

She stopped. Glared at me.

"If Rodale wants me in on this, then I'm all in. Don't micromanage. Let me do my job."

"That's precisely what I'm here to do: to make sure everyone does his job."

She left.

I thought about the case and about Cheyenne.

Call it a quirk, but I don't like unanswered questions, so even though it felt like a vague disloyalty toward Cheyenne, I decided to check on any prior ties she might have with Executive Assistant Director Margaret Wellington.

As I headed for my car, I made a wide berth of the cable news feeding frenzy outside the building.

━━━━━━━━━━━■━━━━━━━━━━━

Ever since arriving at the house nearly three hours ago, Tessa had been trying to make her way through *Boulders Dancing on the Tip of My Tongue*, a collection of poems by Alexi Marēnchivek, a Russian poet mostly unknown in America but someone who understood the paradoxes of life—both its tragedy and its glory.

Tessa didn't know Russian, only Latin and French, so she was stuck reading an English translation, which was sort of annoying.

Finally she put it aside. Her friend Pandora had been bugging her to read some Sherlock Holmes, which she was totally not into, but Tessa had been hoping to check out some Robert Louis Stevenson, who, unlike so many of the writers of "the classics," actually could write.

She opted for Stevenson instead of Doyle and pulled out *The Strange Case of Dr. Jekyll and Mr. Hyde*.

Every five minutes she'd been checking to see if there was an email from Paul. He always sent his emails by 9:00, but for some reason tonight he was late, and that sort of worried her. She'd emailed him over an hour ago, but he still hadn't replied.

She found her bookmarked page and read Stevenson's description of a foggy night in London.

The fog still slept on the wing above the drowned city, where the lamps glimmered like carbuncles; and through the muffle and smother of these fallen clouds, the procession of the town's life was still rolling in through the great arteries with a sound as of a mighty wind.

Nice.

Very nice.

Tessa checked the email again.

Nothing.

She read on, but ten minutes later, distracted by her thoughts, she laid the book on the couch and tried the TV. *American Idol* reruns.

Karaoke on steroids . . .

That would be a no.

Click.

Some kind of Western. Click.

A *Seinfeld* rerun, commercials, commercials, one of the *Star Wars* movies. More commercials. She was about to turn off the stupid thing when she came to a cable news story with footage of a zoo or something in DC where a congressman's daughter had apparently been attacked.

She paused.

The reporter, a perfectly sculpted woman with perfectly styled hair speaking in a perfectly cultivated voice, was explaining that the congressman couldn't be reached for comment. "But we have confirmed that this is a joint investigation and that the FBI is already working closely with local law enforcement. Bob—"

The FBI, huh?

"Thank you, Chelsea." The camera cut back to the news anchor. Then he started interviewing the network's "expert crime analyst" who apparently didn't have any additional information but wasn't about to let that stop him from giving detailed interpretation of the unconfirmed facts concerning the case.

Guesswork about conjecture based on hearsay.

Cable news today.

On the news loop captured "only moments ago" running behind Anchorman Bob's left shoulder, Tessa noticed a man in the background walking toward a car. He was wearing an FBI jacket and might have been just another anonymous agent, but she recognized the way he carried himself. And she knew the car.

Patrick.

Okay.

That's informative.

She waited for more details from the anchorman, but the same footage kept replaying, and Bob kept restating the same information with slightly different wording each time, including a teaser before each commercial break to make it seem like there was breaking news about the case.

Finally, when he invited people to email him their opinions about whether or not this was an act of domestic terrorism, promising to read the messages on the air as they came in, she couldn't deal with it anymore. Actual news reporting had died a swift and certain death in the age of instant messaging and 140-character attention spans.

She clicked off the TV.

Checked her email.

Nothing.

After grabbing a bag of tortilla chips from the kitchen, she flopped onto the couch again and thought back through the night.

Detective Warren had dropped her off at the house just a few minutes after 8:00, the storm churning around them.

They'd talked about surface stuff on the way: what Tessa was hoping to do during the summer (check out the Smithsonian, Library of Congress, maybe the NSA museum, the Spy Museum, things like that), and if she had a boyfriend (nada), and if she was thinking about college yet (yeah, maybe Brown or USC; maybe Duke), what she wanted to study (that's easy—double major in English and Deep Ecology).

When they arrived at the house, Detective Warren had offered to stay with her, but Tessa told her not to worry about it. "I'll be fine. Seriously. But thanks for the ride."

"All right. Lock the doors." And even though she was nowhere near old enough to be Tessa's mother, she sounded parental.

"I will."

"Good night."

Tessa hesitated before climbing out of the car. "You're not just here to take a bunch of classes, are you?" She didn't wait for a reply. "I know how you feel about Patrick. I could tell. In Denver."

A long pause. "Good men are hard to find." At this point, the detective sounded more like a sister than a parent. Guy talk between two girls.

"So you came here to win him back?"

"I never had him, Tessa."

"What about your ex-husband? Aren't you two—"

"Tessa."

She waited, expecting to hear that it wasn't any of her business, but Detective Warren went a different direction. "We're getting along again—and that's a good thing. But we'll never be close like we were. That's over."

It was hard to know how to respond.

Actually, Tessa respected her for her frankness and for pursuing what really mattered to her, and from everything she'd seen, Cheyenne and Patrick really would make a good couple. "He likes you too," she said at last, though she wasn't sure she should have. "Patrick does."

Detective Warren was quiet. "I should probably go. Good night, Tessa."

"G'night."

"And lock those doors, okay?"

"Right."

Then Tessa hurried through the rain, using her body to protect the mail she'd grabbed at the end of the driveway on the way to the house.

Then inside.

Door closed.

Locked.

Ever since being attacked and nearly killed by a serial killer whom Patrick had been tracking last October, she'd learned to be extra cautious. She checked the back door, confirmed that it was locked.

Okay.

Good to go.

But now, three hours later, Patrick still wasn't home.

She knew that he hadn't gotten over Lien-hua yet, but if things weren't going to work out there, she felt like he should totally hook up with Detective Warren.

However, it was obvious he liked them both, and honestly, so did she. It would have been a lot simpler if one of the women had been a real loser, but Detective Warren, the forthright cowgirl, and Agent Jiang, the introspective beauty, were both pretty amazing women.

Tessa checked her laptop once more, and this time she saw the email icon flashing.

With a small shiver of the guilt that comes from going behind someone's back, she tapped the space bar.

Tessa,

Hey! You're not going to believe this. I'm in DC! Only for the next couple days—a friend of mine has a few sculptures that are showing at the Hirshhorn Museum. I have the middle of the day tomorrow free and I'd love to see you. I could meet at 10:30 or so. I'm thinking by the Capitol, maybe? I know a few people and I think I can get you a tour of the House gallery.

Let me know.

Love,

Paul

Oh.

Unbelievable.

Not good.

Not good at all.

She reread the letter.

Tomorrow!

Why didn't he tell you about this sooner? Why would he—

A pair of headlights turned from the road and began meandering down the long, winding driveway to the house.

Oh, man.

Patrick.

Tessa couldn't think of any way of telling him what was going on—no, no, no, not right now. He'd been suspicious of Paul from the start, and if he found out she'd been emailing Paul like this behind his back, he'd be furious.

Besides, even if he *would* give her permission to meet with Paul, there was no way he'd be happy about it.

No way in the world.

Enough with the emails. There's stuff you need to talk to Paul about. Go see him, get your answers, then sort everything out with Patrick tomorrow night.

She typed in her reply to Paul.

The garage door opened.

Patrick was home.

13

I heard Tessa rummaging through the cupboards in the kitchen. "That you?" I called.

"How could the answer to that question possibly be no?"

I paused.

Good point.

She appeared, crossed the room, and plopped onto the couch.

"Did you have a good night?" I asked.

She shrugged. "You? Was it bad? At the primate place?"

I let my eyes ask her how she knew where I'd been, and she flipped her thumb toward the television. "I saw you on TV."

"Perfect."

"It's all over the news."

I sighed. "Yeah, well, the media is going to have a field day with this one."

She'd piled the mail on the coffee table beside her laptop, and I picked up the stack and started shuffling through it as we spoke: the latest issues of *Sports Illustrated* and *Soldier of Fortune*, both addressed to Freeman Runnels, the man who was letting us stay in his home for the summer . . . "Did you thank Detective Warren for the ride?"

"Patrick, I'm not five."

"I know that." A handful of sales flyers, a few credit card offers— all for Runnels.

"So, don't treat me like it. I know when to say please and thank you."

I looked up and saw that she was giving me an irritated stare.

"I'm just making sure you were polite," I said.

"I'm the queen of polite."

I blinked. "You're the queen of polite?"

A raised eyebrow. "Careful."

"I'm just saying."

She laid her book on the couch and stood. "I gotta get to bed."

"Hey, are you feeling all right?"

"Sure, yeah." Her tone softened. "I'm just, you know. Worn out, I guess. I have a big day tomorrow."

Back to the mail again. "I thought you were gonna hang out around here. Read?" Hardly anyone knew we were staying here, so I was surprised to see an official-looking letter addressed to me from a law firm in DC.

"Yeah, I mean, I was thinking I might take the VRE train to the city. Maybe see if I can get a reader's card for the Library of Congress. I hear they're pretty cool about giving them out to students. Is that all right?"

The Library of Congress was the biggest library in the world. A bibliophile's paradise. I knew it was her mandatory mecca for the summer. She'd talked to me earlier about getting a reader's card to get access to the main reading room, so her request wasn't a surprise.

As I ripped open the letter I realized I couldn't think of any good reason not to let her go, except that I didn't really like the idea of her wandering around the District of Columbia alone.

Ease up. She's seventeen.

"Sure, that's fine. I'm teaching most of the day tomorrow anyway." Then a thought. "I'll be in class from 8:00 to 11:00, and then from 2:00 until 5:00. I have a meeting in between there, but I should have enough time to sneak to DC, grab lunch, and get back to the Academy. What do you say? Hang out together for lunch?"

You'll never make it, Pat. Not with the briefing . . . the drive alone could take you—

"Lunch." A slight pause. "Yeah."

Good.

I'd find a way to make it to DC in time.

After an awkward moment, she headed for her room, but I called after her. "You sure you're feeling okay?"

She didn't turn around. "Yeah."

"I love you," I said.

Her bedroom door swung open. "You too."

She went in, clicked it shut.

Yes, definitely spend some time talking tomorrow.

I slipped the envelope's contents into my hand and scanned the pages.

And felt my throat tighten.

The letter was from a law firm representing Paul Lansing.

He was taking me to court to get custody of his daughter.

14

I'd only been in the DC area for a couple weeks, not long enough to get to know any lawyers, but Ralph had lived here for the last decade.

I speed-dialed him, and he answered after two rings. "Yeah?" His voice was hushed.

"You still at the primate center?"

"Naw. I'm at home. Tony's in bed." Tony was Ralph's eleven-year-old son. A boy Tessa called "a Cheetos-eating, soccer-playing, video-gaming fool."

"Sorry to call so late."

"What's up?"

"I think I need a lawyer."

A pause. I had the sense that he was repositioning the phone. "What do you need a lawyer for?"

I told him about the letter from Lansing's law firm. "Here's the thing: I'm her legal guardian, so I don't think there should be any prob—"

"This guy is her father, Pat."

"I know, but he was never in the picture."

"Did he want to be?"

An uncomfortable memory squirmed through me.

Last month Tessa had found an old letter that Christie had kept in which Paul begged her not to abort her unborn child. He'd promised to help raise the baby, but Christie hadn't wanted him to be a part of their lives and had moved away, then raised Tessa alone.

"That's not the point, Ralph."

"The court always favors blood relatives. You know that. And she's still a minor." His voice had softened, and I didn't sense that his sympathy right now was a good sign. "You will need a lawyer," he said. "A good one."

Not what I'd wanted to be hearing. "You know of any?"

"Most of the ones I know don't do divorces, custody, any of that stuff. It's all criminal law." He thought for a moment. "Hang on a sec. Let me talk to Brineesha." I heard him turn away from the phone and exchange a few indecipherable words with his wife, then he was back on the line with me. "Brineesha says hi."

"Hi, back."

"I'll tell her. Anyway, she might have someone for you. One of her friends from work—Tracy—I guess she just went through a divorce, messy custody battle, the whole thing. Whoever Tracy's lawyer was seemed to be really sharp. Brin says she'll ask her for the name first thing in the morning when she gets to the bank."

At least it was a start. "Tell her thanks."

"Hey, don't worry about this thing, okay? It'll work out." His assurances seemed to be having the opposite effect on me.

"Yeah."

"See you at 11:30 tomorrow. My office."

"All right."

Astrid led Brad down the steps to the basement.

Where they were keeping the woman.

"How was it for you?" she asked him. "Tonight, I mean? Being able to watch?"

"It was everything I'd hoped it would be."

She'd been watching things too, from a rather unique vantage point. "The video feed to that store was a great idea," she said.

"Thank you."

"You got the footage I asked for? Afterward?"

He held up his phone.

"Good." She took it from him. Slipped it into her pocket.

She had to admit, Brad's plan was by far their most devastating and brazen one yet. There were a few holes that she would fill in over the next two days, but overall he'd done a satisfactory, even admirable, job, and she was quite proud of him. Two more people would die, and the FBI would never suspect her or Brad of anything.

"How did you learn to reroute the video like that to the television store?"

"Research."

"Research?"

"A job I had before my accident."

He left it at that, and she sensed it was awkward for him to go on. He'd never told her how he got his scars, but ever since the two of them had first met, it'd been evident to her that the memory was painful.

She decided not to press the issue at the moment.

They reached the bottom of the stairs and went to the room Brad had recently remodeled.

Last month, he'd asked her if they could move some of their work to the house. She hadn't liked the idea at first, but he'd been persistent, and when she realized it would be harder to travel after the baby was born, she'd given him permission.

He'd spent the last few weeks working on the room. She'd allowed him free rein, and in the end had been surprised by how thorough he'd been in designing it so that it could serve an array of troubling purposes. He'd even made the room soundproof and added a drain to the floor to make cleanup easier.

For her, the excitement came from the feeling of control, not from inflicting physical pain. Brad, on the other hand, had recently become more and more fascinated with that secondary aspect of their hobby.

His choices for outfitting the room reflected that.

She opened the door.

Brad stood quietly beside her as she made sure the woman was safely tucked away for the night.

When Astrid was done, she locked the door behind them and took Brad upstairs.

Just knowing that the woman was down there, helpless, captive, afraid, only served to add to the thrill, and when Astrid reached the bedroom door, she slid seductively in front of her man. "Ready?"

"I've been looking forward to this all day."

```
And as their prisoner in the basement cried futilely
for help, upstairs in the bedroom, the midnight
games began.
```

15

Wednesday, June 11
491 Riley Road
Stafford, Virginia
5:03 a.m.

I woke up irritated, the letter from Paul Lansing's lawyers on my mind.

And the Mollie Fischer case as well, only a few strides behind it in the race for my attention.

And Calvin's death.

And Basque, of course, the ghost of flesh and blood from a time in my life I thought I'd left behind, lurking, always lurking, in the background.

"Promise me you won't let him do it again," Grant Sikora had begged me as he lay dying.

"I promise," I'd said.

My thoughts circled around everything, evaluating what was at stake in each case, wondering again how Lansing's lawyers could have known our address, sorting, analyzing. All of the issues seemed like cables tightening inside of me, tugging my thoughts in opposite directions.

Too many things to deal with.

My life in a nutshell.

Even though I knew Brineesha wouldn't have arrived at work yet, I checked my messages to see if, for some reason, she might have called with the lawyer's name and number.

She had not.

I looked over my email—nothing important.

Since I didn't need to leave for the Academy until about 7:30, I changed, threw myself into a workout—a thirty-minute run, twenty max-out sets of pull-ups on a tree branch at the edge of the property, and then crunches until I could barely sit up.

But it didn't clear my mind.

A shower.

Breakfast.

After downing some oatmeal and a banana, I grabbed a cup of Lavado Fino coffee from Venezuela and my laptop, and headed for the back deck.

Though barely 6:30, the morning was full of the smells of summer—freshly cut grass, warm sunshine, and steel-blue sky. The slightly fishy smell of a nearby lake.

Songbirds jabbered in the trees.

Steam from my coffee curled, wispy and smoke-like from the cup, then faded away, caught in the soft breath of wind, disappearing into the moment.

I sat there, just *being* in the stillness, in the gentle opening arc of the day. I've never been one to meditate, but I've always been drawn to the clarity that solitude brings.

A small touch of calm in the middle of my tempest life.

A chance to think.

When the DEA moved their Basic Agent training to Quantico a few years ago, one of their crime scene analyst instructors and friend of mine named Freeman Runnels had bought this house. Really, it's more of a cabin—rustic framing, thick oak doors, handmade cherry furniture.

However, this summer he was on assignment in Panama, and when he heard I was teaching for three months at the Academy, he'd graciously offered to let Tessa and me stay here. "Just water the plants," he'd said, and we agreed.

The ten-acre plot was mostly wooded, except for a stretch of lawn here behind the house. An old rock wall, about waist high, skirted along the edge of the woods that lay maybe thirty meters from the deck.

Tessa isn't exactly the outdoorsy type, but she values her privacy, and when she saw the property and found out that a Virginia Railway Express station was just a fifteen-minute walk away, she'd said, "I guess this'll be okay." Which in Tessa-speak means, "Sweet. I'll be able to go to DC whenever I want."

I clicked to the online case files to see if we had any updates on Mollie Fischer's homicide.

The complete police report wasn't posted yet, no statements from the keeper or the security guard, and, while it annoyed me, it didn't surprise me. Law enforcement officers are notoriously slow in filling out paperwork. It's the one part of our job no one seems to like. Including me.

However, I was glad to see that the crime scene photos had been uploaded.

Ninety-four of them.

I scrolled through the jpegs.

No pictures of Mollie alive, only of her dead.

First, hanging from her wrists, then lying on the straw. Photos of her wounds, the restraints, the dead chimps, the entrance and exit doors. Six separate photos of the eyeball Lien-hua had found lying in the straw, a bloodshot orb with a pale blue iris and a ragged penetralia of optic nerve from where the organ had been tugged from—

A small flicker of movement near a break in the rock wall caught my attention.

The leaves parted, and a white-tailed deer stepped delicately into the field.

When I was a teenager growing up in Wisconsin, my father had introduced me to the unofficial religion of the state—deer hunting. And, from what I could remember about the growth cycles of deer, I figured this doe was maybe two or three years old.

She meandered into the yard, silent as a heartbeat, nibbling at the grass until something spooked her and she froze, her head raised, her ears pricked upright.

Maybe she'd caught my scent.

I sat still, watching.

She stayed stationary for only a moment, then whatever had startled her must have seemed too threatening, and she abruptly took off, bolting across the far side of the yard, her tail flagging, until she disappeared into the morning shadows in the woods just past the end of the wall.

A moment of tranquility, of grace, overcome by fear. The jittery race for survival. Life running from death.

Always running.

Always being chased.

I looked at the pictures again.

A race we all lose.

Like Calvin did.

Like Mollie Fischer.

Like so many victims I've seen over the years.

Their dead staring eyes. Their quiet, gray lips.

And their shattered, grieving families.

I thought about those platitudes that don't work as I watched my coffee's ghostly thin steam curl and then fade into the morning air, then mouse-clicked away from the grisly crime scene photos.

My thoughts returned to Basque.

Ever since his release, he'd been at the center of a media whirlwind. His initial conviction, subsequent retrial, and not-guilty verdict just seemed to be too big of a story for the press to let die, and since he was still in their watchful eye, I doubted he would do anything blatantly illegal, at least in the immediate future.

So I'd been careful and meticulous rather than hurried and sloppy in my research regarding the clue Calvin left: H814b Patricia E.

But so far I'd been unsuccessful in finding her.

If she was even a real person.

If she was even a witness.

Or a victim.

Or alive.

I pulled up my notes.

At first I'd dabbled with the idea that the note was a word play of some sort: H814b—"Height won four be" or "Hate one for bee"—but no combinations of the words seemed to make sense.

The sequence didn't have enough digits to be a phone number.

It wasn't an address, at least not in the United States. It wasn't a Dewey decimal number.

After exhausting my ideas I'd contacted Angela Knight, one of the Bureau's top cybercrime analysts, who also has a knack for cryptanalysis.

We'd tried searches involving every combination of Patricia we could think of: Patty, Patsy, Tricia, Trisha, Trish; and yes, my own name, just for kicks: Pat, Patrick, Rick, Eric, Ricci, Erica.

And so on.

Nothing had come up.

We'd done metasearches through all the data collected at Giovanni's and Basque's crime scenes for possible relationships to the name or letter-number sequence. Nothing solid.

Angela suggested that it might be a password for one of Calvin's computer files or for a website he might have visited, but when we did a digital data analysis of everything on his three computers and cross-referenced the letters and numbers to all the websites he'd visited, addresses in his address book, and numbers stored on his cell phone, we came up blank.

I scoured my files, looking for anything we might have missed until 7:30.

Nothing.

I rubbed my head.

Went back inside the house.

As I gathered my things to leave for my class at the Academy, I noticed a voicemail from Ralph: "Hey, man, Brin went to work early, found her friend, just called. Missy Schuel. That's her name. The lawyer. I don't have a number, but she's got an office on 11th St. NW. See you at 11:30."

I looked up the number, phoned her, left my name and number as well as a brief summary of my situation, then asked her to call as soon as possible. Then I stuffed the letter from Lansing's lawyers into my computer bag so I could refer to it to answer any questions she might have.

Finally, before heading to class, I left a note for Tessa: "Call me. We'll set up a time and place to meet for lunch." I thought about adding, "There's some stuff we need to talk about—like your dad trying to take you away."

But that's not the kind of thing you tell someone in a note.

Computer bag in hand, I left for the Academy.

16

Astrid and Brad had met on DuaLife, a website on which you create avatars, or online identities, and live another life as anyone you choose. Marry, if you want to. Have children, get divorced, start over. Whatever you like. You could be a man or a woman, straight or gay, young or old.

A prostitute.

A banker.

A priestess.

Or a serial killer.

Or a victim.

She'd found Brad on one of the newer continents, one that was designed to cater to the unique tastes of adults.

But it wasn't cybersex that brought them together.

She'd been experimenting at the time, exploring ways to control and manipulate people, and ended up deciding to be the continent's first female serial killer.

Of course, since the site's users have invested so much time—and in some cases, money—into creating their online lives, you can't just kill the other avatars without asking for permission or negotiating with their NowLife creators.

So, counting on the fact that, even in DuaLife, people would want their fifteen minutes of fame, Astrid had posted a notice that she was looking for volunteers who wanted to be lured in, overpowered, and then slaughtered.

And she'd been right about people wanting their moment in the sun. Two men and one woman had responded almost immediately.

Those had been her first few games.

But it was only online.

Only imaginary.

And besides, none of those first three victims had been all that relationally or intellectually engaging and, as a woman with an IQ of 142, Astrid started longing for someone a little more intriguing to kill. Then, in one of her online chats with potential victims, she met Brad.

The Brad avatar was a twenty-eight-year-old oncologist. A fundamentalist Mormon who'd never married, he enjoyed hiking, golf, college football, and reading philosophy.

Of course, in NowLife, he might have been a forty-five-year-old Buddhist single mom who liked classic movies and judo.

Or anyone else.

That was part of the fun. A whole new life played out in your imagination.

Though it was possible that in NowLife he might be a woman, in their initial emails, Brad had responded to her questions in a way that seemed unmistakably masculine. He also appeared to exhibit the qualities she was looking for in a NowLife man.

Sometime after meeting him online, she'd begun to wonder what it would be like playing these games of life and death and destiny on real people.

She'd invited him to her DuaLife apartment and was getting him drunk so she could more easily subdue him before killing, but that's when she started to have second thoughts.

"Why do you want to die at my hand?" she'd asked him. "Why do you want me to kill you?"

"Because you're a woman."

"A woman?" On her computer screen she saw that he had finished his vodka. She poured him another.

He took a sip. "In *Thus Spoke Zarathustra*, Nietzsche wrote, 'A real man wants two things: danger and play. Therefore he wants woman as the most dangerous plaything.'"

"So, to a man, a woman is a plaything?"

"Yes." He downed his drink. "And the more dangerous she is, the more desirable. The greatest danger, the greatest pleasure."

"But I would be the one playing with you."

"Yes," he'd typed.

When he didn't elaborate, she'd responded, "I thought you believed in God, and yet you read Nietzsche? The man who said 'God is dead'?"

"You can find flowers even in a field of weeds."

So.

Nice.

Perhaps it was time to see if Brad might just be the one to partner with her. She'd typed, "How much danger and play can you handle?"

And after a pause he'd replied, "How much are you offering?"

Oh yes.

"I think it's time we met," she typed. "In person."

And so they had.

And sex had followed. And so had love. And now, though she hadn't yet told him, so would a child.

A new family grown from their DuaLife encounter.

As they'd gotten to know each other, they'd chosen to keep using their DuaLife names, rather than use their real ones. A way to extend the fantasy. To keep the illusion alive.

DuaLife.

NowLife.

Becoming one and the same thing.

It hadn't taken them long to learn the art of killing, and then the art of setting others up for their crimes.

She'd found that, just like his avatar, the NowLife Brad believed in God, and yet, despite his religious convictions, he seemed surprisingly willing to take the life of other human beings whenever she required him to do so.

Now, as she lay in bed with him, she slid her hand to her stomach, where their child was growing. A second heartbeat inside of her. The child of their passion and desire.

A new life. To be taught and molded. Just like her man.

He stirred.

"You're sleepy this morning," she said.

"I killed two people last night. That can really take the life out of you."

"Ha." She smiled. "Doesn't God say killing is wrong?"

"No one acts in complete congruence with his convictions." He still sounded half asleep. "Admittedly, this is one area I need to work on."

She ran her fingers through his hair. "That sounds like a line from a made-for-TV movie. That's not enough of a reason. Not for you. There's more to it, isn't there?"

"Saint Paul wrote, 'That which I do, I don't understand. For I do not do the good I wish, but the evil I do not wish, this I do. I am a wretched man! Who will rescue me from this body of death?' The inner war is the burden of all who believe."

She trailed her finger along the edge of his scars. "Brad, Brad, Brad, you are my little enigma, aren't you?"

A slight hesitation, perhaps a hint of intimidation. "Do you know anyone who is not?"

"Not?"

"An enigma."

"Well, if you're right about God, darling, I imagine you'll go to hell for the things you've done."

He was quiet.

"Any quotes on that? On the enigma of hell?"

He thought.

She smiled. "I got you this time."

"Francios de Fenelon."

"Who's Francois de Fenelon?"

"He was a priest in the seventeenth century. He observed that you can see God in all things but never so clearly as when you suffer. Perhaps hell, where people suffer the most acutely, is where they begin to see him the most clearly."

She laughed at the absurdity of using a priest to justify a journey to hell in order to discover God. Only Brad could come up with something like that. "Well," she said. "If God exists—"

"There is no 'if.'"

"If he does"—and she let him know by her tone of voice that the subject was not up for debate—"and if people become more aware of him in hell, then I expect both of us will be quite the experts on him someday."

"I expect we will."

After a few more minutes of letting him hold her, she rose, telling him that he could sleep in if he wanted, that she would get everything ready.

"Thank you."

"I'll see you at 2:00."

"Yes."

"You'll take care of the alley video?" she said.

"The surveillance camera will be looping through previous footage when you arrive."

"And the door?"

"I'll leave it propped open."

She flipped open the laptop belonging to the woman in the basement, downloaded the video Brad had taken last night from his cell phone, then she put the computer in the van.

Hopped into her car.

And left for work.

17

The FBI Academy
Classroom 317
7:46 a.m.

Death.

That was the agenda for today.

This morning, videos of murder, then a visit to the body farm this afternoon.

Over the years, the Bureau has collected thousands of DVDs and video tapes from crime scenes, from secret stashes of killers and videos from certain websites we've learned to monitor.

We have the world's largest collection of videos of humans dying at the hands of others.

Disturbing.

But, unfortunately, necessary.

We show these videos to the New Agents and National Academy students so they can understand the true nature of those we hunt. We make the agents and law enforcement officers watch real people die in painful slow motion, rewind, pause, replay.

So that they'll know.

Really know.

Some victims beg, others bribe. Men make threats they must certainly know they're incapable of carrying out. Women try to barter, offering their bodies and vowing not to tell.

Sometimes I wonder how many women actually succeed in exchanging sex for survival. I've only seen the videos of those who failed.

In my classes I've seen even the most hardened cops, the most experienced investigators from around the world, break in half when they see these videos.

Almost always, whether the victim is compliant or struggling, praying or begging, there's that moment when he realizes what is about to happen. You see the knowledge of the inevitable pass across his face.

The undeniable truth we spend our lives denying has finally sunk in: death is coming.

The end is here, only moments away.

That look, when he comes to that final chilling revelation, is the most heartbreaking of all to see. The race is over. Life has lost.

I turned on the video projector to cue up today's first video—a man in San Francisco who did to prepubescent boys the things that nightmares are made of.

For me, the hardest videos to watch are the ones in which people pray, because in so many cases you can see that they really do believe that God will hear them, will intervene, will save them. But in the videos we have here at the Academy, he invariably chose not to.

I often wonder if his silence is proof that he isn't there. That's the easy answer, of course. The intellectually facile one, but still, it's tempting to retreat into skepticism when you see such suffering responded to with silence.

Sometimes I envy people who find a way to live in quiet denial of what we as a species are capable of doing to each other. It'd be so much easier to live with that kind of naivety, closing one eye to the tears of the world, thinking that everything has a Disneyfied ending, a silver lining, a sunset to ride into.

A few months ago when I was speaking with Lien-hua about this, she told me not to dwell on the negative so much.

"I can't pretend that the world isn't what it is," I'd said.

"What do you mean?"

"That these things I see don't happen, that life is better than this."

A small pause. "But can you stop pretending that it's worse?"

It took me a long time to reply. "I'll try," I'd said.

And I still am.

I turned on the projector, tapped the DVD's play button, but the first frame—the one in which the killer zoomed in on the young boy's frightened eyes staring into the camera—today that image alone was too much for me.

I couldn't do this. I needed to look away from suffering, at least for the moment.

So I shut off the projector.

Plan B.

Astrid knew that Brad had money; he'd never kept that a secret, although he hadn't explained where it was from, and she'd never pried.

She'd suspected he'd stolen or extorted it until she saw him working on the computer system at the research facility yesterday. Now she began to wonder if he might actually have earned it as a computer programmer.

Well, what mattered was not where it had come from but what they could do with it if they needed to.

Disappear.

Or, if she needed to, she could do that herself.

Yes, she knew his bank account's pin number. She'd found it jotted on one of his statements two months ago. And this secret knowledge was a sweet and subtle thing.

Now, as she pulled into the parking lot at work, she thought of what would happen to the woman at 3:00 p.m. as the game moved toward its climax.

Tessa had agreed to meet Paul Lansing on the steps of the Library of Congress at 10:30 sharp. And now as she stepped onto the Amtrak train that would take her to the city, she felt somewhat like she was running away.

She told herself that as soon as she got some answers to the questions she hadn't felt comfortable bringing up while Patrick was around, she would explain everything to him and things would get back to normal between them.

Through Paul's emails over the last few weeks she'd found out where he grew up—St. Paul, Minnesota. His pastimes—sculpture (pretty cool), hunting (definitely uncool), hiking, carpentry, and organic gardening (that's better). His birthday—September 9. And so on.

And on.

But the core stuff went a lot deeper.

That's the stuff she needed to know.

The train doors closed, and she took a seat.

She'd chosen a T-shirt that left the scars on her right arm visible, the scars she'd given to herself when she was into cutting. A man stared at her now, his eyes lingering on her arm, and then on the oxymoronic words on her shirt: "Anarchy Rules."

She handled his curiosity with a steady gaze, locking eyes with him until he looked away.

Tessa had saved the biggest questions for a face-to-face meeting with her dad: How long did you date Mom before you slept with her? Did you love her? How come you live by yourself in the mountains? What are you running away from?

It seemed beyond weird to her that a man who lived without a phone or running water, a guy who'd been emailing her from a six-year-old borrowed laptop, had suddenly decided to hop on a plane and fly to the nation's capital just to see some sculptures that one of his friends had made. She'd have to ask him about that too.

He'd said he didn't know that Christie ever had her child, that he thought she'd gone through with the abortion she'd been planning. That's what he'd said, but Tessa didn't believe him. She'd found the postcard he sent to her mother only a few years ago. If he kept tabs on her mom, how could he not have known about her?

And so, perhaps the most important question of all: why didn't you ever come to see me after you two broke up?

And then there was Patrick.

She tried to think of a way to politely cancel lunch with him without making him suspicious. And without lying. She'd done enough of that already.

With a lurch, the train left to take Tessa Bernice Ellis to her father.

Class had started five minutes ago.

There were a number of seminars running concurrently this morning, and though officially the National Academy course didn't begin until Monday, the NA students who'd already arrived were invited to attend any of the lectures this week that they thought would be most helpful to them.

I'd been hoping Cheyenne might sit in on my class so I could thank her for taking Tessa home last night—at least that's the reason I told myself. But when class began and she wasn't in the room, I realized it was probably a good thing, since she has a way of monopolizing my attention and there was already plenty on my mind.

So, no videos today. Just discussion.

I'd kicked things off by telling my students that understanding the process an offender undertakes in planning and carrying out his crime is vital to eliminating suspects.

"Excuse me," a woman in the front row said, two fingers flagged in the air. I'd met her earlier in the week: Annette Larotte, a National Academy student from Houston. A homicide detective. Tall—5′11″. Brunette. Deep, reflective eyes.

"Yes?"

"What was number four? From last night?"

"Number four?"

"At the panel discussion you said there were four premises underlying geospatial investigation. But you only had time to list three before the discussion was cut short. What was number four?"

I quickly reviewed the first three: "Number one—timing and

location. Most crimes occur in the offender's awareness space. Two—rational decisions lead to the criminal act. Three—least amount of effort principle."

When I paused to take a breath, Annette finished my thought for me: "Offenders try to save time and money just like everyone."

I nodded. "Exactly. So here's number four: progression. With each successive crime, offenders become more efficient and experienced, learn from their mistakes, develop tastes and preferences for specific activities over others. They also learn from other people—criminal associates, research, observations—and as they do, two things happen: they become more competent, and typically, they become overconfident, which can lead to carelessness."

A few people took notes, Annette nodded her thanks to me, and I went on, "So to get us rolling today, tell me: what are the secrets to committing a perfect murder?"

The students began by noting the obvious:

1. take precautions to avoid leaving physical evidence,
2. contaminate the scene with other people's skin cells, bodily fluids, or DNA to confound investigators,
3. dispose of the body outdoors where insect activity, scavengers, and the weather will help disperse and destroy physical evidence—or better yet, don't allow the body to be found at all,
4. never murder someone you have a close relationship with, but rather choose someone whose disappearance will go unnoticed (runaways, transients, vagrants, hitchhikers, prostitutes, etc.).

Self-evident, rudimentary ideas.

I knew that the students in my class could do better, and I challenged them to go deeper.

And they didn't disappoint me:

5. since the authorities begin by searching for people who would most likely be present at the time and place of the murder,

it's wise to counterintuitively break your habits rather than keep them when you commit the crime,

6. kill alone because as soon as you have an accomplice you have a loose end,

7. if possible, artificially, microscopically, fake the DNA evidence you leave. Ever since two years ago when Israeli researchers discovered how easy it is to do—that even first-year college biology students could do it—it's become more and more common among educated criminals, and even with the Bureau's technological advances over the last year, it's still frustratingly hard to detect,

8. don't kill close to your activity nodes (home, work, preferred recreational areas, and commercial businesses) or the travel routes between them.

"Good," I said, building on the idea. "Very good. Most current research indicates that proximity of a series of crimes might be an even more accurate indicator of crime linkage than modus operandi or signature."

Then a suggestion came from a man in the third row, a detective from Bangkok, a member of the Royal Thai Police: "Keep it simple."

The door in the back of the room eased open and Cheyenne surreptitiously slipped into the room and took a seat in the back row.

Detective Nantakarn went on, "The more unique the crime, the more attention you'll draw from investigators. And the more arrows will lead back to you."

I nodded.

Annette suggested using an untraceable means of death, and because of the famous forensics dictum that whenever you leave a room you take something with you and leave something behind, the class debated about whether or not that was possible. However, I'd worked cases where the principle hadn't borne out, so I let the suggestion stand.

"Anything else?"

Cheyenne lifted her hand, and I nodded to her.

"Don't make your alibi airtight. Only a person with something to hide would remember the details of her whereabouts well enough to present a rock-solid alibi. The more perfect the alibi, the more suspicion it should draw."

"Good."

With Cheyenne we'd have another mind on Mollie Fischer's murder. Another good mind . . . It shouldn't be a problem clearing her to be part of the Joint Op program.

A quick look at the clock.

9:44.

I had a break scheduled at 10:00.

Yes. I would ask her then if she would like to join our team.

I was confident she would agree.

The two of us would work together again.

18

"Time to get up."

Brad gently shook the woman who, after being left alone in the pitch-black basement for nearly ten hours, had no doubt lost all sense of time.

She groaned.

"Come on, wake up." He flicked on a heat lamp, and she cringed at the harsh, sudden light.

He smiled at her. He had some things to tell her, some advice for how to prepare for her death in just over five hours. "I thought we could talk for a few minutes," he said. "Now that we're alone."

■

At the break, Cheyenne stepped into the hall before I could catch her, and hurrying after her seemed too middle-schoolish to me, so instead I fiddled around with my notes for a few minutes waiting for her to return, then decided to check my messages.

Missy Schuel had not returned my call.

I tried her number again but only reached an answering machine.

After evaluating things, I decided that if I didn't hear from Ms. Schuel by noon I would look for someone a little more responsive to potential clients.

I did have one voicemail, however, from Tessa, bowing out of lunch: *"It looks like things might take a little longer than I expected. Is it cool if we just connect tonight? That would rock. See you later."*

Brief. To the point.

All right.

I felt a little let down but not frustrated—it freed up the middle of my day, and without a trip to the city I wouldn't need to rush out of my 11:30 meeting with Ralph. Maybe we could actually make some headway on the Fischer case.

The students were filtering back into the classroom.

Just before the end of the break, Cheyenne returned, followed closely by Annette. They sat in the back, and since we were about to start, I figured it would be best to wait until after class to speak with Cheyenne. Until then, it was back to getting away with murder.

Tessa found Paul Lansing waiting for her on the west steps of the Library of Congress's Jefferson building.

For some reason, when she saw him, she thought of how Patrick would describe him: Caucasian. Late thirties. Brown hair. Beard. Six-foot-one. Two hundred pounds. Blue jeans, hiking boots, checkered shirt with the sleeves rolled up to the elbows.

And then—even though she had to chastise herself for doing it—she thought of how she would: *Paul Bunyan Visits the City.*

"Tessa," he called. He was smiling. He ambled toward her and gave her a shoulder hug, then a kiss on the cheek, and even though he was her dad, he'd never kissed her before and it felt slightly awkward.

"Hey." She gave him a sort of half hug, then backed away. "How was your flight?"

"Long. Got in last night, about 10:00. Two layovers. There aren't any direct flights from Riverton, Wyoming, to Washington DC."

"No, I guess not."

All this just to see a sculpture your friend made?

She wondered what kind of friend this was.

But then, a realization that should have been obvious from the start: *Duh, Tessa. He came to see you, not the sculptor. It's not rocket science.*

He was still smiling. "So what about you? Are you all settled in for the summer?"

"Yeah."

"Where are you guys staying?"

"In the country, at this house near the Academy."

A nod. "Very good."

So.

Her turn. "And you're gonna be in town for a couple days, then?"

"I fly out Saturday," he said.

"Okay."

A pause. "So," he said.

"So."

She waited.

His turn.

"Oh!" His eyes lit up. "I brought you something." He retrieved a North Face hip pack he'd set on the step before she arrived.

"You didn't have to—"

"No, no. I know." He was searching through the pack like a kid through a cereal box. "Here."

He handed her a flat screen BlackBerry.

"A phone?"

"So we can stay in touch." He patted his pocket. "Bought one for myself too."

"I already have a phone." She wasn't trying to be rude, but from what she knew, Paul wasn't rich and maybe he could return it and get his money back.

"Yes, I know. But this way—"

Patrick won't be able to find out about the calls.

"—we can talk anytime we want to."

"We can do that already."

She could see the air slowly going out of his balloon. "It's got that Google GPS thing on it so if we get separated we can find each other."

Okay, that was just plain stupid. "You can just call me on my normal phone."

He looked defeated, undercut by the obvious. "Sure, yeah." A man-sized puppy whose tail had stopped wagging. "I should have thought of that."

Oh, boy.

He held out his hand. "Here, I'll see if I can—"

Go on, Tessa—

"Actually, you know what? This is way better than the phone I have." Accepting the gift felt like another slight betrayal toward Patrick, but she didn't want to get off on the wrong foot with her dad. "Seriously, it's sweet. Thanks."

He waited for her to put the BlackBerry into her purse, then gestured toward the Capitol. "So are you up for a tour?"

"Listen, I was kinda wondering: how do you know someone who works here when you've lived in like the middle of Nowhere, USA, for six years?"

"It's from another life."

For a fraction of a second she thought he said "from another lie," but then caught herself.

What is wrong with you? Just chill!

"I lived in this area for a while," he added, "a long time ago."

"Oh, cool."

He gave her a curious look. "Is something wrong?"

"No. Sorry. Um . . ." She pointed to the Library of Congress's Madison building. "As long as we're here, let me get a reader's card first. Then maybe we can go do the tour thing or check out your friend's sculptures." She wasn't exactly into sculpture because so much of it was sophomoric or abstruse, but she knew it was important to her dad. "I'm sure they're cool."

"So, a reader's card." He held out his hand to indicate that she could go first, and she started down the steps with him beside her but slightly behind her.

"I'm really glad you could make it today," he said. She could tell he was trying overly hard to be friendly, but she didn't hold it against him. It would take them time to connect. It'd taken Patrick and her almost a year to feel natural around each other. "Ever since you and your stepfather showed up at my—"

"Patrick."

"Sorry?"

"His name is Patrick."

But even as she said the words, it occurred to her that her comment probably sounded rude. "I mean, maybe if you could call him Patrick instead of 'your stepfather,' that'd be cool. I call him Patrick."

"Sure, right. I meant no disrespect."

"I know."

They crossed Independence Avenue.

"Well, ever since you two showed up at my cabin, I haven't been able to stop thinking about you."

"Okay."

"We've got a lot to talk about."

"Yes."

Paul Lansing put a hand on her shoulder. A friendly gesture. That was all.

Something a father would do.

For his daughter.

But when a clutch of businessmen approached them, she gently eased away from him so that the men could pass between them.

———————————— ■ ————————————

"Cheyenne, hang on a sec."

Class had just finished, and she was on her way to the door with the rest of the students. When she heard me call her name she paused and glanced my way. She didn't normally wear makeup, but I noticed that she'd put on lipstick today. "Yes?"

"Thanks again for taking Tessa home last night."

"No problem."

My thoughts corkscrewed between her and Lien-hua, bothering me in a way that didn't exactly bother me. "Listen, last night you asked me if there was anything you could do regarding this case. Were you serious?"

"Of course."

"Well, I think I can get you into the Joint Op program; it's where NA students—"

"Sure. Consult on cases in conjunction with NCAVC."

"You know about—"

"It's covered in the application process, Pat. It's not a state secret."

"Oh. Right."

"And, yes. I'd love to work with you."

I noted her choice of words: "with you" not "on the case."

To work with me.

"But I'll be in class most of the time this summer," she said. "Almost every day."

"We'll catch up in the evenings."

A slight pause, and with it, a smile. "That sounds doable."

"Great. So, actually I'm on my way to NCAVC right now for a briefing. If you're not doing anything, why don't you come along? We can put the paperwork through and I'll show you around."

She hesitated. "That'd be nice, but the thing is . . ." She flicked her thumb toward the dining hall. "I missed breakfast. I need to grab a bite or I'll never make it through the afternoon."

"We'll pick up something on the way. My treat. For helping me out by taking Tessa home."

"Pat, you don't owe me anything." Her words had become taut. I might have offended her. "I told you before. I was only trying to help."

"Okay, then. You can treat me."

With my comment, the mood of the conversation softened, and she gave me a light, conspiratorial smile. "And why would I do that?"

I thought for a moment, made a decision. "In exchange for me not prying into why you're really here this summer."

"Well, then, your car or mine?"

"Mine."

We started down the Gerbil Tube. "And where exactly did you have in mind?" she asked. "For lunch?"

"Billy Bongo's Burger Hut. It's right on the way."

"Billy Bongo's Burger Hut? You're kidding me."

"Nope. Fastest fast food in town."

She shook her head. "You and your cheeseburgers." That's what she said, but underlying her words was a subtle message: *I know you. What you like. We have a history together.*

"Well, I never get any burgers at home—one of the disadvantages of living with a teenage PETA member. I have to sneak out for one whenever I can."

"So now I know your dirty little secret."

"Everyone needs a couple of those."

And we stepped outside, into the day.

■

Okay, so something wasn't right.

When the Library of Congress staff member asked to see the driver's licenses of the couple in front of them in line, Paul whispered to Tessa that he needed to make a quick call and that he would be back in a minute, would meet up with her by the door. "You're going to be all right?" he asked.

"Sure, yeah."

"Good. Okay, I'll be right back."

And as he walked away Tessa felt a quiet, tiny twitch inside of her, in the part of her where she needed most to feel safe. She didn't know this man very well. Patrick was suspicious of him. She wasn't supposed to be here, in the city, alone with him.

Just chill.

He's your dad.

She reminded herself that her mother had trusted him enough to sleep with him. And if her mom could trust him, she could too.

Tessa moved forward in line, pulled out her wallet, and handed her license to the man.

19

The NCAVC building was actually an old warehouse that still had a sign out front for Tarry Lawnmower Supply. Posters of lawnmowers still filled the front lobby, the receptionist still answered the phone, "Tarry Lawnmower Supply, how can we meet your lawn service needs?"

No sense advertising the headquarters for the FBI's investigative group dedicated to studying and solving the nation's most violent crimes, as well as the location of ViCAP, and the offices of the fifteen top behavioral profilers in the world.

Cheyenne and I passed through security, I picked up the Joint Op paperwork at the front desk, signed the recommendation forms, and told her, "You'll need to fill out the rest of these. Don't worry, Ralph'll send 'em through." I handed her the pack of papers. "Try not to get writer's cramp."

She weighed the stack in her hands. "I'll try to not throw out my back first."

Ralph was on the phone when we entered his office. He gave Cheyenne a quick glance, and I realized that even though he'd visited me in Denver, the two of them had never met. I signaled to him that she was with me, then pointed to the Joint Op forms in her hand and he waved us through to the conference room.

I led her inside.

And found Lien-hua sitting at the table, paging through a file folder.

Oh.

She looked up as we entered. Her eyes flitted to Cheyenne.

The phrase "unintended consequences" came to mind.

"Lien-hua." I said. "This is Detective Warren. From Denver."

"From Denver," Lien-hua said.

"We've worked together a few times."

"Seven," Cheyenne said.

"I see." Lien-hua stood, extended her hand to Cheyenne. "Lien-hua Jiang."

Cheyenne shook her hand convivially. "Cheyenne Warren. So you must be the profiler Pat talks so much about."

"Really?"

She gave Lien-hua a warm smile. "It's all good, though, I assure you."

Lien-hua looked like she was about to respond, but before she could, Cheyenne added, "Pat and I just had lunch together, and he offered to show me around the center." She held up the Joint Op papers. "And it looks like I'll be helping with the case."

"Welcome to the team, then," Lien-hua said in a tone that was impossible to read. "Detective."

"Thank you, I'm glad I'll have the chance to work with you."

The two women had started talking around me, as if I weren't even in the room.

"And where did you go?" Lien-hua asked.

"Oh, we just got here."

"No, for lunch."

"Billy Bongo's Burger Hut."

For some reason I felt like I needed to defend myself. "It's right on the way."

"Of course." Lien-hua gave Cheyenne a wink. "Let me guess: he got the Ultimate Deluxe Classic Cheeseyburg Extreme, curly fries, and a medium Cherry Coke?"

Cheyenne looked at Lien-hua oddly. "Right on the very first try."

"Old habits die hard," Lien-hua said.

Okay. This was officially awkward.

I heard heavy footsteps just outside the door, and I was relieved when Ralph flung it open and joined us. He tossed a stack of bulging manila folders onto the table and looked like he was about to launch right into the case, but took a moment first to introduce himself to Cheyenne, and based on my recommendation, he immediately signed her forms. "Finish it up, hand it in tomorrow," he mumbled, but I could tell something was definitely weighing heavily on his mind.

"Thank you," she said.

"So here's what's up." His tone was rough and hard. "That was Doehring on the phone. They just found Rusty Mahan. Dead. Hung himself sometime last night. Left a note confessing to Mollie's murder."

A stretch of elegiac silence filled the room. Lien-hua slowly lowered herself into one of the chairs circling the conference room table. "Where was he found?"

"Underneath the Connecticut Avenue bridge, near the riverbank. He was hidden in the trees. Never would have found him if the phone in his pocket hadn't started ringing. A jogger heard it, saw the body."

"Was the note handwritten or typed?" I asked.

"Typed. On his phone."

"Did we identify the caller?"

"No." He shook his head. "I know, it's all too convenient, but Doehring doesn't think so. The kid had motive, means, and opportunity. You know Doehring. And here's the clincher: he's planning to go public with this at the top of the hour."

He glanced at the clock on the wall.

11:35.

"Just twenty-five minutes before this thing explodes," Lien-hua said.

Ralph motioned for us to take a seat. "That's what we have to stop from happening."

Cheyenne chose the chair between me and Lien-hua.

"Quick update," Ralph said. "Margaret is in DC running point on the joint task force. We've set up the command post at Metro PD headquarters, third floor. So far we've got FBI, Metro PD, Capitol police, US Marshals on this." He shook his head. "Probably call in the freakin' Boy Scouts before this thing is over."

A deep breath, then he flipped open one of the folders. "All right. Here we go. Here's what we know so far."

━━━━━━━━━━━━━ ■ ━━━━━━━━━━━━━

The woman wasn't being cooperative.

Okay. Enough with that.

Brad forced a gag into her mouth.

Tugged it tight.

Looked at his watch.

11:39.

"You have until 3:00 this afternoon to live: three hours and twenty-one minutes left to reflect on eternity." He took a breath. "I was hoping it wouldn't have to go down this way. If you'd been more willing, things might have turned out differently."

She tried to cry out, but the gag swallowed the sounds.

"I'll be back."

Then he left her again, lying there alone in the dark. He went to check the wiring and timer on the explosive device that he had created. A one of a kind. A work of art.

An elegant surprise for Special Agent Patrick Bowers.

20

Ralph spent five minutes filling us in, mostly reviewing information I'd already read in the online case files.

I was anxious to find out what else we'd learned since I left the scene last night but tried not to appear as impatient as I felt.

"By the way," he said. "There's no sign of Mollie Fischer's laptop—we were hoping that might get us somewhere."

When he mentioned Mollie's laptop, I realized Cheyenne would need more than Ralph's cursory summary, so I flipped open my computer, clicked to the online case files, and turned the screen so that it faced her. "So you can catch up as we talk."

"Thanks." She tapped the mouse pad, began to scroll through the files.

"Where's Doehring?" Lien-hua asked.

"Command post. His team is back at the primate center interviewing the staff." Ralph pulled out a notepad. "All right, let's run down the timeline. What do we know?"

"Perhaps," Lien-hua said, "the key right now isn't focusing on what we do know but on what we don't." She ticked off her points one at a time on her fingers as she listed them: "We don't know if Rusty drove his car to the scene, accessed the facility, was present at the storefront, wrote the suicide note, or killed himself—or even for sure that he and Mollie broke up."

"So basically, nothing," Cheyenne observed, her eyes still glued to the laptop screen. "Square one."

"Okay, let's think about this." I stood. Began to pace. "Let's say someone is trying to set up Rusty. Considering the technical and tactical aspects of this crime, doesn't leaving his car at the scene seem like an odd way to frame him? Taking into account the typed confession, the ideally timed phone call just as a jogger is going past Mahan's body—"

"Too obvious," Ralph said. "Amateurish."

"Yes. And why leave Mollie's purse with her in the chimp's habitat?"

"But if someone *wasn't* trying to set Mahan up," Cheyenne said, "then it might have been him—all the circumstantial evidence points to him as the killer."

"That's true." Lien-hua nodded. "But Rusty is almost certainly not the killer, so . . ."

"Square one," Ralph said.

Even though my specialty is working serial crimes in which there are half a dozen or more primary or secondary crime scenes, the key to all investigations is zeroing in on timing and location, and that's where we needed to look more carefully right now. "The research center's video surveillance footage was deleted from 5:00 to 7:00, right?"

Nods.

"And Mollie's death appears to have been between 6:00 and 7:00 . . ." I was thinking aloud now, reevaluating an idea I'd toyed with but never really pursued. "And yet, the killers—let's say it's plural for now—exited the scene at some point—most likely after her death, but possibly before. In either case, they weren't caught on tape leaving the building . . . so unless there was some way to circumnavigate the cameras or preprogram the security system to start videotaping again after they left—"

"They stayed inside." Lien-hua leaned forward. "Then left after they'd turned on the cameras again."

A spark.

A possibility.

"And they would be caught on tape leaving sometime after 7:00." Ralph said.

"Let's try this," I said. "If we review the videotapes starting at 7:00, we should be able to identify everyone who entered or left the building after the keeper's 911 call—all the law enforcement personnel, EMTs, everybody."

"Yes," Lien-hua said. "So if we find footage of someone who left the building—"

"But no footage of 'em entering it," Ralph interrupted, "we have our inside man."

"Or woman," Cheyenne said.

I nodded. "That's right."

The logic of it was simple, but admittedly, there were holes. There might have been a way we didn't know about to avoid the cameras, but it was an avenue to pursue. A place to start.

Ralph scribbled on his pad. "I'll get some agents on this ASAP."

"Do we know any more about Sandra Reynolds, the keeper?" Cheyenne was studying the computer screen. "The woman who shot the chimps? She was present when the officers arrived."

"She looks clean," Ralph said. "Doehring and his guys interviewed her pretty extensively. We'll see if they get anything else from her this morning."

"And the security guard?"

"We had a tox screen done to see if he might have been lying about being knocked out, but he still had tranqs in his system. I'd say he's clear too. Neither of them saw anyone else there."

Ralph sounded convinced. I decided to move on. "And Mollie was deceased when the responding officers arrived? They confirmed it?"

"Oh yeah," he said, his voice somber. "There was no question about that."

A moment of uncomfortable stillness crawled through the room. The pieces just weren't coming together.

Cheyenne tipped her gaze away from the laptop and toward me. "I'm wondering, what if the chimps didn't kill her?"

"What do you mean?"

"I mean, is it possible she might have been dead before the chimpanzees maimed her?" She pointed to a crime scene photo of the straw-covered floor of the habitat she'd pulled up on the screen. "There's blood on the straw, but it's not as pervasive as you might expect, considering the wounds on the jugular vein in her neck, and once her heart stopped beating, she would have stopped bleeding."

"Gravity." Ralph nodded. "Blood pools to the lowest part of the body."

"Yes," she said.

I glanced at Ralph. "Is the autopsy finished yet?"

A look at the clock. "In progress."

"Let's see if the ME can establish for certain the mechanism of death."

More notes.

Lots to do.

He rose. "Actually, let me put this stuff into play. I think there're enough questions to hold off Doehring's announcement. I'll be right back."

As he left, Cheyenne discreetly asked Lien-hua where the ladies room was. "I'll show you," she replied, and they stepped into the hall.

I took the opportunity to connect my laptop to the USB hub for the flat screen wall monitor so we'd all be able to view the images when the three of them returned.

Then I began scrolling through the crime scene photos, focusing on the contents of Mollie's purse, trying to find anything that didn't mesh with the theory that Mahan was innocent.

■

"It's remarkable," Tessa whispered as she and Paul approached the sculpture.

Nearby, a mother was corralling two young boys toward the stairs, but even with that annoying little drama going on, the sculpture still held Tessa's attention.

It was a three-foot-tall mixed media sculpture of a girl with her hands wrapped around a boy's waist. Somehow the sculptor had captured the moment in such a way that it made it appear as if the girl was both clinging to the boy and pushing him away at the same time.

Even though Tessa had been hesitant about the whole idea of

the art museum, after seeing this sculpture she was hopeful that it might not be a complete waste of time. Without glass enclosures around the sculptures, you could get really close, and she stepped forward and inspected it admiringly.

Here you had the tension of a life captured in wire and plastic resin: holding on and pushing away; we want to be close but separate, independent but needed, free but constrained by love. Human nature in a nutshell.

"I'm glad you like it." Paul seemed pleased, almost proud.

"Yeah. It's really nice."

Out of the corner of her eye, Tessa noticed the woman turn her back on one of the boys. Without her supervision, the boy apparently felt free to approach a ceramic sculpture on a short wooden stand.

"Is it one of the pieces your friend made?" Tessa said, but her eyes were on the small boy who was reaching for the sculpture.

"Julia? No. Hers are—"

She could see disaster written all over this and called out to the woman to warn her, "Hey, your son!"

But the woman turned toward Tessa instead of looking at the boy. Tessa pointed at him as his hand found the sculpture—

The ceramic piece smacked to the floor.

And in that instant, Paul whipped around, his back to Tessa, shielding her from the direction of the sound—but of course there was nothing to protect her from.

Then an alarm was ringing and two staff members were rushing to the family. The mother was already scolding her son, and now Paul was herding Tessa to the other end of the exhibit hall.

"What was that all about?" she asked him. "You were like crazy fast. Were you ever a cop or something?"

"No," he said simply. "Come on, we'll work our way up to the fourth floor."

It would make sense if he was. Mom always was into the law-enforcement type.

"Seriously, you—"

"No." And he guided her onto the escalator in front of him.

21

I didn't find anything significant while they were gone, and when the four of us reconvened, Ralph announced, "All right, Doehring said he'll hold off on releasing any info to the press for now, but the congressman isn't going to. He scheduled a press conference for 1:00. And that's in stone. So unless we have something more by then, he's going to tell the press that his daughter's killer was Rusty Mahan."

"We need to rein him in," I said. "That could seriously hamper the investigation."

"I called Margaret to ask about this, but Rodale seems to be behind the congressman."

"That's unbelievable," Lien-hua said. "What's going on here?"

Politics as usual.

He shook his head. "I don't know," he said gruffly. "But it doesn't smell right to me either."

Forget the press, focus on the evidence.

I closed my eyes and reviewed the street layout surrounding the research facility, mentally following the route I'd taken to get there, forming a three-dimensional map in my head. But my memory wasn't nearly as accurate as a satellite image would be, so I opened my eyes, pulled out my phone, and projected the 3-D hologram of DC above the table.

All four of us gathered around it. Studied it.

I drew my finger across the phone's screen to zoom in on South Capitol Street where the research center lay, then rotated the image, studying the sight-lines from the parking garage's exit, the building's other exits in relationship to the streets, the parking lot . . . the traffic lights . . . the looming stadium.

Wait.

A thought.

On the laptop, I clicked to the DC Metro police site. Typed in my federal ID number.

Oh yes.

A small thrill. The moment opening up.

"What is it?" Ralph asked.

"Cameras," I mumbled.

"The footage was deleted." I could hear his growing impatience in his voice. "We just went through all that. We need to—"

"No. Traffic cams." I felt the juices flowing. The case beginning to enter my system in the way it's supposed to; the way I like. "We might not have footage of the killer arriving at the research center, but we might have video of him approaching it. If we caught Mahan's car on the way to the facility, we should be able to get a look at the driver."

"Confirm for sure whether or not it was Mahan." He was tracking with me now, step by step.

"Exactly."

It took me less than a minute to log in, pull up DC's traffic camera database, and find the video archives.

Mollie was last seen leaving the Clarendon Metro station.

I chose the traffic lights two blocks north of the facility, since it would be in a more direct route from the area of the city where she was last seen.

And, starting at 4:00, the time Mollie was last seen alive, we began to study the footage at 8x speed, looking for Rusty Mahan's '09 Volvo.

Brad carried the duffel bag containing everything he and Astrid would need to the van. Set it inside.

According to the plan, Astrid would meet him at the hotel at

2:00, but he liked the idea of having the woman alone with him in the room for a little while before Astrid arrived.

Leaving now would give him plenty of time.

He chambered a round in his gun, a Walther P99, holstered it, then went back downstairs, grabbed the woman by the hair, and, as she squirmed desperately to get away, dragged her toward the stairs.

———————————■———————————

It didn't take Tessa long to realize that the sculpture of the boy and the girl was the exception, not the rule.

Most of the sculptures were completely lame—trying too hard to say too much, or so esoteric that they failed to say anything at all. In the latter case, the museum staff had placed little plaques next to the sculptures describing why the artist made them, what was going on in his or her life, and what the sculpture was supposed to mean.

How helpful was that.

But the thing is, true art, real art, needs no explanation. There's no epilogue at the end of a novel telling you what the story was supposed to mean. No commentary at the end of a symphony explaining what the composer was trying to communicate with those specific notes. No footnotes clarifying the meaning of poems—at least not any that are worth reading. Art either stands on its own or it does not. As soon as it needs to be explained, it ceases to be art.

She didn't say any of this to Paul, though. Probably not the ideal dad/daughter conversation, since she would undoubtedly end up dissing this whole reclusive-sculpture-guy-thing he had going on, and she didn't want to do that.

They were still on the second floor, and the journey upstairs to Julia's exhibit was going excruciatingly slowly since Paul was studying each sculpture for way too long.

Finally, when he paused to read the plaque beside a bronze sculpture of two gray apples with red wigs kissing each other, Tessa said, "So you never got married?"

"No."

"Why not?"

"I guess I never met the right woman at the right time."

"So for Mom, was it the wrong time or the wrong woman?"

He looked at her. "I was the wrong man. I guess."

Not the answer she'd expected. She let his words sink in.

He led her to a large UPS box encased in glass. A sword had been driven through it, as if it were Excalibur piercing a stone.

Another explanatory plaque.

Oh, joy.

"So, no other kids?"

"No."

"That you know about."

The smile he'd been wearing when they first met on the steps of the Library of Congress had slowly been fading throughout the morning, and now he gazed at her curiously. Perhaps with a hint of hostility.

"I mean, you've made it clear that you didn't know about *me*," she explained. "But here I am. So, what I'm saying is: you mean there are no other kids that you *know* about."

"There aren't any others."

He sounded certain, but she couldn't believe that over the last seventeen years he'd never slept with any other women.

"How do you know?"

"I don't have any other children, Tessa." Something cold and uncertain had wormed its way into the space between them.

She repeated herself, speaking more slowly this time. "How do you know?"

"I had a vasectomy, Tessa."

It was too blunt, not the kind of thing a father tells his teenage daughter. Sure, she'd pressed him, but still—

"Come on." He pointed to the elevator. "I'll show you Julia's sculptures."

"Okay," she said. "And you can tell me a little more about her on the way."

22

Nothing.

No Volvo.

But we did have footage of the guard's car moving through the intersection at 5:53 p.m., and the GM Volt of the keeper, Sandra Reynolds, at 7:02.

I made a mental note of the times. However, the storm, traffic, any number of factors could have affected their arrival times.

Try the traffic lights south of the facility.

It would be a more circuitous route from the Metro station where Mollie had been seen last, perhaps indicating that her abductors left the city and then returned with her. And if that was the case, when I drew up the geoprofile, depending on the hot zone's location, it might prove significant.

Home? Did they take her to their place of residence?

Questions, questions.

I needed facts.

Only seconds after I'd started the second video, Ralph nailed his finger to the screen. "Gotcha."

At 5:32 p.m. Rusty Mahan's '09 Volvo passed through the intersection.

They arrived and then waited for the shift change?

Maybe.

I paused the image, backed it up to the moment the car first appeared onscreen.

Pressed play.

"That's it," Lien-hua said, but there was a note of disappointment in her voice. "But you can't see the driver, too much glare from the rain."

"Play it again," Cheyenne said.

I did, twice, and at different speeds. But the glare obscured the driver's face.

Ralph pulled out his cell. "The lab guys can pull some of that off—"

"No," I mumbled. I was staring at the image. "That's not right."

"What?"

"Look." I zoomed in on the license plate. "It's a different plate. The Volvo in the parking garage had 134-UU7 for its tags; this one has IPR-OMI."

Ralph lowered his phone. "But that is the same car."

"Let's make sure." I tapped the play button again.

Lien-hua ran the second set of plates while Cheyenne, Ralph, and I reviewed the footage to the point at which the emergency vehicles passed through the intersection at 7:14 p.m. on their way to the scene. No other Volvo sedans.

"OK," Lien-hua said. "Both sets of plates are registered to Rusty Mahan."

"Two sets of plates for the same car?" Cheyenne turned the keyboard toward her so she could tap at the keys, bring up the case files. "You'd need someone on the inside at the Department of Motor Vehicles to pull that off."

Ralph shook his head. "No. A driver's license, address, and a few bucks'll get you plates."

"Fake ID?" Lien-hua asked.

"Sixty bucks on the street."

I shook my head. "I could see switching plates to avoid apprehension, but why switch them if you're just going to leave the vehicle at the scene? Especially if you use plates registered to the same owner?"

The case seemed to be skewing into a completely different direction.

"All right, let's think about this," Lien-hua said. "IPR-OMI. Does that mean anything to anyone?"

"IP is your Internet Protocol," Cheyenne said. "Your computer's address within a network. ROM has something to do with computer memory."

"Read-only memory," Lien-hua said.

Cheyenne tapped at the keyboard. "IPROM stands for University of Illinois Probability Modules. A software program students use in their probability courses."

Ralph cut in, "Lien-hua, you said our guy might be a hacker?"

"Yes. But what about the *I* at the end?"

We were quickly sinking into the quagmire of conjecture.

He shook his head. "OMI could mean 'oh, my.'"

"Hang on a minute," I said. "Rather than worry about what kind of hidden message the plates might contain, let's find the DMV clerk who filed the registration papers and see if we can get a description of the person who applied for them. See if it was Mahan or not. We can have Angela Knight or the NSA's cryptographers work the plate angle for us."

No arguments.

"All right, bring up the video again, Cheyenne." Then I addressed all three of them. "Is there anything else here? Anything we're missing?"

She played the footage again.

The traffic light.

Red. Yellow.

"The facility's cameras . . ." I mumbled, "the electronics store . . . the killers know video . . ."

Green.

"Wait," I said. "Replay it."

And at last I saw it.

I couldn't believe I'd missed it earlier.

"Here, here, here. Watch it again. The traffic lights." I leaned close to Cheyenne. Hit play. I caught the light, sweet scent of her perfume, tried to ignore it.

As the video played, I could see from the looks on everyone's face that none of my colleagues had any idea what I was talking about. I moved the cursor back and pressed play one last time. "The light. Notice when it changes."

We all watched as the car approached, the light turned green, the vehicle slowed, passed through the intersection, accelerated.

"He slows down," Lien-hua said, "as he approaches the light."

"Yes, *as* he approaches," I said. "But it turns green while he's at least thirty meters away. So why would he slow down on an empty street as he approached a light that just turned green?"

"It could be almost anything." Ralph put an edge to his words, and it was clear he didn't think this was significant at all. "He could have been distracted, on the phone, fiddling with the radio . . ." A stretch of thoughtful silence, then he mumbled the same thing I'd been thinking, "Or he *wanted* to get caught on camera."

"That's what I'm wondering," I said. "Everything else so far has been set up to make us look in one direction while missing the obvious facts in another. They switched the plates and it looks like they wanted us to notice—but not right away."

"Who would even guess that we would check this?" Lien-hua asked. "The traffic cams?"

"Someone who thinks like Pat," Cheyenne said.

"But why?" Ralph asked. "Why would—"

My phone rang and my caller ID told me it was Missy Schuel, the lawyer.

Her timing couldn't have been worse. I hated to step away from this conversation, but this was one phone call I couldn't afford to miss.

It rang again.

"Hold that thought," I told my friends. "I'll be right back."

I slipped into the hallway and answered my cell.

23

"Pat Bowers here."

"Dr. Bowers, Missy Schuel. I received your message. I'm sorry I didn't get back to your sooner, but my daughter threw up this morning, and I had to take her out of daycare."

Of all the excuses to not return a call, taking care of your sick child had to rank near the top of the list, but it seemed oddly forthcoming for a lawyer to share that with a potential client.

"Is she all right?"

"Yes. Thank you for asking. She's with a friend." A brief transitional pause, presumably meant to bridge the conversation from personal matters to business. "Normally I'm not able to see new clients on such short notice, but I had a cancellation at 12:50. I can meet with you then for perhaps fifty minutes. It's my only opening until the seventeenth."

I glanced at my watch.

12:20.

Not gonna happen.

I knew that Missy Schuel's office was in downtown DC, at least a thirty minute drive from NCAVC, so even if I left immediately and sped all the way there, I'd barely make it, and considering how much Missy and I needed to discuss, I couldn't think of any way I'd make it back to Quantico in time for my 2:00 class. "There's nothing else? You're sure?"

"Dr. Bowers, I can meet with you at 12:50." No irritation in her voice, just professional formality. "Otherwise, I'll be glad to give you the names and numbers of other lawyers I would recommend. Which would you prefer?"

"Are they as good as you are?"

"No." A simple, frank assessment that impressed me.

I thought of Ralph's list of all the agencies involved in this investigation, all the people on the case. *They can get by for a couple of hours without you, Pat. Don't mess around here. Do what's best for Tessa.*

"I'll be there at 12:50."

"All right. My office is located at 1213 11th St. NW. Park at the liquor store across the street. They don't mind."

"The liquor store?"

"I don't have any parking here at my office, so I tell my clients to use their lot. Just don't linger or they'll think you're there for a drug deal."

My confidence in Ms. Schuel was beginning to falter.

"Okay."

"I'll see you soon, Agent Bowers."

"Hang on. I told you I was a doctor; I didn't say anything about being an agent."

"I looked you up. I don't like surprises." And that was all.

We ended the call, and I hurried back to the conference room and collected my things, leaving my laptop for the team to use. "I need to go."

Lien-hua gave me a look of concern. "Are you all right?"

"Yes." I gestured toward the hallway. "Can I talk to you a moment?" As we left I noticed Cheyenne watching us curiously, but when she saw me look her way she focused on the computer monitor again.

When Lien-hua and I were alone in the hall, I said, "Could you do me a favor? Are you heading back to the Academy?"

A pause. "I can."

"Could you take my 2:00 class?" I could hear that my voice was urgent, rushed. "Just thirty minutes maybe. We're supposed to do a walk-around of the body farm."

"Pat, what's going on?"

Go on, lay it out. Then move.

"It's Tessa's father. We found him last month, and he's trying to take her away from me. He's suing for custody. I need to meet with a lawyer, and it can't wait."

There. On the table.

"I'll take the whole class period. Go."

"Thanks, I owe—oh man. Cheyenne. She rode here with me. She'll need a ride back to the Academy."

"Don't worry about it. I'll give her a lift."

"You sure?"

"If we're going to be working together, we'll need to get to know each other."

Unintended consequences.

Without thinking about it, I squeezed her shoulder lightly. "Thank you." Touching her felt both familiar and unfamiliar at the same time. Different tones of the past.

I was about to pull my hand away, but she put her hand on it and her fingers curled around mine, ever so slightly, but they did. "You don't have to thank me. Now get going."

Then the moment disappeared. She returned to the conference room and I jogged to the parking lot, my thoughts flying ahead to my meeting with Missy Schuel.

24

So, according to Tessa's dad, Julia Rasmussen was someone he'd met when he lived in DC six years ago. Apparently, she was the one who introduced him to sculpting.

She was a sculptress.

How nice.

"Will you be seeing her while you're in the city?" Tessa asked.

He was slow in answering. "Tomorrow. Yes." He gestured toward a sculpture about twenty feet away. "Well, here we are."

Tessa stared at the figure Paul was walking toward: four-feet tall, made out of some kind of plastic resin. The sculpture's feet were fins that slowly morphed into thickly muscled, hairy legs and then changed into a naked torso and neck, then a face of a girl with a tragically sad smile but optimistic eyes.

It had an explanatory plaque. Of course.

Paul was beaming. "Amazing, isn't it?"

Julia, huh?

The sculptress.

"It's . . . interesting."

"What does it say to you?"

"Honestly?"

"Yes. Of course."

"It says she couldn't decide what to make—a frog, a gorilla, or Shirley Temple."

He looked at her oddly.

"I'm sorry, I mean, okay, how about this: it's the history of life on this planet, from fish to ape to man, moving inexorably toward happiness. But our race hasn't reached it yet—we're still dragged down by our animal nature, and that's why her face is so downcast. She's hopeful, optimistic, but has yet to reach enlightenment."

He blinked. Glanced at the plaque. Looked again at Tessa.

"No, I haven't seen it before," she said.

"That's extraordinary."

"Yeah, but it's not honest."

"Not honest?"

"The sculpture. About life. It assumes natural selection always moves toward happiness, which is imposing a value judgment on it, which is illogical. And who's to say animals aren't happier than we are? Not too many of them commit suicide. Besides, a lot of people think we're shaped by the hand of God, not simply natural processes. Mom believed that. I do too."

A pause. "You've thought about this before."

"Yeah." She considered telling him that Patrick had told her more than once that truth is not afraid of scrutiny. But she held her tongue.

"Do you believe in God, Paul?"

He was slow to answer. "I'm not sure."

"Does Julia?"

"Tessa, this is — "

"None of my business?"

He looked at her closely. "No, I don't think Julia believes in God."

Tessa felt it in the air: awkwardness, awkwardness, awkwardness.

"So." He pointed to a nearby sculpture: a toilet seat surrounded by fake fur and framed inside a giant green triangle. "What about this one? Let's see if you can get two in a row."

Oh, please don't tell me Julia the Sculptress made that thing too.

Tessa glanced at the name on the placard.

Good.

"Well?"

"Come on, Paul. I just want to talk. I'm really not into this whole sculpture-interpretation-thing."

"You nailed the last one."

"Luck."

"I don't believe you."

She held back a sigh. "It's a toilet seat in a giant triangle. Can we move on? Please?"

"Come on, you can do better than that. Can you tell me what it means?"

All right.

Enough with this.

"I'm no artist, but I don't think the point of art is to *mean*, I think it's to *render*. If it doesn't do that, if it needs a plaque to explain it, it's not art. It's like nature—what does a bird mean by its song? What does a flower mean when it blooms? It means beauty. Any explanation beyond that is superfluous."

He stared at her.

"Look, what did you do before moving to Wyoming and becoming a recluse?"

"I worked for the government. I told you that before. How do you know so much about—"

"Yeah. The game and fish department."

"That's right."

"Why are you living out there in the middle of nowhere? Are you running from something?"

"I needed a place to be alone to work on my sculptures; we went through all of this when you and your stepfather came to my cabin. Did you study art or—"

"Patrick. When Patrick and I came to your cabin. Please use his name."

A hard look. "I'm not sure what you're trying to do here. Are you angry at me?"

"No."

"Let's try to switch this from an interrogation to a conversation, okay?"

She felt a sharp itch of anger. "I'm not interrogating you."

"How about we just go back and forth, okay? You ask me a

question, then I'll ask you one." He gestured toward some leather chairs near the window, but she didn't move.

"How long did you and Mom go out?" she said.

"Three weeks."

"And did you—"

A smile. "It's my turn, Tessa."

She said nothing.

"Do you love Patrick?"

"I love him. Yes. What about Mom? Did you love her?"

A pause. "We went out for three weeks, Tessa."

"And?"

He didn't answer.

"So," she said, "you slept with her even though you didn't love her?"

"We slept together. Yes. Three or four times."

"Three or four? You don't *remember*?"

"My turn for a question. Has he ever done anything to hurt you?"

"Who?"

"Patrick."

"To hurt me? What are you talking about?"

He pointed to her right arm, to her scars. "Did he do that to you?"

"How could you even think that? I did that to myself. You can't remember how many times you slept with my mom? How many other women were you sleeping with at the time that made it so hard for you to keep track?"

"There weren't any others." Then back to the scars. "Some of those look recent. Why didn't he stop you?"

She stared at him coolly. "I think I'm done with this little conversation-bonding-time." She slung her purse strap over her shoulder. "And I've had enough art appreciation for one day. I'm leaving."

He reached out for her arm to stop her, but she glared at him. "Don't even."

He stopped just short of actually touching her.

"I care about you." He let his hand retreat. "I want you to be safe. During Basque's trial last month, your stepfather—Patrick—admitted to physically assaulting him, to breaking Basque's jaw when he arrested him."

"The guy was trying to kill him."

"That's not exactly how the press portrayed—"

"Patrick would never hurt me. Ever."

A drop of silence. "I'm glad to hear that."

She narrowed her eyes. "What's with all the questions about Patrick?"

"You're my daughter. I just want to make sure you're in a safe environment. You're important to—"

"Oh yeah? Well, then, answer me this: if I'm so important to you, why didn't you ever come to see me? And *please* don't tell me it's because you thought Mom was going to abort me. You kept tabs on her. You wrote to her fifteen years later—*I found the postcard*! You would have known about me."

She watched him closely. His face. His body language.

"Honestly, I always thought your mother went ahead with the abortion."

"Yeah, right."

"I'm telling you the truth. I didn't know you were born, Tessa. I had no way of knowing. Before your mom moved away she made it very clear that she didn't want me in her life." A pause. "But now we're here; we're together, and I'm just trying to make sure that this man who is taking care of—"

"Patrick! His name is Patrick! And he's more than just the guy who takes care of me, okay?"

"Okay."

Show him, Tessa. Prove it.

She yanked up her left sleeve, revealing the raven tattoo she'd gotten to conceal the scar Sevren Adkins had given her when he slit her brachial artery and left her to bleed to death.

"Patrick saved my life last year when this serial killer attacked me. He risked his life. He almost got killed doing it."

"A serial killer?"

"That's right."

He was looking carefully at the tattoo. And at the scar.

"I didn't know that."

She let go of her sleeve. "Yeah, well, now you do."

"I'm sorry you were hurt like this. I would never have let some-one—"

"I am so done with this." She turned to go.

"Tessa, don't walk away from me when I'm talking to you."

She whirled around. Got in his face. "Patrick would do any-thing for me, and while you were out there in your little Una-bomber cabin playing with papier-mâché, he was busy being a dad to me. Don't email me anymore. I think I know everything I need to."

"There's still a lot we need to discuss. I'll—"

"Discussion's over. Paul."

"I told you before. In my emails. You don't need to call me Paul. I'm your father. You can call me Dad."

Unbelievable.

"Patrick's my dad. You're just the man who impregnated my mom."

She strode away, but as she boarded the elevator, she shot a glance at him, and saw that he hadn't moved from where he'd been stand-ing. He was still watching her with clear, unswerving eyes.

It creeped her out.

The elevator doors closed.

He used your mom. He didn't love her.

He used her . . .

She felt a rush of hot anger and a tight coil of disappointment.

He didn't love Mom. How could he have ever loved you?

And as soon as she reached the ground floor she escaped to the bathroom to think. To hide. And despite herself, to cry.

25

The woman in the back of the van was silent now, and still.

Earlier, as Brad had transferred her from the basement to the vehicle, she'd struggled more than he would have liked, but he'd put a stop to it.

Now, compliant once again, she lay next to the wheelchair that he would use to take her to the room where she would die on the eighth floor of the newly renovated Lincoln Towers Hotel, best known as the place where a would-be assassin tried to kill the vice president six years ago.

He and Astrid had taken a room at the hotel last month and, using the television's volume, had tested how much sound was noticeable in the hallway. They'd found that, while the room wasn't as soundproof as the one in their basement, with the television turned up to hide the woman's cries, it would work just fine.

In a sweet curl of irony, the woman would die in a room that the corpse from the primate center was paying for—at a tidy sum of $598 per night. And no one would find that out until it was too late.

He hopped off I-95.

12:41 p.m.

The hotel wasn't far at all.

Let the games begin.

26

I was less than five minutes from Missy Schuel's office, and in anticipation of our meeting, my thoughts were revolving around Tessa and her father.

We met him in Wyoming at the end of last month.

The air in the mountains had been smudged with rain that day, and the peaks surrounding his cabin were swallowed in a thick gray mist.

A weary, drizzling sky.

As we stepped out of the car, Tessa slid a wisp of hair away from her eye. For some reason I remember that. A small gesture. Frozen in time. "I want to do this by myself."

"That's not going to happen."

"I'm serious."

"So am I. Tessa, I'm not leaving you alone with him. Not until I know more about him."

"He's my father."

Though I knew the words were true, they stung a part of my heart I'd never known existed until after Christie's death when Tessa became the most important person in my life. "Yes, he is," I said. "But if you're going in there, I'm coming with you."

A pause. "Fine."

So together we'd approached the cabin. The fog snaking around us. The mud thick underfoot.

I wasn't sure how Paul would respond to having us show up like this unannounced. We hadn't phoned to tell him we were coming; after all, he didn't own a phone. Or have a bank account. Or a credit history. On paper the man didn't exist.

And that was one of the reasons I wasn't going to leave Tessa alone with him. He'd left society behind, and I wanted to know why.

When he answered the door I decided that mentioning I was a federal agent might not be the best way to get off on the right foot. "My name is Patrick Bowers," I said. "Are you Paul Lansing?"

His eyes traveled back and forth from me to Tessa. "I am."

I was about to explain the purpose of our visit, but before I could, Tessa held out the diary, opened to a note that a man named Paul had written to her mother seventeen years earlier asking her not to have an abortion. "Did you write this?"

He gazed at the page, and his expression changed from curiosity to mild suspicion. "Who are you?"

"My name is Tessa Bernice Ellis. My mother was Christie Rose Ellis. Seventeen years ago you slept with her and she wanted to abort me and you begged her not to. I'm your daughter."

I waited for Paul to speak, to say something, anything. But he just studied Tessa for an infinitely long moment, and finally whispered, "So she didn't . . ." Neither Tessa or I moved. "I always thought . . ."

And then a soft tear formed in his eye and he invited us inside.

And in that moment I realized that he had loved Tessa for the last seventeen years even though he hadn't known she was alive.

Just down the block from Missy's office, my phone's ringer snapped me out of my thoughts about that gray day in Wyoming. I answered.

Ralph: "Where are you, man?"

"DC."

"Good. Congressman Fischer wants to see you."

"What are you talking about?"

"He asked for you. I think it's about Mahan."

"Me? Why?"

"Didn't say. I know it doesn't make sense, but I need you to—"

"Listen, I'm on my way to see the lawyer Brin told you about. Have Margaret deal with—"

"I know you need to do that, but those things take weeks. You have time. Fischer has a press conference in less than fifteen minutes."

I pulled into the liquor store's parking lot across the street from Missy Schuel's office. "Ralph, this doesn't make sense. There are plenty of people who can talk to Fischer. Sic Doehring on him."

"You can stop him from—"

"What about a phone call? Why don't I just call him?"

"He asked to see you." Agitation rising in his voice. "I don't need to tell you that right now is not the time to get him pissed off at the Bureau."

"Wait." I was losing my patience too. "Am I talking to Ralph, or is this Margaret?"

A slice of silence.

"The meeting with the lawyer can wait." Ralph's tone had turned cold. "You have ten minutes to get to the house minority leader's office so Fischer can talk with you before he meets with the press, and I don't want you to be late."

"Get ready to be disappointed."

"Pat, the priority right now needs to be—"

"My daughter," I said and I ended the call.

Then I turned off the ringer, grabbed my satchel with the letter from Lansing's lawyers in it, climbed out of the car.

And headed across the street to Missy's building.

■

Tessa was washing her face, but her black mascara had smeared really bad and she still looked terrible.

How can that man actually be your dad? It's not possible!

She felt like hitting something, *hitting him*, and of course, cutting again. Trying to slice the pain away.

Her eyes went to the scars on her arm.

She'd seriously been trying to move past that chapter in her life, didn't even carry a razor blade or X-acto knife with her anymore. But she could get one. She could buy—

142

Don't go there, Tessa. Not again.

She finished at the sink, dried her face, left the restroom.

She needed to talk to Patrick.

Now.

Tell him everything, apologize.

Oh great. That's right.

The phone. The BlackBerry Paul had given her with his little Google GPS program on it so he could *track* her.

She pulled it out and left him a rather unambiguous message on the screen of what he could do with his little gift phone, then dropped it in the trash can beside the front door as she left the museum. Go ahead, let him track it, find it, read it.

Enjoy that, *Dad*.

She fished out her own phone. Speed-dialed Patrick.

No answer.

Come on, pick up, pick up.

Nothing.

Dang.

She left a message, trying to make it seem like she wasn't totally about to lose it, but it wasn't easy.

Get back home.

Back to the house. Just get out of here.

At the street corner, she found a placard showing the location of the city's Metro stations, located the nearest one that could get her to the VRE back to Virginia, and headed toward it.

Missy Schuel's reception area was a small, cluttered nook of a room containing a desk piled high with papers, invoices, and legal pads filled with illegibly scribbled notes. No receptionist. An old TV sat in the corner of the room, sound off, mutely showing an empty podium with a flag beside it. Text at the bottom of the screen told me that Congressman Fischer's press conference would be starting momentarily.

I'd dealt with enough crimes in the DC area to recognize the press corps room just outside the house minority leader's office.

The place Ralph had told me to go.

A door to my left had a sticky note on it: "I'm in here."

A sticky note.

Wonderful.

Brineesha said she's good. At least give her a chance.

I knocked.

"C'mon in, Dr. Bowers."

I stepped inside.

27

A simple office.

Law manuals packed the bookshelves, a small window on the east wall faced another building less than five meters away. A laptop computer sat centered on her desk flanked by a small digital clock and a picture of three smiling children—one boy and two girls, all of whom appeared to be ten years old or younger. A neat, nearly empty inbox.

Missy Schuel was neither hefty nor slim, neither beautiful nor unattractive. Early forties, black hair fringed with a touch of gray. She made me think of an elementary school principal rather than a hard-nosed divorce attorney.

She stood and took my hand. "Dr. Bowers, pleased to meet you."

"Call me Pat."

"Missy."

Before asking me about my situation with Lansing, she dove into an explanation of her own story: she was a mother of three who'd recently gone back to work after her husband left her last summer, he was a good man, she said, and it hadn't been for another woman and she didn't hold it against him.

Once again, strangely forthcoming.

And although I found it hard to believe, she really didn't seem bitter toward her ex-husband, just wounded by him. I got the feeling that she'd been shattered by the fact that the man she'd given her life to had decided he would rather be alone than with her—a blow that I could only imagine might take a person a lifetime to recover from.

Still, as sympathetic as I felt toward her situation, I just wanted to get started and I think she could tell. "I only share this with you," she explained, "so that you know I'm a single parent myself and that I can understand the types of struggles and issues you deal with. Every case is personal to me."

"I'm glad to hear that."

We promptly discussed her fees, and in contrast to her office surroundings, she wasn't cheap, but I accepted her terms. Then she told me she would only be able to meet until 1:20, twenty minutes less than I had thought, and we both took a seat. She positioned a legal pad in front of her. "I won't lie to you, Agent Bowers. These things, these custody cases—they can be . . ." She seemed to be searching for the right word.

"Tricky," I said.

A nod. "Yes. And painful. And confusing. Especially for the children."

I felt a twist of anxiety, maybe even guilt, although I couldn't think of anything I'd done that I should feel guilty about. "I'm aware of that."

She lifted an impossibly sharp pencil, held it in her hand just so, the tip against the top line of the legal pad. "All right. From the voicemail you left me this morning, I understand that your step-daughter's biological father is trying to get custody of her."

"Yes."

I handed her the letter from Paul Lansing's lawyers.

She studied it. Set it aside.

"Talk me through this. You first met Tessa when?"

My cell phone vibrated in my pocket, and I ignored it.

"About three months before her mother and I got married."

"Three months."

"Yes. Christie and I were engaged for only a short time." I gave her the dates.

She wrote.

The phone continued to vibrate and I continued to ignore it.

A new habit of mine.

I kind of liked it.

She glanced toward my pocket. She must have noticed the muted sound of my phone. "And your marriage lasted?"

"Christie died four months after we married."

Missy paused. "I'm very sorry." The sympathy in her voice seemed honest and heartfelt, and I began to trust Missy Schuel with my case.

"Thank you."

My phone stopped.

"Go on," I said.

"May I ask—if you only knew Tessa for such a short time when her mother passed away, why didn't you contact another relative to have him or her raise Tessa after Christie's death?"

"Both of Christie's parents died when Tessa was young. Christie didn't have any siblings. And I had no way of knowing who, or where, her biological father was."

"So there were no close relatives."

"Not that I was aware of, no. Before she died, Christie asked me to take care of Tessa." Another call was coming in, but I didn't want any distractions, so I took a moment to still the vibrate function on my phone.

"Then you do have custody? Legal custody?"

"Yes."

"Good."

A ray of optimism. Things were going to be okay after all.

But that's not what Missy's face told me as she asked me for more background. I took her through the story of how, after Christie's death, I'd moved with Tessa from New York City to Denver in the hopes of putting some distance between us and our grief. At first we'd struggled to get along, but since my work schedule required seven or eight days of travel each month, mostly weekends, we were both able to get enough space to stay sane.

"And where did she stay during those times? When you were gone?"

"With my parents."

I mentioned Tessa's difficult times with self-inflicting—or cutting, as kids today call it—and then concluded by telling Missy about the weekend last October when our relationship began to improve. Pain had brought us together.

"She was abducted by a serial killer. He cut her and left her to die."

"That's horrible."

"Yes, but I got to her in time. After that, I don't know . . . maybe we both realized how much we'd always loved each other, needed each other, but had never really understood how to show it."

"Does she have scars?"

"Pardon me?"

"You said he cut her. Does she have scars?"

The question seemed a bit intrusive. "Yes. She has a scar on her left arm. There's a tattoo covering it, but it's still visible."

Missy wrote a few notes on her pad. I didn't like that she scribbled in a style of shorthand that was impossible for me to read upside down. "And Paul Lansing," she said, "what do we know about his relationship with Christie?"

"The few times I asked her about who Tessa's father was, she only told me that he was no longer a part of their lives."

Missy had her head down, staring at the paper, but now raised her eyes, gave me a slow, measured look. I sensed that she did not believe me.

"I didn't press the issue with her. We all have some things that are too painful or awkward to share. Things we need to put behind us."

"All right."

"Tessa only found the diary with Paul's name in it recently, a few weeks ago."

A head tilt. "Diary?"

"Yes, Christie's. From when she was in college. According to what she wrote, she had a short-lived relationship with Paul and that was all."

"And did he choose to assert his rights as Tessa's father at that time?"

I hesitated.

Missy watched me. Reading my face, my silence.

"Tell me."

"When Christie found out she was pregnant she decided to have an abortion. He wrote to her, Paul did, begging her not to. She kept his letter in her diary. After she chose to have Tessa, there's no mention of him again in the diary entries. But it wasn't the letter that persuaded her. It was—"

Missy set down her pencil.

"I'll need to see that letter. The diary too."

Even though I knew it was wishful thinking, I'd hoped to keep those two items out of this. There was no way either Paul's letter or the diary was going to help our case. "All right."

"And after Christie passed away, you didn't put any paperwork through to legally adopt Tessa?"

"I had custody. It never occurred to me to adopt her." The more we spoke, the more off balance I felt, as if everything I'd thought was solid in my life was sinking, shifting.

A slim breath. "Tell me a little more about your stepdaughter."

■

Brad was parked in the handicapped parking spot beside the Lincoln Towers Hotel.

He crawled into the back of the van, held the woman's arm still, and slid the needle into her vein. Depressed the plunger.

The drug he was using would work quickly. It wouldn't take long until she would be unconscious.

He removed the needle, sat back, and watched as her breathing slowed.

As her eyelids drooped.

As her body went limp.

She lay helpless beside him.

He unpocketed his phone and took some video. It wasn't officially part of the plan. This video was just for fun. For his own personal use.

Then he pulled out the woman's computer to hack into the hotel's security system and loop the video footage on the back alley's surveillance camera.

28

Missy Schuel tapped her pencil against her desk.

"You mentioned that in the first eight months following Christie's death, that you two—you and Tessa—struggled relationally."

"Yes. Things were a little rough between us at first, but like I said, we didn't know each other well, we were both hurting." Our time was almost up, and I didn't feel like we'd made much progress. There was still a lot to cover.

"All right." Missy let out a careful sigh. "Here's what I would say if I were Paul Lansing's lawyer: after her mother's tragic death, you uprooted the girl, moved across the country, and there, in Denver, pursued a job that took you away most weekends, forcing her to stay with your parents, whom she barely knew. You endangered her by allowing her into a life that no grieving teenager should have to experience. In fact, as a direct result of one of your investigations, she was abducted, suffered unimaginable mental duress, and was nearly killed."

When Missy put things like that, I couldn't imagine any judge landing on my side. "She was at an FBI safe house when she was taken." The words seemed weightless. Without merit. "I did all I could to make sure she was safe."

"I'm afraid that might not matter. The fact that this killer managed to find her and attack her, that's all the judge is going to hear— especially if he sees that scar, and you can be sure Lansing's attorneys will make that happen."

I repositioned myself in my seat. "So where do we go from here?"

150

Rather than answering my question, she asked one of her own: "Do we know for certain that Paul Lansing is Tessa's biological father?"

"We did a DNA test. It's confirmed. He's her dad."

She slid her notebook aside. "I'm going to be honest with you, this diary, this letter, they trouble me."

"It wasn't the letter that convinced Christie to keep her baby."

"I understand that, but his lawyers will argue that it was, and we can't prove that his words didn't influence her, at least to some extent." After a pause, "Can we?"

"No." I hated to admit it. "We can't."

Over the years I'd worked enough with the judicial system to know where all of this was leading. "He's got a good case." I didn't ask it as a question.

"A tenuous case," she corrected, but then hesitated for a long time before going on, and I had the sense that she was trying to find a way to put a positive spin on things. "Tessa would prefer being with you, rather than Paul, correct?"

Her question felt acidic, not because of her tone, but because I wasn't certain of the answer. "Does that matter?"

"When a girl's her age, yes, it does."

"I think so."

A nod. "And you are her legal guardian. You've been her sole caregiver and provider for over a year. That counts for a lot. It really does."

She paused.

There was more.

"But?"

"But, Lansing apparently desired to be involved in her upbringing, and her mother denied him that. If indeed he is her biological father and took legal steps during Christie's pregnancy to establish his paternal rights, he might . . . well, he might gain some sympathy from the judge. But listen to me, I'm good at what I do, and I promise I will do my best to help you keep sole custody of your daughter."

"Stepdaughter."

"No, your daughter," she said simply, leaving me to interpret that as I chose.

She glanced at the clock on her desk, and my eyes followed hers.

1:18 p.m.

"I need to go," she said. "We'll talk soon."

We both stood. "Get me that diary and the letter. Today." She jotted an address on the back of a business card. "If you can't get it here before 6:00, drop it off at my house." She handed me the card. "And I'll contact Paul Lansing's lawyers. I'll want to meet with them as soon as possible."

I hesitated. "Why as soon as possible?"

"People only cower when they're afraid or have something to hide. We don't want it to look like we're stalling or dragging our feet. If we move forward quickly and confidently, it'll show the judge the truth: that we have a solid case and nothing to fear."

I liked the way she thought. "I'll get them to you."

"One last thing. Does Paul Lansing know that you have his letter and Christie's diary?"

I let out a small breath. "We showed it to him when we met in Wyoming, when we first met him."

She kept her face expressionless. Pointed to her card. "Call my cell if you think of anything else that might be helpful. Anything at all. No secrets. Remember—"

"You don't like surprises."

"See you soon."

As I left her office, I glanced at the television screen in the corner of the receptionistless reception area. The congressman was stepping away from the podium. I punched up the volume just in time to hear a female correspondent say, "Bob, to reiterate, Congressman Fischer has just announced that Rusty Mahan, the primary suspect in the case, has been found dead in an apparent suicide. We don't know the details yet, but we will be covering this breaking story closely as events unfold."

Great.

While the reporter went on to summarize Fischer's press conference, his daughter's smiling photo floated in the upper left-hand corner of the screen and I realized that, apart from the brief glimpse at Cheyenne's cell before I left the Academy to go to the scene, I had yet to see Mollie's face.

I observed her closely now. She had a thin jawline, jade eyes, an attractive dimple—I caught myself overlaying her features against the gruesome, chewed-off remains I'd seen the night before, and quickly I blinked the image away . . . light complexion, a pair of earrings in each ear, a small, delicate nose—

A shiver ran through me.

It can't be!

I yanked out my phone, speed-dialed Ralph. He answered immediately, harshly: "Pat, you are in deep—"

"Listen to me," I said. "Did Mollie Fischer wear contacts?"

"What?"

The picture disappeared from the television screen.

"Contacts. Did she wear contact lenses?"

"What are you—"

"Check it, Ralph. The case files!"

A long pause accompanied by the click of keystrokes.

"No," he said. "No glasses either. What's going on?" The hot anger I'd heard in his voice only a moment ago was gone. I felt like we were on the same page again.

"It's not her."

"What?"

"The woman we found at the primate facility, it's not Mollie Fischer. The dead woman had only a single piercing in each ear, Mollie has two; and the iris found at the scene was blue. In her AP photo, Mollie's eyes are green, and since she didn't wear contacts—"

"But she was positively IDed by her own father," he mumbled, and I couldn't tell if he was disagreeing with me or simply thinking aloud.

"Her face was missing." I was rushing out the door.

Of course she was positively IDed, everything else pointed to her. The killers had dressed her in Mollie's clothes, left her with Mollie's driver's license, purse, ring, necklace, phone. The depth of the deception we'd fallen for was staggering.

Mollie Fischer might still be alive.

I hit the sidewalk running.

Mollie had been missing for nearly twenty-one hours, and with every minute our chances of finding her grew slimmer; Ralph knew all of this, I didn't need to tell him. "Call the congressman," I said. "Tell him to announce it now, at this press conference. If Mollie is alive—"

"Yeah, I know. The public can help. Get to the Capitol, Pat. If he doesn't listen to me, you can talk to him in person."

"I'm close. I'll be there in less than five minutes."

"I'll try to get an ID on the dead woman," he said.

End call.

I bolted to my car.

◼

Brad closed the computer. Done.

The woman lay unconscious; only her chest was moving, rising and falling. Steadily, steadily. With each gentle breath.

For a moment Brad felt a thrill, the same excitement he felt when he was alone with Astrid after each game. He hesitated for a moment, then kissed the woman on the cheek, but that was all. He didn't touch her, not in an intimate way. After all, he was a gentleman and would never take advantage of an unconscious lady.

No, he would not touch her, not like that. It wasn't part of the plan. Instead he held her hand gently for a few moments, then positioned her in the wheelchair and lowered it to the ground with the handicapped lift.

Then he wheeled her through a side entrance and into the hotel.

◼

I burst through the door to the press corps room just outside the house minority leader's office.

The press conference was over, but the room was still full of lurking reporters hoping to snag congressional staff members for comments, and as I entered, every head turned my way.

Why fake Mollie's death?

Why last night?

Why there?

And who is the woman we found at the primate center?

I'd already flashed my creds at three previous security checkpoints, and now I did the same for the Capitol police officer beside the door. "Where's Congressman Fischer?"

Giving me a somewhat curious look, he pointed to the house minority leader's office.

I let myself in.

Four people in the room—three men, one woman. The congressman was the only one I recognized: mid-fifties, slightly overweight, but he carried it well. Wire-rimmed glasses, a finely tailored suit, assiduously combed brown hair.

Everyone stared at me, obviously not used to being interrupted like this.

"I'm Patrick Bowers," I said, "with the FBI."

"You're Bowers?" Congressman Fischer said.

"Yes."

"You're the one who noticed it? That the dead woman isn't Mollie?"

"Just a few minutes ago, sir. Yes. And I need to tell you—"

"Give us a minute," he interrupted me, then glanced around the room at his people, who dutifully, and without a word, grabbed their things and filed out the door.

Fischer crossed the room and closed the door behind them.

"Congressman Fischer, I—"

"Is my daughter still alive?"

"Unfortunately, at this point we have no way of knowing. I came here to—"

"And who's this girl who was killed? The one they found?"

"I don't believe she's been identified yet. Listen to me, we have a good opportunity here. The press is already outside that door. All you have to do is walk back out there and tell them the truth."

"I just made a fool of myself." He was shaking his head.

"Excuse me?"

He pointed to the door. "Out there. Just now. I told them Mollie was dead, that her killer committed suicide last night."

"We can fix that if you just—"

"Dr. Bowers, don't you understand? I'm the one who identified her body. They'll say I didn't even know my own daughter."

I could hardly believe I was hearing this.

Maybe he was in shock.

"With all due respect, Congressman, there's a very real chance your daughter is still alive; you need to stop worrying about what people might think of you and start focusing on the best way to help her."

He was quiet. "Let's not be hasty here."

"What? Do you have any idea what—"

"I just had a chat with your superiors at the Bureau, right before you came in. They told me you would be showing up."

That had to be Margaret.

Or Rodale.

But why would either of them—

"And," Fischer went on, "they have assured me that waiting until a more strategic time before making this announcement will give us the upper hand in finding Mollie as quickly as possible."

"A more strategic time? Who did you talk to?"

He ignored the questions. "Besides, we don't even know for sure that Mollie was abducted. She might have just run off with some friends."

This was ridiculous.

"Listen to me. The people who killed the woman in the primate facility found someone who was the same height and weight as Mollie. They dressed her in your daughter's clothes, put Mollie's necklace on her, and then murdered her in one of the most disturbing ways I've ever seen. Your daughter did not run away. Rusty Mahan did not kill himself, this is an elaborate setup—"

"To do what?"

"I don't know."

"Why my daughter?"

"I don't know that either, but—"

"Well, what *do* you know, Agent Bowers?" His voice had turned oddly diplomatic, cultivated by years of careful political posturing, and considering the circumstances, his emotional detachment was unfathomable to me. "Do you know for certain that revealing all of this information will be in the best interest of my daughter?"

"Here's what I know: if your daughter is still alive, she's in grave danger, and the sooner we get the public to start looking for her and phoning in tips, the better chance we have of—"

"You're what, Agent Bowers? A doctor? A criminologist? Is that correct?"

I felt a flare of anger. "I'm the guy who finds and stops killers like this. I do it better than anyone. And manipulating the facts, misleading the public rather than allowing them to help is not the way to do that."

The Bureau only releases carefully prepared statements to the press, of course I knew that, but at this point I didn't care. Although it was possible Mollie was already dead, she might be alive, and time was of the essence. "If you don't go out there and make this announcement," I said, "I will."

He eyed me. "I understand that you are involved in a custody battle involving your stepdaughter."

"What did you just say?"

"I'm sure you would hate to lose your job at the Bureau because you did something rash. Being unemployed might endanger your chances to keep her."

I took a step toward him. "Are you threatening me?"

How does he know about the custody case?

"No. Just offering a free word of advice. One father to another."

"If you were a real father, you would do whatever it takes to protect your daughter. Congressman."

Do it, Pat.

Go.

I left his office; he called after me, but I ignored him.

In the press corps room I approached the podium, stepped to the microphone, and after I had everyone's attention, I said, "I'm Special Agent Bowers with the FBI, and I have an announcement to make."

And then, I told the world that Mollie Fischer was not the woman we'd found at the Gunderson Foundation Primate Research Center.

29

I was blunt, quick, to the point.

The press conference was over in minutes, and the aftermath was swift and certain.

A clump of reporters rushed me for additional comments, but I shouldered my way through them to a restricted area. Only then did they scurry away to write their articles, file their reports, film their live remotes.

I looked at my phone.

Four missed calls.

Two since I'd initiated my impromptu press conference.

How about that.

One from Margaret, one from FBI Director Rodale. In addition, Tessa had called twice while my ringer had been turned off during my meeting with Missy Schuel.

She'd left me two voicemails.

"Patrick, um, I know you have like class or whatever, but I . . . Well, I was wondering if we could talk, maybe. If you have a break or something. I'm going home . . . So anyway. Call me when you get a chance."

And the second: *"Just seeing if you were still in your meeting. That's all. Okay, talk to you later."*

Beneath the words I heard an urgency that concerned me. I tried her number, but there wasn't a signal and I realized that if she was on her way home, she might be on a Metro train where her cell wouldn't work.

Try her again in a bit. For now, get out of here. Get to the command post at police headquarters.

Leaving the ringer on, I pocketed the phone and was heading

for the tunnels leading to the underground parking garage where I'd left my car when I found Lieutenant Doehring scouring the corridor, looking for me.

He jogged toward me. "That was ballsy."

"Thanks."

"The right call too. Despite what Wellington is gonna say."

I recalled the congressman's words: *Do you know for certain that revealing all this information will be in the best interest of my daughter?*

"Yeah, well, we'll see."

"I shouldn't have assumed Mahan was involved." His voice was sharp with anger directed at himself. "I jumped the gun."

"None of that matters. We just need to—"

"Find these psychos."

"Yeah. Let's get to the command post."

He pointed toward the exit door. "My car is this way."

"Is it close?"

"Right outside." I could worry about my car later. We headed in the direction he'd pointed. "Fill me in," I said. "What do we know?"

"My officers just finished interviewing the primate center's staff." He sounded exasperated. "Keepers, researchers, custodians, administrators, interns—everyone who's not on vacation."

"And?"

"Nothing solid. I can't see any connection between them and the crime."

I trusted he'd been thorough. "Forensics?"

"The chimps managed to destroy or contaminate nearly all the evidence we might have pulled from the habitat. Also, there weren't any incriminating prints on the leather straps or the contents of Mollie's purse. All wiped clean. Nothing so far on the rope used to hang Mahan either."

Of course.

We made it to the door, left the building.

"There must be something. Do we know where Mahan's

abduction took place? Where his car might have been parked prior to appearing in the parking garage?"

Now we were at Doehring's squad. Both of us climbed in.

"I'm not sure," he said.

I didn't need to tell him to make the call to find out. He had the radio in one hand and was cranking the ignition with the other.

I recalled my class discussion earlier in the day about planning the perfect murder. So far, these killers were right on target.

Except for one thing: if our hypothesis was correct that there were multiple offenders, that meant there was at least one accomplice. And that meant there was a loose end.

The DC streets were clogged, but we pulled into traffic and headed toward Metro police headquarters.

2:12 p.m.

Astrid finally arrived at the hotel, wearing a wig, sunglasses, a small disguise. She was somewhat rushed, somewhat frustrated: the task force had made the discovery much quicker than she'd expected.

But it wouldn't change things. Everything else was still in play.

She peered into the van and saw that Brad had forgotten the duffel bag and the woman's laptop computer. She sighed, retrieved them, then entered the hotel through the alley door where Brad had made sure the video footage was looping. At least he'd remembered to leave that propped open for her.

She went to the stairwell.

Because of the FBI's progress, they would move up the schedule.

Mollie would die at 2:45 instead of 3:00. Just to make sure.

"Did the lab remove the glare from last night's video?" I asked Doehring. "The footage of the Volvo?"

"Most of it, from what I heard, but not enough for us to ID the driver."

Come on, Pat. What are you missing here? What are you missing?

The Volvo's driver slowed down as he approached the light . . . He switched plates so that you'd notice . . . So that you'd notice . . .

I phoned Ralph. "Any ID on the woman yet?"

"No. We've got a list of possibles, Metro PD is going through them."

"Did the agents find footage of any unidentified people leaving the facility last night?"

"They should finish in about ten minutes."

"They should have finished an hour ago!" I snapped.

"They gave me some crap about a lot of people being there." His tone was fiercer than mine had been. "A lot of partial faces, having to analyze stride length, posture, height, weight, whatever."

"Just tell 'em to hurry."

"Oh, believe me, they know."

End call.

Doehring threw on his siren and overheads. Slowly, cars began to edge to the side as much as they could to let us through, but with the congestion in both lanes, it didn't make that much of a difference.

I considered the locations we knew of so far . . . the electronics store . . . the primate research facility . . . the Metro stop where Mollie had been seen yesterday afternoon . . . the Connecticut Avenue bridge where Rusty had been found . . .

The killers approached the primate center from the south, less than ninety minutes after Mollie was last seen.

Oh.

Obvious!

I could hardly believe I'd missed it.

I tapped at my phone, pulled up the videos of Mahan's car approaching the facility.

Doehring glanced at me. "What are you thinking?"

"The Volvo would have traveled through more than one light."

Astrid opened the hotel room door and saw Mollie Fischer sitting on the bed, shivering with fear, her hands bound behind her, her legs tied together. Blood oozed down the left side of her forehead from something Brad must have done to her. Now he dabbed at the blood, even though in a few minutes none of that would matter.

Both of them looked her way. She entered the room, closed, then dead-bolted the door behind her.

And the voice inside of her, the one that Astrid realized was beginning to sound more and more like her father, narrated:

```
Most people do not scream as they die, they move
through the doorway with a slight gasp or a soft
breath, or a faint and final moan.
    One would think that the culminating act of life
would be more dramatic, more exciting, but that final
moment is not nearly as fascinating as the movies
make it seem. More often than not, it's disappoint-
ingly anticlimactic. Passing away is actually a good
phrase to describe it. We slip into the eternal sea,
and the ripples of our lives quickly fade and settle
and disappear.
    And soon, so soon, we are forgotten.
```

Astrid looked at the woman and thought of death—the ones she'd witnessed, the ones she'd helped arrange—thought of the pain and meaninglessness of the life that precedes it. Sometimes the passing away starts years before passing through the doorway.

Just like Dad's.

Brad finished wiping the woman's forehead and turned on the television, clicked through the channels until he found a car chase that seemed loud enough to hide any sounds Mollie might make when they removed her gag.

Astrid didn't like the idea of having Brad inflict undue physical harm, but Mollie's compliance was important, so she told her, "In a moment we're going to remove that gag. And if you make any sound, I'll have my friend beat you until you're unconscious, and then do things to you that I can guarantee you would not want done. Do you understand what I'm saying?"

A small and terrified nod.

Power.

Power over hope.

Astrid motioned for Brad to loosen the gag.

No!

I'd been hoping to track the Volvo's path backward to its point of origin, but I came up empty. Admittedly, I was flying through the footage too quickly to be absolutely certain, but I wasn't able to locate the Volvo at any other traffic lights, and there were plenty of routes he might have taken to evade the city's traffic cameras if he knew their location.

If only we knew the identity of the Jane Doe at the research center . . .

Timing, timing, timing.

We were almost to HQ, but I didn't want to wait. Using the radio in Doehring's cruiser I called the command post, identified myself, spoke with one of the officers. "The missing persons you've been following up on. Have you checked their recent phone calls, credit card usage, emails?"

"Of course, sir."

"Send them to me."

Astrid had studied acting when she was an undergrad, and now she was enjoying her role.

She flipped open Mollie's laptop, logged into the hotel's wireless connection, and then positioned the screen so that Mollie could see it. "I am going to give you a gift that very few people have ever been offered."

"You're gonna let me go?" Mollie's voice was shaking. She was a mouse staring into the eyes of a snake.

Predator.

Prey.

"The last thing you see."

A question crossed Mollie's face, and Astrid said to her, "What do you want it to be? I'll pull up any image from the world, any picture you like."

Yes.

Control.

"No." Mollie's voice was shaky. "Please."

Prey.

Astrid stared at her for a moment, then let her gaze drift toward Brad.

He spoke softly, reassuringly. "Mollie, I need to tell you something." He nodded toward Astrid. "My friend is a persistent woman. She'll make you choose eventually, but it'll be less trouble for everyone if you choose something now. Whatever you want. Any picture. Any video. Just say something."

His acting was almost as good as hers.

Mollie gulped. "I don't know."

Brad took over the keyboard and clicked to an Internet search engine. "Think of something calming. It might help. A seashore, maybe? Or a mountain meadow or a sunset? Just tell her something."

"Please." She shook her head. "Stop."

Brad said, "It doesn't matter what."

Predator. Prey.

Control over hope.

"Time's up," Astrid said.

"No, no, no," Mollie cried. "Rusty. Okay, Rusty, please."

And as the woman asked to see the face of the young man she had loved, the man who was already a corpse, Astrid felt sweet excitement, the same frisson of dark pleasure she'd felt last month when the EMS dispatcher kept asking the corpse of Jeanne Styles if it was okay.

"Are you hurt?"

No, hurt is a whole different thing.

Rusty had been in the van with her, tied, gagged, blindfolded, last night. But she hadn't even known.

Prey.

"All right." Astrid gestured toward the woman's computer. "Do you have a picture of him?" The schedule was tight, but she wasn't willing to give up this part of the game.

A nod.

"Where?"

"My photos." Mollie sounded frightened, desperate as she nodded toward the computer. "In iPhoto."

Astrid gestured to Brad, and he opened the computer's directory to find the files.

Twana Summie.

She was a college student from northern Virginia who attended Gallaudet, hadn't been seen since Tuesday morning, and her Visa card had been used to book two nights—last night and tonight—at the Lincoln Towers Hotel.

So: a college student booking two nights at a hotel that charges six hundred dollars per night for a room? At a hotel that close to her college?

"Turn around," I told Doehring. "Get us to the Lincoln Towers Hotel." It was downtown. Close.

"You have something?"

"I might." As I told him what I'd found, he whipped the car around and I pulled up Twana's DMV records to see if she shared enough physical characteristics with Mollie to have been the victim we found in the Gunderson Foundation Primate Research Center.

Astrid found the photos of Rusty and Mollie, and when she pulled up one of the young couple on the beach, Mollie nodded, closed her eyes, nodded again.

It was a quaint picture. A dock with a sailboat in the background. A lightly clouded horizon and blue ocean beyond them—sun and sea and scalloped sky. Rusty's arm was draped around her shoulder, and she was leaning tenderly against his chest.

"It's nice."

"I'll do anything. Please, just—"

"Shh." Brad laid a hand on the woman's shoulder. A nurturing gesture. "Calm down. All will be well."

Astrid looked at him and loved him and desired him.

She let her finger graze across the picture of Rusty. "He's very handsome. You made a good choice. To die looking at him." Then to Brad: "Turn up the volume on the television."

Yes.

Although Twana was slightly taller than Mollie, she had the same build and hair color.

"That's it."

I felt the net tightening.

Twana's credit card had been used to book a room at the hotel tonight, her abductors might be there . . . if they brought Mollie . . .

Too many ifs.

The hotel was two blocks away.

I called their number to find out which room Twana Summie was staying in.

And they put me on hold.

Astrid used the cursor to highlight the picture of Mollie and Rusty at the seashore, hit delete, and then emptied the trash so that the picture was gone now and forever. "How did I do?"

Mollie's fear subsided briefly, turned to confusion. "What?"

"Did I have you convinced?"

"You're going to let me go?" A glimmer of hope in her voice. "You're not gonna hurt me?"

"No. I mean did you think I was going to let you look at that picture while you died?"

Astrid noticed that Brad looked as surprised as the woman.

"What is this?" Brad asked.

"I had you too?" Astrid felt a tickle of satisfaction.

"Had me?"

"Believing that I would let her look at something pleasant while you killed her?" She spoke to him as if Mollie were not there. As if she were already dead.

Mollie begged, "No, no . . ." Terror rising in her eyes.

Brad looked slightly betrayed, and that bothered Astrid. What was his problem? It was all part of the game. "Don't pout."

"It wasn't in the plan."

"I thought it would be more fun this way. And it was, wasn't it? It was more fun." She kept her eyes locked on his until at last he looked away.

"Yes," he said quietly. "It was more fun."

"Why do you think I had you take the video of Rusty last night?"

Brad was quiet.

"Video of Rusty?" the woman said. "What did you do to him!"

Astrid had a feeling what would happen when she showed Mollie the footage of her boyfriend struggling for breath at the end of the rope.

She picked up the gag and turned to her.

"I'll show you."

■

Doehring and I rushed through the doors of the Lincoln Towers Hotel.

Adrian Lees, the manager, was waiting for us.

Mid-forties. Slim. Tailored suit. Small goatee, neatly trimmed. "I'm the CEO," he said. "Here at the Lincoln Towers. We checked the system." He paused at awkward intervals as he spoke, chopping his sentence into odd, bite-sized pieces. "No one by the name of Twana Summie has a room here."

What?

"No credit card charges?"

He shook his head.

But that's not possible . . .

"Take us to your control center," I said.

His face was flushed. "Is everything all right?"

"No," Doehring growled. "The control center! Now!"

Lees motioned toward the hallway behind the registration desk. "This way."

After my initial surprise that there were no rooms reserved in Twana's name, I realized that the glitch, the inconsistency, was a clue that we were on the right track—but we still had no way to know if our suspects were on-site. As soon as we could confirm—

My phone rang.

Ralph.

"Yes?" I answered. I was hurrying down the hallway, following Lees.

"The videos. I just got word."

"Tell me."

"A cleaning lady—name of Aria Petic. No video of her entering the building either before 5:00 or after 7:00, but she left immediately after the EMTs arrived. We're looking for her."

"Do we have her face on tape?"

"Mostly obscured. Only a partial."

At least we could get her pace, stride, approximate height. "Send it."

End call.

Game on.

30

Astrid played the two-minute-and-fifty-one-second video chronicling Rusty's death, first the preparation, then footage of him dangling beneath the bridge, clawing uselessly at the rope cinched around his neck, and the voice of her father, her dead father, spoke to her,

```
With each passing second, the young man became less
and less animated. Less frantic. More submissive to
the inevitable. The final denouement of his ever-
shrinking world.
```

Mollie had stopped trying to scream now and was watching the video with large, terrified, broken eyes.

Predator.

Prey.

The game.

Astrid tapped the space bar to pause the video, then said to Brad, "All right. Let's send that message to the FBI."

He went to the duffel bag to pull out the items he would need.

On the way to the control center, I asked Doehring if he'd interviewed anyone named Aria Petic, and he mentally clicked through his list of names. "No, I don't think so."

We arrived, and I immediately noted that the hotel had a better security surveillance system than most FBI field offices. Six attendants monitored an array of video screens stretching across the wall, each person's eyes flickering from one screen to the next as the images changed to show different angles and hallways of the hotel.

Twenty-eight screens.

State of the art.

Adrian Lees introduced us to his head of security. "This is Marianne Keye-Wallace. Used to work for the NSA. She'll help you. With anything you want." Platinum blonde. Careful, steady eyes. She couldn't have been more than thirty, but high-tech security positions rely more on brains and adaptability than either brawn or experience.

Without waiting for our names, she told Lees, "We'll call you if we need you." Then she promptly took a seat beside one of the computers turned to us. "Talk to me."

"Are there any guests here by the name of Aria Petic, Twana Summie, or Mollie Fischer?" I said.

Marianne's fingers were light and spidery on the keyboard. Lees hovered for a moment, then disappeared. "No," she said. "What are we looking for here?"

It would take too long to explain. I pulled up the video of Aria Petic that Ralph had just sent me. "Do you have facial recognition on your video surveillance system?"

"Of course. Facial, audio, video."

I handed her the phone. "Upload this picture. I need to know if this woman is in this hotel."

The folded-up wheelchair leaned against the wall beside the room door, the duffel bag next to it. The suitcases that Astrid had brought into the hotel last night sat beside that.

Brad was busy with Mollie.

Astrid made the call to the front desk.

No footage of Aria Petic.

"You gotta be kidding me." Doehring smacked the wall.

"What else?" Marianne asked, fingers poised at the keyboard.

Come on, come on, come on.

"We're looking for . . ." I began, but my thoughts distracted me.

The key is Mollie. Everything revolves around her.

"Yes?" Marianne asked.

"Go online. Pull up the AP photo of Mollie Fischer."

It took seconds.

"Do a search. If she's here, I want to know what room she's in. Pull up any video of her entering or leaving the hotel since 7:00 last night." I figured we'd start there and work backward, if necessary to 4:00, when she was last seen.

A few minutes later Marianne found footage of Mollie in a wheelchair, being pushed into the hotel by an unidentified man wearing a baseball cap that completely hid his face from the camera, which told me he knew the camera's angle and location before he even approached the building.

Follow up on that. If he knows where the cameras are, he's likely to have been here before, scouting out the site.

Later, later, later.

Because, for now, we also had footage of them entering a service elevator inside the hotel. "Where do they exit the elevator?" I asked. "Which floor?"

"There's no way to know. We only have surveillance cameras covering the guest elevators on each floor, not the service elevators."

"Have they left the building?" Doehring said.

"Let me find out." Marianne let her fingers loose on the keyboard.

She did another facial recognition search, then shook her head. "Unless they found a way to get past our cameras, they're still inside."

But that was enough for Doehring. He was on his radio calling for backup to set up a perimeter around the hotel; in less than five minutes, we would have the area secured.

"Have security seal off all the exit doors," I said to her. "The suspect transported Mollie into the hotel in a wheelchair, so look for a handicapped-accessible vehicle outside. And go back to the footage of him entering the elevator. I've got an idea."

31

The video revealed that after the man entered the elevator, he reached out to press one of the floor's buttons before the doors closed and the two of them were gone.

"Back it up."

She did.

"Pause it."

The image froze.

I pointed. "There. Which button is he pressing? Which floor?"

"Hang on." Marianne slid the cursor, zoomed in, then cursed. "I can't tell. The angle is wrong."

"Download that to my phone."

She connected my cell to her system, tapped at her keyboard, then seconds later handed back the phone, the image frozen on the screen.

"He might have changed clothes, but circulate this image to security," I said. "Let's see if we can get an ID. And call every room, leave a recorded message that security's looking for a missing wheelchair. Let's see who tries to sneak away. And no one leaves this hotel." I started for the door. "Where's the service elevator he used?"

"Take a left out the door, at the end of the hall go through housekeeping. The elevator will be on your right."

Doehring and I took off.

Everything had been arranged.

Mollie was not going to be a problem for them.

Astrid glanced at her watch.

"We need to move," she said to Brad, who was taking care of the room.

"Almost done."

———————————◼———————————

We made it to the elevators.

I studied the video on my phone, the height of the man's hand in relationship to the floor numbers . . . the angle of the camera in the hall . . . then I stood in the same place he had, raised my hand to the same level as his, and played the video again.

It was possible the suspect pressed a second button after the elevator doors closed, but we had to start somewhere.

Doehring and I scrutinized the video. "What do you think?" I said. "Floor eight or nine?"

He shook his head. "I can't tell."

"Send security to both floors, sweep the rooms. You take nine. I'll get eight." I sprinted for the stairwell at the end of the hall.

———————————◼———————————

Astrid and Brad were just about to leave the room when the phone rang.

Both of them stared at it.

Another ring.

Then, ever so faintly, they heard simultaneously ringing phones in the adjoining rooms.

"They know," Brad said. "Somehow they know."

She shook her head. "That's impossible. You took care of the cameras, right?"

"Yes."

But as the phones continued to ring, Astrid felt, for the first time since they'd started their games, a small nervous twitch of anxiety. She hesitated for a moment, then, with a gloved hand, picked up the room phone, listened to the message. Hung it up. "We need to leave."

Brad said nothing, went to the door, peered out the peephole, then eased the door open a crack. Checked the hallway. "It's clear."

She picked up the laptop.

"Careful," he said. "You don't want to—"

"Drop it. I know." She nodded toward the door, where their things were sitting. "Get those."

He did.

They slipped into the hall.

Eighth floor.

Legs screaming from the sprint up the stairs.

My .357 SIG P229 in hand, I threw open the door to the hallway.

Two maids, a few kids in swimming suits running down the hall to their room, a bellhop pulling a luggage cart, two security personnel knocking on doors.

They'd gotten here fast. Good.

Good.

No sign of the suspect.

I flashed my creds. "Anything?" I called to the guards.

"No," one of them replied.

"No one leaves this floor. Understand?"

"Got it."

I bolted down the hallway, then to an adjacent hall to the east.

And as I flared around the corner, I saw a man pause at the door to the stairwell at the far end of the hallway about thirty-five meters from me. He wore the same clothes as the man who'd been caught on the security video pushing the wheelchair.

"Stop," I shouted, "FBI!"

He glanced over his shoulder, his face shadowed by the cap. He reached toward his belt.

A gun.

He's going for a gun!

I leveled my SIG. "Hands to the side!"

He hesitated.

"Now!"

But a door opened between us, and an elderly couple left their room. "Get down!" I yelled.

They were terrified and hesitated. The man by the stairwell door ducked through and disappeared.

"Get back in your room!" I shouted to the couple, and I raced down the hallway even as I yanked out my cell, called Doehring. "Get someone to the southeast stairwell. First floor. Now!"

Past the terrified couple.

Seconds ticked.

Ticked.

To the stairwell door.

Readied myself.

Threw it open.

Footsteps below me.

Weapon ready, I swung around the corner, scanned the area, and saw someone rounding the stairwell far below me. "Stop!"

I tried to tell if there were two sets of footsteps or just one.

Two, I thought, but I couldn't be sure.

One suspect or two?

Advice from my training: *Always assume the greater threat.*

Two.

Quickly I checked the landing above me for any accomplices.

No one.

Then I flew down the stairs, taking them three at a time.

Astrid and Brad had made it to the first floor.

Brad had his Walther P99 in one hand and cautiously pushed the door open with the other.

No cops.

Two doors before her. She pointed to the underground parking garage sign, just ahead on the left.

"Wait," Brad said. His eyes were on the oversized freight elevator. "I have an idea."

Ground level.

I burst through the door.

No one.

But the doors of a freight elevator at the end of the hall were closing. "Stop!"

I rushed forward, my heart hammering from my sprint up, then down eight flights of stairs.

And from adrenaline.

And from the hunt.

By the time I arrived, the doors had closed. I pressed the up button. Steadied myself. Leveled my gun.

They slid open.

Empty.

I raced to the parking garage.

Scanned the stretch of concrete and cars.

And saw a latex glove on the ground about five meters away, directly to my right.

32

I saw no movement in the parking area. Heard no footsteps.

No, no, no!

The door behind me burst open, and I spun, aiming, saw Doehring rush in. I immediately lowered my weapon and turned my attention to the parking area again. "Mollie," I said, "is she safe?"

He shook his head. "Haven't found her yet." He was out of breath. His eyes had found the latex glove. "Is the guy in here?"

"I don't know. You go left. I'll go—"

Wait a minute.

The freight elevator, Pat . . . they opened the elevator doors to slow you down . . . last night Aria waited at the scene . . . didn't leave until after emergency personnel arrived . . .

After.

After.

Assume the greater threat.

Two not one.

Doehring noticed my hesitation. "What is it?"

"Stay here by the door. Make sure no one doubles back. Get this garage sealed off. And have security check every car. Trunks included."

"What about you?"

"I've got an idea."

I ran back inside and surveyed the hallway: the elevator, the hall I'd come down, and saw a door I hadn't noticed before because my eyes were on the elevator.

A sign read: Restricted Access. Authorized Personnel Only.

Oh yeah.
That would be it.

Astrid and Brad were making their way through a sprawling room, dark and cluttered, their path lit only by an exit sign fifty feet ahead of them. "The glove," she said. "It was a good idea."

"I hope so." Brad seemed unsure. Uneasy. "This one's smart. This agent. Somehow he found us."

I felt along the wall, found a light switch, flicked it on. A line of fluorescents blinked on one at a time, in a long, methodical row. "There's no way out," I called, hoped it was true.

I saw no one in the vast room.

Stall, stall, stall.

Slow them down.

"We have this hotel sealed off." I moved forward cautiously. "Step out now with your hands in the air!"

The storage room was cavernous, stretching nearly the length of the hotel, and was filled with stacks of chairs, end tables, beds, TV cabinets, and mirrors—the leftover furniture from the hotel's recent renovations.

Literally hundreds of places to hide. But a cleared path led straight through the middle.

I took another quiet step.

Heard a scraping sound ahead of me to the left and swung my gun toward it.

Then a gunshot.

Impact.

The bullet slammed into my left arm as the sound reverberated, echoed, thundered through the room. The force spun me around, nearly threw me to the ground, but I managed to pivot behind an old television cabinet with four mirrors leaning against it before dropping to the concrete floor.

Astrid was standing next to the exit door when Brad shot the FBI agent.

"What are you doing?" she asked, her voice low, accusatory.

"Sending him a message."

He scurried across the aisle to join her.

"You're not playing this smart anymore." She grabbed his hand, pulled him outside; she heard sirens whining. "You're going to ruin everything."

"No, I—"

"Quiet."

The alley stretched in both directions.

Left or right?

A choice. She made it.

They ran.

◼

Blood all over.

It felt like someone had slammed a sledgehammer against my left biceps, and the pain made it almost impossible to think.

I squeezed my eyes shut, tried to concentrate on the scene.

The scene.

The scene.

A moment ago, I'd heard the exit door at the far end of the room bang shut.

Oh, man, that hurts.

Three possibilities: both suspects left the building, one was still here, or both were still inside and they'd just opened the door to trick me, lure me out.

Thick pain chugged through my shoulder, up my neck, then broke apart like an explosion of glass in my head.

Focus, Pat.

Focus!

I'd passed my gun to my left hand and was instinctively pressing my right hand against the wound to slow the bleeding, but now I removed it, and a quick check told me the bullet had both entered and exited my arm—a through and through.

It was bleeding heavily but not spurting, so I doubted there was arterial damage, and I didn't see or feel any obvious fractures, so that was a good sign, but the blood and the pain made it impossible to tell.

I needed my gun in my right hand, and that meant I had to find another way to put pressure on the wound to stop the bleeding. I yanked off my belt and braced myself because the pain was about to get a lot worse.

Gritting my teeth, I wrapped the belt around the wound, slipped the end through the buckle. I didn't need a tourniquet, but by tugging it tightly I could make a crude pressure bandage.

Do it, Pat.

Come on, come on!

I clenched my teeth and pulled the belt snug.

A shower of hot light broke apart inside my head. Breath escaped me.

Focus.

Focus!

I secured the belt. My arm flared again. Dizzying pain.

Eyes squinched shut, I leaned back against the cabinet.

Tried to catch my breath.

The exit door.

Don't let them get away.

Before I could make a move, I needed to know where the suspects were, so I tilted one of the nearby mirrors to see down the corridor between the pieces of furniture.

No one.

Strategically they had the advantage. There were two of them, at least one was armed. They might be anywhere.

I pulled out my phone, called Doehring, whispered, hoarse, out of breath, "The perimeter. Is it up?"

"It should be."

Should be.

The suspects could already be gone.

"The south side of the building," I struggled to keep the pain out of my voice, "get officers there now. The suspects are armed. Proceed with extreme caution—there might be only one person; I'm not sure."

End call.

You're hit. They're armed.

I ought to wait. I really ought—

Screw it.

I stood and leveled my gun, then spun around the cabinet, and trying to move my left arm as little as possible, headed toward the exit door watching for any movement as I raced through the room.

Saw nothing.

No one.

I arrived at the exit. Threw my body against the pressure bar, and the door flew open.

A quick visual sweep.

Just an alley, a dumpster.

No fleeing suspects.

No one.

I checked in and around the dumpster.

Clear.

Both streets lay about forty meters away, and I had no idea which direction the suspects might have fled.

Sirens, but no officers in sight.

Would the suspects split up? Go different directions?

Splitting up made sense, but obviously I could only check one street at a time. I chose the one to the right and ran toward it.

At the corner, here's what I saw: a ponytailed jogger, typical DC traffic, a woman facing the crosswalk pushing a stroller, three young children straggling behind her. Across the intersection four businessmen were looking the other way waiting for a light to change.

No one who fit either Aria's or the unidentified man's build. No one who was acting suspicious or even looking in this direction.

No!

The other street. They went the other way through the alley.

With this much time elapsed since they'd left the building, I doubted it would do any good to check the other street, but I needed to be thorough. I started toward it.

But only seconds later two burly officers burst through the basement door and swept into the alley. "I'm Agent Bowers, FBI." I pointed to one of the men. "Check the other street"—then to the other—"Get back in there and guard the exit. They might still be inside."

The officers obeyed.

More sirens.

The streets were being sealed off.

Too late. It's all too late!

Every time my heart beat, my arm throbbed. My vision blurred. I leaned my weight against the wall.

Another officer emerged from the door, and I had him radio dispatch to stop traffic and have officers detain and question everyone on the streets on both ends of the alley.

"Are you all right, sir?" he asked.

"Go."

When he left, I noticed that the woman with the young children was staring at me. She looked pale. I saw her swallow and then direct her children to follow her toward the pedestrian crosswalk.

The blood.

The blood on your arm.

Wait.

She hadn't been facing the alley when I ran to the street, but there was a good chance one of her kids might have seen something.

I holstered my weapon and, pressing my right hand against the wound to hide the blood as much as possible, I approached the woman. "Excuse me, ma'am. I need to ask you a few questions."

33

She didn't give me her first name, just said that she was "Mrs. Rainey," and then proceeded to tell me she hadn't seen anyone leave the alley. "I'm sorry." She was staring at my arm. "We were going the other way. Shouldn't you be in a hospital?"

Probably.

I looked at her children. A sleeping baby in the stroller. Twin girls about three or four years old. A boy, maybe six. I knelt beside them. The twins eased back, grabbed the legs of their mother. One of them bit the corner of her lower lip and looked like she was about to cry. I couldn't hide the blood completely, but I turned to the side to hide it as much as I could.

"I need to get them home," Mrs. Rainey said.

"Just one moment. I won't upset your children. I promise." She looked at me uneasily, then at my arm, then at the alley where more officers had arrived, and then at the police cars screeching to a stop nearby. Though she was clearly reluctant, she must have realized the importance of my request, because at last she nodded. "Okay."

"Listen," I said to the kids. "Did you see anyone come out of this alley? Just a little while ago? It's very important."

None of them responded.

I held up the phone's screen with the picture of Aria Petic that Ralph had sent me. "Did this woman come through here?"

The children just stared at me.

I showed them the man pushing the wheelchair. "Or him?"

Silence.

"Go on," their mother said. "Did any of you see them come out from between those two buildings?"

The girls clung to her. The boy just looked at me suspiciously.

All right, this was going nowhere. I was feeling queasy from the pain, and I was only upsetting the children.

Normally, we'd detain potential witnesses a little longer, have another officer follow up, but I didn't like it that the kids were here at a time like this.

"I really should go," Mrs. Rainey said.

I took down her address and phone number so I could follow up, then I handed her one of my cards. "If any of your children remember anything, anything at all, call me."

She accepted the card, and I headed unsteadily toward a park bench to sit down and catch my breath.

But I hadn't made it more than three steps when I heard her voice: "Wait."

I turned and saw one of her daughters pointing.

At a taxicab.

34

The driver, who astonishingly spoke English as his first language, told me he'd just made a drop off, but hadn't picked up anyone from this curb for hours.

Mrs. Rainey asked her daughter again and found out she'd meant that she saw someone get into *a* taxicab, not *that* taxicab, which, of course made sense, but still, it frustrated me.

Another setback.

The streets were surrounded by officers. No other taxis in sight.

Margaret had arrived and was walking down the sidewalk toward me.

This day was just getting better and better.

I called to the officer I'd spoken to a few minutes ago and told him to get some men to check all the drop-offs and pickups of DC cab companies along this street over the last twenty minutes.

He eyed my arm. "Are you okay, sir?"

"I'm fine. Are you listening to me?"

He didn't look away from the bloody sleeve. "Yes, sir."

I described the suspects and explained that we didn't know if they were traveling together or separately.

"If we find their cab and they're in it, don't let the driver stop until we can get some undercover officers there waiting for the suspects. Got it?"

"Yeah." He was still looking at the blood.

"Go."

He hesitated. "Is your arm—"

"Go on."

He left.

I started for the bench again, but Margaret was catching up to me. "So you got shot?" It sounded more like an accusation than a question.

"I did."

"Apprehend anyone?"

"No."

"Shoot anyone?"

"No."

"Did you see the suspects well enough to identify them?"

"No, Margaret." I made it to the bench. "I did not."

A small sigh. "Well, then, sit down before you collapse."

"Good idea. Did we find Mollie?"

"Not yet."

I lowered myself onto the bench and cradled my arm in my lap. Tried to calm my breathing.

She took out her radio and called for a paramedic — ASAP — then addressed me again. "That stunt you pulled at the press conference, oh, that was . . ." She shook her head in lieu of finishing her sentence, then added, "You have no idea how tenuous your job is right now."

Firing someone with my seniority wasn't easy, but Margaret was a resourceful woman, and with the congressman on her side it wouldn't be a tough sell to Rodale. "I might," I said.

"I will be writing an official reprimand to be placed in your personnel file."

That wasn't exactly at the top of my list of concerns at the moment. "Okay."

"But, you led us here. You were close to catching the suspects, and you were wounded by adversarial action, so I won't be submitting the reprimand. At this time."

I blinked.

How about that.

"Thank you."

"Tell me what happened."

She listened carefully as I filled her in on the chase and the shooting. "Mollie Fischer must be somewhere in that hotel," I concluded.

"Yes," Margaret said vaguely. She was looking at Mrs. Rainey and her kids, who were still standing amidst the swirl of law enforcement activity. "You said those children saw something?"

Beyond her, at the end of the block, I saw an ambulance pulling to a stop at the hotel entrance.

"Just someone entering a taxi—I think. I'm not even sure about that. They're not really excited about talking to strangers."

"I'll speak with them."

"Um, I'm not sure that's such a good idea."

"I'm good with children," she said, and before I could dissuade her, she'd paced over and knelt beside the twin girls.

35

"Hello. My name is Mrs. Weeeeeeellington." Margaret drew out her name in a long, comical way. "That's kind of a funny name, isn't it?"

One of the girls nodded.

"What's your name?" Margaret asked.

"Her name is Lizzie," Mrs. Rainey answered before the girl had a chance to reply.

"I'll bet you're five years old, aren't you?" said Margaret, keeping her eyes on the girl and sounding impressed.

Lizzie shook her head.

"Six?"

Lizzie held up four fingers.

Margaret dropped her jaw, widened her eyes. "No, you must be more than four! You're seven, right?"

Lizzie shook her head. She was smiling.

"We're both four," her sister said.

Two EMTs in their early thirties—a stocky Caucasian man and a petite Persian woman—stepped out of the ambulance and began walking toward me. The woman carried a large paramedics response kit, the man was pushing a gurney. I had no intention of lying on the gurney, but I didn't mind seeing that first aid kit.

"Wow." Margaret was looking back and forth at the sisters. "You two look like you might be related."

"We're twins!" they shouted.

Fake surprise. "Really?"

Both girls nodded.

To the second girl: "So, is your name Lizzie too?"

"No!" The girls squealed in unison.

"I'm Jill," Lizzie's twin replied, then pointed to her brother. "And he's Danny. He's six."

I could hardly believe my eyes. Margaret really was good with kids.

"You two are big girls," Margaret said. "And smart too. I can tell. And it's nice to meet you too, Stanley."

He looked at her curiously. "It's Danny."

"Oh, I'm sorry, Mannie."

"My name is Danny!" he said impatiently, but he was smiling.

"Frannie?"

"Danny!"

She hit her forehead with the heel of her hand. "Right. Yes. Oh, I'm so sorry, Granny."

All three children laughed. He had his hands on his hips. "Danny, Danny, my name is Danny!"

"Hi, Danny," she said. "Good to meet you."

He groaned.

Margaret had those kids in the palm of her hand.

Amazing.

The paramedics saw where I was sitting and picked up the pace.

Margaret pointed to the alley. "Tell me about the people who came out of there." She nodded toward me. "Before this silly-looking man showed up."

I'm a silly-looking man. I see.

"Is he hurt bad?" Danny asked.

Their eyes shifted to my bloody shirt, and I turned in my seat to show them my good arm.

"Oh no," she told them, then said to me, "Show them a funny face, Agent Bowers. Show them you're not hurt badly."

I did my best.

"See?" Margaret said.

I was so glad she was enjoying this.

Danny didn't seem to buy it, but the girls laughed and Lizzie said, "They were in a hurry."

The paramedics arrived, and the man, whose name tag read Neil Blane, said, "Sir, we need to have a look at that arm."

I rose awkwardly, and the female paramedic, who introduced herself as Parvaneh Bihmardi and looked like she hadn't gotten enough sleep last night, saw me wobble. "Wait. Sit back down."

"No." I shook my head, spoke softly, "Away from the children."

Neil Blane gestured toward the gurney, but I declined. He reluctantly offered his arm to me; I declined that as well. They followed me toward a short concrete-barrier wall surrounding a treed-off area. The wall looked about a meter high, acceptable for me to sit on, and it appeared to be out of the sight-line of the Rainey family.

On the way there I heard Margaret ask, "So how many people were there? How many did you see?"

I glanced back and saw Lizzie holding up two fingers.

"A man and a woman?"

The girl nodded.

"Were they carrying anything?"

"The woman had a computer," Danny offered. "The man had a big black bag."

I paused.

Margaret asked, "What color was the computer?"

"White."

If that was Mollie's missing laptop, we could back trace its location as soon as they went online and, depending on the model, remotely turn on its video chat camera to catch a glimpse of the killers . . .

I phoned Doehring; he told me he would get on it, then I eased myself onto the concrete wall that encircled the trees, and Parvaneh pulled out large fabric shears. "All right, let's get that shirt off and see what we've got here."

36

Astrid waited impatiently as Brad finished breaking into the Honda Accord parked on Eisenhower Drive, across the highway from the Pentagon.

She hated that things had spun off in this direction, but they had, and now she would just have to deal with it.

"You were supposed to hack in, loop the video in the alley," she said.

"I did."

"Then how did they—"

"I don't know."

"Why did you shoot that agent?"

"I was afraid."

The lock popped open. She was better at hot-wiring cars than he was, so after he got the doors open, she started the engine, then slid to the passenger seat to fix her hair.

"We need to get back to the house," he said.

"No, I need to get back to work or it won't look right. You know that."

Silence.

"Drop me off, switch cars, then meet me later."

Brad didn't look happy to hear that, but she didn't care.

He guided the car onto the street. "What about Wellington?" he said. "She'll be at the scene."

"Tomorrow. We'll do that tomorrow, unless . . ." Astrid said. "Unless . . ."

"Unless?"

"Let's just see how things play out."

With gloved hands, she set the computer in the backseat. The

FBI would find it later. And the plan would work. The timing would work.

Everything would sort itself out, as long as Brad didn't screw things up any worse.

Neil and Parvaneh worked fast.

It took them only a couple minutes to clean the wound, pour on some QuickClot, and wrap my arm with a pressure bandage. While they tended to the gunshot wound, I tried to regroup, to think through all that I'd been through over the last two hours . . . the emotionally draining meeting with Missy Schuel . . . the revelation that the victim at the primate center was not Mollie Fischer . . . the confrontation with the congressman . . . the press conference . . . the chase through the hotel . . . getting shot.

Nothing had gone right, and to top things off, the suspects had apparently slipped away.

Taking a deep breath, I felt myself beginning to relax, but Parvaneh's words put an end to that: "This might prick a little."

I opened my eyes just in time to see her swab my right forearm with an alcohol wipe and position a ridiculously long IV needle against my skin.

Oh bad.

I hate needles.

She pressed.

And it went in, leaving a small ridge of raised flesh in its wake as it descended through my muscle and punctured my vein. The sight was more unsettling to me than the gunshot wound had been.

I had to look away.

"For your blood loss," she explained.

"I see," I managed to say. I could feel a tug of skin as she removed the needle, leaving the catheter behind.

Neil pulled out his radio and told someone that we were on our way in, then ended the transmission and wheeled the gurney closer to me. "We need to get you to a hospital."

I didn't want to miss anything here at the scene. I shook my head. "I'm staying here."

"That's not going to happen."

"I'll get my arm taken care of after things settle down. I just need a few minutes to brief the officers here—"

Parvaneh and Neil glanced at each other, and then she said, "We're taking you to Mercy Medical."

"No," a gruff voice called, and I saw Ralph quickly approaching us. Behind him, more squads, news vans, and ambulances were pulling up to the hotel—Metro police, FBI, Capitol Hill police.

Spaghetti.

"I'll take him in." Ralph strode toward us. "Come on, Pat. We need to talk."

"I'm sorry, sir," Neil said. "This man has been shot, he's losing blood, he has an IV in his arm. We can't let you—"

Ralph reached down, grabbed the IV's tube—

"Um, Ralph—"

Jerked it out of my arm.

Oh yeah.

That didn't feel so good.

"There we are," Ralph said. "Fast and clean." The sheath of the plastic catheter glistened, wet with my blood, as he set it onto the gurney and said to Parvaneh, "I'll let you take care of that." He pressed the plastic tape that had been holding the IV in place over the needle hole.

Parvaneh was staring at us wide-eyed.

"All right." He helped me to my feet. "Good to go."

My phone rang. Tessa's ring tone.

Unbelievable.

I needed a cup of coffee in a big way. A little caffeine to calm me down.

"Listen, Ralph." I debated whether or not to answer the phone. "If this is about the press conference—"

Ringing.

"No." Ignoring the continued objections of the two paramedics, he led me toward his car. "It's about Richard Basque."

"What? Basque?"

Still ringing.

Go on, Pat. Tessa needs you. She already left two messages.

"Hang on," I said to Ralph. "It's Tessa."

As I answered the phone, I saw his car at the curb. Not far.

"It's me," I told her.

"Hey."

"Are you all right? Your message from earlier, I was concerned."
Agents Tanner Cassidy and Natasha Farraday along with the other
members of the FBI's Evidence Response Team were entering the
hotel.

"Sure, yeah," Tessa said. "I'm okay."

"What is it? What's going on?"

"It's just . . . when are you coming home? Are you in class?"

"Not quite. Something came up."

"Oh." Then, "You sound kind of . . . I don't know. Out of
breath."

"I was exercising." I tried to keep my voice even and measured.
"Did I do something? Are you upset because of something I—"

"No-no-no-no." She scrunched all the no's into one word. "Nothing like that. But when do you think you're gonna get home?"

"Tessa, I . . ." A glance at Ralph. "The truth is, I'm kind of in
the middle of something here. But if you need me, if it's urgent, I
could be home in about half an hour."

Ralph shook his head, mouthed "No you can't."

I mouthed "Yes, I can."

"No, that's . . . it's no big deal," Tessa said. "Later's okay."

"Give me . . ." I checked the time.

3:36 p.m.

"I'll try to be home by 7:00, okay?" That gave me just about
three and a half hours to get to the hospital, get seen, get out, and
get home, which would be a minor miracle, but maybe I could find
a way to hurry the hospital staff up.

"Sure, yeah. I'm okay, so don't worry or anything. It's just . . .
I need to tell you about something."

"Tell me now."

"It can wait."

"It's okay, you can—"

"It can wait," she repeated.

I was growing increasingly impatient but also more concerned. "Tessa, listen to me. Are you safe? Are you all right?"

"Yeah."

"If you're in any kind of danger or trouble right now, ask me to stop bugging you with so many questions. I'll get the police there in—"

"No, it's not that. I'll see you at 7:00? I'm fine. I'll be fine."

We ended the call.

But things didn't feel right.

Ralph and I arrived at his car, and he put his news about Basque on the back burner for the moment. "She okay?"

"I don't know."

"Want me to have Brineesha go check on her?"

"When's she off work?"

"4:30."

From the bank, the drive to our house would take at least thirty-five minutes. I shook my head. "No good. That's too late."

"She could probably leave early."

I had a thought.

"Hang on."

Cheyenne.

She knows where you live . . . Tessa trusts her . . . If she decided not to go to the body farm . . . If she's free . . .

"Give me one more sec." We climbed into his car. Accidentally, I bumped my wounded arm, and a jolt of pain made me cringe. I had to close my eyes and take a deep breath to steady myself.

Easy, easy.

"You all right?" Ralph said.

"Yeah."

I repositioned myself in the seat. It didn't really help. Ralph pulled into the street while I called Cheyenne, found out she'd bypassed the body farm tour and spent her time reading through the case files and filling out the Joint Op paperwork.

"Listen," I said, "there's been a lot going on with this case and I'll brief you on everything, I promise, but right now, I need to ask a favor."

"What is it?"

"Something's up with Tessa. I'm not sure what, I'm worried about her. She's at home. I think she needs someone there with her right now, but I have to swing by the hospital. Can you go over there? Just for—"

"The hospital?"

"I hurt my arm a little. It'll be all right. But if you can check on her, it would help. She knows you. She trusts you."

"Pat, you wouldn't go to the hospital if your arm was only hurt a little. What happened?"

"A through and through," I said. "No arterial damage. No apparent fractures."

Cheyenne knew guns like I know coffee, but she didn't ask about the caliber, the proximity of the shooter, the angle of penetration, she just said instead, "Oh, Pat, I'm sorry."

"I'll be all right, just don't tell Tessa. Okay? I don't want her to worry."

"I won't tell her. I'll get there as soon as I can."

"Thanks."

"Are you sure you're okay?"

"Yes."

"Take care of that arm."

"I will."

I hung up.

"All right," I said to Ralph. I took a small breath. "Tell me about Basque."

"He's missing," he said. "And so is Dr. Renée Lebreau."

37

"What?"

"Both of them."

The news sent my thoughts back to Basque's trial.

Last autumn Professor Lebreau and her Michigan State University law students were the ones who'd found the discrepancies in the eyewitness testimony and DNA evidence from Basque's trial thirteen years ago. Their findings had played a pivotal role in the Seventh District Court's decision to give Richard Devin Basque a retrial and had also been influential in swaying the jury to acquit him.

"When was she last seen?"

"She failed to show up for her legal ethics class about twenty-nine hours ago. Her SUV's still in the parking lot. She hasn't been seen since."

"And Basque?"

"We're not sure, but he dropped off the radar screen a couple days ago. Chicago PD is looking for him, but as you know . . ."

"He's a free man."

"Not just free." Ralph said the words with a dark tone that showed he didn't agree with the verdict either. "Innocent."

"According to the courts."

"Yeah. And an innocent man doesn't have to check in with the police when he goes on a road trip." His words were grated with anger.

I thought again of Grant Sikora's dying wish: "Promise me you won't let him do it again."

"I promise," I'd said.

A stretch of silence, then I asked Ralph who was working Professor Lebreau's disappearance.

"Director Rodale sent Kreger to head it up."

"I don't think I know him."

"Good man. Smart. Cool under pressure. He's working with the East Lansing Police."

Basque was one of the most elusive killers I'd ever encountered, and if he was involved in Professor Lebreau's disappearance, even with Kreger's help, I wondered if a city the size of East Lansing had the resources to find him.

You promised Grant Sikora you wouldn't let Basque kill again . . . you promised . . .

"Send me up there," I said.

Ralph shook his head. "You know I can't do that. You have your classes, this Fischer case, the whole custody thing with Tessa that you need to straighten out—not to mention that scratch on your arm."

"My gunshot wound is a scratch?"

"No bones sticking out. Can't be that serious."

"Nice criterion. Listen, find a way for me to help search for Basque. I know more about him than anyone—"

"Except for . . . ?"

At last I realized what this conversation was really about—the FBI agent who'd helped me track Basque thirteen years ago.

"You," I said.

He nodded. "My flight leaves in an hour."

We were on Massachusetts Avenue NW. The hospital was two blocks away.

"We need to be careful about this, though," he said. "Not jump to conclusions. For all we know, the professor went on an unscheduled vacation and Basque went fishing for the week."

But I could tell he didn't buy any of that.

I knew Ralph would have already thought of this, but I felt like it needed to be said: "If it's been twenty-nine hours, there's a good chance—"

"Yeah, that she's dead," he said. "Or worse."

A harsh stillness filled the air as we both thought of the things Basque had done to his victims before he killed them.

"Ralph," I said slowly, "what do you think of preemptive justice?"

"I was an Army Ranger, man. Most of the missions we went on were preemptive. Identify a threat and eliminate it before it eliminates you."

"Or someone else," I said.

"Yes."

And I had a feeling we were thinking the same thing.

We arrived at the hospital and parked in front of the emergency room doors.

"Both Basque and Lebreau go missing in the same week?" I said. "It's too much of a coincidence. Basque is involved."

"I know."

We climbed out of the car, and Ralph offered me one of his Herculean arms for support, but I turned him down. "Here's the thing that just doesn't fit," I said. "Dr. Lebreau is the one who ended up providing information that helped exonerate Basque. Why would he go after her?"

"I've been wondering the same thing. I have no idea." His voice grew dark. "But, trust me. I'm gonna find him. And if he hurt her . . . Let's just say the justice would be fast."

"And clean."

"Yeah."

We entered the lobby.

When a law enforcement officer is brought into a hospital with a gunshot wound, the doctors are primed and ready, so I wasn't surprised to see a trauma team waiting for us: half a dozen surgeons and nurses in gowns, booties, gloves standing poised around a gurney.

But apparently they must have been expecting something a little more exciting, because the doctors looked at each other uncertainly, and one of them asked, "You're the GSW?" He sounded disappointed.

"Sorry it's not more life-threatening," Ralph said. "Next time we'll try to make sure he gets shot in the chest."

"Hey, thanks, Ralph."

They didn't seem to appreciate our comments, and one by one they dispersed. Ralph excused himself so he could get to the airport, and a severe-looking nurse carrying a stack of paperwork appeared and gestured toward a nearby exam room.

38

Tessa needed to get her mind off the whole deal with Paul Lansing, but it was still gonna be more than three hours before Patrick was supposed to show up.

Great.

Not exactly in the mood for crossword puzzles or poetry. Not today.

Maybe do something to make up for keeping the emails from him, for going behind his back, that would be a major plus.

So? Clean?

Um . . . not.

Supper?

Ouch—that was painful just to think about. She'd tried cooking a few times, and those had not exactly been her best hours.

Okay, so what does he care about—besides you—what matters to him?

Well, that was obvious.

His work.

And right now that meant finding whoever killed the congressman's daughter in that whole weird, totally disturbing, chimpanzee attack.

She tried to think like Patrick would:

Location and timing.

Why then?

Why there?

What does the choice of this location tell us about the killer's familiarity with the region, about his travel patterns? About his perception of the area and his relationship with the victims?

Timing: last night.

Location: the primate research place.

The cable news last night had said that the place was studying cognition in higher primates.

She knew a little about primate cognition, but maybe . . .

The Internet was a possibility, but she had a better idea.

She went online and, using her freshly acquired reader's card verification number, logged onto the Library of Congress's archives, the world's largest collection of scientific journals, and then typed in "Gunderson Foundation Primate Research."

A nurse checked my blood pressure and pulse and then put a bandage on my seeping IV needle mark, and after she left the exam room, I spent ten minutes filling in the hospital's paperwork while I waited for the doctor to arrive.

But at last I set the forms aside, borrowed some paper from a receptionist, and began analyzing the details of the hotel chase, the shooting, the locations related to the crimes, jotting notes as I did.

After a while I realized that it'd been an hour since I'd spoken with Tessa or checked in on the case, and I still hadn't gotten back with Director Rodale, who'd left me a message earlier for me to call him.

I phoned Tessa first, and she assured me she was fine. "Detective Warren is here." She lowered her voice. "I didn't need a babysitter."

"That's not why I asked her to stop by. You know that."

A slight pause. "I guess so."

"What are you two doing?"

"Talking about boys."

"No, we're not," Cheyenne called from the background.

"Boys?"

"She thinks you should let me date older guys."

"No, I don't," Cheyenne said.

"Whatever."

Despite Tessa's reluctance to have someone check in on her, she sounded much more relaxed than when we'd spoken earlier, and I was relieved. "Anyway," she said, "we're playing chess. She's a lot better than you are."

"Well, that's not too hard."

"True."

I tapped a finger against the chair. Since I was still waiting for a doctor, my chances of getting home in time were growing slimmer, but I said, "I'm still hoping to make it by 7:00."

I heard Cheyenne again: "Check."

"All right, I'll see you." Tessa sounded distracted, and I pictured her studying the board.

She hung up, I called Doehring.

We talked for a few minutes about the case—still no sign of Mollie Fischer, but they were checking the hotel room by room. "Farraday found the wheelchair in room 809."

"Whose name was the room reserved under?"

"The manager's. It's a comp room he keeps reserved for foreign dignitaries visiting Washington."

Unbelievable.

"Fourteen sets of prints on the chair—so far mostly partials, DNA from Mollie, two maids, some still unidentified. No matches to anyone in the system, though. And the alley? Well, somehow these guys hacked in and looped the video feed. That's why we didn't see the woman enter. Marianne's furious she didn't catch it."

So the question remained—where was Mollie?

I remembered reading about a case from the 1990s in which a Belgian couple abducted young children and kept them in a specially designed dungeon. The police searched the house twice and heard children crying each time, but assumed the sounds came from kids playing outside somewhere. Two girls starved to death while the husband was serving time and his wife, who was an elementary school teacher, stayed in the house and ignored the girls' cries for weeks until the two children finally died.

"Take the room apart," I said. "Check under the bed frame, move the furniture, assume nothing."

"It's done."

"A maid's cart? Could they have put her in a laundry cart?"

"We checked. Listen, how is your—"

"I'm fine. The freezers at the hotel? The roof? What about the elevators? Check on top of them—" And then, thinking of the hotel's state-of-the-art security and ultramodern renovations, I had a grisly thought. "Any document shredding machines at the hotel? Large ones, I mean industrial-sized?"

"Don't worry. My men are thorough."

At last, as we were finishing the call, I asked him if he could send an officer to pick me up when I was finished here, take me back to my car.

"You were shot, Pat. I'll have Anderson take you all the way home."

"No, I just need to get to my car. I'll call you when I'm ready to leave the hospital."

We hung up.

Finally, under the pretext of returning the call he'd made to my cell earlier in the afternoon—but primarily hoping to find out if he was the one who'd told Fischer to keep the information about Mollie from the press—I punched in Director Rodale's number.

His secretary told me he'd just gone home for the day. "He wants to speak to you too," she said.

That was no surprise.

We set up a meeting at his office tomorrow at noon, between my classes.

Then I went back to my notes, and a few minutes later the doctor arrived.

39

After unwrapping the bandages that the paramedics had snugged around the arm, Dr. Stearn washed out the QuikClot, carefully inspected the entrance and exit holes, then ordered an X-ray to make sure there were no bone or bullet fragments in my arm.

Which only ate up more time.

Afterward, I convinced him to take me to a patient's room rather than the exam room so I could watch the news on the in-room television. He irrigated the wound and said, "Prepare yourself." He was getting a scalpel out to debride the area—a process that involves cutting away the dead tissue surrounding the injured area.

I tried to focus on the news.

Chelsea Traye, Channel 11's on-site reporter, announced that they were expecting a statement "at any moment" from the FBI concerning "an alleged shooting in the basement of the historic Lincoln Towers Hotel."

"Alleged, huh?" Dr. Stearn said.

A deep needle prick as he numbed the area.

"Until it goes through the Bureau's public affairs department, I'm not officially wounded."

"How nice."

As I watched the news, Dr. Stearn finished the debridement and as tenderly as possible put a non-occlusive dressing on the wound. WXTN's news team was explaining that according to their sources, the authorities were looking for a man and a woman as possibly being responsible for Mollie Fischer's disappearance and the death of Twana Summie.

An orderly holding a doctor's scrub top for me appeared at the door—something to wear, since my shirt had been stained with blood and scissored to pieces by Parvaneh. "Compliments of Mercy Medical," he said.

"Pink?" I said. "I thought scrubs were supposed to be green?"

"Discourages people from stealing them."

"I can't imagine why." I pointed at the chair in the corner of the room. "Just set it over there."

As soon as he was gone, I called for a nurse and handed her a twenty dollar bill. "Can you stop by the hospital gift shop and pick up a T-shirt for me? I'm a federal agent and I'd consider this a great service to your country."

She smiled. "Sure."

The doctor had a sling out and was adjusting it to fit my arm. I told him I wouldn't need it; he told me I would.

The news program cut to the press conference, and Margaret appeared on the screen. I turned up the volume. Even though she was only giving a perfunctory explanation, I had to admit that her statement was much more carefully worded than mine had been earlier in the day.

She finished by announcing that one of the Bureau's "finest agents" had sustained "minor injuries from adversarial action at a shooting in the basement of the Lincoln Towers."

A few hours ago I was silly looking, now I was one of the FBI's finest agents.

Maybe Margaret was just plain warming up to me.

"Minor injuries?" Dr. Stearn said dubiously, and I realized that so far he had only communicated to me in two-word sentences.

"Hurts though," I said.

In the end, Margaret didn't say anything that I didn't already know, then the news program shifted to an "expert's analysis" of the incident.

The doc finished with my arm and told me to come back and have it checked on Monday for infection. Finally he gave me some pain meds and antibiotics. "No narcotics," I said. He reluctantly agreed, switched the meds, then said, "Twice daily." He pointed to one of the bottles of pills and then tipped out two. "Swallow these."

"For pain," I said.

He nodded and then stunned me with three complete sentences in a row. "Take another two before going to bed. The next couple days are going to be rough. I'll give you a prescription."

I thanked him and was standing up to go when the nurse returned with a hot pink "DC Rules!" tourist T-shirt.

"You've gotta be kidding me," I said.

"The only extra large they had left." She handed me the shirt and my change. "Don't worry, pink is the new black."

"Oh. Is that it."

Dr. Stearn was scribbling his signature on a sheet of paper clamped to his clipboard.

"No driving," he said.

Okay, back to two-word sentences.

"I understand," I replied.

The two of them helped me put on the shirt and position my arm in the sling, I grabbed the notes I'd jotted down, and then went outside, eased off the sling, and called Doehring to ask if Anderson was available to take me to my car.

40

Tessa was getting frustrated.

Cheyenne had actually beaten her at chess.

Twice.

"Where'd you learn to play?" Tessa asked her.

"My dad. You know I grew up on a ranch? Well, he wasn't too thrilled about us watching TV, so in the evenings we'd play games— mostly chess. He was nationally ranked in college. Over the years he taught me a couple strategies."

A couple.

Yeah, right.

Tessa focused in, scrutinized the board. And made her move.

6:57 p.m.

Using an undercover car, which he proudly notified me was his typical vehicle, Officer Lee Anderson had dropped me off at my car about thirty minutes ago. The meds hadn't really kicked in yet, and every time I moved my arm or shifted my weight it felt like someone was driving a giant needle through my arm and wrenching it back and forth.

Needles again.

Man, I just couldn't get them off my mind.

To make matters worse, traffic had stalled. Maybe there was an accident up ahead.

I shifted my weight.

Needles.

Think about something else.

Okay. Ralph's news: Basque and Professor Lebreau's disappearance. Unbelievable.

For a flickering moment, I considered the possibility that Basque might somehow be involved in the crimes here in DC, this week. A quick calculation told me the drive time from Michigan would have been tight but workable.

But even as I considered that, I realized the scenario didn't work. The build of the unidentified man pushing the wheelchair into the Lincoln wasn't right: Basque was nearly my height and stocky; that man was shorter and had a medium build.

So . . .

What could I do from here to help find him?

At first I couldn't think of anything, but then—

Ah yes.

Not me.

Angela Knight, my friend in the cybercrime division. She and her computer she'd named Lacey could find just about anyone.

Traffic was at a standstill, so I pulled up a few jpegs from Basque's case files on my cell and then called Angela and started by telling her about the IPR-OMI license plate. She told me she'd gotten word that the NSA guys were on it. "I'm backed up here like you wouldn't believe."

Considering how busy she was, I wondered if I should even tell her the main reason I'd called, but since I really didn't have anything to lose, I just went ahead. "One more thing—"

"Pat, I know what you're going to ask, but I haven't had any more time to work on your Patricia E. cipher." She sounded exhausted.

"This is about something else."

"Oh." A pause. "Let me guess: you need confidential information, you need it now, and you don't want to fill out any paperwork."

"You're amazing. You read my mind."

"What can I say, I'm psychic."

"I had my suspicions." I took the phone from my ear and tapped the screen to email her the jpegs while I edged the car forward a few feet, holding the steering wheel in position with my knees.

A small sigh. "What do you need?"

"I need you to find Richard Devin Basque. I don't care how you do it—credit card use, driver's license, his cell phone's GPS. Hack into his lawyer's computer. Her name is Priscilla Eldridge-Gorman. I can get her address for—"

"Hold on. What's this about?"

I told her about Dr. Lebreau's possible abduction and the all-too-conveniently timed disappearance of Basque.

"Who's the agent in charge?"

"Kreger's on Lebreau. Ralph's flying up there right now to help look for Basque."

Traffic moved forward slightly, then stopped again.

"Then why isn't he the one calling me?"

"He's playing this close to the chest," I said evasively.

"Oh. I see. Richard Basque is a free man and not—let me see, how shall I phrase this?" A slight sting in her words. "'A person of interest in the case,' so placing an official locate on him could be considered harassment."

"I wouldn't put it quite like that."

"How about like this: Ralph is going about this within the bounds of the law."

I heard a ping. The email with the attached photos I'd just sent her had arrived.

She noticed it. "What's that?"

"Pictures of his victims. To help convince you to help me."

"I'm deleting them."

"No."

"I can't do this, Pat. He's a free man."

"This woman who went missing yesterday, she's the one who uncovered the DNA evidence that helped free him. It's very likely he's involved somehow. Her life is in danger."

"If this locate doesn't come from Ralph, I'm going to need authorization from Assistant Director Wellington."

"Open the jpegs," I said. "Look at what he did to his victims."

"He was declared not guilty."

"The jury made a mistake."

A small pause. I wondered if she was looking at the photographs. She said, "This missing woman, that's not the only reason that you want to find him, is it?"

"Finding her, making sure she's okay, that's our primary concern."

"But not the only one. Not for you."

I felt an uncomfortable itch on the back of my neck. "Okay, yes. I need to talk with Mr. Basque."

"Talk."

"Yes."

"That's it? Just talk?"

"Angela, you and I have worked together for five years." It wasn't an answer to her question. "Trust me on this."

"I know how long we've worked together, that's why I'm asking you the question. I'm concerned you might do something reckless."

"Have I ever done anything reckless?"

"Are you being serious?"

"Okay, but I mean, apart from those times—whichever ones you're thinking of."

I heard a small snort-laugh.

Ah, good.

A chink in her armor.

"Help me out here, Angela. If anyone can find Basque, you and Lacey can."

Angela treated her computer as if it were a real person. She claimed Lacey had emotions, good days and bad days, and was self-aware. I'd seen them work together enough to wonder if Angela might actually be right.

A pause. "We could get in trouble for this, you know that." I wondered if "we" referred to me and her, or her and Lacey. "I could lose my job."

"Your skills are very transferable. I wouldn't worry too much."

A small sigh. "Remind me again why I'm friends with you?"

"My scintillating personality."

"Really."

"Probably, that or my striking good looks." I guided the car down the Garrisonville exit. "As soon as I hang up, I'll send you everything I have on Basque."

"Pat, if I find him, you have to promise you won't hurt him, that you won't do anything that would make me regret helping you."

"Angela—"

"Promise, or I'll wait to hear from Margaret, and we both know that's something that's not going to happen. Give me your word and I'll trust you."

I weighed my options.

"Pat?"

"I promise I won't hurt him," I said.

"Then I'll find him."

I thanked her and then the conversation was over. I sent her the information and then spent the rest of the drive home wondering how I would keep both my promise to her and my promise to Grant Sikora.

And I couldn't think of any way to honor them both.

41

At the house I found Tessa and Cheyenne in the living room, seated across from each other at a chessboard.

"Check," Tessa said, moving her knight to h7. When she looked at me, her gaze went immediately to the bandages on my arm. "What happened?"

"I got a little scrape. How are you doing?"

"A scrape?"

Cheyenne gave me a look of concern. "Is your arm all right?"

"I'm good."

"Really?"

"Yeah."

"A scrape?" Tessa repeated.

"I'm all right."

She considered that for a moment, then her eyes drifted to my new T-shirt. "Wow. You're really stylin' tonight."

"Pink is the new black."

"Really."

Cheyenne momentarily went back to examining the board.

"It's hip," I assured Tessa.

She grimaced. "Hip?"

"Trust me. I have my finger on the pulse of all that is cool."

"Please tell me you did not just say that."

Cheyenne slid her rook across the board, took Tessa's knight, and said, "Mate."

Tessa refocused on the board, and her mouth gaped open.

"Seriously, Pat." Cheyenne rose, came toward me. "Are you okay?"

"It's fine. I'm fine. Now, no more questions about my arm."

Tessa evaluated the board, then let out a groan. "You were setting that up for like five moves."

"Six."

Nice.

Tessa slumped back in her chair.

Cheyenne stood beside me now, closer than a mere co-worker would have stood. The proximity spoke for itself. "Is there anything I can do for you?" she said. "I could stay if you want, I'd just need to make a couple calls . . ."

Man, was that tempting. "I'll be all right. But thanks. Really."

She didn't look like she exactly believed me but seemed willing to let it drop for the moment. "I brought your laptop back from the NCAVC meeting." She pointed to the kitchen. "It's on the table."

"Great. Thank you."

A slight awkwardness filtered its way into the room, and even though I'd just told her that I didn't need her to stay, I felt a growing desire to rescind that. Cheyenne picked up her purse. "Well, I should probably be going, then."

"Wait," I said. "Did you guys eat yet?" It was a lame attempt at finding a way to tell her I wouldn't mind if she hung around. "Do you need some dinner?"

"Actually, I'm supposed to be meeting someone for dinner in the city."

"Oh."

"Lien-hua."

"Oh."

"We really hit it off this afternoon. Seems we have a lot in common. She's going to fill me in." I expected her to elaborate, but she stopped abruptly, leaving her words open for interpretation.

Unintended consequences.

"Well, I'll walk you to the door." I glanced toward Tessa. "Hey, can you get your mom's diary?"

"Why?"

"Please."

She gave me a disapproving look but at last left for her bedroom.

Cheyenne and I crossed the room. "There've been a lot of developments in the case," I said. "I'm sure Lien-hua will bring you up to speed."

"Actually, I spoke with your boss on the phone about twenty minutes ago. She gave me a rundown."

"Margaret?"

She nodded. "I handed in the Joint Op paperwork this afternoon. She said that as the head of the task force, she wanted to introduce herself. She told me to attend class in the morning and then come to the afternoon briefing with the rest of the team."

"So you've never met her before?"

"Uh-uh."

Huh.

"What time is the briefing?" I asked.

"It's scheduled for 2:00, but I think it'll depend on how the investigation progresses in the morning."

My class started at 2:00. "I won't make it, but maybe we can connect afterward. Catch up on the case."

"Sounds good."

We were at the door. "Hey," I said, "you've really been a big help to me. Last night and then tonight, coming to my rescue again."

"Didn't I tell you? It's my new hobby."

"In addition to target shooting and line dancing."

"A girl's gotta be well-rounded." She gave me a concerned smile. "You sure your arm is all right?"

"Yes. Listen, did Tessa tell you anything about what was going on with her this afternoon? Anything I need to know?"

Cheyenne shook her head. "She didn't say, but it did seem to help that I was here."

I hesitated for a moment. "I hate to keep asking you for favors, but you mentioned you're having dinner in DC?"

"Yes."

"Could you come to my rescue again?"

"Any time."

I pulled out Missy Schuel's card and jotted her home address on a sheet of paper, then handed it to Cheyenne. "Can you take the diary to Missy? She's a lawyer for—"

"A lawyer?" Tessa was standing at the end of the hallway, holding the diary. "Why are you giving the diary to a lawyer?"

"I'll explain everything in a couple minutes."

"Now is good."

"Tessa." I tried to sound stern, fatherly. "Detective Warren needs to go." I held out my hand. "The diary. Please. And then we can talk things through in a few minutes."

After a brief consideration, Tessa gave me the diary, I paged through it to make sure that the letter Paul Lansing had written to Christie was still inside, then slipped a scrap sheet of paper in to bookmark it and handed the diary to Cheyenne.

Tessa watched.

"Okay," Cheyenne said. "See you soon."

"Thanks again."

Then she left and Tessa and I were alone.

"All right." My stepdaughter had her hands on her hips. "What's going on—why did you give her my mom's diary?"

42

"In a minute," I said. "You first. I want to know why you were so upset this afternoon and why you were so eager for me to get home."

She seemed to debate with herself whether or not to press me but then said, "Okay, so I have something to tell you, but I don't want you to get mad." Her eyes focused on the thick bandage again. "What'd you scrape your arm on, anyway?"

"A bullet, and I can't promise that I won't get mad until I know—"

"You got shot!"

"Yes, but right now we're not talking about me, we're talking about—"

"Who shot you?"

"One of the bad guys. Now, listen—"

"Are you okay? Seriously?"

"Tessa." I'm sure my tone reflected my growing impatience. "I did my best to hurry home because you were anxious to tell me something. What is it?"

She stared at me for a long uncertain moment, then unexpectedly left the room, returned with her laptop, set it beside me on the couch, and tilted the screen so I could see it clearly.

Her email application was open, and she'd highlighted a thread of messages.

When I saw who they were from, a sharp bite of anger cut through me.

"You've been emailing him!" Paul Lansing's first email had been sent the day after we'd visited Wyoming. I scrolled down the list and saw that the most recent had been sent less than twenty-four hours ago. "I specifically told you not to email him without letting me read over—"

"Does it hurt?"

I went back to the top of the list and started scanning the messages. "What?"

"Your arm. Does it hurt?"

"Of course it hurts. A bullet went through it. I can't believe you've been—"

"Ew." She looked pale. Sat down. "I wish you hadn't told me that."

With every email I read, I felt a fresh surge of betrayal.

"How could you do this? Go behind my back and email him like this?"

"Why is it going behind your back to email my dad?"

"Because I didn't give you permission to."

"He's my . . ." She paused, must have reconsidered what she was about to say because she left the sentence unfinished, stranded there in midair between us.

"Anything else?" I said. "Any other bombshells you want to drop on me?"

She hesitated for a moment.

"Well?"

She leaned over, tapped the keyboard to open an Internet browser window, clicked to her facebook page.

Another email.

From 2:21 p.m. this afternoon.

Tessa,

I'm sorry I got angry at you today at the museum. I just wanted to make sure you were safe. I tried calling the phone I gave you, but you didn't answer. (Don't worry, I found it.) I'd rather not call your cell, I don't want your stepfather to find out we met. I wouldn't want him to get mad and then take it out on you.

But we need to talk. Call me or email me as soon as you can.

Love,

Dad

I felt a rising quiver of rage. "You saw him? That's why you went to DC? To see Paul? That's why you cancelled lunch with me?"

"I . . ."

"You lied to me."

"No, I just—"

"You said you were going to the Library of Congress."

"I did."

Half truths.

Deception.

"Love, Dad" . . . He signed the message "Love, Dad."

I could feel my whole body growing tense, the ache in my arm tightening.

Tessa watched me uneasily. "I'm sorry."

I pointed to the computer screen. "What is this about him giving you a phone?"

"I threw it out."

I waited.

"No. I did. I promise." She pointed to the screen. "He even says he found it."

"And just when exactly were you going to tell me about all these emails?"

"I tried to this afternoon, but—"

"You've been emailing him for three weeks!"

"I was scared you'd be mad."

I smacked the couch. "Well, I am mad."

Then I stood and I was towering over her and she was easing backward.

"I needed to find out why he never came looking for me and whether or not he loved Mom, things like that. And he didn't." Her voice cracked slightly. "He didn't love her."

Despite how distraught she sounded, I was still furious. "He says here that he doesn't want me to find out about any of this; that he was afraid I'd take things out on you. Why would he write that? Is that what you told him?"

"No! I swear! I told him how much you love me, how you'd do

anything for me, how you saved my life. But he kept asking me all these questions about you, and that's when I left."

Her voice was crisp with pain, and I felt the delicate bridge we'd been building for the last sixteen months splintering apart. But I had a right to be angry. I said nothing.

"Please. You have to believe me."

I wanted to ask her why I should believe her now. Why, when she'd been deceiving me for the last three weeks? And I probably would have said it if the realization of what Paul had been doing hadn't hit me so hard.

He was doing research for his lawsuit.

He was using Tessa to dig up dirt on you.

Something cold and uncertain began crawling around inside of me. "Did you tell him where we were staying for the summer? Is that how his lawyers found out where to send the letter?"

She was quiet. "What letter?"

I hesitated.

"You just said his lawyers sent a letter," she said. "What letter?"

"Tessa, right now, what matters is—"

"Tell me!"

I took a breath, evaluated things, finally plowed forward. "Paul Lansing is trying to assert his rights as your biological father. That's probably why he—"

"Assert his rights?" It took her only seconds to connect the dots. "You mean custody. He's trying to get custody of me?"

"Don't worry. I've already spoken to a lawyer—"

"Oh?" Now, it was her turn to look betrayed. "Really? And when were *you* planning on telling me all *this*?"

"I only found out about the letter last night after you went to bed, and then this morning you were asleep when I left." A seismic shift had happened in the conversation. It was a little disorienting. "I wasn't keeping it from you. I was going to tell you at lunch."

As I watched her, I could almost see the anger she'd felt toward me only a moment ago evaporating and something darker taking its place. A shiver of fear. "This isn't happening," she said. "This can't be happening."

Her hands were shaking slightly.

I held my good arm out to her. "Come here."

She came to me then, and, careful to avoid touching my injured arm, she leaned against my chest. And she held me in a way that broke my heart.

I didn't feel right telling her that things were going to be okay, that it would all work out, because I couldn't guarantee any of that, but then I realized she was crying and I knew I had to say something. "Shh," I whispered. "Don't worry. I'm here." I've never been good at this sort of thing. "I'll always be here for you. You know that."

After a long, painful moment, she eased back to look at me. A single, round tear traced down her cheek. "I love you," she said, and her words were soft and deep and real.

I wiped the tear away. "I love you too, Tessa."

"You can't let this happen. You can't let him take me."

Then I said what I'd been hesitant to tell her only a moment before: "I won't let him take you away. I promise."

And this was one promise that I swore to myself I was going to keep.

No.

Matter.

What.

43

Thirty minutes later, after things had calmed down somewhat and Tessa was feeling at least a little better, she asked me to tell her about how I got shot, but to leave out any gross parts.

Obviously, I couldn't divulge details about the case, but I did tell her as much as I could about the race through the hotel and the shooting in the basement.

And in that strange way that shared tragedy seems to draw people together, my story about the shooting made me feel closer to her, reassured me that we could both be vulnerable in front of each other and it was okay.

When we finally went to the fridge for supper, it was after 8:00.

She found some leftover Thai and headed to the microwave. "Aren't you guys always supposed to wait for backup?"

"Ideally, yes." I grabbed a couple cans of root beer. "But it doesn't always work out like that."

"So, what is this? The third time? Fourth time you've been shot?"

"Only the third, but I've been doing this for over fifteen years and—"

"Maybe you wouldn't get shot so much if you'd follow the rules."

"That's never exactly been my strong suit, Raven."

A stretch of silence.

"You could have gotten killed, Patrick."

Honestly, I hadn't thought about the shooting in those terms, and her words brought a sudden seriousness to the conversation. "I suppose that's possible."

"Do me a favor."

"Yeah?"

"Don't let that happen."

Unsure where to go with this, I replied simply, "I'll do my best."

After supper, we talked for a long time about things we'd never really shared before: her years growing up in Minnesota, her first boyfriend, my high school basketball days, the two women I'd loved before meeting her mother.

Eventually, for a late dessert, we broke into my secret stash of vegan brownies I'd bought for her at a bakery a few days ago. I anticipated that they would taste like baked chalk, but they were amazingly good.

"This lawyer you have," she said, her mouth full of brownie, "is he good?"

"It's a woman, and I think she is. I've never worked with her before, but she comes highly recommended."

"And she's the one who wanted the diary?"

"That's right."

We both munched for a moment, then she said, "Don't go after him, okay?"

"Who?"

"Paul." Another bite. "Just leave it to the lawyer."

I felt a tug of disappointment for being the kind of person to whom she needed to say something like that.

I'm sure my hesitation telegraphed my thoughts, and I decided to change the subject. "I have to make a few calls," I told her. "I need to tell the lawyer about Paul contacting you, and I should probably touch base with my boss, let her know there aren't any broken bones in my arm, that I'll be fine to teach my classes tomorrow."

"Maybe you should take a day off?"

"I'll be okay."

"Yeah," she said, and it almost sounded like she was disappointed. She stood. "I gotta print out some stuff anyway. I did some research for you."

"Really?"

"On that Gunderson Foundation place, and on primates. I think it might help you with your case."

Hmm. Nice.

"Forward Paul's emails to me first," I said, "so I can send them to the lawyer."

A pause. "Okay."

She left the room, and I dialed Missy's home number.

44

Missy Schuel listened silently as I told her about Paul Lansing's emails to Tessa and his rendezvous with her earlier in the day.

"Who initiated the electronic communication between them?"

"I'm not sure."

"What about the meeting?"

"He did."

"Forward the emails to me."

"I'm doing it right now." I tapped at my keyboard.

"It might be considered intimidation if you contact him, so don't. I can guarantee you that it wouldn't help our case. Also, your friend dropped off the diary. Thank you."

"Yes."

"I have a few other cases on my plate, but I'll read as much of it as I can tomorrow."

"Good. Thank you."

"I left a message for Lansing's lawyers; they haven't returned my calls. I'll try again in the morning. Hopefully we can still set up a meeting next week. They might not like it, but I think we should move forward as soon as we can."

I thanked her again, and when I ended the call, I saw a text from Lien-hua asking how I was doing—she'd heard about the shooting and was concerned.

Considering all that was on my mind and my tumultuous feelings toward her, I didn't think I was up for the emotional roller-coaster ride of talking to her right now. I texted her that I was fine, thanked her for teaching my class today, and then told her I'd call her first thing in the morning.

Finally, I phoned Margaret and asked if Mollie Fischer had been found.

"Not yet."

"You've searched every room in the hotel?"

"Yes, we—"

"Any video of her leaving?"

"No. There's been no word from her, and there's nothing on video. We're wondering if the killers somehow managed to get her into a car and out of the parking garage before the perimeter was set up. Patrick, I spoke with the doctor who treated your arm—"

"No."

"No what?"

"The timing doesn't work. I was right behind them. They couldn't have gotten her out, especially if they used the taxi."

Unless only one of them was in the storage room.

But how would they have gotten Mollie down eight flights of stairs?

And who were the two people the Rainey children saw?

"We'll find her," Margaret responded.

"But if she didn't leave the hotel, she has to be inside it."

"We're on it." Her tone had become more terse, and since I'd already gone over most of this with Doehring earlier, I moved the discussion into a slightly different direction. "Did you follow up on the laptop and duffel bag Danny Rainey mentioned?"

"Nothing was left in the cab they used. But we did find the bullet that traveled through your arm. The lab says it's a 9mm, fired from a Walther P99." She told me a few more details that the Rainey children had shared with her: the man and woman were walking; she was thinner than their mom and was really pretty. Danny thought he'd seen her somewhere before on a TV show. The man had black hair and a lot of scars on his face and was "pretty much normal sized."

Scars.

Hmm. Should make him easier to identify.

That was a lot of good information from the children who hadn't told me anything. "Where did you learn to do that, by the way?"

"Do what?"

"Talk to kids like that. You seem like an old pro."

"I work with children every weekend," she replied. "Yesterday you informed me that you didn't see the man you were chasing . . ." Since eyewitnesses don't often recall specific details until hours or even days after a traumatic event, I had a feeling I knew where she was going with this. "Have you thought more about it? Can you give us any kind of description?"

"I only caught a glimpse of him at the doorway to the stairwell, and I never saw his face. But based on the security video footage of him wheeling Mollie into the hotel, we know he's Caucasian, medium build, approximately five-foot-eleven or six foot tall. He used his left hand to press the elevator button and to open the stairwell door."

"So, left-handed."

"Most likely, yes. And he favors his right leg." My curiosity was getting the best of me. "You work with children on the weekends?"

"I volunteer at a shelter for battered women; I watch their children for them. When you say he favors that leg, do you mean he puts more weight on it or less?"

"Less weight." It was as if we were carrying on two conversations at the same time. "Margaret, helping at the shelter, that's impressive. That's a side of you I never knew existed."

"Agent Bowers, there are many sides of me you have never seen."

A comment like that begged for a different context, but as I considered her words, it occurred to me that Margaret Wellington actually had a life outside the Bureau.

Fascinating.

At last she asked about the gunshot wound, and I assured her that I was fine. "One more thing." I took a seat in the living room. "Are you the one who told Congressman Fischer not to release the information about his daughter, that it might jeopardize the investigation?"

"No."

"What about my daughter? Did you tell him about the custody case?"

A small silence. "What custody case?"

I heard no hint of deception in her voice.

All right, then, I would deal with all that when I met with Rodale tomorrow. "Never mind."

"One last thing," Margaret said formally. "Because of your injury, I'm excusing you from your teaching responsibilities for the rest of the week. If you're feeling up to it, you can return to the classroom when the NA classes begin on Monday."

"I'm not teaching arm wrestling, I'm teaching geospatial investigative strategies. I'll be all right."

"I'm not debating this with you. There are liability issues at stake here that the Bureau needs to be cognizant of and responsive to."

"Honestly, Margaret, it's not that big of a deal."

"I've already spoken with Agent Vanderveld, and he's agreed to take your classes."

Not Jake.

Please, not Jake.

"Margaret, he's screwed up two major investigations he's worked with me."

"He's a valued member of the NCAVC and one of the most experienced profilers we have. He's qualified to take your classes for two days." She took a breath. "Besides, I looked it up: Bureau policy clearly states that anyone with a firearm injury caused by adversarial action must be released from duty, with pay, for a minimum of forty-eight hours."

"I don't remember that policy."

"How many policies *do* you remember?"

Okay, now that wasn't even nice.

"But what about the case?" I said. "Mollie is still missing. You can't just expect me to step away and then—"

"I'll keep you posted on our progress, but for the next forty-eight hours, you are officially on medical leave."

I didn't respond.

"Do you understand?"

I said nothing.

"Are we on the same page here or not?"

"I hear you," I said noncommittally, and left it at that.

A pause, as she no doubt considered how far to press things, but finally she moved on: "Don't forget, I'll need your incident report. I'd like it on my desk by 9:00. Also, I spoke with the hospital. They said you need to complete the forms they gave you, that filling in the d's and b's was not sufficient."

I'd had a feeling that would come back to haunt me.

"Paperwork. Good. Sounds like fun."

"I'll see you in a couple days. Just get some rest. Good night, Agent Bowers."

"Good night, Margaret."

End call.

And when I looked up I saw Tessa standing in the doorway. "Did you hear that?" I said.

"Sort of. I mean, your part at least. I could pretty much fill in the rest."

She placed a stack of manila folders filled with printouts on the table. The folders had been labeled "Primate Metacognition," "Primate Aggression," and "Altruism in Higher Primates."

Primate metacognition? Altruism in higher primates?

"That was Assistant Director Wellington." My eyes were on the folders. "I'm not sure you've ever had the pleasure of meeting her."

"Has anyone?"

Ooh. Nice line.

That one was worth remembering.

Tessa took a seat beside me. "Is she always like that?"

"Pretty much." Curious, I flipped through the altruism folder. Tessa had printed out more than a dozen scientific journal articles on reciprocal altruism, cognitive empathy, primate intentionality, and partner-specific reciprocity among chimpanzees. I caught the gist of what the phrases were referring to, but I wasn't sure how these articles could possibly relate to the case.

"The word *uptight* doesn't even come close, does it?" Tessa said, referring to Margaret again.

"The words that come close would not be appropriate for a seventeen-year-old girl to hear."

"I'll bet I can guess 'em."

"I'll bet you can."

As I paged through the printouts I was impressed with the thoroughness of Tessa's research. "You did a lot of good work here. I'm proud of you."

"I hope it helps." She was setting up the chessboard.

I closed the folder. "I'll take a look at these in the morning when I have a little more time."

When she'd finished arranging the pieces, she quietly rotated the board so that the white pieces were in front of her, and then without a word, moved her king's pawn to e4 and glanced at me.

I positioned myself across from her and played e5. Tessa favored a Ruy Lopez opening, so I wasn't surprised when she countered with knight f3.

But I went with Petrov's Defense to see how she'd respond, so instead of knight to c6, I played knight to f6.

She eyed me.

Smiled in a soft, confident way.

And as the game progressed, the stress from the case began to drain away, the pain in my arm became less and less noticeable, and although Tessa and I hardly spoke, it seemed like we were both opening up to each other in ways deeper than words.

I was just a dad spending time with his daughter.

It struck me that it was times like these that Paul Lansing was trying to steal away from me.

Then I made a move, she took my knight, and I realized that I needed to change my entire strategy or I might end up losing this match before it had barely begun.

45

Oasis Hotel
Vienna, Virginia
11:47 p.m.

After the debacle at the Lincoln, Astrid had suggested that she and Brad stay at a hotel tonight rather than the house, just to play it safe.

"At least it all worked out," Brad had told her as he locked the door.

"But shooting an FBI—it was rash. Careless."

"Okay."

"You understand?"

"Yes."

So that was an hour ago.

Now, she was slipping into something a little more comfortable for bed, and he was watching her.

Over the last few minutes, for whatever reason, they'd gotten onto the topic of serial killers. "They take souvenirs," Brad said. "The serial killers do. So that they can relive their crimes, so they can feel that sense of power and control again."

She already knew this of course, but decided to pretend that she didn't. "What kind of souvenirs?"

"Jewelry, underwear, body parts. In a surprisingly high number of cases, shoes."

Serial killers.

Like Brad.

But not like her. She'd never killed anyone, not in NowLife. It'd always been him.

She'd planned it that way from the start.

Just in case they ever got caught.

No, she was not a murderer. Just a bystander. "We keep a different kind of souvenir," she said, getting back to the conversation.

He stared at her quizzically.

"In the freezer," she added.

"The freezer?"

"Prison, our little fishbowl."

A questioning look.

"I never told you about that? About the fishbowl?"

"I don't think so."

She stepped into the bathroom to freshen up. "You mentioned once that you had a dog, when you were a kid."

"Brandi, yes. She was a Sheltie."

"I never had a pet myself, but my sister did." She'd told him stories about her sister Annie before. "A goldfish named Goldie."

"Annie had a goldfish named Goldie."

"What can I say, I was always the more inventive one in the family." She washed her face. "Goldie lived in a fishbowl on the dresser in our bedroom; anyway, one night Annie and I got into a fight. I don't remember what it was about—who was supposed to help Dad with the dishes, maybe. Something like that. But I ended up being the one who got into trouble, and Annie spent the rest of the night teasing me. Well, the next morning when she woke up, Goldie was gone."

"You flushed her goldfish?"

"No."

Astrid finished in the bathroom. "Goldie's bowl was gone, and Annie looked all over for it. It was Saturday but my father worked weekends, so we were home alone. Annie was bigger than I was, stronger, and she hit me. A lot. But I didn't say a word. She emptied out the garbage, didn't find any glass, looked everywhere outside. No sign of the fish or the bowl anywhere."

She glanced at him to see his reaction.

He was listening intently. She had him, she could tell.

"I guess Annie must have searched for three or four hours that morning. Finally, at lunch, I figured it'd been long enough. I told her to check—"

"The freezer," he said.

She smiled. "Yes. Annie cried for three days. My dad beat me for doing it, but every time he hit me I hardly noticed, all I could think of was how it had felt when Annie was looking. The feeling was . . ." She searched for the right word, couldn't find it. "It was like nothing I'd ever experienced before."

"Exquisite," he said. "It was exquisite."

"Yes." She joined him beside the bed. "All I'd done was set the bowl in the freezer and close the door. It was that simple. And then the water began to freeze and I knew that slowly, slowly, it would become a solid block of ice."

"It made you feel powerful."

"Yes."

"Is that how you got started?"

"It wasn't the only thing." She reflected for a moment. "You set things in motion and then life simply goes on, but you have a secret, and in a way you want someone to open the freezer to see what you did, to see your handiwork, but you don't tell them because while they search, while they wonder, while they worry, you own a piece of them."

"Like the FBI, right now," he said. "Searching for Mollie, for us. We control a part of them."

She thought of the current game, but also of the four men in prison because of her. The goldfish from the previous games. She could get them released at any time; all she needed to do was tell the authorities the truth. "Yes."

Then, after watching him for a moment, she stepped back and smiled. "So, how did I do?"

"With what?"

"The story. Did I have you?"

A question mark on his face. Then dawning disappointment. "You made it up?"

"It was good, wasn't it?"

"I didn't know it was a story."

So, yes, he had believed her. He was staring at her with a wounded, confused look, the same look he'd had at the hotel when she deleted the picture of Rusty.

"Don't sulk." She trailed a finger along his cheek. "It was a good story, wasn't it?"

After a moment: "Yes. It was a good story."

"Time for bed."

"Okay."

The novel that was her life played out in her head.

He remained distant and distracted throughout the
night and that bothered her, especially since he was
the one who had failed her earlier in the day—being
so impulsive, so remiss, shooting the FBI agent.

Yes, it was true she'd deceived him, now, twice
in one day, but it shouldn't have been a shock to
him. After all, so much of their relationship had
been built on the sand of half truths and lies. Ever
since the beginning. Ever since DuaLife.

This moodiness, his carelessness, were not acceptable.

In a quiet, slow U-turn of emotion, she found herself considering possibilities she had never fully
explored before.

She began to wonder if he might be turning into a
liability.

The idea made her uncomfortable. He was the father
of her unborn child and she loved him, but now she
realized that if things came down to it, she might
need to be ready to swing the freezer door shut on
this scarred little pet resting in her arms.

And to her surprise, she found the idea enticing.

Maybe even exquisite.

46

My arm was killing me.

I'm not a big fan of drugs, so last night, even though I took the antibiotics, I'd passed on the second dose of meds the doctor had offered me, and as a result, the gunshot wound had ached and throbbed throughout the night, keeping my sleep light and fitful and sporadic.

At last, when daybreak cut through my window, I gave up fighting for sleep and climbed out of bed.

And took the stupid painkillers.

No workout today, but I washed up, and as I was getting dressed I noticed the St. Francis of Assisi pendant that Cheyenne had given me lying on my dresser where I'd left it when we moved into the house for the summer.

Last month when I was preparing to leave to testify at Richard Basque's retrial, she'd offered the pendant to me, explaining that St. Francis is the patron saint against dying alone. "It helps remind me why I do what I do. It'll be good for you to have at the trial. To remember the women he killed." I knew she was Catholic, and her words had underscored to me how seriously she took her faith. "Don't worry, I can get another one."

I'm not very religious or superstitious, but the gesture meant a lot to me, and I'd accepted the pendant.

Now, as I picked it up, I couldn't help but think of what Lienhua had mentioned about how Mollie Fischer would've gotten rid of the locket that Rusty had given her if she'd really broken up with him.

So maybe you shouldn't keep the pendant . . . ?

But Cheyenne and I had never broken up, never been a couple—in fact, we'd only gone out once, and that was just a pseudo-date since Tessa had tagged along.

Pseudo-date or not, I slipped the pendant into my pocket, chose a shirt that was baggy enough to hide the bandages on my arm, bypassed the sling, and went to the kitchen for breakfast.

Margaret had made it clear that she didn't want me working on the case today, but there was no way I could shut off that part of my brain for forty-eight hours.

Besides, we hadn't found Mollie yet, and there was a remote chance that she was still alive. I figured job security wasn't all that big of a deal when there were lives at stake, so after grabbing some breakfast and brewing a pot of Ethiopian Yirgacheffe, I went online and logged onto the case files to see what had been added since last night.

The FBI Lab had established with certainty that the woman who'd been found in the primate research facility was indeed Twana Summie. Her family had been contacted, and as I read through the autopsy report, I thought of the words that had likely been said to them:

"Her condition proved to be fatal."

"We arrived too late to save her."

Platitudes.

Undoubtedly, officers would be following up with the family and friends, asking the typical questions: Do you know of anyone who might have wanted to harm her in any way? Did she mention any people she was meeting on the day she disappeared? Was she acting unusual prior to her disappearance? Did she know Rusty Mahan or Mollie Fischer?

And of course, they would be checking her address book and calendar, looking into her recent phone calls, searching for and then interviewing the last people who had seen her alive.

During my six years as a homicide detective in Milwaukee, I'd done my share of asking those questions and pursuing those types of leads, and I remembered how discouraging it can be to run into dead-end after dead-end.

Yet now, given the inscrutable actions of this week's killers—switching the license plates, staging the crime scenes, using elaborate misdirection techniques, daring us to decipher their clues and anticipate their next move—I had a feeling even more dead-ends than usual were on the horizon.

I read on.

The task force was compiling a list of other potential suspects. So far they'd collected hundreds of names from tips and the case histories of hundreds of known offenders who'd committed violent crimes in DC and its neighboring states. The suspect pool was growing larger, not smaller, by the hour. In fact, two more names appeared on the active screen even as I was reading the report.

The team was still looking for Aria Petic.

No DNA had been found on the latex glove left in the parking garage. Apparently, it had never been worn.

Amazingly, the ERT hadn't pulled anything useful from the handicap accessible van, except for a gas station receipt from last week that had no prints on it and DNA evidence that Mollie, Twana, and Rusty had been in the back. They followed up, but the receipt didn't lead anywhere. No usable prints on the elevator button that the suspect had pressed, so evidently, he'd avoided touching it with the pad of his finger or had wiped it clean.

Dead-end after dead-end.

Dr. Trower, the District of Columbia's medical examiner, confirmed that Twana had died from the chimpanzees' attack. The bites on her neck had caused her to die from exsanguination.

However, according to him, there were lacerations on her face that could not have been caused by the chimpanzees. He speculated that since chimpanzees consume blood, the killers had inflicted these wounds prior to her death to attract the chimps' attention. Although his theory was still unconfirmed, it seemed like a plausible explanation to me.

As of yet, there were no clear ties between Twana Summie and Mollie Fischer, Rusty Mahan, Congressman Fischer, or the research center. And the only connection Twana seemed to have to the Lincoln Towers Hotel was the use of her credit card to pay for the room—the credit card number that somehow did not show up on the hotel's records. Which served as further evidence that one of the killers was a skilled hacker.

I considered Twana for a moment. It was entirely possible that the killers had chosen her simply because of her physical similarities to Mollie Fischer, but if that were true, they still would have needed to find her and follow her before abducting her. And that was a clue as to where they'd been earlier this week.

And since awareness space correlates to movement patterns, it was also a clue as to where they might be right now.

I pulled out the notes I'd scribbled yesterday afternoon while waiting for the doctor to look at my arm, and paged through them until I came to the list of locations related to the crimes.

- The Gunderson Foundation Primate Research Center—chimp habitat, parking garage, research room (for the drug), security control center, other??
- The Lincoln Towers Hotel—room 809, the parking garage, the service elevator, the lower level storage room, other??
- The van in the handicapped parking space.
- The taxicab's pickup and drop-off points, the taxi itself.
- The Connecticut Street bridge where Rusty's body had been found.
- Williamson's Electronics Store—possibly.
- The residences, work addresses, and travel patterns of Rusty Mahan, Mollie Fischer, Twana Summie, and Aria Petic.

Just a cursory look at the list told me that I had enough information for an initial geoprofile to begin narrowing down the most likely location for the killer's home base.

I jotted a few questions:

1. What significance do these crime scene locations hold for the killers? Why the primate center? The Lincoln Towers? What's the connection between the two of them?
2. How might the killer's life have intersected with Mollie Fischer's? Rusty Mahan's? Twana Summie's? The congressman's?
3. Who was the woman who fled the Lincoln Towers Hotel with the unidentified man? Aria Petic?
4. How could the killers have gotten Mollie Fischer out of the hotel?
5. Did they?

I gazed at those last two words, considered once again what I knew about the case, and then wrote down one final question, a troubling one, but something that needed to be considered: was Mollie Fischer really abducted after all?

47

I stared at the question, thought about what we knew so far: Mollie was missing, she was not the victim we'd found at the research center, she'd been wheeled, apparently unconscious, through the door by an unidentified man, but as of yet there was no evidence that he'd harmed her. As far as we could tell, only two people had snuck out of the hotel, and if the male suspect was one of those two people and Mollie Fischer rather than Aria Petic was the second, it would explain why her body hadn't been found.

The scenario seemed unbelievable to me, but I'd worked cases before with so many twists and turns that I didn't want to discount anything.

Ralph was in Michigan and Margaret had ordered me not to work today, so I emailed Doehring with my thoughts and asked him to have an officer follow up on everyone who actually *was* registered at the Lincoln Towers Hotel yesterday to see if we could connect the dots between one of the guests and either Mollie or Twana. I also asked him to look more closely at Mollie Fischer's background for any possible connections to alleged or confirmed criminal activity.

Then I dove into the geoprofile.

Cognitive maps differ not only in respect to people's relationship with their surroundings but also in regard to their relationships with each other—married, single, divorced, as well as their age, sex, race, socioeconomic status, and the actual layout of the city in which they live.

Every one of us is only intimately familiar with a small fraction of our city's or rural region's overall area. And here is the key: the awareness space of a victim almost always overlaps, at least to some extent, with the awareness space of the offender. Which makes sense, because their lives intersected at least at the moment of the crime.

So that's where I would start—the known travel routes and awareness space of the victims. And I could determine those by the locations of their most frequent credit card purchases, their club memberships, GPS locations of their past phone calls, and so on.

I placed the phone with the hologram projector onto the table in front of me, used a fire wire to connect it to my laptop, positioned my coffee cup next to the computer, and went to work.

6:02 a.m.

FBI Executive Assistant Director Margaret Wellington did not feed canned dog food to her purebred golden retriever, Lewis.

Absolutely not.

Gourmet food only, and now as she ripped open the bag, he must have heard the sound because he came trotting into the kitchen. Wagged his tail cheerily.

"Good morning, Lewis." She scratched his neck and filled his bowl. After Lewis had taken a moment to nuzzle her hand, he turned to the food.

She collected her things and headed for the door.

Margaret was in the habit of leaving for work by 5:30 a.m., primarily to avoid the DC traffic but also to get in as much work as possible before Rodale loaded her plate with even more.

Today, however, she was already more than thirty minutes behind. And that did not make her happy, especially in light of her packed schedule for the day.

In addition to the drive to the city, she had at least three hours of work to do before the press conference scheduled at 9:00 a.m.

Impossible, but still she would be expected to do it.

She didn't mind speaking to the press, it suited her, but she did not like cleaning up other people's messes. And so far, that's what this case was turning into—a complete mess.

First, she had the public outcry from Fischer's misidentification of the homicide victim on Tuesday night. The right-wing bloggers were having a field day with that: "If he doesn't even know his own daughter, how can he know what's best for the country?"

Idiocy.

As well as unconscionable—taking advantage of a family's loss solely for political gain.

It made her furious.

Fischer's mistake might result in a lawsuit against the Bureau—even though the ME who failed to verify the young woman's identity worked for the city and not the FBI. That's what comes from these joint investigations—incompetency and unclear lines of authority. And in this case, since Rodale had assigned her to head things up, the buck stopped at her.

Not only did she need to deal with the Bureau's public-relations black eye but also the distraught Summie family, the self-possessed congressman and his cronies, and an ever-shrinking investigative team.

Agent Hawkins was in Michigan.

Agent Bowers was recuperating.

Yesterday evening, before she'd spoken with Bowers, she'd read over the hospital's report concerning his GSW and knew that it was more serious than he was letting on.

His recovery was necessary for the good of the investigation as well as the National Academy classes beginning on Monday. Despite his impertinence, he was the Bureau's most qualified instructor in crime mapping and site analysis, environmental criminology and geospatial investigation, and she couldn't afford to have him out of action and chance diminishing the Academy's reputation as the premier law enforcement training facility in the world.

So yes, he needed rest, but she knew him well enough to guess that he was not the kind of person to listen to a doctor's advice. So, for his own good, she'd quoted a bogus Bureau policy about agents who are injured in action being on mandatory medical leave for forty-eight hours.

And he'd actually seemed to buy it.

As she thought about him, she noted that one of the few characteristics she shared with Patrick Bowers was this: neither of them believed in coincidences.

She'd served on a committee last winter for a Defense Department program that had been terminated in February, and because of the nature of the project that the committee had been overseeing, she was almost certain it was no coincidence that the killers had chosen the Gunderson facility—however, because of the social and political implications of Project Rukh, she needed to tread lightly and confirm her suspicions before bringing them up with the task force.

For the moment, it was her job to keep all of these plates spinning in the air, and despite her experience and administrative acumen, she wasn't sure she could do it.

But as she merged onto the highway and drove to work, she told herself that she could.

48

It took more than two hours to narrow down a possible hot zone where the killer might live or work, and I ended up with a ten-block radius in the business district of the city—not as precise as I would have hoped for, but at least it was a starting place for us as we began evaluating the home and work addresses of the people on the burgeoning suspect list.

I was emailing the data to Doehring when I heard Tessa moving around in her bedroom.

She doesn't usually crawl out of bed until at least 10:00, and it wasn't even 8:30 yet. I supposed that the emotional impact of finding out about the custody suit had stolen some of her sleep.

Since I didn't want her to get a glimpse of my work, I shut off the hologram, and a few minutes later she shuffled into the kitchen, still bleary-eyed and in her pajamas but at least remotely conscious.

"Morning, Raven," I said.

"Morning," she managed to say. She moved in slow motion. She might have been a zombie.

"Trouble sleeping?"

She poured herself a cup of coffee, took a long, slow drink. "Yeah." Then she gestured toward my arm. "I was worried about you."

"About me?"

"Your scratch."

"Well, thank you. It's doing better. So, there's a tender side to you after all."

"Yeah, right." She glanced at my phone, laptop, handwritten notes. "I see you're already hard at work disobeying your boss."

"I thought I'd get an early start."

"Let me guess . . ." A yawn. "Trying to brush off conjecture with the facts until only the truth remains? Something like that?"

I stared at her. "Did you just make that up?"

She shrugged, rubbed a tired hand through her hair. "Sounded like something you might say."

"I might want to use that in my lectures."

"You must be desperate for material." She drained her cup and went for a refill.

I slid my computer to the side. "Really, Tessa. Are you doing all right?"

She shrugged again. "You know." Another yawn. "I gotta get dressed."

While she took a shower, I spent some time finishing the paperwork for Margaret and the forms for the hospital. Soon the water in the bathroom turned off, and I started paging through some of the primate research Tessa had printed out.

I'd gotten through two articles when my computer's video chat program blinked on and told me that Lien-hua was online.

After a moment's consideration, I typed in, "Good morning." Waited.

It wasn't long.

"Turn on your camera," she wrote. "So we can talk."

I did.

Her face appeared, a vase of artfully arranged flowers beside her. So, she was in her kitchen. Her sable hair was still unkempt, but it didn't quiet her beauty.

Lien-hua appraised me for a moment, then said, "I would ask about your arm, but you're just going to tell me that it's okay, so let's just skip that part. How are you, Pat? Really?"

"It feels like a bullet went through my biceps and I only got a few hours of sleep."

My comment brought a smile and a small nod. "Thank you. And they're saying it's going to be okay?"

"No rock climbing for a few days. Other than that, I should be fine."

"Ooh . . . that's going to be rough. Think you'll make it?"

"I'm not sure. Maybe I'll have to take up something less strenuous. Like kickboxing."

"Whenever you want a lesson, just let me know."

I felt the intimate attraction I'd had for her returning. Maybe it had never left. "Be careful, I might take you up on that."

"I'll hold you to it."

It wasn't easy stifling my curiosity about what she and Cheyenne might have talked about last night when they had dinner together, but it wasn't really my business and I refrained from asking about it. "How was the body farm yesterday?"

"Disturbing. That's not really my thing."

"I hear you."

A pause. "Pat, I heard through the grapevine that Margaret put you on bed rest for the next couple days."

"Just a nasty rumor."

She nodded softly.

Silence took over the conversation, and I could sense the mood shifting, deepening. At last she said, "I have to tell you something."

I waited.

She was slow in responding. "When I heard you were shot, I . . . Pat, everything between us, whatever it was that went wrong, when I found out you'd been hurt like that, it all seemed so minor. So inconsequential." She pushed a rogue strand of hair from her eye. "I was so worried about you."

Despite myself, I noticed thoughts of Cheyenne skirting around inside of me, vying for my attention. I pushed them aside. "I should have called you last night—"

Lien-hua swept her hand through the air, as if she were erasing any missteps from our past. "It's all right. I ended up calling Ralph, he'd just arrived in Michigan. He told me you were going to survive, unless he kills you for whining."

I wanted to tell her that he'd yanked an IV out of my arm and that hurts and there were a lot of needles and everything, but realized that didn't sound very macho. "Well, that's thoughtful of him."

Another pause—and again it seemed to move the moment deeper, shrink the space between us. "I'd like to see you," she said, "but I'll be at the command post at police headquarters for most of the day. Will you be in the city at all?"

"Actually, Vanderveld's covering my classes. I have a meeting with Rodale at noon. So, yeah. I'll be in DC for that."

"There's a briefing scheduled for 2:00. If your meeting doesn't go too long, would you like to grab lunch with me afterwards? I just need to be done by 1:30."

"Lunch sounds good. I'll give you a shout when I'm ready to leave HQ."

"Okay." She let her eyes smile at me and drew me inescapably into her world. "I'll talk with you later."

"Talk to you soon."

As I tapped the keyboard to end the chat, I noticed Tessa with her eyebrow ring, fresh black fingernail polish, and wearing a neobeatnik skirt over black tights, watching me from the doorway.

Patrick was staring at her judgmentally.

"What?" she asked him.

"You've gotten into a bad habit of eavesdropping on my conversations."

"Actually, I've always had it, you're just now noticing." She stepped into the room. "Girl problems, huh?"

"No."

"Mmm-hmm." She took a seat facing him. "So, you're confused about the two of them? Which one to pursue?"

"I'm not having girl problems," he grumbled. "I'm not confused. And who are you supposed to be? Dr. Phil?"

"Denial. Not a good sign."

She waited him out and eventually, probably sensing that in the end evading her questions would be a losing battle, he let out a small sigh and admitted, "All right, maybe a little confused. Last month, Lien-hua breaks up with me, and now, well . . . I don't know what to think."

"Duh. Detective Warren is here."

He looked at her blankly.

Okay, you have got to be kidding me.

"Relationships 101, Patrick: what makes a girl more interested in a guy than anything else?"

"I'm not sure. I—"

"Hello. Another girl interested in that guy."

"Oh."

"And the light goes on."

"Gotcha."

"So which one of them do you want to be with?"

He thought for a moment. "Honestly, I'm not sure."

"Well, keep playing things like this, and you'll end up without either one of 'em."

Curiosity on his face. "What makes you say that?"

"No woman wants to be strung along while you play the field looking for someone better."

"I'm not stringing anyone along."

"You're being flirty with 'em both."

"No, I'm not."

A pause. "If you say so."

"That's not what I'm doing."

"Okay."

"I'm serious."

She shrugged. "Right. I get it."

He folded his arms. "Stop that."

"Stop what?"

"Agreeing with me."

"You don't want me to agree with you?"

"Every time you agree with me, I can tell, it's just another way for you to unobtrusively *disagree* with me."

"Am I supposed to agree with that? Or not?"

He opened his mouth as if he were going to reply, then closed it.

He glanced at the clock, obviously trying to find a way to escape the conversation. Then he stood, collected the primate notes, his phone, a clipboard, and his laptop, and stuffed them into his computer bag. "I need to get going, Tessa."

"Where?"

"I have a meeting with FBI Director Rodale."

She nodded toward the computer. "During your chat you said that you weren't meeting him until noon. That's like three hours away."

"I'm hoping I'll be able to get in a little sooner."

"So you can have more time for lunch with Agent Jiang?"

He pulled out his car keys. "I'm leaving now."

"What about me?"

"Well, I was thinking you could stay here."

"By myself?"

He eyed her. "You're a big girl."

"Paul knows where we live, and he's trying to find me, remember? To talk to me without you around? You sure you want to leave me here alone?"

Her words seemed to bring him pause.

"All right," he said at last. "C'mon."

She grabbed her purse. "I hope Agent Jiang doesn't mind vegetarian."

49

Astrid was nine when it happened.

Her mother had died in childbirth, and she'd been an only child.

There was no sister Annie, of course. She'd lied to Brad about that from the beginning . . . Her dad did not work on weekends . . . The goldfish had been Astrid's pet, and it was a neighbor boy who'd put Goldie in the freezer, telling her later that it was all just a joke and not to make such a big deal out of it.

Astrid was the one, not the imaginary Annie, who'd cried for three days when Goldie was found dead.

And of course, her father had not hit her, never would have laid a hand on her, he was not that kind of a man.

But she hadn't wanted to appear vulnerable or weak to Brad, so she'd invented a second past, a dual life, with just enough truth in it to keep things believable.

Though her father was a good dad, even as a child Astrid could tell something wasn't right. Often, she would hear him crying when he was alone. Sometimes in the morning before work, sometimes late at night, sometimes in his study when he was supposed to be preparing for the college classes he taught.

She'd finally decided that maybe he cried because something inside of him was broken.

It was an explanation that made sense to a child.

She was the one who found him that night in May.

He hadn't cried that day. Just stared at her with a distant, sad look and told her how much he loved her and how he would always love her and did she understand that? Did she really? And she'd told him that of course she did, and then he'd held her close in a way that frightened her.

"I need to do some work tonight," he explained to her, "after you go to bed. So if you hear me in the study, don't worry."

"Okay, Daddy," she'd said.

Then he tucked her in.

And soon afterward, when she'd finished reading the Nancy Drew book he'd given her for her birthday and had just turned off the light, there was a harsh scraping sound in his study, and then all at once she heard the clatter of a wooden chair against the floor, and the house shuddered around her.

She sat up. "Daddy?"

Silence, except for a thin creaking sound coming from the study. Almost like the sound of a swing in motion on a windy day at the park.

She called again. "Daddy? What happened?"

No answer.

She picked up her favorite stuffed animal, a kitten named Patches. "Daddy?"

No reply.

She slipped out of bed and she was afraid again, like she'd been when he'd told her earlier that night, with some urgency, how much he loved her.

"Daddy?"

Silence.

She padded to the hall, but it was dark and lonely and seemed to stretch forever in front of her, as if it'd grown longer since the last time she'd walked down it.

The sound of the tired creak was now growing quiet and dim.

She held Patches close.

Walked toward the study.

Her dad almost never locked the door because, as he liked to say, "You're more important to me than work, honey. So anytime you need me, just come in. A daddy has to have his priorities straight, you know."

But tonight it was locked, and when she called to him, he didn't answer. So it was a good thing she knew where he hid the key—in the kitchen, in the cupboard where he kept the nice china dishes, right above the sink.

It didn't take her long to find it.

She returned to the study.

Then unlocked the door, put her hand against it, and pressed.

The door slowly mouthed open before her.

She saw his feet first, about a foot off the ground, and then her eyes traveled up his legs, his body, past his head to the rope that stretched taut and straight and tight to the rafters that had stopped creaking now. Then her father's body pivoted toward her.

And she saw his face.

And screamed.

Dropping Patches, she ran down the hall as fast as she could and dove under her bed. She was crying and trembling and wished, wished, wished she hadn't left her kitty behind in the hall. Wished she hadn't seen what she had.

Her daddy's face.

Terrible, terrible thoughts tumbled through her mind. Scary thoughts and frightening thoughts and bad, bad images that she did not want to think about.

Her daddy in the study.

His face.

The tight, tight rope.

But the thoughts wouldn't go away.

She wanted to help him, wanted to, but couldn't.

Couldn't do anything.

But pray.

Maybe she could pray.

So even though she wasn't sure if God was there or was even listening, she prayed and prayed that her daddy would be okay.

But nothing changed. Her daddy didn't come to be with her.

God ignored her. The house remained silent.

So quiet.

So lonely.

So still.

Until morning, when she heard the cook arrive, and then she ran past the study—somehow made it past the study, grabbing Patches as she did—and found the cook standing in the kitchen getting things ready for breakfast, and she told her everything.

Her father had left a note with only five words: "I'm sorry I wasn't stronger."

Then came the foster families who would shuffle her off to new homes if she cried all the time or if she refused to go to bed because she was too terrified of her dreams. And for a long time she couldn't help but cry and disappear into herself and stay up all night sitting on the bed, staring at her door, but it was lonely going to new families all the time, so she'd learned to act like a good little girl, a girl who wasn't broken inside.

Acting, acting, always acting.

The good little girl.

But now.

Now.

She was no longer the frightened little child who'd trembled under the bed and lost her faith in the Almighty on a cool night in May. Now she was a woman, strong and confident and self-assured, everything people expected from someone in her highly respected, much sought after position.

Something about the memory of that night when she found her father began to chew away at the anger and disappointment she'd felt toward her man last night.

After all, he hadn't deviated far from the plan. Yes, he'd made a few mistakes, but those were forgivable.

She glanced at her reflection in the mirror. She was showing some, had put on a little weight, but Brad hadn't seemed to notice.

A child.

A baby growing inside her.

She hadn't felt the baby kick yet, but soon, soon the evidence of her life, or his, would come.

The more she thought about her own father and the father of her child, the more she considered telling him about the baby.

Maybe it was time.

According to the plan, she would go to work today, Brad would get the plates and the car, then pay a visit to FBI Executive Assistant Director Wellington's home, and tonight, after the explosion, they would swing by the FBI Academy to leave a little surprise. And then this game would be over. Then they would move on.

So for now.

Watch.

Watch and see.

Keep an eye on him and only if necessary put him in the freezer and close the door.

Only if absolutely necessary.

———————————— ∎ ————————————

9:48 a.m.

Margaret Wellington did not like the feeling that something had gotten by her, so after the press conference, rather than go directly to the task force command post at police headquarters, she returned to the Lincoln Towers to see if there was anything the officers might have missed in their search for Mollie Fischer.

She spent twenty-five minutes retracing the route Bowers had taken as he chased the killers through the hotel, looking for any place they might have found to hide a body.

Nothing.

Now, she scanned the lobby.

The atrium extended up all twelve floors, with terraced gardens and a narrow waterfall that spilled out of a faux rock wall on her left. The water tumbled into a goldfish stream that meandered along the ground beneath a network of bridges and walkways.

She still believed that somehow the killers had managed to get Mollie Fischer out of the building, perhaps through the parking garage, which might explain the glove that had been left behind.

Or maybe they'd found another way.

Or maybe she was wrong and Mollie was still here some-where.

Margaret rubbed her head.

Room 809, the room in which they'd found the wheelchair, was still sealed of course, but the rest of the hotel was open. Last night Agent Cassidy and the new transfer from St. Louis, Natasha Far-raday, had cleared it.

Still no news about the laptop or the duffel bag that the Rainey boy had seen the man and woman carrying when they left the alley and climbed into the taxicab.

And, honestly, Margaret had no idea where else to look for Mol-lie.

A different perspective might be helpful, a fresh set of eyes, so with Hawkins and Bowers out of the picture for the moment, she phoned the next most qualified agent on the team.

"Lien-hua here."

"This is Executive Assistant Director Wellington. I'd like you to meet me at the Lincoln Towers Hotel. We're going to do a walk-around. Together."

50

On the drive to DC, I'd managed to move up the meeting with FBI Director Rodale one hour, to 11:00. "Actually," his secretary had informed me, "the director is anxious to see you."

"Great."

Since Tessa and I had some time, she'd suggested coffee, and although we'd already had some this morning, she persuaded me. While we were at the coffeehouse I called Doehring, and he told me that nothing had come of his search into Mollie Fischer's background and so, once again, I moved forward with the working hypothesis that she indeed was a victim in this crime spree, not an offender.

By the time we'd left the coffeehouse, battled traffic, driven to FBI headquarters, parked, cleared security, and obtained Tessa's visitor's pass, it was almost 11:00.

"You'll be good waiting for me?"

She nodded and took a seat in the reception area just outside Rodale's office.

"I'll see you as soon as I'm done." I gave her the guest password for HQ's Wi-Fi. She plugged in her earbuds, opened up her laptop to read more about primate cognition, and I knocked on Rodale's door.

"Come in."

I entered and found him standing beside his corner window overlooking downtown DC.

Congressman Fischer stood beside him.

Maybe Mollie's body was found.

I waited for one of them to tell me the news, whatever it might be.

"Pat," Rodale said. "I believe you've met Congressman Fischer?"

I nodded to him. "Congressman."

"I heard you almost caught Mollie's abductors yesterday," he said. "I need to thank you for going after them like that. Especially after our . . . well, my . . . the words I had with you in my office."

Today he sounded a lot more shattered by what had happened, a lot more like a man whose daughter was missing. "I know you were upset."

"They tell me you were shot yesterday?"

"Yes, but I'm all right."

I waited; no explanations came.

Rodale gestured toward a chair. "Please, Pat, have a seat."

Neither of the two men moved toward a chair or elaborated on why the congressman was here, and a tense kind of awkwardness sifted through the room. "I've been sitting all morning," I said. "If you don't mind, I think I'll stretch my legs too."

A nod. "Sure. Yes."

"Has there been a break in the case?" I asked at last.

Rodale shook his head.

"No," Fischer said soberly.

Then Rodale walked to his bookcase and let out a tired-sounding sigh. He was six months from retirement but looked ready to bail on his job this afternoon. "I'm in a quandary here, Pat. I want to commend you on your valor yesterday, on your insights into this case, but I also feel the professional obligation to reprimand you for the reckless nature of your actions."

I wasn't exactly sure how to respond to that. "That's understandable."

"No more spur-of-the moment press conferences."

"Agreed."

"All right." I could tell this was just the tip of the iceberg. "Moving on. There's a sensitive aspect of this case that I need to tell you about, and I need you to keep it in the strictest confidence."

I let my eyes pass from him to the congressman, then back to Rodale. "What aspect?"

Congressman Fischer spoke up. "The Gunderson facility. I believe I might know the reason the young woman was killed there."

"And that is?"

"You remember Project Rukh?" Rodale said. "In San Diego?"

"Of course."

Last February, Lien-hua, Ralph, and I had uncovered a biotech conspiracy that involved marine biology research and recent advances in neuroscience to create a top-secret weapon for the Pentagon. The device could be used to damage, in an untraceable manner, specific parts of a person's frontal cortex to cause permanent brain damage or a stroke.

The case would always stick in my mind not just for professional reasons but for personal ones as well: while in San Diego a young man had tried to sexually assault Tessa, and one of the killers we were tracking had attacked and drowned Lien-hua; I'd barely been able to revive her.

"I thought the Pentagon pulled the plug on all that?" I said, referring to Project Rukh.

"They did," Congressman Fischer responded. "But a private firm managed to acquire the neuroscientific research that survived. For an unrelated project."

Unrelated.

Yeah, right.

"The Gunderson Foundation," I said.

Both men confirmed my words by their silence.

"So you're involved with the foundation somehow, is that it?" I said to the congressman. "Is there some legislation before the House that relates to—"

"I've contributed financially to the foundation in the past. Yes," he replied. "But that's something I would rather the public not be apprised of at this time."

"Thank you."

He looked confused. "For what?"

"For narrowing things down. I can guarantee that if you don't want the information released, there's somebody out there who does. And that person may very well be involved in your daughter's abduction. So, the obvious question: who would want the facts about your donations made public?"

"Every Republican in Congress."

Although that seemed like a gross overstatement, if the primate research were in some way ethically controversial, he might just be right. Rodale glanced at Congressman Fischer, who nodded. I did not find it reassuring that the Bureau's director was taking cues from a congressman.

Rodale said, "I know that Margaret pulled you off this case so you could get some rest, but I'd like you to keep pursuing whatever leads you can. I'll speak with her. Arrange it. If you're up to it."

"I'm up to it."

I turned to Fischer. "Send me a list detailing all of your contributions to the foundation. Forward all emails sent or received. Everything. And I want your phone records."

He hesitated.

"Don't fool yourself, Congressman. Someone will find out this information. The task force should see it before the press does."

"You can trust him," Rodale said to Fischer.

He looked uncomfortable with the idea but finally agreed.

Then I turned to Director Rodale. "A few minutes ago you asked me to keep this all in the strictest confidence. How can I work with the task force if I'm not able to share this information with them?"

"For now, only command level staff hears about the congressman's contributions to the center. I don't want anything leaking to the press and slowing down the investigation."

Admittedly, if this information was as sensitive as I was being led to believe, his concern made sense, but something didn't feel right. I still wasn't sure why these two men had chosen to share this information with me, but I figured I could bring that up with

Rodale after the congressman left and we were alone. I nodded and he said he'd send me the files.

I gave Fischer my email address, he excused himself, but as he was getting ready to leave I asked, "Congressman, who told you about the custody case?"

"Custody case?"

"Yesterday. You mentioned the custody case involving my step-daughter."

This time, unlike yesterday, he was forthcoming: "My brother."

Shock.

As far I knew, he had only one brother. "The former vice president told you?"

"Yes."

"How does he know about a custody case involving my step-daughter?"

"He's acquainted with your stepdaughter's biological father. That's all he said."

What?

"How?"

He shook his head. "Honestly, I don't know. He didn't say."

The congressman seemed to be telling the truth, and if he was, it added a whole new layer of complexity to what was going on. It meant Lansing had friends in very high places—and that would not be to my advantage in keeping custody of Tessa.

"But why?" I said to him. "Why did he tell you this?"

"Since it involved an FBI agent"—he avoided looking at Rodale—"and I've proposed budget cuts to the Bureau, I suspect he was trying to get me to . . . well . . ."

"What? Threaten me?"

"Suggest cuts in strategic departments."

He didn't have to spell it out for me.

Get rid of the agent; help his buddy get custody of the child . . .

"When I found out you were on the case involving Mollie, I felt torn, and I knew we needed to talk. In the end, I said things to you I shouldn't have."

I didn't find his explanation entirely satisfying, but it was a start. I needed to give all this some thought.

He offered us both a departure nod. "I do need to get back to the House floor."

After he left, the mood of the room still felt full of static. There was too much being left unspoken here. "Director," I said, "did you tell the congressman to refrain from announcing the news about the victim's true identity yesterday?"

"An announcement like that should come from the public affairs office or one of the ADs, you know that, Pat. It doesn't come from the father of a missing girl. Or from an NCAVC field agent. We have a system in place for the release of pertinent information, and that system serves the good of everyone."

"Not Mollie," I said. "Not yesterday." He eyed me severely, but I didn't care. I went on. "Why did you call me in on this case to begin with? You know my specialty is serial offenses, but when we started on this we knew of only one homicide."

"We haven't always agreed on everything over the years, but we've always respected each other." He made it sound like an answer, but I couldn't see how it was.

"Yes, I would say that's true."

"You're not the kind of man who plays politics, who's always looking for a way to get ahead."

His comments were making me a little uncomfortable. "I'm an investigator not a bureaucrat, if that's what you mean."

"Yes. That's what I mean. And that's why I want you on this."

But if he doesn't want people working this case with an eye on a promotion, why did he assign Margaret to head it up?

"If I can be frank, sir, none of this makes any sense. It seems like politics and personal agendas are taking precedent over finding a missing person."

Welcome to Washington, Pat.

"You know that's not true."

"I'm not sure that I do."

A dark cloud was crossing his face—

And then it hit me.

"The budget cuts. Is that what this is about? Maybe, 'Find my daughter, keep my involvement with this research place under wraps, and I won't push through the legislation to cut Bureau funding.' You scratch my back and I'll scratch yours?"

Rodale looked at me icily. "I will pretend that you did not just say that."

"Don't bother." I headed for the door. "I'll keep you informed," I said. "Of our progress."

Tessa could tell I was upset when I met her in the lobby. "You all right?" she asked.

"Oh yeah."

Then I was on my way to the exit and she was hastily grabbing her things and catching up with me. "Agent Jiang called while you were in there. She told me she can meet us at Jacob's Deli at about 12:30, if that works. She said you'd know where it is."

"I'm afraid we're going to have to cancel. There's someplace else I need to go."

"Where's that?"

"The Gunderson Primate Research Center."

51

The Lincoln Towers Hotel
Room 809

Nothing.

Margaret Wellington shook her head.

Mollie Fischer couldn't have just disappeared. Where is she!

Lien-hua was standing beside the bed, carefully studying the room. "We found the wheelchair in here but no other physical evidence?"

"That's right."

"But how could that be? The video of the suspect wheeling Mollie into the hotel shows that they entered at 1:29 p.m. And Pat was shot just after 3:00."

"That means at least one of them was in a room with an abducted woman for approximately an hour and a half," Margaret said, following Lien-hua's train of thought, "but yet managed to leave no forensic evidence behind."

"That's not likely."

"No, it isn't."

Margaret thought, *They faked Mollie's death . . . left her purse in the habitat . . . left Mahan's car at the scene. . . left the glove in the parking garage . . .*

They used misdirection every step of the way . . .

Of course.

"They used another room," she said. "Just left the wheelchair in here to mislead us."

Lien-hua considered that for a moment. "According to Pat's report, there were two maids in the hall when he was pursuing the subjects. I wonder—"

"Come on," Margaret said, heading for the door. "We need to have a talk with those maids."

———————————■———————————

Tessa and I grabbed drive-thru bean burritos for lunch and were on our way to the primate center.

I convinced her to listen to her iPod for a few minutes so I could make a call, then I speed-dialed Lien-hua's number, and, speaking quietly so Tessa wouldn't overhear me, I cancelled lunch, then summarized my meeting with Rodale and Fischer. Lien-hua listened attentively, and toward the end of my explanation, I heard Margaret speaking incredulously somewhere near her. "What's going on?" I asked.

"We're wondering if the killers kept Mollie in a room other than—"

I heard Margaret's voice again, the words were indistinguishable, but she was obviously upset. "Just a sec," Lien-hua said. She spoke off-phone for a few seconds, then said to me, "You're not going to believe this: there is no Aria Petic."

"What do you mean? We have footage of her leaving the facility."

She took another break from talking with me to get an update from Margaret, then spoke into the phone again. "Margaret just got a call from Doehring. Apparently, the primate facility contracts out their janitorial services. Aria's name appears on the computerized records, but that's all. No one by that name has ever worked for them."

"How come we're just finding this out now?"

"Why do you think Margaret is so upset?"

Unbelievable.

"So," I was thinking aloud, "the killers get into the research facility, they enter a fictional name onto the janitorial records so if the woman is seen leaving the building it won't raise any immediate red flags."

Plus, as a contract employee, the security guard and keeper wouldn't be expected to recognize her if she were detained.

"But as it turned out, she wasn't even questioned," Lien-hua said. "In the confusion she just walked away. Slipped out one of the side doors after the EMTs arrived."

Spaghetti.

I heard Margaret call for Lien-hua, who subsequently told me, "I have to go."

"Listen." I was thinking of Lien-hua's drowning incident in San Diego during the Project Rukh case. "Remember how things went down in February? If these killers are involved in any way with the conspirators from San Diego—"

"I'll be careful," she said. "I promise."

"Be extra careful."

"I will."

After we'd ended the call, I saw that Tessa was staring out the passenger-side window, still listening to her music. We were only a few minutes from the research center. "Look, college guys," I said softly, quieter than I'd been speaking to Lien-hua, and Tessa's head snapped in my direction.

She realized her mistake and quickly averted eye contact.

"You heard my conversation," I said.

She unplugged the earbuds. "What?"

"Yeah, right. You need to forget anything you just heard."

"I only heard my music." And then: "If anyone asks."

Great.

We arrived at the research facility, and I pulled into the lower level of the parking garage.

Although I was certain the glass-enclosed habitat in which Twana's body had been found would be sealed off, the Gunderson facility itself was no longer considered an active crime scene. And I was thankful, because this way I wouldn't have to leave Tessa in the car.

"You've read more about this place than I have," I said. "You're coming with me. But you can't ask any questions related to the case. You're only looking for information concerning the primate research."

"Seriously? You're letting me help?"

"Just with monkey intel, not with the investigation. I want to find out more about the metacognition research." *And finances . . . ethically controversial research . . . politically charged implications—*

"Did you just say monkey intel?"

"I'll introduce you as my research assistant." I opened my computer bag and pulled out a clipboard. "Maybe you're an intern or something." I handed it to her.

Dressed like she was with her black tights and black fingernail polish, I wasn't quite sure my plan would work, but she did look old enough to be a college student if it came down to that.

She stared at the clipboard. "What's this for?"

"That's the most powerful ID in the world. If you walk into any building with an air of confidence and a clipboard, no one will question why you're there."

"Nice." She looked impressed. "I can *so* do an air of confidence." Then a pause. "Just don't say monkey intel again while we're in there."

"Right."

I popped open the car door.

But then I had realization.

Closed it again.

"What is it?" she asked.

"Are you sure you want to do this? This is a research center, after all. The animals are all going to be—"

"Caged. Yeah, I know."

There was really no subtle way to put this. "I'm not sure exactly what their research involves, but—"

"Medical tests. I thought of that too."

"Are you cool with that?"

A long silence. "Almost all medical advances in the last hundred years have come from animal testing. And I've never heard of anyone, not even a PETA board member, denying himself life-saving medical treatment in conscientious objection to the fact that research has been done on nonhuman subjects."

Her carefully phrased response made it clear that she really had been thinking about this. "Well put."

"But that doesn't make cruelty right. It doesn't make suffering okay."

"No, it doesn't."

By the look on her face I could tell she was dealing with a torrent of conflicting emotions.

Finally she spoke, and her voice was on fire with both loneliness and resolve. "A few more cancer tests and Mom might still be alive." She opened her door. "Let's go."

52

The director of the research center, a slim, white-haired man in his early fifties with the unusual name of Janz Olan, led Tessa and me to the research rooms that lay behind the glassed-in habitats.

As I'd suspected, the habitat in which Twana's body had been found was still closed off to the primates, and for Tessa's sake, I was glad to see that the floor, although no longer covered with straw, had been mopped and sanitized and there was no visible sign of blood. Still, Tessa's eyes wandered around the area as we passed by, and I had no doubt that she was able to discern why the floor had been so thoroughly cleaned.

"So," Mr. Olan said, glancing at Tessa, "how long have you been Agent Bowers's . . . assistant?"

"Ever since he began researching the politics, culture, and moral development of pongids."

I assumed that meant apes.

"Oh," he said. "I see."

"Mr. Olan." I gestured toward one of the testing rooms. "Explain to me more about your work here. What exactly are you doing with the CAT scans, MRIs, MEGs?"

"Well, our research focuses on two primary areas—neuroscience and cognition."

I remembered Lien-hua's words from Tuesday night. "And aggression?"

"That would fall under neuroscience. Brain-imaging studies have shown that the amygdala and frontal cortex are the areas of the brain most associated with fear, aggression, and violent behavior. Specifically, we look at the neural activity of chimpanzees, the closest relatives to humans. They're also the only species, besides humans, who regularly kill adult conspecifics."

"Adults of the same species," Tessa said, taking notes.

A pause, then, "Yes. Chimps also form raiding parties and have wars against other communities of chimps. Some even use their skills in toolmaking to form clubs that kill more effectively."

That sounded astonishing to me.

And also chillingly human.

"So, in a sense, you're studying the neurology of violence," I said.

A pause. "That might be one way of putting it."

I let that sink in, wondering what implications the findings might have if taken in the context of the congressman's comments over the last few weeks about the proposed budget cuts to the Bureau in lieu of "a more progressive approach to curbing criminal behavior."

Every Republican in Congress would want his connection to the center made public . . .

"Yeah, well," Tessa said to Olan, "chimps aren't so closely related, if you accept that Ardi was a biped."

He was slow in responding. "Yes. If you accept that she was," he acknowledged at last. "But it's clear that in trees she was a quadruped."

"Who's Ardi?" I asked.

"Doesn't matter." Tessa was answering Olan, not me. "She proves we didn't evolve from knuckle-walkers like chimpanzees and gorillas."

"Who is Ardi?" I repeated, directing the question to them both. Olan answered, "She was a female *Ardipithecus ramidus.* Her fossil was found in Ethiopia in 1994, but it took fifteen years of study before the findings were released to the public in 2009. And some scientists believe she walked upright."

"Most," Tessa corrected him, "not some."

I shook my head. "I'm still not quite—"

"She lived 4.4 million years ago," Olan said impatiently, "and if she was a biped it would seem to indicate that we did not evolve from modern primates but rather separately from them, from some ancient ancestor."

"Which means," Tessa interjected, "there is no missing link between us and modern apes, and postulating human origins from modern primate behavior or biology is casuistic."

Olan stared at her. Blinked.

"Well," he said, "since no members of the *Ardipithecus ramidus* family are still with us today, we study chimps, whose DNA is 96 percent the same as human DNA."

She looked ready to counter, but I stopped her with a small head shake. I was more concerned about the focus of the center's research than resolving how someone might have walked four and a half million years ago. "Tell me about the second area," I said to Olan. "The cognition research."

"Yes, well, perhaps I should have specified that it's mainly in the field of metacognition."

This time I was familiar with what he was referring to, but Tessa beat me to the punch. "Theory of mind," she said. "Consciousness, empathy, understanding."

He nodded. "Yes. Self-awareness, the roots of empathy, the ability to understand that others have thoughts, feelings, sensations just as you do."

We arrived at a fully equipped research room with a metal meshed-off area that led to the gorilla habitat.

"Are you saying apes have those abilities?" I asked.

"Different species of primates exhibit varying degrees of altruistic behavior," he replied, not exactly answering my question.

I thought of the sections of Tessa's research that I'd perused. "As well as cognitive empathy, right? And partner-specific reciprocity?"

"Yes." Olan seemed somewhat taken aback that Tessa and I appeared to know what we were talking about, and as he went on, he seemed bent on proving that he knew more.

"Chimpanzees kiss and hold each other after fighting, sometimes jump into water to save other chimps—even though no chimps are able to swim. In some cases, gorillas have warned keepers when young gorillas are in danger—thus showing that they are both cognizant of the plight of other creatures and able to identify a possible means of rescue for them. And as far as intelligence and problem solving, some gorillas have scored 90 on human IQ tests, others have learned more than 3,500 sign language words, even made up signs to describe themselves."

I'd never heard about apes trying to save each other or taking human IQ tests, and I was surprised—and for some reason that I couldn't quite pinpoint, vaguely troubled.

"One ape even made up a sign for contact lens cleaning solution after watching his keeper wash and then put in her contacts."

"What was it?" Tessa asked.

"The gorilla combined the words *eye* and *drink*," he said.

That was just plain impressive.

I asked a few follow-up questions, and Olan seemed to become more and more antsy with each one. "I'm very sorry," he said at last. "But I'm terribly busy—still dealing with the aftermath of the incident on Tuesday night as it concerns our board, our donors. We're a nonprofit organization and donations are essential for our survival. I'm sure you understand. Perhaps it would be best if one of our researchers or keepers answered any additional questions."

Actually, that might not be a bad idea.

I asked if we could speak with Sandra Reynolds, the keeper who'd found Twana's body and killed the two chimps who were attacking her, but Olan told me she'd taken the rest of the week off. "For counseling," he added in a somewhat ominous tone.

He called to a studious-looking woman in her late twenties who was bent over a computer keyboard in an adjoining room. "Dr. Risel, can you spare a few moments?"

She didn't bother to look up. "I'm in the middle of my bibliography." From her outfit, it was clear that she liked the color brown in all of its many shades and hues.

"Dr. Bowers here is investigating the tragedy Tuesday night."

"That's nice."

"He works for the FBI."

At last Dr. Risel looked our way, hesitated for a moment, then joined us.

After introductions, Mr. Olan left for his office and Dr. Risel informed us that she was a psychobiologist and was under a strict deadline for her next journal article, then waited, arms folded, for me to tell her what I needed, but I wasn't exactly sure what that was.

Tessa bailed me out. "Tell us about the MSR research."

"Mirror self-recognition," Dr. Risel said, as if Tessa couldn't possibly have already known what the initials stood for.

"Um, *yeah*."

Dr. Risel looked around the room absently for a moment, then sighed. "It might be just as quick if I showed you." She pulled out a set of keys and headed for the gorilla habitats.

Astrid had asked Brad to lay low for the day.

Yes, he needed to arrange everything for tonight. But that wouldn't take him long.

So, keep tabs on him.

She'd asked him to check in with her every hour by phone, which he had faithfully done so far.

Good.

One step at a time, make sure that he was not slipping up again.

She decided that tonight she was going to tell him about her child.

Today they would stay on schedule.

Finish the game.

And then tonight at the body farm, she would tell him about the baby.

53

Tessa and I watched from the other side of the mesh enclosure as Dr. Risel led one of the apes, a young female named Belle, out of the habitat and into the room.

To my surprise, the doctor stayed with the gorilla in the enclosed area, and when I commented on it, she just said, "Gorillas are gentle creatures. Very timid and shy. She's harmless." She stroked the ape's fur to show me how harmless the thickly muscled primate was.

"Belle is our newest arrival," she explained. The more time she spent with the gorilla, the less urgent she seemed to be about finishing her article. "She's never done this test before, so hopefully, she won't let us down."

"She's so cute," Tessa cooed as she stared at Belle.

Cute was not exactly the word I would have used.

Dr. Risel grabbed a mirror that was attached to a pivoting metal arm hanging from the ceiling. She positioned the mirror so that Belle could look into it, which she did.

Belle seemed immediately fascinated by her reflection, and grunted softly, then leaned forward, tilted her head, and studied the ape in the mirror. She raised one arm, then dropped it heavily onto her lap, grunted again, then lifted it once more, watching how the gorilla in the mirror responded.

"Initially, chimps look behind the mirror," Tessa explained to me softly, "to try and find the other chimpanzee, or they reach out and try to touch 'em. So do monkeys, baboons, all other primates. But chimpanzees can learn to identify themselves. Orangs can too." She hesitated. "Most gorillas have a hard time with this."

While Belle was observing herself in the mirror, Dr. Risel retrieved a small container of vanilla frosting from a cooler and eased off the lid.

Belle was too fascinated by the mirror to pay attention to her.

"All right," Dr. Risel said. "Here we go." She dipped a finger into the frosting, and then, while speaking softly and reassuringly to Belle, waved her other hand in front of her to get her attention.

The gorilla responded by turning from the mirror and looking at the doctor. Risel brushed her hand gently along the side of the gorilla's head and then surreptitiously dabbed the glob of frosting onto Belle's forehead.

But she did it so lightly that the gorilla didn't notice.

Then, Risel tilted the mirror so that Belle could see her reflection again, and this time, when she peered at the gorilla in front of her, Belle made a loud guttural sound in the back of her throat and then raised her left hand and extended one finger.

I expected her to touch the mark on the forehead of the gorilla in the mirror, but she didn't. Instead, watching how the ape in the mirror moved, she reached to her own forehead, brushed off the frosting, and then licked it from her finger.

Fascinating.

"Gorillas like frosting," Tessa told me.

Dr. Risel looked triumphantly at us and then gave Belle a treat of a handful of grapes from the cooler. After a few moments, she led her back to her habitat.

It was an impressive demonstration, and it took me a few moments to process the implications.

Somehow Belle had been able to understand that her movements were mirrored identically by the ape she could see, and from that fact she'd concluded that the ape she was looking at was really her, and that the frosting would be on her own forehead and not on the head of another gorilla.

I was considering all of this when Dr. Risel reappeared.

"That's one of the cruder tests," she said. "But you can see what it means, can't you?"

Tessa stood beside me quietly, clipboard in hand, but I was the one who answered. "She understands that she is a unique creature," I said, "separate and distinct from her counterpart in the mirror."

Dr. Risel nodded.

I went on. "She exhibited one of the core characteristics of consciousness—Belle is self-aware."

Dr. Risel bent her head slightly to one side, then to the other, as if she were weighing the validity of what I'd just said. "We have to be careful not to anthropomorphize too much, but Belle was clearly aware that she was the ape she saw and was also able to use the mirror to help locate the frosting on her own forehead."

"Besides higher primates, how many other species have this self-differentiating ability?" I asked.

"Just elephants and dolphins—although there's some growing evidence for pigs—but obviously we have a slightly different test for those species. They don't like frosting as much as apes do." She looked at me expectantly as if I were supposed to laugh at that. I smiled.

Tessa remained silent.

We spent a few more minutes speaking with Dr. Risel about theory of mind research, then she explained that because of natural selection, we would expect that all human behavior and states of consciousness would appear, at least in rudimentary form, in the animal kingdom.

"And the more we study animals," she said, "the more we find this to be true—emotions, intention, language use, inquisitiveness, use of tools. Dolphins communicate with each other by using different pitches to mean different things and understand the importance of word order syntax. Some types of birds experience REM sleep, cows mourn the loss of their young, ants and wolves form cooperative communities with a complex social order."

Tessa had become withdrawn, and I noticed that not even Dr. Risel's litany of animal accomplishments seemed to perk her up. I caught her eye, smiled at her, and she gave me a forced half-smile in reply. Something was up.

"Chimps can be taught to use fractions," Dr. Risel went on enthusiastically. "Sea lions understand equivalence relationships and basic logic. Many species of primates live in complex societies and compete, cooperate, deceive, and manipulate each other—just like humans do. They have power struggles, privileged classes, form alliances, use bargaining and networking to get ahead. Most of my colleagues believe that because of this, there is, at least in a primitive form, politics in the animal kingdom."

From my research in environmental criminology, I already knew that some species of primates in western Africa form cognitive maps to remember the location of large rocks to crack nuts, understanding their awareness space similarly to the way humans do.

And of course, recent studies have shown that human serial killers follow predatory movement patterns similar to those of great white sharks and lions, but Dr. Risel didn't pause long enough for me to add any of this to the conversation. She seemed to have completely forgotten about her journal article deadline.

According to her, animal behavior had been studied for centuries, but the questions of whether or not apes and other higher primates were self-aware, had the ability to think in abstract terms, or had free will were still relatively unexplored fields.

"The neuroscience and primate metacognition research is still in its infancy." She was beaming, obviously proud to be a pioneer in this field. "Imagine how well we'll understand the workings of the brain in *Homo sapiens* and in other animals in fifty years. A hundred. A hundred thousand."

Even though I was only marginally familiar with the advances in neuroscience over the last twenty years, I knew they'd been exponential, and I couldn't even begin to imagine the knowledge we might have unearthed in hundreds or thousands of years.

At last Dr. Risel glanced at the time, frowned, and quickly excused herself and went back to finish writing her article. When she was gone I asked Tessa if something was the matter, but she brushed off my concern.

For the better part of an hour I investigated the facility, looking for any evidence of controversial biotech or medical research or anything else that might be highly politically charged, but found nothing. I also inspected the entrances and exits again and the sight-lines from the sealed-off habitat in which Twana had died to see if I could find any clue that might lead us to Mollie's whereabouts, but came up empty there as well.

While I looked around, Tessa tagged along, sometimes jotting notes on her clipboard, mostly staring introspectively at the apes.

By the time I was ready to leave, I'd scrutinized every room, briefly interviewed three other researchers, even reviewed some of the computer files detailing research procedures and results, but apart from being wary of scientific inquiry, I couldn't see any good reasons why other congressmen might find Fischer's involvement here politically advantageous to them.

Neither did I find any procedures that seemed overly invasive, cruel, or tendentious.

The closest thing to animal cruelty might have been the use of the drug 1-phenyl-2-aminopropane, but the records showed that it was only administered in miniscule amounts to the primates in the course of the typical research.

Maybe I'd been wrong. Maybe the congressman's connection to this facility was insignificant to the case.

On the way out, I asked Olan if I could see the facility's financial records, and, as I suspected, he told me that I would need a warrant. Of all the federal law enforcement agencies, the FBI has some of the quickest access to warrants, but still, at this point we didn't have any good reason to get one. Olan was polite enough about denying my request, but not being able to look them over was discouraging.

It struck me that rather than finding answers here, I was leaving with more questions than I'd had when I arrived two hours ago. As Tessa and I headed toward the elevator to the parking garage, a sense of frustration ate away at me.

Think in a different direction, Pat. Don't get caught on a one track—

The elevator doors opened at almost the same time my phone rang. The ringtone was Cheyenne's, and I convinced Tessa to go ahead of me to the car, then answered, "Hey."

"It's me."

"Out of the briefing already?"

"Pat, it's already past 3:00."

"Oh."

"How's your arm?"

"It's all right. I told you to stop worrying about that. How was class?"

"When I heard that Vanderveld was teaching, I bowed out." Jake had worked the Giovanni case with Cheyenne and me last month, and she'd come to respect him as much as I did, so I wasn't surprised she'd found another way to spend her morning.

"Lien-hua mentioned the suspects may have used another room at the hotel," I said. "Any more on that?"

"Nothing solid. A couple things: WXTN has been scooping. We might have a leak. And oh yeah, Margaret thinks there might be a connection between these crimes and the assassination attempt on Vice President Fischer six years ago at the Lincoln Towers."

Hmm.

The former vice president had stayed mostly out of the limelight since leaving office, and I hadn't even thought of that assassination attempt in years.

I considered the possible implications.

The gunman, a pro-death penalty activist named Hadron Brady, had tried to kill Vice President Fischer as he was entering the hotel to give a speech at a constitutional law symposium being held there. I remembered that Brady was fatally wounded when the Secret Service returned fire. Other than that, the details were fuzzy.

So maybe it wasn't Mollie Fischer's father who had ties to these killers. Maybe it was her uncle.

"Cheyenne, get a couple officers to find out more about the shooter and the exact topic of Vice President Fischer's speech that day. I want to find out if it had anything at all to do with the meta-cognition of primates."

A pause. "I'll talk to Margaret about it," she answered. "What about you?"

By faking Mollie's death at the primate center and then taking her to the hotel, the killers had tied the two locations together. I had no idea what the assassination attempt might have to do with this case, but it appeared that there was a connection worth exploring—

"Pat?" She jolted me out of my thoughts.

"I'm going to stop by the hotel," I said. "Take another look around."

"All right. I'll talk with you soon."

"Okay."

My thoughts jumped to Paul Lansing's friendship with the former VP. I wasn't sure if it would be relevant to the custody case, but since Tessa had gone to the car and I still had some privacy, I gave our lawyer, Missy Schuel, a call and told her what I knew. She took note of it and explained that she was still reading through the diary and that she'd left two more messages for Lansing's lawyers. "I'm still hoping to convince them to meet with us next week."

Finally, before catching up with Tessa, I took a moment to check in with Ralph. He told me that Lebreau went through boyfriends "amazingly fast for a law professor," so it wasn't easy eliminating potential suspects. Also, there was still no sign of Lebreau or Basque, but he was following up on two possible eyewitnesses: one who claimed to have seen Basque's car in the parking lot where Lebreau's SUV was found, the other who said she saw a man fitting Basque's description leave a gas station in Lansing, Michigan, an hour after Lebreau failed to show up for class. "Says there was a woman in the car with him. But you know how reliable eyewitnesses are."

"Keep me posted."

"I will."

I debated whether or not to tell him that Angela Knight was working this from another angle; but for the time being, I decided not to mention it.

I ended the call, met Tessa at the car, and we drove to the Lincoln Towers Hotel.

Brad checked the girl's email.

Last month when he'd contacted Dr. Calvin Werjonic, when he'd asked Astrid to research the federal agent's presence at the assassination attempt, he hadn't had any idea how neatly his plan would come together.

But fate seemed to be on his side. Everyone who mattered was in the Metro area now this week.

Just a little tweak in the agenda for today to make the climax as exciting as possible: the special gift for EAD Wellington would have to wait until tomorrow night. But the delay would only serve to make the game better, more complete.

No doubt the task force's command level staff were busy trying to connect the Lincoln Towers Hotel with the primate center, diving into the possible implications, the importance each location might hold in the mind of the killers. But there were so many layers to Brad's plan that the authorities would never unpeel them all in time.

Astrid had asked him to call and check in every hour, and this was not the time to displease her.

He punched in her number.

"Do you have the car?" she asked.

"Yes."

"And the plates?"

"I'll be leaving to get them in a few minutes."

"Don't wait too long."

"All right."

"We'll talk soon."

"Yes."

The call ended, and he pulled up the video he'd taken of Mollie Fischer yesterday in the van and watched it in one corner of his screen while he scanned the email program in the other.

After reading the most recent emails, he googled the FBI Academy. It was amazing what you could find online, and last week he'd located a page on their official site that showed a map of the Academy grounds. Now, he confirmed that there were no changes, then printed the helpful little map that the Federal Bureau of Investigation had posted for all the world to see.

54

After I'd grabbed a pair of latex gloves from the car, I led Tessa into the hotel.

She watched me slip the gloves into my pocket. "What are those for?"

"Examining stuff."

"Wow. Never would have guessed." Her sarcasm felt friendly and familiar, but under her words I could tell there was something deeply troubling her.

"Stick with me long enough and you'll learn all kinds of cool things."

She was quiet.

"You all right?" I said.

"Yeah."

We stepped into the expansive atrium. "So you'll be okay hanging out here for a few minutes?"

She nodded as she glanced at the hanging gardens, waterfall, and streams, and I realized I'd never brought her to this hotel before. She was obviously impressed.

"I just need to see if I can slide a few pieces of the puzzle together," I said. "I won't be long."

She didn't reply or complain, and I almost wished she would have argued with me; at least then I would have known she was feeling okay.

"So we're cool? You're sure you're okay?"

"Yeah."

As she took a seat, I suggested she might want to touch base with her friends in Denver, give Pandora or Jessie a call.

That seemed agreeable to her; she pulled out her computer and clicked to her video chat program.

I was turning toward the front desk when she said, "Do you think she's dead?"

When I faced her again, I saw that her eyes were on a WXTN News cameraman filming a reporter who was interviewing Mr. Lees, the hotel manager. They stood at the other end of the atrium.

"Do you mean—"

"The congressman's daughter."

Careful, Pat.

"I don't think we should jump to conclusions," I said. "Stay here and wait for me, okay? Just give me maybe fifteen or twenty minutes. Then we'll take off." I thought for a second. "And I'll get you home."

She was repositioning herself so that her back was to the news crew. "Okay."

I wanted to see if the former NSA analyst Marianne Keye-Wallace and her "facial, audio, video" recognition computer system would be able to help me find a connection between the would-be assassin at this hotel six years ago and the killers who brought Mollie Fischer here yesterday.

Leaving Tessa behind, I walked toward the hallway that led to the control center.

55

I was striking out.

Marianne had started out by telling me she didn't have records from that far back. "When the hotel went through its renovations last year, we switched to a new computer system—by the way, are you okay? Weren't you shot yesterday?"

I patted my left arm gently. "It's just a scratch. So, you're telling me the computer records didn't transfer?"

"No, they transferred, it's just that the management decided to only keep records for the last five years—and I'm not just talking about video footage. All the guest room records." She shook her head. "I beat my head against the wall trying to convince them to archive everything, but they wouldn't listen to me."

Working with so many disparate agencies over the years, I knew all too well that arbitrary and ill-informed decisions happen all the time. Often we don't even know why we ourselves do what we do, let alone understand the motivations of others—still another reason why probing for motives is so unreliable.

I explored a few other ideas with Marianne, seeing if either the congressman or former vice president had stayed at the hotel recently or if there'd been any other constitutional law conferences in the last few years related to the one that the vice president had been scheduled to speak at when Hadron Brady tried to kill him.

Nothing.

Okay, so where does that leave us?

"Lien-hua mentioned the maids," I said. "Did she and Margaret talk to you about that?"

"Already looked into it. Housekeeping made up more than twenty rooms on the eighth floor between 2:00 and 4:00, not in any particular order, just as they received word from their superiors. As far as I know, EAD Wellington had agents look through all the rooms on the floor again—some were already occupied—nothing suspicious."

"What about when the hotel was remodeled—could there be a dumb waiter? Some kind of panic room, something like that put in to room 809?"

"The renovations were mostly cosmetic." She brought up a floor plan of the building prior to and after the renovations, overlaid them. Nothing of note.

I tried to think of what else I could do here and came up blank.

Maybe you should just get going, find out what's bugging Tessa. See if Rodale and Fischer forwarded the files to you.

I flicked my eyes across the computer monitors one last time and saw that the cameraman and reporter had finished interviewing Mr. Lees and were packing up their things. He was standing just a few feet away from them. Watching them.

Hang on.

The hotel might not have footage concerning the assassination attempt, but every news network in the country would have covered the story, and I was willing to bet that the producers at WXTN didn't trash their footage after six years.

I jogged back to the atrium to catch the news team before they left the hotel.

56

The cameraman was a twentysomething guy with wild, black hair and thick sideburns who introduced himself simply as Nick, which seemed to be exactly the right name for him. Chelsea Traye, the investigative journalist, was graceful, movie-star beautiful, and moved as if every step she took set a trend. I recognized them both as being present at the press conference I'd given yesterday.

After I'd introduced myself I said, "What would it take for you to access your station's video archives of the coverage following the assassination attempt on Vice President Fischer six years ago?"

They exchanged glances.

"You're the agent who was shot," Chelsea observed. "This is for the Mollie Fischer case, isn't it?"

"It's for an ongoing investigation."

"I see." She gave me a once-over, then asked Nick to give us a minute, and after a small pause, he set his camera on a nearby bench and stepped away.

"If we help you—" she began.

"No deals." I cut her off. "If you won't help me, I'll find a station from another network that will—but that'll just waste time and that's not something either of us would want." I could see that she was mentally trying to fill in the blanks from what I'd left unsaid, undoubtedly calculating costs versus benefits of helping me out.

After a moment she said, "Sure. We can get you the footage."

"Through the web?"

She nodded. "If you have a fast enough connection—otherwise it would take forever. There might be hundreds of hours of unedited footage."

I knew that Angela Knight in the Bureau's cybercrime division could do a metasearch on the computer she affectionately called Lacey, but if Marianne's system was as advanced as she'd indicated to me yesterday, I could take care of this right now.

"Go get Nick," I said. "And follow me."

***

Tessa had ended her video chat with her friend Pandora and was people-watching, pretending to listen to her iPod. She gazed around the atrium at the skylight, the terraces, the rows of hundreds of doors the guests locked themselves behind every night.

As people passed through the revolving doors at the front entrance, she had a thought: *Out of the cage, into the world.*

Last winter, Patrick had taken her to Johannesburg, South Africa, while he taught a three-day seminar at the Council of the Africas Crime Analysts' Symposium, and it had struck her that in one of the most violent cities in the world, the upper class and above live in walled-in subdivisions patrolled by armed guards, with their houses protected by electric fences, security systems, guard dogs, and barred windows and doors.

When Patrick asked what she thought of the city, she'd told him, "The free people live behind bars and the criminals are allowed to run free."

And after a moment, he'd answered, "I guess that's a pretty accurate description."

So here you go again—people deadbolt themselves into their hotel rooms, their cells, while the killers from this week walk around the city. Free.

Cages and freedom.

A zoo by another name.

And that brought the primate center to mind again.

Belle and the mirror self-recognition test.

Even Patrick could tell how much it had troubled her.

The deal wasn't so much the research they were doing; that all seemed humane enough, as far as any research on animals goes. What bothered her were the implications. After all, the researchers weren't just studying the neurology of violence but also the neurology of self-awareness, of morality.

Sure, at school she'd learned about evolution—mostly still the outdated theories that we evolved from gorillas, chimpanzees, or other modern knuckle-walking quadrupeds instead of *Ardipithecus ramidus*, but whatever—whether or not any of that was the case, or if natural selection had any divine intervention, she'd never really considered that there was a continuum of consciousness between humans and other animals.

A continuum of morality.

It didn't take a genius to put two and two together and realize that if, as Dr. Risel had said, all human traits and behavior can be found in rudimentary form in the animal kingdom, then the difference between humans and animals would be merely one of degree, not of kind.

And that was the idea that bothered her.

In essence, nothing except time and mutation would separate us from other animals. Behavior that we consider to be moral would have developed fundamentally out of natural selection as the most beneficial behavior for propagating the species. And if that were the case, morality would be simply functional—determined by the biological imperatives of reproduction and survival.

What is good for the species is good.

What is bad for the species is bad.

Morality would be utilitarian, nothing more.

She was staring at the front doors of this giant human cage sorting through her feelings toward all of this when she saw a man step into the hotel, pause, and look around.

The man was Paul Lansing.

Her father.

57

She quickly slid down in the chair and turned her head to the side so he wouldn't see her.

What is he doing here!

He was following her. He had to be following her!

She unpocketed her cell to call Patrick, but before she could speed-dial him, she had a thought.

Paul thinks Patrick has an anger problem . . . that he's violent . . .

If Paul was following her—which obviously he *was*—then he would definitely have seen Patrick enter the hotel with her. So he would know that her stepfather was close by . . .

What is Paul trying to do?

There was no way to know for sure, but she didn't trust him, and considering the custody suit, she couldn't shake the thought that he was here to somehow ruin her chances of staying with Patrick.

She looked around for a sneak-off route, but as she did, Paul somehow picked out her face from all the others in the crowded lobby and started toward her.

No, no, no!

She put the phone away, grabbed her purse, and was picking up her laptop so she could leave, but as she did, she thought of a way to turn the tables on Paul, especially if he was trying to set up Patrick—if that was his little plan after all.

She left her laptop open.

Tapped at the keys.

◼

Chelsea Traye had covered the shooting six years ago, and it hadn't taken her long to help Marianne find the right raw footage.

Now she was sitting on one side of me, Marianne on the other. Nick stood behind her, taking in the room, obviously impressed.

Marianne was downloading the network's archived video footage, sending it through her system's audio recognition program, flagging references to the words "Mollie Fischer," "Lincoln Towers," "Gunderson," "primate," "metacognition" and a dozen other keywords I'd given her.

"This program tags spoken words," Marianne explained to us, "then grabs twenty seconds of audio on both sides of them so you can listen to the phrase in context."

The files and video clips were piling up by the second. I was astonished by the amount of material the station had, and I realized most law enforcement agencies don't even have the capability for this depth and breadth of research.

I certainly wouldn't have time to listen to all of this audio right now. "Can you transcribe the audio files into text files?" I noticed Nick holding his cell in his right hand, tapping at the keys with the other. "You need to put that away in here," I said. "Or you'll have to leave."

He looked embarrassed. "Sorry."

He pocketed the phone, and Marianne said to me, "Sure, I can get you text files."

She let her fingers loose on the keyboard, and a string of text messages appeared on the screen before me, hyperlinked to place markers in the video footage. And I began scrolling through the hundreds of snippets of text, looking for anything that might relate to Mollie Fischer's abduction.

58

"Paul," Tessa said as he approached her. "What are you doing here?" She tried to keep her voice even.

"I came to apologize."

"Really."

"Yes."

"How did you know where I was?"

"One of my lawyers knows Mr. Lees, the manager. He mentioned that the FBI had showed up again and—"

"You're almost as bad a liar as . . ." She hesitated. "Some people I know."

He eyed her. "Would you believe I followed you here from your house?"

She shook her head. "Patrick would have noticed. He would have seen your car."

Paul spoke softly. "Very few people would have."

She stared at him questioningly. "What's that supposed to mean?"

"Nothing."

"Well, all right, you came to apologize. So apologize."

"There are some things we need to talk about. Can I have a seat?"

"That's not an apology."

"I'm sorry that I was a little overbearing at the museum."

"A *little*?"

"Please?" He gestured toward the chair.

She slid her purse and still-open laptop from the chair beside her to the end table and looked away as a way of acquiescing. He sat down, then she eyed him. "I already know what you're here to talk about—the custody thing."

"Patrick told you."

"Of course he told me. I'm his daughter."

She'd chosen the word *daughter* on purpose and waited for Paul to dare correct her, but he just accepted it and said, "I want what's best for you."

"Then leave me alone. Leave us both alone. You were never a part of my life before, and we all got by just fine. I don't like how you took advantage of my mom and I don't like how you questioned me about Patrick. And I don't want you around me. End of story."

"I hear what you're saying, but remember the letter? The one I sent to your mother when she was planning to abort you? I wanted to be a part of your life. From the very start."

She hated to admit it, but that much was true, the letter had been unequivocal.

"Why?"

"Why what?"

"You barely even knew Mom. You told me you didn't love her. Why did you want to be a part of my life?"

"Because I'm your father." His voice was soft, sincere.

She was quiet.

"Look," he said. "I came here to clear the air, to tell you what I did before I went to live in Wyoming."

"I thought you came here to apologize."

"Both."

"I already know what you did. You worked for the Wyoming Game and Fish Department."

"Not quite."

"Oh, so that was a lie too."

"I worked for the government."

"Yeah? So?"

He waited as if he were expecting her to catch on.

Of course she knew that the phrase "I work for the government" was often used as a thinly veiled way to avoid admitting that you worked for the FBI or the DEA or CIA. Or maybe the ATF. You didn't have to be a Washington insider to know that.

"What?" she said. "Are you telling me you were a spy or something? Oh, or maybe an assassin? A special forces black ops guy?" Then she leaned close and whispered, with faux admiration, "Are you the real G.I. Joe?"

He didn't argue with her. And his silence seemed to be a way of making his case.

Enough of this.

"Either tell me what you came here to tell me or get lost."

"I worked for the Secret Service, Tessa."

"Yeah, right."

"It's true."

"I don't believe you."

"How did I manage to follow you this morning without being seen? Without letting an experienced FBI agent notice he was being tailed?"

Patrick had no reason to think he might have a tail. Duh!

"Prove it. Show me an ID or something."

To her surprise, Paul reached into his pocket and produced a credentials case similar to Patrick's.

Her stepfather had been so intense about her not dating older guys that he'd taught her how to spot fake IDs, and when she studied Paul's creds, even though they were six years out of date, they looked legit.

He tried to protect you when that sculpture shattered at the museum . . . He knows people at the Capitol . . . Used to live in DC . . . Patrick couldn't dig up any dirt on him at all; the Secret Service could have done that—erased his record . . .

She gave him back the ID. "If what you're saying is true, my mom would have told me."

"I was in the middle of the application process when I met her. She knew that having a family, having attachments—especially children—was not . . . Well, let's just say, when the government is looking for people willing to lay down their lives, they don't want you to have any reason to hesitate."

"And children and girlfriends are good reasons to hesitate—is that the deal?"

"Yes. The Secret Service doesn't give the highest priority to applicants with lots of attachments."

The vasectomy? Is that why he got it?

"So you're saying I was a liability to your career. How nice."

He ignored that. "I'm not sure what your mother was thinking, but I've always believed that she left because she wanted to protect both of us."

"Or maybe she just didn't want to be anywhere near you. Have you ever considered that?"

"Yes. I have."

She eyed him. "How would it protect me? If she left you?"

"Family members of Secret Service agents are often targeted by people who might want to compromise that agent."

Though she hated to admit it, some of what he was saying actually seemed to make sense. "Why are you telling me this now?"

"I didn't want there to be any secrets between us."

"Really? Who is Julia?"

"There is no Julia. I visited the Hirshhorn the day I flew in, chose a sculpture, and decided that its creator would be my reason to be in the city."

"When all the while the real reason you're here is to try to get custody of me." She didn't offer that as a question.

"You turn eighteen this fall. I couldn't wait until then or it would be too late to get to know you before you moved away to live on your own."

"You lied to me."

"If I would have told you the truth up front, would you have agreed to see me yesterday?"

"I don't know. But at least I'd trust you more than I do now." As she mentioned that, she felt a slight sting of hypocrisy—after all, she'd deceived Patrick in almost the same way. And it'd probably had the same effect on him.

Paul didn't reply.

Despite herself, she was starting to believe him. "How did you get into sculpting then?"

"I took some classes at a community college."

That would explain why he knows, like, nothing about art and had to read all the explanatory plaques at the museum.

"So how come you live in the middle of nowhere? Were you fired from the Secret Service—and I'm not saying I believe you were ever actually in it, but if you were—were you fired or did you quit?"

"It was a mutually agreeable arrangement that I leave."

"Explain 'mutually agreeable arrangement.'"

He glanced around the atrium for a moment, then leaned closer and lowered his voice even more than he'd been doing for the conversation up until then. "Six years ago I was protecting Vice President Fischer when there was an attempt on his life, here, at the Lincoln Towers Hotel."

59

Tessa said nothing.

"You were only eleven, you probably don't remember that."

"No. I do."

"Really?" He sounded doubtful.

"I have an above average memory."

She thought about the shooting and recalled that the gunman had missed the VP and was killed by—

Oh.

"You shot the guy? Is that what you're saying?"

He shook his head. "No, I didn't kill the assailant."

"Well, then why was it mutually agreeable that you leave?"

He was quiet. Seconds passed. "Tessa, when Hadron Brady began shooting, I dove for cover. I didn't return fire; I didn't throw my body in the line of fire to protect the vice president. Rather than embarrass the service any further, I resigned, and they agreed to help me disappear so my actions wouldn't reflect negatively on the agency."

She processed everything. "You ran for cover?"

He nodded but said nothing.

He's a coward. Your dad is a coward!

She told herself that obviously he'd been afraid when the shots were fired, but then she realized that if Patrick had been there, he might have been afraid, anyone would've been, but he wouldn't have hidden, run away, backed down, dove for cover. He would have protected the person he was guarding. No matter what.

"What are you thinking?" Paul asked her.

"I'm thinking that if all this is true, you should have told me the first time we met, at your cabin."

"I was trying to wait for the right time."

"What makes this the right time?"

A small hesitation. "Apparently, it's not."

She felt a swarm of emotions. None of them good. "I think I'm done talking now."

"Yes, well." He rose. "I'll see you later. I won't meet with you without Patrick's permission next time. I promise."

She had the sense that she should say something about the custody case—*So what's happening with that? Are you still gonna go through with it?*—or maybe she should tell him that she forgave him for not being up-front with her, but instead of any of that she just watched him walk away.

He's a coward. That's all he is.

Your father is a coward.

She waited until he'd left the hotel before she tapped the keyboard to pause her computer's video chat program that she'd been using to tape their entire conversation.

Then she scrolled down.

And clicked "save."

I might have found something.

In the footage, in addition to mentioning room 809, the room in which we'd found the wheelchair, there were several references to room 814. It wasn't clear if Hadron Brady, the shooter, had stayed in it or simply used it temporarily to snap his rifle together, but when I cross-referenced that room number against the maid's records detailing which rooms were made up yesterday afternoon, the timing worked. The maids had cleaned it.

Timing and location.

The two rooms the killers chose were the same ones Brady had used.

Before telling Marianne what I'd noticed, I thanked Nick and Chelsea for their help, excused them, and they grudgingly collected their things and left the room.

"What is it?" Marianne asked.

I pointed at the screen. "Is anybody staying in that room?"

She looked it up. Shook her head. "No. Not since Tuesday."

So if the killers used it; evidence might still be present.

But then why would the maids have serviced it?

This whole case was beginning to remind me of a cave system—a series of subterranean passageways that you can't identify by looking only at the surface—you only find the connections when you actually climb down and start picking your way through the tunnels.

And the next tunnel I needed to explore was above me, on the eighth floor.

———————————————■———————————————

Tessa knew that she could wait here of course, wait for Patrick—however long that might be.

Or she could call him, but this wasn't exactly the kind of thing you tell someone over the phone: "By the way, my dad stopped by to let me know he's a cowardly ex–Secret Service agent. Oh yeah, and he's been following us all morning. Talk to you soon. Ciao."

And if she phoned Patrick and said she wanted to talk to him about something later, he'd just worry.

No, she needed to tell him in person.

Earlier, when he'd left to look around, he'd walked down the hallway that led behind the guest reception counter.

She grabbed her things and headed toward it.

60

I exited the elevator and started down the hallway.

There were only two possibilities—either Mollie was still inside the hotel or she was not. That much was obvious.

I passed room 804.

An axiom came to mind, one I'd taught in my seminars a hundred times over the years: what is obvious is not always what is true.

809.

Either Mollie was alive or dead.

Either she was here or she was not.

812.

What other options were there?

I arrived at the room.

For a moment I thought about the ways the Academy students had come up with on Wednesday for committing the perfect murder: take precautions to avoid leaving physical evidence . . . contaminate the scene with other people's DNA . . . dispose of the body outside, don't allow the body to be found at all . . .

Don't allow the body to be found at all.

I snapped on the latex gloves that I'd brought along.

Pulled out my lock-pick set.

Despite what hotel managers might tell you, keycard locks are some of the easiest ones to pick. Hotels use them because they're cheap, not because they're secure. It's one of the best-kept secrets in the hotel industry.

Most people feel safe in their hotel rooms.

If only they knew.

So, although in my haste to get up here I'd forgotten to get a keycard, it only took me a few seconds to get the door open.

The curtains had been drawn across the windows at the far side of the room, and the muted sunlight that had managed to slip through gave everything a yellowish, pasty glow.

I knew that Doehring and his team had looked for Mollie Fischer in every room of the hotel, that the ERT had processed room 809, that Margaret had sent agents to recheck all the eighth floor rooms the maids had serviced, but as far as I knew, no forensics unit had been in this room.

But the maids had.

Unwittingly vacuuming up the evidence.

Wiping it from the countertops.

Scrubbing it from the sink.

When you're looking for something in a room that's already been searched, you need to consider the conditions under which that initial search occurred, and then alter those conditions so that your attention isn't drawn to the same objects or areas the previous searchers would have focused on.

And since room lights always throw shadows in the same places, they're one of the main determinative factors to alter.

So now I left the lights off and clicked on my Mini MagLite.

The flashlight beam cut a slim crease through the pale, jaundiced light of the room.

I slipped off my shoes to avoid leaving dirt particles on the carpet. Then I stepped inside, closed the door, and began my search for something that might lead us to Mollie Fischer.

61

I knelt and shone my light across the carpeting and, as I'd expected, saw neat rows of tilted fibers that told me the room had recently been vacuumed.

No visible footprints, so apparently the maid had vacuumed the room as she backed toward the door.

I checked the closet, the desk, the chairs. Nothing.

Then the drawers, under the bed, behind the curtains.

Nothing.

I went though the entire room, carefully, methodically, searching each area from different vantage points and various angles until I was satisfied.

And so.

Only one place left to search.

I walked to the bathroom door.

We were looking for Mollie's body, for a corpse.

But this room has already been searched . . .

If Mollie had been killed in this hotel, and the killers didn't have time to transport the body to another location, it was obvious that her corpse had to still be here somewhere.

What is obvious is not always what is true.

I pressed the bathroom door open, and it angled away from me into the dark.

Because of the bathroom's orientation to the window, almost no light filtered into it, just shadows of different depth, different intensity.

I dialed my MagLite's lens, widened the beam, and targeted it inside.

The bathroom appeared empty, but I noted that the shower curtain had been pulled all the way across the curved, silver shower rod, thereby hiding the tub from view.

Unconsciously, I found myself sniffing the air, but I didn't smell the odor that I feared I might find.

I went to the tub.

Holding the flashlight in one hand, I grasped the edge of the shower curtain with the other.

Images from past crime scenes flickered like an old movie reel through my mind. Images of death and terror and gore—

Slowly, I slid the curtain along the rod while shining the light toward the tub.

Empty.

I let out a small breath of relief, but it was tainted with frustration. I wanted so badly to find something. There were just too many passages in this cave that I hadn't been able to connect.

You might have been wrong about this room. About all of this.

I took a breath.

All right.

I'd finish looking around, then get going.

Evaluate the scene systematically, start at the sink.

The flawlessly shiny faucet and clean counter told me that the surfaces had recently been wiped down—the shampoo bottle, soap, lotion, were all new.

Towels folded.

Mirror, spotless.

The maid had done a thorough job.

I turned my attention to the commode. The spotless handle shimmered. No smudges.

No prints.

The bowl held nothing but clear water, but when I knelt and looked behind the base of the commode, I did find one thing.

A small, balled-up facial tissue.

It might have been left behind by the killers, but when I narrowed my flashlight beam and inspected it more closely I saw that it was covered by a thin layer of undisturbed dust, so it had almost certainly been in the room for more than the last twenty-four hours.

The killers might have planted it. They're into that kind of thing.

We would check it for DNA, but whether or not the tissue had been left by the killers, its presence did indicate one thing: there were areas of the bathroom that were easy to miss even for a meticulous maid.

I turned again to the tub.

A little soap scum near the faucet, a few hairs caught in the drain. Hair itself doesn't contain DNA, but hair follicles do, so if we had roots of the—

Mollie was unconscious in the wheelchair . . .

It takes a few hours for drugs to get into the root of someone's hair, and if Mollie had been drugged for more than an hour and this was her hair, it was possible we might find traces of the drug.

And if so, the guys at the lab could test it, identify it, match it.

Mollie is either inside the hotel or she is not.

I stepped into the tub and tugged the shower curtain across the rod again.

Using the MagLite, I carefully investigated the shower curtain itself. A small amount of soap scum. A few water spots. Nothing else.

Only when I knelt and peered at the far end of the curtain, in between two of the curtain folds, did I see it.

A tiny speck.

Dark.

I leaned closer.

Dried blood.

The only way to notice it was from inside the tub, an unlikely place from which to clean, even for an experienced maid.

It might be nothing. Might not be related. Maybe. Maybe.

I phoned Doehring, told him what I'd found, and he said he'd send the CSIU guys over here immediately. We hung up.

Sure, it might be nothing, but at the moment it seemed like

too many tunnels were converging in this room for me to believe that.

The blood.

The lack of DNA in 809.

The proximity of the two rooms.

I closed my eyes and pictured what I'd seen when I arrived on the eighth floor yesterday: two security guards . . . two maids . . . three children in swimming suits . . .

A thought, out of nowhere: *Could they have been the Rainey children?*

No, the children in the hotel were older.

But I'd seen one other thing.

A bellhop pulling a luggage cart.

62

A slow chill crawled down my back.

I called Marianne and asked where the bellhops store the luggage for guests who arrive early, or who need the hotel to hold their bags until a later checkout time.

She told me the location—a room on the lower level near the storage room where I'd been shot. I didn't tell Marianne what I suspected, just asked her to meet me there, then I ended the call.

And, trying to convince myself that I was wrong to suspect what I did, I left for the basement.

◼

"Here we are," Mr. Lees declared as he and Tessa arrived at the hotel's control center.

It'd taken her longer than she'd thought it would to convince him to take her to Patrick, but finally she'd told him how upset *Special Agent Bowers FROM THE FBI* would be if he found out the hotel's president wasn't allowing his daughter to see him, and Mr. Lees had asked her to kindly follow him.

"I believe our head of security is meeting with him right now." He knocked on the door, and a moment later, a slim, sharp-dressed woman in her late twenties appeared.

Mr. Lees said, "Marianne, this is Tessa Ellis, Agent Bowers's stepdaughter."

"I need to talk to him right away," Tessa said.

"Well, I'm on my way to meet him now. Why don't you come along?"

◼

I made it to the luggage storage area before Marianne, and I decided not to wait for her.

After clearing all the bellhops out of the room, I entered it alone and closed the door.

In contrast to the splendor and extravagance of the rest of the hotel, this was a vast, boxy concrete chamber that smelled of dust and mold and stale air. Industrial florescent lights. No carpeting. No windows.

Twelve luggage carts stood empty and waiting in a line along the east wall. Filling the rest of the room were piles of suitcases of various shapes and sizes. With nearly a meter of space between each stack, they'd clearly been arranged to keep the items of the different guests separated.

Yesterday, I'd only momentarily seen the suitcases on the luggage cart that the bellhop was pulling down the hallway, and I wasn't certain what brand they were. So now, as I scanned the piles, I started by looking for the luggage collection with the biggest suitcases. I figured that would be the most likely—

And I saw it.

At the far end of the room.

A cluster of large suitcases that, as I thought about it, did appear to match the style of the ones I'd seen on the luggage cart.

We'd been looking for Mollie's body.

Her whole body.

But that might not be what we were going to find.

I crossed the room toward the pile of suitcases.

63

The luggage looked brand new.

Using new suitcases would make sense if you were a killer who was trying to avoid leaving physical evidence that might be traced back to you—not just DNA, hair, or trace evidence, but also scratches or scuff marks that could give us clues as to where the luggage had been.

I had a feeling these killers would have thought of that.

Using my cell phone, I snapped half a dozen photos of the arrangement of the four suitcases.

Then I stared at the largest bag.

Knelt beside it.

As I did, I caught the faint whiff of the odor I've smelled at far too many crime scenes. And though I tried to reassure myself that the smell would have been more pungent, more sickening by now, I was aware of the methods of taking care of that problem: wrap the item in plastic . . . use chemicals . . .

My fingers trembled slightly as I rolled the suitcase away from the others in the stack and tilted it toward the floor.

It was very heavy and settled onto its side with a disquieting, moist thump.

Heart hammering, I reached for the zipper.

A bellhop rolled these suitcases right past everyone . . .

Right past you.

Carefully, I guided the zipper along its track, making sure it didn't catch on the fabric, didn't snag on my glove. Or get caught on anything else.

Why those two rooms on the eighth floor?

What's the connection between these killers and the assassination attempt six years ago?

The zipper reached the end of its track.

Heart beating.

Beating.

I took another picture with my phone.

Then I braced myself.

And lifted the unzipped flap of the suitcase.

Just as the door behind me swung open.

64

I quickly closed the suitcase.

I'd only needed a glimpse to confirm my worst fears—the killers hadn't used just this one suitcase. Based on what I saw, I suspected they would have needed most of the ones in this stack.

Trying to hide the torrent of grief and anger I felt, I turned to see if it was Marianne at the door behind me.

And it was.

And Tessa was with her.

"What are you doing here?" I shouted.

She was quiet, staring past me at the luggage I was kneeling beside.

"Tessa, you need to leave this room. Now." I didn't intend for my tone to be so harsh, but I did not want her anywhere near this place.

Marianne put a hand on her shoulder. "Let's go, sweetie."

Tessa's face was flushed. She was a smart girl, she could put two and two together. "Is that . . . ?"

"Come on." Marianne ushered her out of the room.

Before joining them, I quickly phoned Doehring and told him to send another forensics team. I felt sick having to say it: "I found Mollie Fischer's remains."

After making sure the bellhops knew not to enter the room, I hurried to the hall and caught up with Tessa and Marianne near the elevator at the south end of the basement. Marianne gave Tessa's shoulder a soft squeeze, said a few words of assurance to her, then left us alone. We entered the elevator quietly, watched the doors close. Stood beside each other in a shroud of silence.

I didn't want to ask Tessa the question, but I knew I had to, so just before we reached the ground floor, I said, "What did you see in there?"

"Just . . ." She hesitated. "A suitcase. A bunch of suitcases."

The elevator dinged.

"That's all?"

The doors slid open.

"And the look on your face."

I felt a deepening sense of failure—first, for not finding Mollie alive, then for letting Tessa see the ragged anger in my eyes. "Come on," I told her. "Let's get you out of here."

As we were leaving the hotel, the first wave of officers, including Officer Tielman, the CSIU member whom I'd met at the primate center on Tuesday, were already rushing through the front doors.

While she was sitting at her desk at the command post, Margaret Wellington got word that Patrick Bowers had found Mollie Fischer's body at the hotel.

Slowly, she set down the phone.

Earlier in the day Rodale had notified her that Bowers was back on the case. She'd felt a wave of indignation toward both Bowers and Rodale, and it hadn't gone away all afternoon.

But now that Bowers had found Mollie, something even she'd failed to do, she felt conflicted.

She'd never liked Bowers's headstrong attitude or his unconventional approach to law enforcement, but she could hardly believe he was the kind of man to go behind her back to Rodale like that. Not only was it a direct challenge to her authority, but it showed contempt for the Bureau's chain of command and its motto: Fidelity, Bravery, Integrity.

She saw none of those three in his actions.

And none in Rodale's decision to contravene her orders and reinstate him.

Just another example of Rodale's inept leadership at the helm of the Bureau.

However, despite all of that, apparently, Bowers had done his job, done it well.

So it was up to her to make the call.

She picked up the phone again.

Congressman Fischer's wife was still on her way back from Australia, so at least she wouldn't have to traumatize her, but as the head of the task force, Margaret did need to call the congressman to ask him to identify his daughter's remains—the second time he'd been asked to do so this week.

She took a deep breath, and then, with a stark mixture of sadness and frustration—both toward herself and at the Bureau for not saving Mollie Fischer—she dialed the number.

On the way home, I tried comforting Tessa, but she told me she didn't want to talk and if I could just leave her alone that would be good.

Over the past year she'd explained to me more than once that usually the best way to help her get through stuff is to just let her be—advice that sounded counterintuitive to me but actually did seem to work.

So for the moment at least, I let things rest and allowed my thoughts to return to the case.

Right now the team would be interviewing the bellhops for a description of the people who'd had suitcases taken from their rooms. Officers would be checking the suitcase for prints, DNA, trace evidence; tracking the luggage claim tag to see if they could tie it to any of the guests who'd recently checked into or out of the hotel; processing the luggage storage room and the hotel room containing the spot of blood.

The nuts and bolts of police work.

But based on what I'd seen so far, the killers this week would have known all that, would have anticipated it.

I was reminded of Sevren Adkins, the killer in North Carolina who called himself the Illusionist and had attacked Tessa and then tried to kill us both. He'd taunted the authorities with clues from future crimes and always seemed to find a way to hide in plain sight, even managing to be at crime scenes without raising suspicion. Right before he died he'd challenged me to a rematch—

"I was looking for you."

Tessa's words jarred me out of my thoughts about Adkins, and it took me a moment to mentally shift gears. "In the luggage room?"

A nod. "I had a visitor."

"A visitor?"

She didn't answer right away. "Paul Lansing."

"What!"

"Don't worry."

"Lansing was there? Did he do anything to—"

"It's okay. I got some good footage."

"Footage?"

I listened as she summarized her meeting with Lansing, but even as she spoke I realized I needed to see this footage for myself, so I exited the highway, parked at a gas station. Then she flipped open her laptop.

And pulled up the video.

65

I watched the digitally recorded conversation three times, shocked by what Lansing had told her, incredulous that he'd followed us, angry at myself for not noticing his car.

His claims seemed outrageous.

But also, though I hated to admit it, perhaps not so outrageous after all.

Actually, if what he was saying was true, it would explain a lot, including how Vice President Fischer knew him and had heard about the custody case, why Christie never told me the identity of Tessa's father or informed him that he had a daughter—and also why I hadn't been able to find out more about Paul Lansing's past.

Of course, I would need to confirm everything, but the more I thought about it, the more I found myself anticipating that his story was going to check out.

Momentarily, I had a disturbing thought, and I was ashamed at myself for even thinking it, but as an investigator I couldn't help it: Tessa's father was in this hotel six years ago when the shooter tried to assassinate the vice president . . . Because of his involvement he would likely know about the two rooms on the eighth floor . . . He was here this week at the time of this crime spree . . . The use of the two rooms pointed to a connection between the crimes . . .

Could he possibly—

No, it couldn't be.

Unlike the man we'd caught on tape pushing Mollie into the hotel, Lansing was over six feet tall and broad shouldered, didn't favor either leg, wasn't left-handed.

Regardless, one thing remained certain: I was going to take a closer look into Paul Lansing's past as soon as we got home.

Another passage.

Another tunnel.

"If he tries to contact you again," I told Tessa, "don't talk with him or respond to his emails. And let me know right away."

"I will."

After a stretch of silence I felt the need to veer the conversation away from Lansing. "Good job, by the way, on getting this video. You'd make a great FBI agent."

She was quiet but seemed pleased by my comment.

"Do you know how to read lips?" I asked her.

She seemed taken aback by my question and shook her head.

"Good." I pulled out my cell.

"What are you doing?"

I cranked the door open. "Two quick calls. I'll be right back."

After telling Missy Schuel about Lansing's claims and assuring her that I would send her a copy of the video when I got home, I spoke briefly with Lien-hua, and she informed me that the congressman had been contacted and was on his way to make a positive ID.

When I told her about Lansing and the Secret Service angle, she offered to do a little poking around to confirm that he really had been an agent. "Thanks," I said, "but I'll take care of it. Listen, it's possible the killers didn't just leave Mollie's body there to confuse us. It's possible they meant to come back for her."

"I already thought of that. With so many responding officers here and all the news coverage, it's probably too late, but I did convince Margaret to get us three undercover agents to surveil the entrances and exits in case."

"As always, you continue to impress me, Agent Jiang."

"Thank you." A pause. "In all seriousness, Pat, nice work on this."

"Thanks. Give me a shout later."

"I will."

I hung up.

And took Tessa home.

Four unzipped suitcases lay at Margaret's feet.

Seeing the contents reminded her of the time a killer had left the torso of one of his victims in the trunk of her car. Just to taunt her.

A tight iciness coursed through her.

Not a good memory.

Congressman Fischer had insisted on making the ID here rather than at the ME's autopsy room, and finally Margaret had agreed. He'd asked for all four suitcases to be opened, and now he was staring into the smallest one, at his daughter's face. And when Margaret did as well, she noticed that Mollie's eyes were still open.

She felt a splinter of anger. As a show of respect, it's standard procedure for the Evidence Response Team to close the victim's eyes before any family members arrive. She glared at Agent Natasha Farraday, the ERT member who should have taken care of this, but obviously had not, then knelt and gently closed Mollie's eyes herself.

The congressman nodded to Margaret in appreciation for the gesture. Then, after a long unsteady moment, he looked into one of the suitcases on the left, pointed to a birthmark on Mollie's left arm. "It's her," he whispered. "There's no doubt."

Despite his apparent certainty, Margaret wanted conclusive DNA testing done before she released any information to the public.

It took Agent Farraday a few moments to do the on-site test. As she did, Margaret couldn't stop thinking about that body in the trunk of her Lexus in North Carolina—

"It's her," Agent Farraday announced. "It's Mollie."

The third confirmed victim since Tuesday night. Still no clear suspects, no persons of interest in the case.

Margaret cleared the room so that the congressman could have some time alone with his daughter, then after a few minutes, he exited and his entourage shuffled him out of the hotel.

As she watched Fischer walk away, she thought again of his

brother's connection to this hotel, and to the attempt on his life by the pro-death penalty activist.

Cheyenne had asked her to see if Vice President Fischer's speech had anything to do with primate metacognition, and she'd found that it had not: it was about the Constitution as a living document and what implications our changing views on the 5th Amendment's rights to life and liberty might have on social issues today.

The right to life.

To liberty.

Knowing the congressman's stand on these issues might help the task force identify potential groups that might be politically motivated to harm his family, and perhaps provide a link to the assassination attempt six years ago.

A look at the clock on her cell phone told her it was almost 5:30.

You've been working for eleven hours straight, Margaret. Go home.

But she doubted she could step completely away from the case. Tonight after dinner she would take a closer look at Congressman Fischer's voting record and what might be at stake in this case.

She left to pick up her things from her office and head home to feed Lewis.

66

As soon as Tessa and I arrived home, I forwarded to Missy Schuel the video Tessa had taken of her conversation with Paul Lansing, and only moments later, as I was getting ready to start looking into Lansing's past, Missy called me.

"I was debating whether or not to contact you," she said, "but now, in light of everything that's happened . . ."

"What is it?"

"One of Lansing's lawyers finally returned my calls. I have a meeting with them tomorrow afternoon."

"Tomorrow? I thought you said you were hoping—"

"Next week. Yes. I expected that would be the earliest they might agree to meet. So now I'm wondering if this sudden eagerness to get together has something do to with Lansing's encounter with Tessa this afternoon." A pause, and then, "Is it possible Paul was aware that their conversation was being taped?"

I considered that. "The way he acted on the video, it didn't appear so."

After a moment she said, "I concur, but in either case, these things never move this fast. Something else is going on here."

Immediately, I thought of Lansing's connection with the former vice president. "I'm coming to the meeting," I said.

"I think it's best if I go alone. At least for this initial—"

"Missy, I'm coming."

"That's not the way to play this."

"You have three children of your own," I replied. "Did you attend the lawyers' meetings after your husband left you? Or did you just trust that someone you barely knew was going to help you keep custody of your kids?"

A thin pause. "Point taken. But if we're going to work together, you'll have to trust me."

"I do."

It's Lansing I don't trust, I thought, but I kept that comment to myself.

"All right," she said. "I advise against it, but it's your decision. The meeting is at 3:30. My car is in the shop, so if you can pick me up at my office at 2:30, that'll give us time to discuss specifics before heading over."

I agreed, and we ended the call.

After my conversation with Missy, I went to the living room to see how Tessa was doing, and I found her lying on the couch reading a collection of Sherlock Holmes stories. "I thought you hated Doyle in favor of—"

"Poe. Yes. I do." She didn't bother to look up.

"So you decided to give Doyle another shot?"

"Pandora likes him. She's always asking me to read these Holmes stories." Finally she looked at me. "But this is definitely Doyle's last chance."

Knowing Tessa, I guessed she'd turned to reading, one of her favorite pastimes, as a way of dealing with the trauma of the day. I tend to do the same thing—retreat into the familiar when faced with the overwhelming. "Tessa, would you like to talk about—"

She went back to the book. "I'm not ready."

"Okay."

I tried to figure out how best to balance my obligations as a dad with my duties as an FBI agent for the rest of the night, but in the end I decided that until Tessa was ready, I'd let her be and get back to seeing what I could dig up on Lansing's amorphous past.

I took my laptop to the back porch, out of Tessa's sight.

From the notes Christie had left in her diary, I knew that Lansing hadn't changed his name since they met, so I logged onto the Federal

Digital Database and typed it in. Both Angela Knight and I had looked into his past when I first found out he was Tessa's father, but I hadn't explored a Secret Service angle and I doubted she had either.

To begin, I targeted my search on the Secret Service's discharges and transfers.

Electronic trails like this are rarely conclusive, but when the government decides to erase your identity, the cover-up is also rarely airtight, so although there were gaps in what I found, there was evidence that one of the agents had moved to Wyoming shortly after the shooting. I worked for nearly an hour, and in time I uncovered enough hints, references, and inconsistencies to convince myself that Lansing's story was true.

In addition, I found that steps had been taken to remove the identity of one of the agents present the day of the assassination attempt.

Yes, Lansing had been an agent and he had been there that day, but I noticed one major discrepancy between his story and the information I found: it appeared that the agent who'd used lethal force on the gunman was the one who had moved out West, not an agent who'd run for cover.

Which in a way made sense, since it did seem odd that Vice President Fischer would remain friends with a disparaged Secret Service Agent whose failure to respond appropriately during an exchange of fire might have cost him his life.

After a few more minutes of looking through the files, I realized I wasn't going to make any more headway here. I would have to ask Lansing about it when I saw him tomorrow at the custody meeting. Deal with it then.

For the moment I had what I needed, and there were a few other things that I needed to check into.

I clicked to my email and found that Director Rodale had sent eight pdf files containing the research articles he'd promised me. In addition, Congressman Fischer had kept his word and forwarded his phone records and the accounts of his Gunderson Foundation financial contributions.

Before reading through any of those files, though, I emailed the congressman expressing my sincere sorrow over what had happened to his daughter.

Finding the right words to say in a situation like that is one of the toughest things to do, and it took me awhile to find ones that were not mere platitudes.

At last when I was done, I cross-referenced the timing of his contributions against the list of potential suspects' bank accounts, credit card statements, and bank deposit records, but found no correlation.

I studied the financial records themselves, but honestly they looked innocuous enough, although his contributions were surprisingly generous.

Nothing striking in the phone records, either, apart from a substantial number of calls to and from Director Rodale since March.

After I was satisfied, I perused the Project Rukh research from Rodale, most of which contained equations about the temporal and spatial correlation of hemodynamic and electrophysiological signals in brain imaging, and although much of it was indecipherable to me, I did recognize that the research centered around the neural impulses that relate to different areas of cognition.

Metacognition?

Theory of mind?

More caverns to the case.

Last February when I was working the case in San Diego in which we'd stumbled across Project Rukh, I'd met a neuropathologist named Dr. Osbourne. He'd mentioned this type of research to me, and I gathered from what I read here that some of his work had survived. I would have contacted him now, but he'd died in a head-on collision in March.

I wondered if there were any unusual circumstances surrounding his death, and I emailed Detective Dunn, a homicide detective in San Diego, to have him look into it for me.

As I was sending the email, I saw Tessa approaching the deck.

She leaned her head out the door to speak to me. "I made supper plans."

I glanced at my watch and realized it was almost 7:30. She must have been starving. "Right on."

"Please don't say 'right on.'"

"Aren't kids saying that again?"

"Yes. Kids are. Adults are not."

"Gotcha. What's for dinner?"

"Chinese. Delivery."

A taste for Chinese food was one of the few things Tessa and I had in common. "Groovy," I said.

She looked at me incredulously. "I hope I just misheard you."

I smiled. "Come here."

She pulled up one of the deck chairs. "It should be here in like twenty minutes or so."

"Okay."

It had been a hard day, and I wanted to comfort her but had no idea what the right words might be. I said, "This afternoon. The primate place, I know it upset you, and then the hotel, that was horrible—believe me, if I'd had any idea that either place—"

"I know, I know—you wouldn't have taken me. Don't worry, I'm just . . ." She shrugged again. "Anyway . . ."

"If you decide you want to talk, I promise to listen and not say 'right on' the whole time."

"Or groovy."

"Or groovy."

It was a long time before she finally spoke, and when she did, she was staring intently into the twilight-enshrouded woods rather than at me. "Patrick, do you believe some people are born pure evil?"

Her words struck me deeply but did not surprise me.

Considering everything that had happened over the past few days, it seemed like a pretty natural question to ask.

I couldn't help but think of psychopaths like Richard Basque, Jeffrey Dahmer, Ted Bundy, Sevren Adkins, Gary Ridgeway, and of course, the killers from this week and their grisly, shocking crimes.

You can't work in law enforcement for any amount of time without the question of evil coming up, and over the years I'd thought about it frequently and eventually formulated an opinion, even if it wasn't a complete answer.

"I guess I think of it more like we're all born with a shell of good around us, but it's fractured—for everyone it is. We all know what's right—even psychopaths who lack empathy are aware of their lack of compassion. I think all people know what's good, even though, all too often, we're attracted to what is not."

"To the fractures."

"Yes."

She thought for a moment. "Are you saying we have an instinct for evil?"

"I wouldn't put it like that. But we definitely have a weakness for it. I guess I'd maybe even say an inclination toward it."

She peered at the forest. "Because sometimes we enjoy doing it."

"Yes." It was troubling to admit. "Sometimes we do."

"And if we're good, then we seal up the fractures? Is that what you're saying?"

This is where things got a little sticky. "Actually, I don't think we can seal them, Tessa. I don't think anyone ever has. That's why we have to be aware of—"

"Dr. Werjonic."

"What?"

"What he said: 'The road to the unthinkable is not paved by slight departures from your heart, but by tentative forays into it.'"

"Yes." I was reminded that I wasn't the only one who was still mourning his death. "He did used to say that."

We were both quiet.

I wasn't quite sure I agreed with Calvin's statement, but knowing that Tessa was familiar with Shakespeare, I said, "I know it sort of flies in the face of that old 'to thine own self be true' quote."

She shook her head softly. "No, it's the same."

I evaluated her words, but the two sayings seemed contradictory to me. "Calvin's words warned against foraying into your heart, Shakespeare promoted the idea. How are they the same?"

At last she stopped studying the shadows across the yard and looked at me. "In *Hamlet*, Shakespeare wrote, 'To thine own self be true, and it must follow as the night the day, thou canst be false to no man,' or 'thou canst not then be false to any man.' There's some controversy about the manuscripts that were preserved, which ones are authoritative—" She caught herself veering into a tangent and redirected her thoughts. "Anyway, that's exactly what these guys that you track do—serial killers, rapists, pedophiles, whatever."

"They're being true to themselves," I said, finding myself agreeing with her, "to their hearts, their desires."

"Yeah. Forays into their hearts, not departures from them."

The observation flew in the face of the popular wisdom that people should be true to themselves, follow their dreams, their heart's desires, but it made sense because when people do that without restraint, they end up committing the worst crimes imaginable.

"That's very incisive," I said. "So then, Shakespeare was wrong in encouraging people to follow their hearts."

"No." She was starting to sound more and more like her typical sardonically-irritated-Tessa-self, and I took that to mean that she was starting to feel better. It was refreshing. "Look at the context. The Hamlet quote isn't advice, it's sarcasm."

Out front, I heard a car pulling up the driveway.

"Supper," she said.

My wallet was on the kitchen table, and I went to grab some cash. "Okay, so how is it sarcasm?" She followed me into the house, carrying my computer for me. "Everyone quotes Shakespeare's words as advice. Besides, 'Follow your heart! Be true to yourself!' is the theme of every Disney movie ever made. How could Disney have gotten it backward?"

"Are you being serious?"

"Only partly." I found my wallet, pulled out a twenty. "But I don't see how it's sarcasm."

"Polonius says the words."

I heard a car door slam.

"Tessa, I have to admit I'm not as familiar with *Hamlet* as you are."

"Polonius is a fool who gets into trouble whenever he does follow his heart, when he actually *is* true to himself. By having him say the line, Shakespeare was underlying how absurd the advice is. Shakespeare wasn't stupid. He's warning people against being true to themselves, not telling them to do it. He understood human nature better than almost any other author in history." Then she added, "Except maybe Poe."

"Of course."

I couldn't help asking myself the obvious follow-up question: if we shouldn't be true to ourselves, what should we be true to?

The doorbell rang. I crossed the living room. "I'm not so sure about the whole Polonius irony thing. I'd have to look that up."

"Trust me."

I answered the door and found Lien-hua standing on the porch holding three bulging bags of Chinese takeout.

"Lien-hua." I stood there holding the door open, staring at her.

She smiled softly. "Can I come in?"

"Oh." I stepped aside. "Sure. Sorry." She walked past me, and I flashed Tessa a look: *What in the world is going on?* She gave me a light conspiratorial smile.

"Hello, Agent Jiang," she said.

"Hey, Tessa."

Lien-hua put the food on the kitchen table.

"I didn't expect you." I was searching for the right words. "So soon."

"Well, the Evidence Response Team and CSIU guys are processing the hotel room and luggage area, so there wasn't much for me to do there. Besides, I needed some space to focus on the profile, and even when you're in the middle of a case—"

"You still need to eat," Tessa said.

"That's right," she replied. "So when Tessa was kind enough to call and tell me how sorry you were that we missed lunch but that you would love to have me join you guys for dinner, well—"

"It was an offer too good to pass up," Tessa said.

"Yes."

"And here you are," I said.

"Here I am."

"Well, it's nice. It's . . . I'm glad you could make it."

"Me too." She was scouring through the cupboards, looking for plates.

I went to the fridge. "Not much to drink, I'm afraid. Pretty much just juice, soy milk, root beer—"

"Water's fine."

"Water it is." I took a glass to the sink and asked Tessa to get out the silverware, but Lien-hua rebuked me with a slender, wagging finger. "This is Chinese food."

"Oh, please not the chopsticks. You know how bad I am with those things."

She smiled. "Practice makes perfect."

67

After five minutes of letting me fumble around with my chopsticks while she and Tessa used theirs with annoying dexterity, Lien-hua finally leaned toward me. "Here, like this."

She gently took my right hand in hers and slid the chopsticks into position between my fingers. Her touch was both cool and full of fire.

"This is very helpful," I said as she glided her fingers across mine, maneuvered the chopsticks for me. "I might never go back to using a fork."

"Hush."

Tessa just shook her head.

Lien-hua took her time teaching my fingers what to do. I didn't mind. "See?" she said.

No. Let's keep the lesson going for a while.

"Reminds me of that night in San Diego," I said. "When you taught me the sign language alphabet."

"I remember that," she replied softly. She patted my hand and then went back to her food.

I'd only managed to take three bites when I heard a car pull into the driveway. I gave Tessa a questioning look, and she said, "That would be our other guest. Why don't you go get the door?"

Lien-hua looked at me. Blinked. "Other guest?"

Knowing Tessa as well as I did, I had a feeling who might be arriving outside. On my way to the door I flicked on the porch lights.

And in the fading evening light I saw Cheyenne getting out of her car.

Oh, Tessa . . .

Cheyenne jogged up the steps.

I opened the door for her. "Hey," I said. "You're here."

"Yup." She was carrying a supermarket brand apple pie. "Dessert has arrived."

68

"Thanks for the invite, Pat," Cheyenne said as I closed the door behind her.

"You're welcome." Then I called to my stepdaughter in the kitchen, "Tessa, you were so kind to pass along the dinner invitation to Detective Warren as well."

"Not a problem," came the reply.

"As well?" Cheyenne said. "So who else is—"

Lien-hua stepped into the kitchen doorway. "Cheyenne."

"Lien-hua."

Both women looked at each other for a moment, and then, almost simultaneously, looked at me.

"Great," I said awkwardly. "So, good . . . um, I'm glad there's plenty of food then."

Neither of them spoke.

Oh, this was just outstanding.

Cheyenne took the pie to the kitchen, Lien-hua joined her, and I asked Tessa if she could kindly come to the hall for a moment. She reluctantly followed, and when we were out of earshot of the two women, I said, "What is this all about?"

"We missed lunch with Agent Jiang."

"I know, but why did you invite them *both* over here tonight? What are you trying to do?"

She gave me a you-are-so-clueless look. "We talked about this earlier. You need to decide who you're more interested in. The best way to do that is to have them both here. That way—"

I didn't buy it. "Why are you suddenly so concerned about me being with a woman?"

A long uncertain pause followed, and somehow it almost made

me regret pressing her for a reason. At last she said softly, "When we got back here tonight, there was so much . . . I don't know . . . I just thought it would be good for both of us if we didn't have to think about death for a while."

I couldn't come up with any argument to that.

"You need to fill me in on these things, okay?"

"It's easier to ask for forgiveness than permission."

"That line doesn't apply to teenage girls."

A tiny smile. "Come on." She started down the hallway. "You have guests to entertain."

Brad arrived at the small country gas station on the isolated road that skirted along the edge of the Quantico Marine Corps Base.

He parked the car.

Astrid had wanted an unforgettable climax to this crime spree, and so he'd suggested leaving the FBI a little surprise in their own backyard. She'd seemed pleased by the idea, and considering where he'd left the laptop, this gas station was in the perfect location.

There were no other cars on the road, none at the gas station.

Seclusion was another reason he and Astrid had chosen this place.

He turned his attention to the man behind the counter in the gas station—Hispanic, mid-twenties, bored, alternating between texting and talking on his cell phone.

Then Brad organized his things and prepared the needle.

69

By consensus the four of us agreed not to talk about dead bodies or blood or, as Tessa put it, "anything even remotely gross," and the conversation wandered through the topics of where we'd each lived, our hobbies, and embarrassing stories from high school.

Safe territory.

The places you go when you need to set the dark things aside.

However, the more we spoke, the more the three of them seemed to jump from topic to topic without any discernible links between the subject matter. I was caught constantly playing catch-up while none of them seemed to have any trouble at all following the conversation. I finally commented that women do this all the time but that guys can't keep track of where the discussion is going because the thinking isn't linear.

The three women stared at me.

"Chauvinist," Tessa said, not completely seriously.

"No. I'm not. You know that. I'm just saying—"

"It's okay, Pat," Cheyenne said. "I'm glad you're aware there's a difference between men and women."

Actually, I'm aware of several of them . . .

"Yes, exactly," I said. "That's my point."

"And you're right. We *are* different—physiologically, chemically, hormonally, psychologically, emotionally. The way we think, prioritize, remember, construct knowledge, and process information—all different."

Good. A way to salvage things.

"There you go," I said. "Men and women think differently. Men are more logical, women are more—"

Lien-hua raised an eyebrow. "Careful, now."

Tessa signaled her agreement. "I second that."

"I'm just saying—" By the looks on their faces I decided I'd better try a different tack. "However, you do know that some feminists might argue that masculine and feminine roles are simply social constructs and not physiological traits."

"Then they're ignoring the research." Cheyenne shook her head. "But that's no surprise. In one of the tragic ironies of the twentieth century, feminists never fought for women to become more feminine."

"What do you mean?"

"Instead of celebrating what it means to be a woman, to be feminine, to be an empowered female, they fought for women to act and be treated more like men. That's why I call them masculinists."

"You call feminists masculinists?" I said.

"That's right."

She must have noticed the surprise on all of our faces because she went on to elaborate, "Yes. Masculinists. Because in their fight for more rights, they ended up devaluing what it means to be a woman and emulating the very things they criticized most in men—imperialism, identity confusion, militaristic propagandism, dehumanizing competition, careerism."

Lien-hua, Tessa, and I glanced at each other. I had the sense that all of us were unsure what to say.

Cheyenne set down her chopsticks. "Women should be extended the same dignity, opportunity, and respect as men but shouldn't be treated in an identical way: equality without uniformity. I want to be treated like a woman, not a pale imitation of a man."

"You go, girl," Tessa said.

Cheyenne took her up on the offer. "Women should never be ashamed to be feminine. Strength comes from conviction, not from acting like a man. Being feminine doesn't mean you're weak, it just means you're proud to be a woman."

All three of them looked at me as if they were daring me to refute her. I had the sense that if they were guys they would have pounded fists with each other, but I decided this might not be the time to point that out.

"Feminine is good," I said at last.

Cheyenne stood. "I'll be right back. I need to use the ladies' room." She'd smiled as she said the words and offered a warm emphasis to the word *ladies*. She left for the hall.

Lien-hua and Tessa watched her sweep away. When she was out of sight, Lien-hua said, "She's not subtle is she?"

Nope, I thought.

"Nope," Tessa said.

"I'm glad she's on our team," Lien-hua said evenly. Then she went back to her meal.

But I noticed that she avoided eye contact with me as she did.

70

After dinner and dessert, we gathered in the living room, and when Lien-hua noted the chess set, Cheyenne complimented Tessa's skill. "She's quite a player."

"Not compared to you," Tessa said. "Just to Patrick."

"Thanks," I said.

Lien-hua picked up the black queen. "I learned to play years ago, but I've never been very good."

"I'm sure Detective Warren could teach you some moves to improve your game," Tessa said.

"I'm sure she could." She set down the queen.

A touch of silence.

"So," Cheyenne said, "your name, Lien-hua, it's lovely."

"Thank you. It means lotus."

"The flower."

"Yes."

Though there was no outward antagonism in their words, I had the sense that the two women were verbally fencing.

Cheyenne looked reflectively at the far wall. Then, concentrating on remembering the words, she said, "Flowers are the hieroglyphics of angels. Loved by all men for the beauty of their character, though few can decipher even fragments of their meaning."

"That's beautiful," Lien-hua said, clearly impressed. "What's it from?"

"I'm not sure, exactly; it's a quote I read once by Lydia M. Child. I'm not a huge reader, but I sometimes stumble across something that's worth holding on to, and I make sure I don't let it slip away." As she said the words, she was looking at me, leaving me to interpret them on more than one level. Then she glanced at Lien-hua. "I like the line about deciphering fragments of their meaning."

"I'd love a copy of it."

"Absolutely."

But at the moment Cheyenne didn't take the initiative to write it down.

More fencing. This time with silence.

"So, speaking of lotuses," Tessa said, "the Lotus Sutra is a teaching, a discourse of Buddha." She paused as we all gave her our attention, then added, "Which brings up the *Nāgas*."

"Nāgas?" Cheyenne said.

"According to legend," Tessa explained, "the Lotus Sutra was given by Buddha himself and kept hidden for five hundred years in the land of the Nāgas until humans were finally ready to understand it."

"What are Nāgas?" asked Cheyenne.

With a glance, Tessa deferred to Lien-hua, who answered, "A Nāga is a serpent. The word is typically translated *dragon*, but a better translation would probably be *cobra*. Usually, Nāgas are kind to humans, unless they're provoked. Then, they can be truly malicious. They guard treasure and represent immortality."

"Yup," Tessa said. "You wouldn't want to cross a Nāga while it's guarding its treasure."

"I'll keep that in mind," Cheyenne said.

With all of the subtext shooting through the room, I wondered how that meal last night between the two women had really gone.

After a moment, Cheyenne, the faithful Catholic, asked Lien-hua, "So, are you Buddhist?"

"No. My mother was." Lien-hua paused. "I don't mean this to be flippant, but I guess I'd say I'm between religions."

Cheyenne waited for her to go on, but when Lien-hua didn't elaborate, she said, "Well, it's a journey."

When Christie and I were dating, she used to tell me that when we pigeonhole people by their faiths, everyone loses out. "Multiculturalism doesn't build bridges," she said. "It puts people into boxes." Maybe it wasn't always true, but I could see it beginning to happen right now.

I wondered if Lien-hua was thinking something along those

lines, because she went on to say, "Last February when Pat and I were working a case in San Diego, I was attacked and left in an empty pool—one that was nearly thirteen feet deep. While I was unconscious, a man who'd already killed at least eight other women—including my sister—chained my ankle to the bottom, and when I awoke he began filling the pool with water."

"That's horrible," Cheyenne said softly, her voice full of empathy. "What happened?"

"Well, I was terrified, of course, and when the water was going over my head, I . . ." Lien-hua hesitated, and I think we could all tell how difficult it was for her to share this story. "Being raised in a Buddhist home, I wasn't even sure if God existed, but I prayed, and someone arrived just in time to save me." Her eyes found mine just as Cheyenne's had a minute ago. "I'm still trying to sort out what all that means."

"It means," Cheyenne said, "that God still has big plans for you."

"I hope you're right."

Then, the conversation veered away from God and fear and treasure-guarding serpents and returned to the tamer territory of favorite books and movies and pastimes, and I was thankful. But not long afterward, Cheyenne mentioned that she really needed to get going. "I'll be sitting in on classes all day tomorrow," she told me. "But I can help with the case in the evening. I'll call you as soon as I'm done. At 5:00."

"Okay," I said.

After we'd all thanked her for coming and said our good-byes, she headed for the door.

I debated whether or not to offer to walk her to her car, but in the end I decided against it. Cheyenne stepped outside, and I joined Lien-hua and Tessa, who were in the kitchen putting away the dishes and leftovers.

A few moments later I heard Cheyenne's car backing down the driveway.

And then she was gone.

71

Brad entered the gas station to get a Mountain Dew.

The clerk glanced up, and for a moment his eyes lingered on Brad's face, at the deep scars. The man, whose name tag had only his first name, Juarez, looked a little uneasy then went back to chewing a glob of gum and texting someone on his phone.

Brad found the soda, brought it to the counter. Set it down. Waited.

Juarez didn't bother to acknowledge him, until, in no particular hurry, he finished sending his text message. Then, without making eye contact with Brad, he muttered with a thick Spanish accent, "That all?"

"Did you ever think about the two things technology tries to deliver us from?" Brad asked.

Juarez finally looked at him. Worked the gum back and forth in his mouth. "*Qué?*"

Brad gestured toward the clerk's phone. "Technology. Whatever field you choose—industry, science, medicine, entertainment—technological advances are there either to create more diversions to occupy our time or to relieve our discomfort: so either to construct a fuller life or an easier one. Would you agree with that?"

He shook his head and mumbled something in Spanish. Brad didn't know the language well but recognized some of the words. He placed his hands flat on the counter beside the soda can. "Paradoxically, do you know the two aspects of human experience that offer us the most wisdom?"

Juarez looked past him then, scanning the store as if he were expecting someone to step out and explain the joke to him. This time as he spoke to Brad, his tone turned caustic. "Did you want anything else with your Mountain Dew, *señor*—" Once again he slipped into speaking to Brad rather rudely in Spanish. Brad waited, studying his eyes, until he was done.

Eventually, Brad saw the smirk fade and a wisp of uneasiness settle in. "Solitude and adversity," he said softly. "Those are the two things that lead us to wisdom. Enough silence to facilitate reflection on the meaning of life, enough pain to cause us to consider its brevity. Quietude and suffering."

Brad still had both hands flat against the countertop, and Juarez was letting his eyes drift from Brad's hands to his face, to his hands. He shifted his weight.

"And yet, every technological advance is another desperate attempt to remove either silence or pain from our lives. Our society is constantly trying to cure itself of the very two things we need the most. Does that sound civilized to you?"

The clerk did not reply. But he had stopped chewing his gum.

Brad slid the soda toward him. "This will be all."

Juarez promptly rang up the purchase. Brad paid for it, then walked to the door, paused, flipped the "open" sign around so that the word "closed" faced the highway, then turned to the clerk. "Maybe I'll have one more thing. Before I go."

72

Tessa told me and Lien-hua that she was going to call it a day, even though I think we all knew she wouldn't be heading to bed quite yet, then she left us alone in the living room. After a few minutes, Lien-hua mentioned she could use some fresh air, and I suggested we go to the back deck.

As we entered the cool night I noticed there was just enough light from the moon for me to see across the yard to the stone wall where the doe had appeared yesterday morning.

Grace and beauty. Pursued by fear.

A small glance of kitchen light slipped out the window.

For a little while Lien-hua and I spoke about the case, focusing on the possible links between the locations of the crimes. "I think we need to speak with the former vice president," she concluded.

"Yes," I said. "But I might not be the right one to do that. Apparently, he's on Lansing's side in this custody dispute."

"I'll talk to Margaret. We'll take care of it."

A moment slid by, but it didn't hold any awkwardness. The silence between us felt safe and familiar, almost inviting.

At last she said, "I never really had the chance to talk with you about Calvin's death. Are you doing all right?"

"He was a good friend. He lived a full life, but even if he hadn't been attacked like he was, he didn't have much time left. He had congestive heart failure."

She saw right through my answer. "That sounds like something a counselor told you to say. How are you doing, really?"

I hesitated. "I'm doing all right. I miss him, but it is what it is."

"Grief has different hues, Pat." No psychoanalysis in her voice, just friendship. Understanding.

"And they change over time."

"Yes, they do."

Then we were quiet again.

The night was full of stillness and crickets and dewy moonlight.

"What are you thinking?" she asked at last.

"I was thinking about him again. Calvin. About the last time we were together before his coma."

She waited for me to go on.

"We talked about justice, and I remember him asking me, 'How far is one willing to go to see justice is carried out?' I'll never forget that question."

She processed that. "There's no easy answer to that."

"No, there isn't."

I recalled the promise I'd made to Grant Sikora that I would not let Richard Basque hurt any more women, a promise I probably shouldn't have made, but nevertheless felt compelled to carry out. And I remembered Ralph's take on preemptive justice: "Identify a threat and eliminate it before it eliminates you."

"Or someone else," I'd added.

I walked to the edge of the deck, away from the light that fell from the kitchen window. "What do you think about preemptive justice?"

"I don't believe we should judge people on what they might do," she said, "only on what they have done."

"And yet plotting a terrorist attack is a crime, right?"

A slight pause. "Yes, it is."

I turned toward her. "And so is conspiracy—to commit murder, fraud, corrupt public morals, and so on. In those cases, we hold people accountable for their intentions, not their actions. In almost every country in the world, you don't have to take any—"

"Yes, I know: concrete or specific steps to put the crime into effect and you can still be convicted of conspiracy." Her words were terse, but I sensed that she was more upset about the laws than at me for pointing them out. She went on, "But just because something is illegal doesn't make it morally wrong; just because something is legal doesn't make it morally right. In the 1940s it was legal to kill Jews in Germany."

Cheyenne's words from our dinner conversation must have still been on my mind because I found myself thinking of the Middle Eastern countries where I'd consulted on cases and the Islamic laws that make it illegal to treat women with the dignity and respect they deserve. "That's true," I said. "Just because something is illegal doesn't mean it's wrong."

"And in the cases you mentioned," she replied, "crimes of conspiracy or plotting terrorism—people are convicted for their thoughts and intentions, not for their actions. But at different times all of us have desires and intentions that are immoral."

I thought I could see where this was going. "So if you take preemptive justice to its logical end, all of us would end up in prison."

"That's overstating things, Pat, but my point is, we can change our minds. That's part of what makes us human. Call it preemptive justice if you want to, but I don't think there's any justice in predicting what someone might do and then punishing him for it. It's not our job to police people's thoughts or imprison them for things they haven't done."

I was quiet.

She looked at me with concern. "What is this about?"

"It's something that's been on my mind lately."

"Something you want to talk about?"

"Something I need to think about."

Even though I wasn't sure it would help get my mind off Basque and my promise to Sikora, I transitioned the conversation back to the case and reviewed the results of my geoprofile, but all the while I sensed that Lien-hua was listening to something that lay beneath my words; that she was reading my inner thoughts and . . . well . . . my truer, deeper motives.

Brad climbed into his car and started the engine.

He'd made sure the gas station's video surveillance footage was destroyed and that the young man who'd been working behind the counter would not be sharing news of their conversation with anyone.

He guided the car onto the road and had driven about a quarter of a mile when he heard the explosion behind him and, in the rearview, saw the plume of fire mushrooming toward the sky.

Based on the rural location, the lack of traffic, the time of night, and the probable emergency services response time, he figured it would be at least fifteen minutes before any fire suppression units or ambulances arrived.

He made the anonymous call to WXTN News, crushed the prepaid cell phone beneath the wheels of the car, discarded the splintered fragments of technology in the woods. Then, he drove to a parking lot beside the entrance to the state park eight miles down the road from the burning gas station.

To wait for Astrid.

When I was done summarizing the geoprofile, I asked Lien-hua about the psychological profile she'd been working on, and she commiserated with me about the difficulty of forming a profile for multiple offenders. I agreed that I couldn't even begin to imagine how hard that would be.

"Is that a touch of cynicism I hear?"

"No, admiration."

Inside the house, Tessa flicked off the kitchen lights, leaving the deck unlit. Moonlight washed across the yard and gently embraced Lien-hua. I told her, "Understanding people, probing their motives, it's not something I've ever been . . ."

"Very excited about."

"Very good at. I read people about as good as I use chop-sticks."

She looked at me closely. "If you were profiling me, Pat, what would you say?"

"Oh, I can't do that."

"Give it a shot."

"Lien-hua, I'm neither trained nor qualified to—"

"Humor me." Her voice had a light smile in it. "Then we can both just laugh about it when you're done."

"Let's just laugh about it now; save some time."

She tilted her head. "How about this: when you're finished, I'll profile you."

"You're not going to let this drop, are you?"

"I'm a persistent woman. I usually end up getting what I want."

Oh, boy.

I gave in. "All right. Let's see . . . The suspect is—"

"Suspect?"

"Of course."

"What am I suspected of?"

Let's see . . . crimes of passion . . . stealing hearts . . .

"Just trying to be official here." Then I cleared my throat slightly. "The suspect is of Asian descent, early thirties, slim build—"

"Thank you."

"You're welcome. Black hair. Athletic. Attractive."

She nodded her appreciation for that last one. "You're doing very nicely so far."

"Thank you. Poised but not overbearing, she has a deeply reflective mind, keen mental acuity . . ."

I debated whether or not to go on, to say the things I was really thinking. If I did, if I said them, a line would be drawn through the sand of this moment, there was no doubt about that.

Tell her, Pat.

You'll regret it if you don't, if you shy away.

"Is that all?" she asked.

"No." I took a small breath. "She feels both strongest and weakest, safest and most free when she's in the arms of a confident man.

She's a woman who can take care of herself but is flattered and honored when a man offers himself to her, to take care of her."

She stood quietly beside me in the moonlight.

I waited for her to reply, heart pounding in my chest.

"Your turn," I said.

"Caucasian." Her voice was soft. Velvet. "Mid-thirties. Tall. Athletic."

"Handsome," I offered, in case she needed any additional ideas.

"Hmm . . . Good-looking. In a scruffy sort of way."

"Thank you."

"You're welcome. He believes in justice, is courageous enough to look for truth despite the consequences, and gets shot too many times because he doesn't like waiting for backup."

"You've been talking with Tessa."

"Maybe."

She paused, spoke more slowly now. "He loves life deeply, passionately, and does not do anything halfway." She hesitated but then went on, "Since the death of his wife, he's had trouble entrusting his feelings to others, and that's caused him to drift away from the people he cares about most. He aches for intimacy yet is losing confidence that he will ever find it again."

The truth of her words shattered me and lifted me. A healing wound—

"Still," she said, "his heart has moved past Christie, and he's in love with another suspect, but he's confused because he doesn't want to take what she's not willing to give."

We were both quiet then, and the sound of crickets beneath the porch filled the space left open in the night.

He's in love with another suspect . . .

He aches for intimacy . . .

But then her comments from Tuesday night came to mind: "We need to move on . . . People see each other, they break up, they find a way to work together again."

I found myself resisting her and giving in at the same time, the strange give and take of attraction. "And what is she willing to give?" I said softly. "This subject with whom he is in love?"

Her eyes left mine, wandered toward the deep woods. "First, a question."

"Yes?"

"I need to know." Then a long pause. "Are you seeing her?"

I knew immediately. "Cheyenne?"

"Yes."

"We're just friends."

She waited for more.

No woman wants to be strung along while you play the field looking for someone better.

"It's true." I felt no duplicity in saying the words, but, because I knew how Cheyenne felt about me, I did feel a ripple of sadness. It seemed like no matter what I chose to say to Lien-hua, I would end up hurting someone in the end.

I repeated, maybe for Lien-hua's sake, maybe for mine, "Cheyenne and I are just friends."

"Pat, when a woman looks at a man the way she looks at you, she's more than a friend. Or she wants to be."

My heart was hammering, not just from the desire to take Lien-hua in my arms and see where the moment might lead, but also from the terrifying truth of her words: *He's in love . . . he aches for intimacy . . . he's confused . . .*

"At one time," I said, "we were almost more than friends, but . . ." There was so much to say, to explain, but right now, only one thing really mattered, and I let myself say it. "Whenever I was alone with her, I ended up thinking about you."

Lien-hua gazed at me in the gentle night, the moonlight playing in her rich ebony hair. "If I were to ask you what you want, Patrick Bowers, right now, in this moment, what would you say?"

The answer was simple. Clear. Immediate. "That I want to be with you." I took a tight, uncertain breath. "What about you? What do you want?"

Softly, she put her hand on the side of my neck, her thumb

gracing my cheek, and for a long tenuous moment she looked into my eyes, hiding nothing.

Then, she drew me close and answered my question with a kiss.

And I answered her back.

73

Astrid joined Brad in the car he'd stolen especially for tonight.

"Are you ready?"

"Yes," he said.

She slipped on the wig.

Tucked her hair beneath it.

As far as they knew, the Marine at the gate to Quantico had never seen Brad, so that wouldn't be a problem, but the soldier had almost certainly seen her.

Long ago she'd discovered that even though women tend to remember the features of a man's face, men recognize women not so much by their facial features but rather by their figure, clothing, and hair. Most women learn this eventually: if you change your hair color, put on a distinctively different outfit, lose some weight, the men in your life, at least those on the periphery, will barely recognize you.

And so she was confident that tonight, even if the guard had already seen the woman she was impersonating, it wouldn't matter. Especially since Astrid was using the fake driver's license Brad had acquired and the same model car as the woman drove—he'd even borrowed the actual plates from her vehicle for this evening.

"She won't notice that they're missing," he'd told Astrid yesterday. "No one would notice that their license plates were changed. It's one of those things you just don't pay attention to."

"Why not just steal her car?"

"Because, that she would notice."

She'd given him permission to do it.

She finished with the wig. "I'll take the wheel."

"Okay."

He got out of the car, and she slid into the driver's seat. When he'd climbed in again, she asked him, "Do you have him? Is he in the—"

"Yes."

"And the dog?"

"It's all taken care of."

"And you have the shovel?"

"Yes."

Then Astrid aimed the car toward the entrance to the FBI Academy.

Tonight, the greatest taunt, the greatest thrill of all—an extra body in the FBI Academy's body farm. And as she and her man buried it, she would tell him about their child.

Predator.

Prey.

Death and life.

The climax of their game. The cycle of all things.

People see what they expect to see.

With the actual license plates and the same model car, with the driver's license, wig, and similar outfit, she did not expect that the sentry would give her any trouble. After all, why hassle two National Academy students returning to their dorm?

But just in case the Marine did, her partner had his Walther P99 hidden beneath the jacket lying on his lap. And more than one body would be left behind at the farm.

Predator. Prey. Death and life.

Their child.

The cycle of all things.

"When we get there," she told him, "I've got a surprise for you. Something I need to tell you."

◾

As I watched Lien-hua drive away, I tried to sort out my feelings.

Holding her, kissing her, had brought everything back.

The hope.

The electric desire.

The confusion.

As well as the struggles to make things work and the biting pain I'd felt when we parted ways last month.

Maybe she was right about me, maybe I hadn't been able to open up the deep parts of my heart since Christie's death and that's what had caused me to drift away from the people I loved.

All because of a lingering hue of grief still crawling around inside me.

The lights of her car flickered into and out of the trees. Fog was circling into the night and made the taillights look like blurred brushstrokes from a watercolor painting.

Few can decipher even fragments of their meaning . . .

Finally, the night mist swallowed the car's lights, and I returned to the living room, where I found Tessa lounging on the couch channel surfing.

Click.

Click. Through the stations.

The Sherlock Holmes book and a copy of *The Strange Case of Dr. Jekyll and Mr. Hyde* sat next to her on a pillow.

"You said good night to her?" she asked.

"I did."

Click.

I took a seat on the couch. "I'm not sure if I should thank you or be mad at you for inviting those two over here without asking me first."

"Let's go with the thanking me one." She landed on the news. A gas station nearby had exploded, and the authorities were speculating that it had been caused by a gas leak from an underground storage tank.

"From now on, keep me in the loop," I said.

"Right on." Click.

Click. A baseball game in extra innings.

"Did it help?" she asked. "Having them both here?"

Honestly, it seemed to make them simpler and more complicated at the same time, but I just said, "Go back."

"To what?"

"The fire."

Click. Click. She found it.

A young man who'd been working at the station was missing, and it was feared he'd been trapped inside. Gas lines were fueling the fire so the fire crews were having a hard time suppressing it.

The gas station was located on a road that ran along the outer perimeter of the Quantico Marine Corps Base.

"So," she said. "More confusing."

"Yes." My attention was on the news.

Timing.

Location.

It's random, Pat. Forget it.

Tessa waved her hand in front of my face. "Hey. You still there?"

"Sorry. What were you saying?"

"No, you were: that things are more confusing now that you made out with Agent Jiang."

I blinked. "I wasn't going to say that."

"You were thinking it."

"No, I—you were spying on us."

She shook her head. "Not this time, but thanks for confirming my suspicions."

Man, I hate it when she does that.

I took the remote from her, turned off the television, and tried to sound stern and parental. "Go to bed, young lady."

"All right, Dad."

A few minutes later as I was getting ready for bed myself, I realized that the St. Francis of Assisi pendant Cheyenne had given me was still in my pocket.

I pulled it out, hesitated for a moment, then set it in my dresser drawer and slowly eased it shut.

■

The Marine standing guard at the front gate to Quantico leaned toward the car window. "Good evening, ma'am."

"Hello."

He accepted their driver's licenses and shone his light toward Brad. "Sir."

"Good evening, Sergeant."

Astrid watched him pause slightly as he noticed Brad's scars. He looked away, but only after staring a moment too long.

He studied the licenses. "From Houston, huh?"

"Yes," she said. "We're here for the National Academy."

"We're staying in Washington Dormitory," Brad added.

The Marine didn't look at him again, just compared their names to those on his list. Made note of the car's license plates. "Have a good night, Ms. Larotte. Mr. Collins." He returned their fake IDs to them.

"Thank you," she said.

And he waved them through.

No trouble. Just as Astrid had anticipated.

Brad had printed a map of the Academy grounds that afternoon. So now, as they passed out of sight of the checkpoint, he pulled it out and studied it under a flashlight. "Turn left," he said.

He directed her past the FBI Forensics Lab, past Hogan's Alley to a gravel lot at the end of the road.

She parked beside a trail disappearing into the mist-filled woods.

The entrance to the body farm.

She left the wig between the seats, grabbed a flashlight of her own, and climbed out of the car.

74

Astrid heard her story unfolding in her head.

    Fog had fingered its way between the trees and inter-
    twined in the dense, thorny underbrush beside the
    path.
        For a moment it made her think of the fairy tale
    where the misty hedge encircles the castle impris-
    oning the sleeping princess—the girl who is oblivi-
    ous to all the princes who've failed to find her; the
    princes whose bodies hang in the deep, secret heart
    of the thicket.

She paused to look at a body lying face-down in a stream about twenty feet to her left.

Brad stopped walking. Stood beside her.

He'd suggested that they find the location first, then return to the car to get everything they needed, rather than "dragging 'em through the woods."

It might have been a waste of time, but Astrid had put up with the idea. Honestly, at this point she was thinking more about the news she was going to share with him than about the young man they'd come here to bury.

The uncomfortable odor of death drifted through the forest.

Brad consulted his map. "Okay. I'm thinking we head west about two hundred yards or so. No class is scheduled to visit that area until Monday."

"How do you know that?"

"Research," he said simply.

"Let me see that."

He handed her the map, and she tipped her flashlight beam

across it. He stood beside her. "No," she said, "we should just do it here."

"I was thinking it might be better over—"

"No."

After a moment. "All right."

"Let's go get the—"

The deep, sharp prick on the side of her neck startled her; shocked her, made her jerk backward. "What the—" Her hand flew instinctively to her neck, found the needle still protruding from it. She would have yanked it out, but it was embedded deeply and she was already feeling dizzy.

Her hands dropped to her sides.

Brad had his arms out to catch her. "Easy."

She was aware, but somehow unaware, of the map and flashlight she'd been holding spinning to the ground. She must have let go of them.

Must have . . .

Now her legs were giving way and Brad was supporting her. "Don't fight it, Astrid," he said. "Don't worry, it's what we used on the guard the other night, what I used on Mollie. It won't kill you."

"What are you . . ." The words felt thick and raw in her mouth.

He was lowering her to the ground. "Shh. Stay calm. All will be well."

She was on her back now and he was removing the needle from her neck. "Just relax," she heard him say, or thought she did. Nothing was certain anymore.

Time rippled forward and backward. She moved her mouth, tried to speak, but nothing came out. A fairy tale. The thick fog seemed to enter her, become part of her.

And the last thing she saw before the world disappeared was her lover brushing a stray tendril of hair from her face, kneeling beside her in the veiled moonlight, telling her softly, softly, to go to sleep.

75

I lay propped in bed, my computer on my lap, exploring one of the as-of-yet unmapped caverns of this case.

Several of the neuroscience articles Rodale had sent me cited the Nobel-prize-winning research of Benjamin Libet, who'd done experiments in the late twentieth-century on initiation of action, intention, volitional acts, and consciousness.

Now I was scouring the Internet, reading about his work.

Apparently, Dr. Libet would record unconscious neural impulses while research participants anticipated and then performed simple tasks such as tapping a button or squeezing a ball. For example he might tell them, "As soon as you are aware of which button you wish to press, do so."

By noting on a cathode ray oscilloscope the millisecond at which the participant was first aware of the urge to act and then measuring that against the brain's electrical activity (and taking into account the time it took for their muscles to respond), he would compare the timing of the unconscious neural activity to that of the participant's awareness of their intention to act.

And he found something surprising.

In almost every case, unconscious neural synapses preceded the conscious choice, or volitional act, that the person made—usually by about half a second.

Some skeptics have pointed out that the simple act of being observed or of rehearsing in your mind how you will respond during the experiment could be partially responsible for the precognitive neural responses. However, if you took the research findings at face value, you'd be forced to conclude that the unconscious mind determined the action or, to put it bluntly, a decision was made, and then five hundred milliseconds later, the test subject believed that she was making it.

The conscious mind took credit for a course of action that the unconscious had already determined.

And that's where things got interesting.

Scientists have long known that some spinal reflexes, such as pulling your hand away from a flame, happen without a decision or any rational thought processes. But now, in the wake of Dr. Libet's experiments and the recent discoveries in neuroscience, many scientists were apparently becoming convinced that complex decision-making also happens unconsciously, as a result of genetic coding being influenced by an individual's environment and the context of a person's experience and conditioning.

An uneasy thought began to squirm around inside of me.

This line of thinking—that our response to stimuli is shaped solely by natural processes: genetic makeup, brain chemistry, and neural synapses that are triggered by certain environmental cues— would mean that in all practicality, we are not free to consciously choose our actions. And if we are not free to choose, we are not at liberty to chart the course of our lives.

The inevitable conclusion, of course, was that "free will" would be an illusion.

And consequently, people would not be morally responsible for their behavior, because, in a sense, they would simply be acting out of instinct. After all, it would be unjust to hold someone accountable for something over which he had no control.

A few online searches confirmed what I feared: some killers had already called on neuroscientists to testify that their behavior was, in essence, hard-wired into their brains and that, given the environmental cues to which they were exposed, they had no choice but to act in the manner that they had. Thus, they could not be held responsible for the crime.

Because they were acting out of instinct . . .

An instinct for evil.

And astonishingly, this defense had been successful in at least half a dozen capital murder cases since October of last year; and now that the precedent had been set, it would undoubtedly become a more and more popular defense.

Science meets justice.

And justice loses.

But of course it wasn't science itself that was battling justice, but rather the interpretation of one specific set of scientific experiments.

Yet it appeared that in this case, that was all it took.

The implications that this could have on criminal investigation and justice systems throughout the world was staggering.

Rapists, pedophiles, human rights violators could argue that they weren't able to refrain from their actions because they were genetically determined to act the way they had, given the environmental cues present at the time of the crime. Therefore they should not be held accountable for their natural, instinctual response.

Cavern after cavern appeared before me . . . the Gunderson Foundation's metacognition research . . . Dr. Libet's intentionality experiments . . . the Project Rukh neurological findings . . . Congressman Fischer's commitment to "a more progressive approach to curbing criminal behavior . . ."

For nearly an hour I considered the relationships between all of the dark tunnels of the case, and saw a number of possible directions they might be leading, but I ended up mired in conjecture rather than leaning on conclusions buttressed by solid evidence.

In time, the emotional toll of the day began to wear on me. I felt my concentration ebbing and exhaustion taking over.

At last, I set the computer aside and closed my eyes, but sleep did not come easily as I found myself drifting into and out of dreams of dead chimps and bloody luggage and black rain slanting around me and splashing like bleeding shadows on the ground.

While nearby, gorillas smashed mirrors into angular shards that reflected a splintered, skewed reality.

That I had become an intimate part of.

76

She woke up slowly.
Back to the world. Back to herself.
She was lying on the ground. She could tell that much, lying on her back. Her eyes were closed and her eyelids felt oppressively heavy, too heavy to open. She tried to move, but her body didn't respond.
Everything within her, around her, was a thick, vague dream. She smelled the moist, piney scent of a forest, laced with the harsh stench of death.
The body farm.
She heard a damp, crunching sound nearby, in a small rhythm with itself. Grating, pausing. Grating again.
But all the smells, all the sounds were contained in a warm, liquid darkness that curled around, slowly, inside her head.
And though her eyes were still closed, worms of color skirted in front of her, floated through the strange visions we all have while passing from sleep into the waking world.
Time passed.
With every moment the foul smell of decay grew worse.
More of the rough scraping sound beside her.
Scrape and crunch.
Until finally, and with much effort, she opened her eyes and managed to tilt her head toward the sound.
And in the diaphanous, mist-drenched moonlight, she saw a man nearby.
Digging.

Brad must have noticed the movement as she turned her head toward him because he stopped what he was doing, drove the shovel's blade into the ground, and rested one arm against the handle.

"It's good to see you awake," he said. "I was concerned I might have used too much Propotol, that your heart might have stopped. I'm really glad it didn't. If you would have died, it would have completely ruined my surprise."

"What?" she mumbled. "No . . ." Not because she didn't understand, but because she was just beginning to.

"I'll explain everything in a few minutes." He raised the shovel again. "Let me just finish up here first."

He scooped out a few more shovelfuls of dirt, and a sharp, rancid smell crawled across the ground.

The stench of rotten flesh was overwhelming, and Astrid felt like throwing up, but for some reason her body did not let her. Her throat clenched, but she didn't vomit. And Brad didn't appear bothered at all by the smell.

She had no idea how that could be.

He knelt and began alternating using a small brush and a gardening trowel to remove dirt from the hole.

Astrid's eyes were starting to adjust to the night now, and she could tell by his movements that the hole wasn't deep.

And she believed she knew what lay inside.

```
The passage of time began to erase the weakness that
had been pinning her to the ground. She could move
her head more easily now, and she felt her strength
gradually returning to her legs, her arms. She could
wiggle her fingers and tip her feet to the side.
    Misty moonlight soaked the forest all around her.
```

Though she wasn't strong enough to sit up, or fight, or run, at least she was finally able to think more clearly.

"What are you doing?" Her voice sounded weak. Distant. As if someone else were saying the words for her.

"I'm finishing what I started when I first found you on DuaLife." He was still digging with the garden tools. "When I first chose you."

"No," she muttered. "I chose you."

"Yes," he said ambiguously, but she could tell he wasn't actually agreeing with her. "For a while I was concerned that you might catch on, guess my intentions, predict the ending." He was troweling out dirt as he spoke. "But it looks like you must have been too distracted by your little power trip to notice."

He finished his work in the hole, set the trowel and brush aside.

She tried to make her voice sound steady, controlled, authoritative. "Take me back home. We'll talk about this at the house."

He walked around her so that he was no longer between her and the hole. Then he knelt beside her. "Do you know what causes fear?"

She was trying to gather her strength to sit up. "Brad, take me home."

"When a person feels threatened in that place—that physical, emotional, or psychological place—"

"Brad—"

He put a finger to her lips. "Threatened in that place where she feels the most secure, there, in that moment, fear is born. And the more profound her sense of safety, the more acute the fear."

"No," she said. "It's . . . you don't understand—"

Softly, he brushed aside a fleck of dirt that must have dropped onto her cheek while he was shoveling. "That power, that sense of absolute mastery over life and death that you've become so addicted to, let's see how you handle the opposite."

He slid one hand beneath her back, the other beneath her legs, and lifted her.

She tried to squirm free but hadn't yet regained enough strength. "I don't . . ." Her words faded away. "I have to tell you something . . ."

He carried her toward the hole. "Yes?"

"I'm pregnant, Brad. Stop this. Now."

He set her down beside the hole, but he did not reply, simply straightened out her arms and legs.

"I'm going to have your baby."

The smell was terrible, overpowering.

She saw him reach to the side, into the darkness, retrieve a gag.

"I said I'm pregnant!"

He was leaning over her. "Astrid, you know how this goes. The victim begs, grovels, tells the oppressor whatever she can think of to get him to change his mind, but it's not going to work. We both know it doesn't—"

"I'll prove it." Desperation shot through her words. "Take me home!"

He paused and seemed to consider her request.

"It's true," she said. Despite herself, her voice cracked. "Please, please."

"If you are telling the truth, if you really are pregnant, then this night will be even more special to me." He bent over her and stretched out the gag. "Two for the price of one." And before she could cry out or yell for help, he forced the gag into her mouth and secured it in place.

"Welcome to the fishbowl."

Then he rolled her face-first into the hole.

On top of the rotting corpse.

77

She would have screamed if she were not gagged.

She tried to push herself up, struggled to, but was still too weak, and he was pressing her down firmly, a knee bent against the small of her back.

"Astrid, I'd like you to meet Riah Everson," he said. "She was a thirty-eight-year-old mother of three. Died from a head injury two days ago after she slipped on a doll that her youngest daughter left at the top of the stairs."

Her cheek was resting against the moist skin of the corpse's face. Desperately, desperately, she struggled to get away, but the lingering sedative and his weight pinned her down. Two fat grubs wriggled across the dead woman's putrid skin, and she felt them squirm momentarily against her own cheek before dropping out of sight.

Again she felt like retching, again she did not.

He was positioning her right arm, laying something across her wrist, but he must have seen her throat clench. "It was a little hard to figure that part out. With the smell, I knew you'd instinctively regurgitate, and with that cloth in your mouth, you'd choke on your vomit and die. And that's really not what we're looking for here."

She felt a strap tighten around her wrist. She tried, tried, tried to pull free, but he'd buckled it securely in place. Fastening her wrist to something beneath her.

The arm of the dead woman.

Another scream erupted from her throat but went nowhere.

"There aren't many drugs that paralyze the gag reflex. I'm not sure the Dotracaine I gave you will work. It's supposed to last sixteen hours. Let's hope so."

She frantically twisted her head to the side to try and work the gag loose, but it did not come free, and from seeing the proficiency of his work in the past, she doubted she would ever be able to get the gag off without the use of her hands.

He was holding down her other arm now, binding it to Riah Everson's. "I wish I could take credit for this idea, but actually the Romans came up with it. They would strap a corpse to the back of a guilty man and make him carry it around until he was dead as well. They didn't understand infection back then, but they did understand death. The Romans were also fans of crucifixion. They did not let the guilty get off lightly."

He was almost done with her left arm. She tried to yank it free from his grip. Useless.

"Remember Saint Paul? We spoke about this on Wednesday. He referred to this technique: 'The evil I do not wish, this I do. I am a wretched man! Who will rescue me from this body of death?' You see how he does that? The body of death? It's a play on words—sin metonymically becomes the dead body he's carrying around."

He tugged the second strap tight. Buckled it.

Then went to work on her legs.

78

After Brad finished with her ankles, he looped the final strap under the neck of the dead woman, and then around the neck of his lover.

As he did, Astrid, who was lying facedown, managed to lift her cheek slightly away from the corpse. Brad grabbed a handful of her hair and forced her head down to keep her face properly positioned as he buckled the strap around her neck with his other hand.

He didn't want to constrict Astrid's breathing so he was gentle, careful, as he bound her neck to the neck of Riah Everson's corpse.

Then he let go of her hair, stood, and pulled out his cell phone to get some video.

For later.

He made sure he got some close-ups. Thousands of law enforcement officers would eventually watch this tape in the classrooms of the FBI Academy, and he wanted to make sure they would be able to get a good look at Astrid's pretty, terror-stricken face.

At last he pocketed the phone and went for the shovel. "Just so you know." He tossed a shovelful of dirt onto her legs. "I won't put any soil over your face. I don't want you to suffocate. And it's not too cold tonight, so hypothermia might not be an immediate concern. It'll probably end up being the scavengers that bother you the most. I imagine there's plenty of them in a body farm. With the degree of Riah's decomp, it shouldn't take them long to arrive. I'm afraid that by this weekend, you'll be a permanent addition to this farm."

He packed some dirt around Astrid's ankles and wrists to make certain she wouldn't be able to wiggle free.

"By the way," he said, "I never had a pet Sheltie." He was snugging the dirt around her feet. "No dog, although there were times when I entertained myself with some of the neighborhood cats."

He could tell she was trying to cry out, and he was pleased by how little sound she was able to make.

After satisfying himself that she was secure, he tossed a thin layer of dirt across her, scattered the remainder of the soil nearby, and spread leaves over the area to hide the evidence of the shoveling.

At last he stood back and studied his work.

Astrid's head was still visible, but unless you knew where to look, it wasn't something you would notice. Her back was jerkily rising and falling as she drew in short, frantic breaths. Based on the rapidity of her respiration, he guessed that she might hyperventilate, but he'd studied human anatomy enough to know that even if she did pass out, she would almost certainly regain consciousness again. At least for the first ten or twelve hours. The human body is amazingly adept at survival.

He began to gather his things.

She had suited him well in the role he'd chosen her to play.

Yes.

He'd killed before he met her, of course he had, but this had been the longest, the most exquisite game yet—all of that time playing the submissive one, the easily controlled, subservient one, all of it had paid off so nicely in gaining her implicit trust.

Danger and play.

Yes.

Exquisite.

Astrid tried to cry out again, but it wasn't possible. She would never make another recognizable sound, never say another word.

He leaned over her one last time. "At first I was planning to take you to the basement, to the room I spent so much time remodeling, but then I decided it would be more fun like this." He ran his hand softly through her hair. "And it was more fun this way, wasn't it?"

She tried to shake his hand free. Failed.

As he'd planned for this night, he'd anticipated seeing panic in her eyes, but the depth of terror and final desperation he now saw in her moonlit face was even more satisfying than what he'd imagined.

A tear slanted down the side of her nose, and he gently wiped it away. "Sleep tight, Astrid."

Then he picked up the shovels and trowel and walked through the fog-enshrouded moonlight to the car.

No, this wasn't the climax to the story.

Things were just beginning to get interesting.

79

Friday, June 13
7:29 a.m.

Considering all the traumatic experiences Tessa had been through during the last couple days, I knew she needed sleep, so I was careful not to wake her as I put on some coffee.

Stepping into the bathroom, I took my meds and checked the gunshot wound. My arm ached, of course, but the pain had morphed from sharp blasts of fire to a deep tenderness that ran all through the left side of my body. A thick, continuous blur of pain that was impossible to ignore.

The wound itself had been draining overnight, and the bandages were now blood-soaked. I spent some time cleaning the wound, put some topical antibiotic on both the entrance and exit holes, then wrapped the arm with fresh bandages—but all of that served to make the wound itself tender and sore all over again.

As I ate breakfast, I tried to direct my attention away from my arm.

Curious about the gas station explosion, I checked the online news and discovered that the body of the young man who'd been working at the gas station, Juarez Hernandez, had been found behind the sales counter.

No sign of foul play.

That's what they said.

Another death.

Another dose of grief for another distraught family.

As I considered the possible implications of the explosion, I checked my email and noticed a message from Margaret notifying all the task force members about an 11:00 meeting at the command post. Our paths hadn't crossed since Rodale had put me back on the case, and I assumed she would not be thrilled by his decision, but I decided not to worry about that unless she brought it up.

Thankfully, another instructor was covering my classes again today, so that would give me the chance to focus the majority of my day on the case—even though, admittedly, I wasn't thrilled that the other instructor was Jake Vanderveld.

After uploading the files from Rodale and the financial reports from Fischer onto the task force's command level database, I reviewed the updates to the case. I remembered that a gas station receipt had been found in the van parked at the hotel, and when I pulled up the jpeg of it, I saw that it was from the same gas station that had exploded.

Knowing how these killers worked, I suspected they had left that receipt in the van on purpose, just to taunt us.

Or to give you a clue to another crime they're planning to commit.

A future crime.

They left the receipt from the gas station, then killed Juarez . . . left Mahan's car, then killed him later that night . . . left Mollie's purse, then killed her the next day.

Hmm.

I was reminded again of Adkins, the only murderer I'd ever faced who'd followed this pattern of leaving clues to future victims, but he was dead after an ambulance chased him to the bottom of a North Carolina gorge. Perhaps someone had found access to his case files and was imitating his pattern.

I spent more than an hour looking into that possibility but found nothing, and at 9:02 I was scrolling through yesterday's DNA reports from the lab when my phone rang.

Caller ID told me it was Angela Knight.

When I answered she didn't waste any time: "I found Richard Basque."

"What?" Immediately, I moved toward the back deck so if Tessa woke up she wouldn't overhear the conversation. "You found him? Where?"

"He's here, in DC—or at least he was an hour ago."

"Where is he now?"

"I'm not sure."

I was on the deck now, closing the door behind me. "How do you know he was in the city?"

"At first when you asked me to look for him, I did the usual—you know, looked for GPS, credit card use, reviewed airline flight manifests, routine traffic stops—nothing. I even tried the defense system's satellite video archives to see if we had footage of his car leaving Chicago; they started keeping old footage, you know—"

"Yes, for six months. I know." I was anxious to hear how she'd found him. "So you found his car?"

"No, that's the thing. I didn't." I heard her yawn and ended up doing so myself. Power of suggestion. She went on, "So I turned to the next best thing—"

"Mass transit surveillance."

"Yes." She sounded disappointed that I'd guessed what she was going to say. "I started a metasearch of the twenty largest US cities' transit video footage since Tuesday. You can't even imagine how long it takes to access some of that data. The bandwidth most of those cities still use is from—" She yawned again.

"How long have you been up, Angela?"

She thought. "I'm not sure. Anyway, there he was, walking through the Metro Central Station in DC at 7:31 this morning. I know that's over an hour and a half ago. Sorry I didn't catch it earlier."

I didn't think she needed to apologize for anything. "No, you did great. Are you sure it's him?"

"Eighty-four percent. According to Lacey."

Her computer. Good old Lacey.

"Did you tell Ralph yet?" I asked.

"I thought I'd let you do that. Considering you're the one who asked me to locate Basque."

I tried to process what she'd told me within the broader context of the case. "All right. Anything on Patricia E.?"

"Pat, I'm way behind here," she said, which was not exactly an answer. "Just before I punched in your number, I got word that Metro found a stolen car with Mollie Fischer's laptop in the backseat, and guess who gets to do the data recovery?"

"They found the computer?"

Oh yes, good.

Things were popping.

"Yes, and you're gonna love this—the car is sitting in front of police headquarters."

Why didn't that surprise me.

"Who found it?"

"Lee Anderson." He was the Metro PD officer who'd shuttled me from the hospital to my car Wednesday afternoon. The one who'd been surprised by my take on motives when we first met.

"Call me if you find anything, Angela. Thanks again. You're the best there is."

Another yawn. Once more I found myself following her lead. I wished she would stop doing that. "See you soon, Pat."

"Okay."

End call.

Obviously, in order to understand the foot traffic patterns as well as the potential pedestrian entrance and exit routes from the car, I needed to have a look at the vehicle and evaluate its orientation in respect to the neighboring streets as well as its actual distance from the entrance to the police headquarters. However, I didn't want to leave Tessa here alone, especially after yesterday when Lansing cornered her at the hotel. In addition, even though Basque had never threatened her in any way, just knowing that he was in the vicinity made me uneasy.

But I couldn't take Tessa to a secondary crime scene that was still being actively processed.

Figure that out in a few minutes.

First things first.

I punched in Ralph's number, and he listened in cold silence as I explained that Angela Knight had found Basque.

"You should have told me yesterday that you had her working on this."

"It wasn't exactly aboveboard," I said. "I didn't want to involve you."

"You involved her."

A pause. "Yes. I did."

"If Basque's lawyer finds out about this, and it comes back to bite us in the butt—"

"I know. Don't worry. I'll take the heat, but you remember the promise I made to Grant Sikora. I need to stop Basque."

"Right now you need to let me worry about him."

It wasn't the time to argue with my friend. "All right."

Last year when Sevren Adkins was murdering young women in the southeast, Ralph had been the one who called me in to help, so I took a moment to mention the observation that the killers seemed to be leaving clues to future crimes just as he had.

He was quiet. "They never found his body, Pat."

"Ralph, there was barely anything left of the ambulance."

He didn't reply.

"No one could have survived a fall like that." But even as I said the words I remembered hearing about instances of parachutists who'd survived falls from thousands of feet when their chutes didn't open.

"You should keep it open as a possibility," he said.

Part of me knew he was right, part of me didn't even want to entertain the prospect that Sevren was still alive.

Theorize, evaluate, eliminate possibilities.

"I'll have the lab go back over all DNA and prints," I said. "We'll look for any other evidence that he might have surfaced somewhere since October. What about Basque? Are you going to stay up there or come back?"

I expected, of course, that he'd tell me he was going to be on the next flight to DC, but instead there was a long pause. "Last night

Kreger uncovered some correspondence that Basque and his lawyer had with Professor Lebreau a couple years ago when they asked her to reevaluate their case."

"I remember when it hit the news," I said. "She was an anti-death penalty advocate."

"Crusader," he corrected me. "Anyway, we're looking into all that. Seems he's written to her off and on over the years. We're not sure if she wrote him back. If I find any evidence that Basque contacted her since his release it might give us something to go on. Until then, we still don't have anything solid that ties him to Lebreau's disappearance."

"Except the timing."

"Yes."

"And these connections from their past."

"You and I both know that's not enough to bring him in. And if we question him without anything but assumptions and—"

"Yeah. I know. The press will have a field day."

"And his lawyers will too."

He thought for a moment. "Here's how this'll go down. I'll stay up here for now and follow up on Basque and Lebreau's address book contacts in the DC area, talk with some of her friends, see if there's anyone they might have gone to the Capital to visit. In the meantime, we'll have Metro PD look for his car, monitor those mass transit videos." He took a breath. "How's that scratch on your arm, anyway?"

"It's fine. By the way, that was just plain rude when you yanked out that IV."

"Man up. When I was a Ranger we used to—"

"No alpha Ralph stories, please. You heard we located Mollie's body yesterday?"

"Yeah. At the hotel. It's all over the news."

"Anderson found her laptop this morning in a car parked in front of police headquarters."

When Ralph heard the location he cussed under his breath. "So, you looking into that?"

"Well, I'd like to, but Tessa's dad has been contacting her. He knows where we're staying, so I don't want her here at the house alone, however, as far as I know, they're still processing the scene so I can't take her with me."

He thought for a moment. "What about Brineesha? They know each other, and Brin's not working today. Shouldn't be a problem."

Actually, Ralph's wife would be perfect.

"I'll give her a shout," I said. "Thanks."

We agreed to keep each other in the loop, then he hung up.

I contacted Brineesha and set everything up: I'd drop Tessa off at their house at 10:15, they'd hit the mall—oh, Tessa would just love that—then, after my briefing, I'd meet up with them at the food court at about 2:00.

It would give the two of us just enough time to get to Missy Schuel's office by 2:30 and touch base with her before the 3:30 custody meeting.

Whew.

Based on Missy's reaction yesterday when I'd told her that I was coming to the custody meeting, I could only imagine what she would say when I showed up with Tessa, but this was about Tessa's future, her life, and I wanted her to be present.

All of that, later.

I gave the command post a quick call to get Sevren Adkins's name on the radar screen. "See if he's shown up anywhere in the system since last fall. ViCAP search, AFIS, CODIS, the whole deal."

"Yes, sir."

After ending the call I glanced at my watch and saw that it was already 9:16. Normally, it's a forty-minute drive to Ralph and Brineesha's house from here, but with Friday morning traffic it would take even longer, and Tessa still wasn't out of bed.

10:15 would be tight. I headed to her room to wake her up.

Which might very well be the most challenging thing I would do for the rest of the day.

80

Tessa groaned when I nudged her awake.

"Turn off the lights." She wrapped a pillow around her head.

"The lights are off. That's the sun."

"Well, turn off the sun."

"Tessa, I need you to get up. It's important."

"Why?"

"Because something was found, some evidence, and I have to follow up on it and then get to a briefing."

She moaned. "I don't want to sit around lobbies all day while you meet with people. I'll be fine here. Paul's not gonna come by, his lawyers would never let him. Just leave me a gun or something."

"I'm not leaving you a gun. I'm going to drop you off with Mrs. Hawkins."

"Where?"

"Where what?"

Finally, she unpeeled the pillow and looked at me. "Where are you dropping me off? Last time she took me shopping."

A slight pause. "She did say something about the mall, but it's just for—"

"You know how I feel about shopping," she complained.

"Like I feel about briefings."

"Worse." With every moment she sounded more lucid, and I could tell it was annoying her. "Way worse."

"It'll just be for three or four hours—"

Tessa grimaced. "How about this: drop me off at the Library of Congress. I'll hang out in the main reading room. Cell phones aren't allowed in there so Paul can't call me. And it's the world's most secure library. They guard it better than anything in DC except maybe the Capitol and the White House."

"I'm not so sure about that."

"Whatever." She propped herself up on one elbow. "Besides, if I see him anywhere I'll just tell a police officer that he's stalking me and then call you. Come on, don't make me go shopping. How's your arm, by the way?"

"My arm is fine, and going shopping wouldn't be that . . ."

Actually, the more I thought about it, the more I found myself considering her request to go to the library. In contrast to the mall, which was at least a fifteen minute drive from the command post, the Library of Congress was just down the street, so I'd be close. And Tessa would certainly be more protected in there than in public with Brineesha.

"All right, you can go to the Library of Congress. But we need to get moving. Get dressed. We leave in fifteen minutes."

I stepped into the hall, cancelled with Brineesha, and went to collect my notes and laptop.

The scavengers had arrived sometime in the middle of the night.

Rats, she guessed, but the way her head was positioned she hadn't been able to see them clearly enough to be certain.

They had bitten her ankles, chewed on the flesh next to the straps that held her down. She'd tried to scream, but gagged; she couldn't even do that.

All night she'd wrestled unsuccessfully to get free but had only managed to loosen the dirt around her, which might have been what attracted the rodents—the ripe smell that seeped out from the body beneath her.

At least, now in the daylight, they'd left her alone.

But her strength was gone, wasted in her useless efforts to get free.

Her courage had died, her tears were used up, and now she was lying flat against the putrid corpse, exhausted.

Cold.

Broken.

She had become again that fragile little girl, trembling under a bed on a night in May, praying to a silent God.

She hadn't prayed since that night, hadn't ventured to believe God was there to listen. But now, with no other recourse left, she prayed.

However, this time she was not asking for anyone's life but for her own death. For a quicker and more merciful release from the terror of all that had befallen her.

Death.

For herself and her child.

Yet even in this, the Almighty offered her only silence in reply.

81

12 hours left . . .
9:29 a.m.

It took Tessa less time than I expected to get ready.

She foraged in the kitchen for some food and ended up with a plate of some of the leftover Chinese from the meal Lien-hua had brought last night, and a slice of apple pie from Cheyenne.

Two distinctively different flavors.

Okay, Pat. Do not even go there.

"You can eat in the car," I told her. "I won't bug you about it. Let's get going."

She grabbed her collection of Sherlock Holmes stories, and before I could ask her about it, she said, "Yeah, I know, but I promised Dora I'd finish it. I'm almost done."

We climbed into the car and started down the driveway. "So are you a fan yet?" I asked her.

"Of what?" She was eating dessert first, and her mouth was full of apple pie. "Holmes?"

"Yeah."

"Um." She swallowed. "That would be a no. Doyle cheated."

She'd contrasted Doyle and Poe to me before, and I drew from our previous discussions: "You mean by shamelessly basing Holmes on Poe's Dupin character?"

"Well, that and the solutions to his mysteries." Balancing the plate of food on her lap, she flipped open the book. "Okay, so this one, *The Silver Blaze*, the one I was reading last night. Holmes solves it when he notices . . ." She took a moment to page through the story. "Yeah. Here: 'The curious incident of the dog in the nighttime . . . the dog did nothing in the nighttime . . . that was the curious incident.'"

I recognized it as one of Sherlock Holmes's most famous lines. "Sure, the dog didn't bark—Holmes realized that it should have, and that was the clue—not what did happen but what didn't happen that should have; the thing you would've expected."

"Right," she said, "well, it *would* have been curious if the dog didn't bark, but up till that point in the story, Doyle doesn't *tell* you the dog didn't bark. It's cheating to let your detective suddenly know something your readers don't. How convenient is that? I mean, if you're gonna write a mystery, you have to at least play fair and include enough clues for astute readers to solve the case."

We turned onto the county road in front of the house. Six minutes to the interstate.

"That makes sense," I said. "But at least Holmes's reasoning was sound, I mean, the investigative principle is true."

"And which Holmes would you be referring to?" She was working on the Chinese food now, and her mouth was full. In lieu of chopsticks she was using a fork.

"You're just prejudiced against him," I said, "because you don't like his author."

"No, seriously, his entire approach to solving crimes is based on a logical fallacy."

"A logical fallacy? Sherlock Holmes? I don't buy it."

She swallowed her food. "Doyle has Holmes say—I don't know, I think it's in *The Hound of the Baskervilles* or maybe *The Sign of Four*—anyway, he says: 'When you have eliminated the impossible, whatever remains, however improbable, must be the truth.' I'm not sure if that's word-for-word, but you get it, right?"

"Sure, Spock even quoted it in the 2009 *Star Trek* movie."

"Well, if he did, he was being illogical too."

"Now you're saying Spock was illogical."

"Yeah."

"Heresy."

"Whatever."

She took another bite.

I evaluated the investigative principle. "Tessa, I have to say, this time I think you're wrong. That reasoning is perfectly logical."

She polished off the rest of her food, set the plate aside. "Let's say you're trying to eliminate the impossible—how do you know you have?"

"Eliminated the impossible?"

"Yeah."

I looked at her curiously, and she explained, "Just because something hasn't been done before doesn't mean it's impossible. If you told Holmes that you could restart someone's heart after she was dead . . ." She held up her cell. "Or that he could use this thing to talk to anyone else in the world any time he wanted to, he would've said it was impossible."

"It was. Then."

She gave me a withering, annoyed look. "Obviously."

"So what are you saying? That in theory it's true, but in practice—"

"Yeah. Consider this: how could you ever be certain that you've eliminated *all* possibilities? That somehow you've considered every eventuality, every combination of the facts, that you've foreseen every unforeseeable contingency?"

"Well." I was reluctant to admit it. "Unless you had infinite knowledge, you couldn't."

"Exactly, so that's the thing: there's no way to ever be certain you've eliminated the impossible. And absolute certainty that you've eliminated every possibility—"

"Is the prerequisite for applying Holmes's axiom."

"Yes."

"And it's illogical," I said, anticipating her conclusion, "to base your investigative strategy on a methodology that cannot in essence be practiced in the real world."

A pause. "That's a good way to put it."

So both Mr. Spock and Sherlock Holmes were wrong because they weren't being logical enough.

I didn't see that one coming.

For the rest of the drive to the Library of Congress while Tessa read and mumbled invectives about Holmes's "specious deductive abilities," I tried to consider the impossible possibilities related to this case.

What was I assuming to be impossible that might not be? How was that affecting my perspective? And where in this tangled mess of clues and killings was the dog failing to bark?

We arrived.

I dropped off Tessa at the library's Independence Avenue entrance, waited until she was inside, and then parked in police headquarters' underground garage, and, taking latex gloves and my computer bag with me, headed to the street to have a look at the car that the killers had left right under our noses.

Brad had hacked into the girl's gmail account the day before he killed the Styles woman and the two police officers in Maryland last month.

And that was one of the reasons he'd proposed the plan for this week to Astrid.

Because of what he'd read in the young lady's emails.

Tonight held so many possibilities, but to make them happen, he needed a little more information.

Hacking into secure sites was quickly becoming one of Brad's favorite hobbies, so now he clicked to his computer's Internet browser and surfed to the website of the Law Offices of Wilby, Chase & Lombrowski.

And he began his work.

82

11 hours left . . .

10:29 a.m.

A perimeter had been set up along the two adjacent streets. A swarm of curious onlookers stood just beyond the barricade while a bevy of bored-looking officers monitored them from this side of the line.

Lieutenant Doehring and Officer Tielman, the CSIU member I'd met Tuesday evening, were standing beside the Honda Accord in which the laptop had been found.

Doehring was filling out a stack of paperwork on a clipboard and Tielman was peering into the car's open trunk, but his forensics kit was nowhere in sight. The Evidence Response Team must have already completed their work.

When Doehring saw me, he called, "How's that arm?"

My eyes were on the crowd. "Hanging in there."

"Ah. You should be a comedian."

"Not according to my stepdaughter." I gestured toward the road-block at the end of the street and asked Doehring, "We're taking video of that crowd, right?"

"Of course."

"Let's see if we can get any probables on body type and posture that might match Aria Petic or the unidentified man we captured on tape pushing the wheelchair into the Lincoln Towers." As far as we knew, Aria Petic was a fictional name, but I could tell Doehring was tracking with me.

"Good call."

"Also compare the facial characteristics of the people here with

379

those of Richard Devin Basque." I took a deep breath. "And Sevren Adkins. The Illusionist."

He stared at me. "Richard Devin Basque and Sevren Adkins?"

"Yes. I think Basque might be in the city. I want to know if he's in that crowd. Adkins is a long shot, but it's something I need to check. I'll fill you in later." Then a thought. Why not. "And Dr. Renée Lebreau. You should be able to get her photo, height, and weight from Agent Kreger up in Michigan. Let's see if she's here."

I saw him tap through his fingers, reviewing the five names. "I'll be right back." He pulled out his radio and stepped away.

I said to Tielman, "Tell me about the car."

"Well, somebody gave a homeless guy a hundred dollars in quarters yesterday afternoon. He's been feeding the meter every hour or so. Anderson saw him, figured he couldn't possibly be the car's owner. And, well, there you go."

"Someone gave a homeless man a hundred dollars? What motivated him to keep feeding the—"

"The promise of more money, if he kept it going for twenty-four hours—and no, the homeless guy couldn't give us a description of the man who gave him the money."

Hmm.

"No one else besides Anderson noticed this?"

"Apparently not."

I studied the vehicle. "Did your team find anything significant here?"

"Well, the luggage claim tag."

"What?" Angela hadn't mentioned that.

"Yeah. Cassidy found it. Farraday swept the car first, must have missed it. No prints on it, though. No DNA."

Why would killers this careful leave a claim tag behind?

"What else?"

"We ran the plates, examined the carpeting for soil samples, no red flags; Cassidy checked the steering wheel, door handles, trunk for DNA and prints, but so far the only ones come from the owner's family, two friends, and the guy who owned the car before they bought it last year."

He had a look of satisfaction on his face, as if he were proud of how well he'd done his job. "The owners are clean. They were both at an art reception at the time of the chase at the hotel. Their car was gone when they left."

"They reported it missing?"

"Yes."

"No candy wrappers in the car?" I said. "Gum? Straws, napkins, anything else you could get DNA from?"

"I'm good at what I do, Agent Bowers." His voice had turned cold.

"I'm glad to hear that." Donning the latex gloves, I slipped into the car, sat in the driver's seat, peered out the windshield.

This is the last thing the driver saw before exiting the vehicle.

From here, I could see the panning surveillance camera above the police station's front entrance. I waited, it rotated toward me, then away from me, then toward me again, but by its position in relationship to the entrance and the panning angle, I guessed this car wouldn't appear in the frame.

I asked Tielman about it, and he confirmed my suspicions—the team had checked the footage, he told me, but nothing came up. "If the killers'd parked thirty feet further up the block we would've had 'em." His tone seemed to praise the police department's potential cleverness rather than the killers' anticipation of it.

Man, these guys were good.

And it was video again.

Always something to do with video.

Angles.

Orientation.

I recalled the cameras at the research facility, the deleted footage from 5:00 to 7:00, the video feed to the electronics store, the traffic camera catching the plates of the Volvo, the looping video footage of an empty alley. The killers seemed to be experts at turning against us the very tools we were using to try to find them.

And yet.

Yet . . .

The man who wheeled Mollie into the hotel had gotten caught on camera twice—entering the hotel and then entering the service elevator.

He's too good for that.

Why didn't he just use the alley entrance or the—

The dog didn't bark.

He wanted us to chase him through the hotel.

I considered that.

Why would he want that?

I had no idea, but either the killers had been careless or they were so far ahead of us that they were orchestrating everything. Six moves ahead of us the whole time. They seemed to know the cave and were only showing us the tunnels they wanted us to see.

I stepped out of the car, asked Tielman, "This vagrant who was feeding the parking meter, did he remember when the guy gave him the money?"

"Just sometime yesterday afternoon." He folded his arms: *I've thought of everything. Go ahead, try to come up with something I missed.*

"Any change left? If so—"

"He used about half of the money on booze," Tielman interrupted me harshly. "We checked the coins he had left for prints, nothing came up in AFIS." He looked past me, toward HQ. "I'll see you at the briefing."

"Good work here."

After a pause. "Thank you."

As I watched him leave, I noticed that three TV news vehicles were lined up at the end of the street, and Nick, the cameraman who'd been at the Lincoln Towers Hotel yesterday when I arrived, was climbing into the WXTN van.

And as he did, I had a few thoughts about an entrance to the cave I hadn't yet peered down.

83

I pulled out my cell. It only took a few moments to find WXTN's phone number online. I tapped it in as I entered headquarters.

Security was tight, but I knew one of the agents working the metal detector, and when I held up my creds and flipped up my jacket to show him my weapon, he waved me through.

The command post was on the third floor.

A WXTN secretary put me on hold, and by the time I was finally transferred to the station's president, I'd made it up the three flights of stairs. "This is Bryan Tait," he said. "I understand you're with the FBI?"

I opted to stay in the privacy of the stairwell for our conversation. "Just doing a little fact checking. You have a cameraman working for you with the first name of Nick; can you confirm his last name for me?" I made up a name. "Is it Verhooven?"

"We have a large staff. I'm not familiar with all of our employees. Just a moment." A pause as he looked up the name. "Trichek."

"Can you spell that for me?"

"T-r-i-c-h-e-k."

"I need you to send me a copy of his work schedule for this last week." I figured I could pull up his address and phone number myself.

A pause. "Has he done something illegal?"

"Not that I'm aware of."

Another pause. "I'm afraid that's privileged information. I'd need to speak with legal affairs about this."

"Sounds good. And while you're on the phone with them, I'll just call in for a warrant, save us both some time." A small bluff. "We can chat again in fifteen minutes. Meanwhile, I hope word doesn't leak out that WXTN was hesitant to cooperate with the authorities. You know how these things can get around — "

A brief silence. "I suppose Mr. Trichek's work schedule is nothing extraordinarily confidential."

Didn't think so.

"Good." I gave him an email address to one of the Bureau's secure online drop boxes, then said, "And also Chelsea Traye's records. I'd like hers as well."

A final stretch of hesitation. "Of course."

I thanked him, ended the call, and headed down the hallway to the command post, trying not to assume anything.

And failing.

84

Work stations were set up throughout the sprawling conference room. I counted twenty-two people present, either tapping at computers, making phone calls, conferring in small groups, or poring over crime scene photos that'd been spread across the tables. I recognized some of the officers and agents; most of them I did not.

Lien-hua and Margaret were standing beside a few hastily arranged rows of folding chairs facing a large screen with a 2-D map of the city projected onto it, the locations of the crimes pinpointed with glowing red dots. A nearby eight-foot table strewn with papers, half-empty coffee cups, and two laptop computers lay just to Margaret's left.

My eyes met Lien-hua's, and neither of us were in a hurry to look away.

For a moment I thought of Cheyenne's comment last evening that she would be in class all day, then call me tonight, and a curl of confusion wandered through me again.

Lien-hua.

Cheyenne.

Pat, don't do this to yourself! Last night you—

Margaret dialed her gaze in my direction. "There you are." Her words were full of her characteristic charm, but I sensed more antagonism than usual. "There's a lot to cover." She gestured toward the chairs. "Let's get started."

Often, agents in charge of task forces such as this will hold command level meetings and then have the lieutenants, detectives, and so on brief everyone else. However, it wasn't unheard of to bring everyone together, and I knew that Margaret liked saving time and making sure her people were on the same page, so I wasn't surprised when she paced toward the center of the room and called for everyone to gather for the briefing.

As the task force members left their work stations and began assembling in the chairs, Lien-hua gave me a furtive glance. "Good morning, Agent Bowers."

"Good morning, Agent Jiang."

"How's the arm?"

"It hurts. But it'll be okay."

"I'm sorry for the first part, thankful for the second," she said, then, "I enjoyed our briefing last night."

I blinked. "Our briefing?"

"Yes. On the deck."

"Oh. Yes. Our briefing. Perhaps tonight we can go a little more in-depth. About the subject matter."

"Hm . . . I'll be sure to prepare my notes."

Oh, man.

Easy, Pat.

Lien-hua took a seat, and I pulled up a chair beside her.

Margaret waited until everyone was seated, then said, "All right, let's begin."

The door to the hallway wisped open, and Lieutenant Doehring and Agent Cassidy snuck in and grabbed chairs near Tielman. When I glanced at Doehring, he shook his head, answering my unspoken question about the crowd outside.

No one who resembled the suspects, Basque, Adkins, or Lebreau.

"Now," Margaret announced, "in addition to the luggage claim tag, Mollie's laptop was recovered inside the vehicle out front, and our cybercrime team is currently analyzing it. Already, they've found a two-minute-fifty-one-second video of Rusty Mahan's death, recorded sometime after midnight on Wednesday morning. I've seen the footage." She paused, then added somberly, "He did not die well."

The room fell silent.

Though it was not something I wanted to see, I knew I needed to watch that footage as soon as this briefing was over. For now, I opened my laptop so I could look up Chelsea Traye's and Nick Trichek's home addresses.

Margaret went on, "So far we have a suspect list of 758 names. However, none of the DNA or prints found at the scenes match any of them."

I found the addresses—Chelsea lived near Reagan National Airport, Nick near the zoo—neither address was in the hot zone. As I thought of Nick, I remembered him finger-typing on his phone with his left hand. The killer had used his left hand to open the door, press the elevator buttons.

He tried using his phone in the hotel's control center.

Was he taking video?

Once again I caught myself assuming way too much and tried to slide the thoughts aside.

Margaret took some time to summarize various forensic aspects of the case, most of which I was already familiar with, and at last she nodded toward Lien-hua. "Agent Jiang has been working on the psychological profile of the killers." She gestured toward the front. "Please."

Margaret took a seat, Lien-hua rose. "Thank you."

Carrying a remote control, she went to the front and addressed the group. "We have two unknown suspects. One male, one female. Both Caucasian, age uncertain, but based on an analysis of their posture, stride length, and the partial facials in the video footage we have, they're most likely late-twenties to mid-thirties. Because of the level of complexity and sophistication of these crimes, I would lean toward the higher number."

She tapped the remote to change the image on the screen to a bullet-point summary of her profile of the killers. "The killers' actions and crime scene behavior show that they are experienced perpetrators, but the flagrant nature of their acts might indicate that they do not have any recent criminal convictions in their records."

"That they do not?" someone asked.

"As a general rule, serving time makes you careful," she explained. "Getting away with crimes makes you careless."

True.

"The killers are intimately familiar with the DC Metro area, including traffic camera locations, and they're forensically aware and adaptive to our investigative approach. The staged crime scenes and strategic misdirection techniques indicate possible law enforcement, forensic, or military training."

That was a troubling thought. I clicked to the suspect list and noted the current or former law enforcement and military personnel whose names appeared on it.

Six out of the 758. Two ex-cops, four ex-military.

No one I knew.

Lien-hua went on. "Considering the deliberate shock factor of the crimes—the chimpanzee attack, filming Rusty Mahan's death and then leaving the video for us to find, dismembering Mollie Fischer—all of these actions point to a motive beyond that of hatred, anger, greed, or malice."

"It's a game," Anderson said, cutting in almost before she could finish her sentence. "They're doing it for fun. Mocking us."

Despite my best efforts to remain objective, I had a feeling he was right.

"Taunting the authorities," she said. "Yes, I agree. So far we find no apparent sexual sadism directed toward the victims, nevertheless there are clearly sadistic tendencies in both perpetrators. They will closely monitor news coverage of the crimes, possibly try to insert themselves into the investigation, perhaps as hotline volunteers, vigil organizers, or community watch coordinators. One will be more dominant—almost certainly the male, but both are narcissistic and have pathologically high self-esteem."

"Wait a minute," an officer in the second row said. "Did you just say high self-esteem? Don't you mean low self-esteem?"

"Esteem incorporates love and respect," she replied, "but the only people whom these killers esteem, value, or love is themselves. They seek only their own pleasure, care only about their own future.

Contrary to popular belief, it's almost unheard of for a person to commit a criminal act because he has low self-esteem or 'doesn't feel good enough about himself.' People who kill, steal, rape . . . or even break the speed limit . . . do so because they place their own desires and needs above those of other people."

Hmm. Good point.

"Low other-esteem," the officer said poignantly.

Lien-hua nodded, and as she went on, the email from Bryan Tait, WXTN's president, arrived in the online drop box. The work hours for Nick and Chelsea coincided with the crimes—they'd arrived at the primate center on Tuesday at 7:29 to film their remote and at 3:44 on Wednesday afternoon at the Lincoln Towers.

Of course they did, Pat. It's their job. To report on-site.

During an investigation you should never do what I caught myself doing now: associating a name with a crime before it's solved. Once you start down that road, you'll begin to conveniently find all sorts of evidence to prove yourself right. It's just human nature.

Still—

Lien-hua finished, and Margaret turned to me. She had a slight gleam in her eye, and that's never a good sign.

"Agent Bowers." She was well aware of how much I hate giving briefings, and even before she went on, I had a feeling what she was going to say. "Anything to add? I'd love to get your perspective on this case."

Great.

"Great," I said flatly.

As Lien-hua sat down, I took the floor, set my cell phone on the table beside me, and turned on the 3-D hologram projector.

85

11:29 a.m.

The hologram hovered above the table.

Glowing pathways, one for each victim, wavered along the city streets, sometimes intersecting wherever shared travel routes overlapped.

As I summarized the geoprofile, I input the street on which Mollie's laptop had been found, as well as the location of last night's gas station explosion. The hot zone shifted west.

"You think that's related?" Margaret asked, referring to the gas station.

"The receipt found in the van is from that station. Also, the killers left a stolen vehicle and laptop in front of police headquarters, and last night there was an explosion on the county road running along the perimeter of the FBI Academy at Quantico Marine Base. So here we have—"

Doehring leaned forward. "The roads bordering the two agencies who are running point on this case."

"Yes," I said. "But those aren't the only agencies involved in this investigation. Capitol Police, US Marshals. It's very possible the killers might leave a clue at their offices as well."

Margaret assigned an officer to notify the other agencies' headquarters. He left the room, and I went on, "I don't believe we've probed deeply enough into the possible links between these crimes and others in the past. We need to see if there are any other known faked deaths with related dismemberments, videotaped staged suicides, or . . ."—and this was the kicker—"video traffic footage of two different license plates for the same vehicle—either the suspect's or the victim's."

Blank stares.

"Different license plates?" Tielman asked.

"I know it's unlikely that responding officers would record this type of information on ViCAP, but we're looking for patterns here. We don't know why the killers switched Rusty Mahan's plates, but it appears likely that they wanted us to find out that they had. I want to know if they've done it before."

"So, a message?" Anderson said.

"Possibly, but I'm more interested in locating the killers than in deciphering their—"

Lien-hua gave me a slight head shake, and I backpedaled a little. "What I mean to say is, it's possible that this is a red herring. But whatever the killers' motives are, it's likely that in a crime spree this elaborate, they would follow patterns established or learned during previous crimes. And if that's the case, linking the crimes from this week to earlier offenses will help us shrink the suspect pool and better focus our investigative efforts—and let's go beyond simply prior convictions and explore similar crime patterns and associated behavior. Anything at all, even if it appears insignificant at first."

Margaret assigned Anderson and two other officers to the comparative case analysis.

"Finally," I said, "I think we can narrow down the search area, focus our efforts more efficiently on eliminating suspects."

I tapped at my phone and cross-referenced the hot zone against the suspect list. "Only 19 percent of the people on our suspect list live or work within this nine-block perimeter. Let's take a closer look at them first."

But as I stared at the hologram, I began to wonder about the geoprofile itself, whether this was even the right approach to be taking.

I flashed back to a discussion I'd once had with Calvin: *"From where does your familiarity with a region, your cognitive map of an area, derive?"* he'd asked me.

"Your movement patterns, obviously; your activity nodes and the routes to and from them."

"So how are those formed?"

"Agent Bowers?" Margaret caught me lost in my thoughts. "You were saying?"

"How are those formed?" I mumbled.

"Pardon me?"

The task force members were staring at me curiously. "I was saying . . ." My eyes went back to the hologram. "I think I might be wrong."

"You think you might be wrong," Margaret replied.

With my finger, I traced a holographic street through the air. "For most people the origination of their movement patterns is their place of residence. But if their work place is the locus of their activity, then they would likely get to know the city from that point instead."

After a pause, Cassidy said, "So, a pizza delivery guy who shows up at work and then leaves from there, travels to a part of the city, then returns. Doing this over and over, he gets to know the street layout."

"Yes." I nodded. "Exactly."

"And with two offenders," Lien-hua said, "the cognitive map of the dominant partner would be the more determinative factor in the selection of the crime scenes."

"So," Margaret said, tracking, "we should focus on identifying and following the cognitive map of the dominant offender."

"Typically, yes," I replied, still distracted by my thoughts.

"Typically." She was sounding more and more unimpressed by my briefing.

I switched the hologram mode so that it only showed the crime scene locations, not the victims' travel routes. "Apart from perhaps the Connecticut Street bridge, these locations—the primate center, the hotel, the car in front of the police station, the gas station bordering Quantico—it wasn't simply familiarity with the DC area that led the offenders to choose them. And it wasn't simply victim availability that caused them to choose Rusty, Mollie, and Twana."

Lien-hua was following my train of thought. "It's likely they chose Mollie because of her father, Twana because she resembled Mollie, Rusty, because he was Mollie's boyfriend."

"Yes."

"And the primate center, and hotel." Margaret added. "They chose those because of the congressman and the vice president."

Lien-hua nodded. "And the police station and Quantico because of their relationship to the investigation."

"It appears so," I said. "So it looks like the choice of locations isn't based on the killers' cognitive maps of the city but on whatever message they're trying to send. The metanarrative they're working from."

"Their motive," Anderson said.

I hated the thought of having to say that word. "Their ultimate agenda. Yes."

"And do you have any idea what that is?" Margaret looked like she regretted asking me to share my thoughts.

"Justice reform." The words just came out.

Everyone stared at me

"And you're referring to . . . what exactly?" Margaret asked.

I shook my head and turned off the hologram. "I don't really know."

As I took my seat, I felt defeated by the evidence, by the dead-ends. Figuring out the killers' motives might be the key to solving this case after all.

For a few minutes, the team explored the relationship between the Fischer family and the crime locations, but when we didn't seem to be making any headway, Margaret handed out assignments to make sure all of the investigative avenues were covered.

I was lost in thought.

It would have to be a combination, Pat—cognitive mapping and metanarrative. Crimes are almost always committed within the offender's awareness space. So the killers had to have been familiar with the hotel and primate center to pull this off.

Margaret concluded by saying, "We'll meet tomorrow morning at 10:00—unless there's a break in the case, in which case I will apprise you of any changes in the schedule. You are dismissed."

As people dispersed to their work stations to begin their assignments, Margaret called to me, "Agent Bowers, may I have a moment, please?"

Okay, here we go.

"Certainly."

86

9 hours left . . .
12:29 p.m.

Margaret and I stepped to a corner of the room, and she hardly waited until we were alone before ripping into me. "The next time you go above my head to Director Rodale . . ." Her words scorched the air between us, but she paused mid-threat, and I took advantage of it. "I didn't go above your head, Margaret. I went to talk with Rodale about something else, and he asked me to work the case."

"Mmm-hmm." It was not her way of agreeing with me.

"I don't care if you believe me or not," I said. "Let's just focus on catching these guys. We can argue about all this later."

A moment passed. I had the sense she was trying to slice me in half with her eyes. "I have a question for you," she said.

"What's that?"

She leaned close and spoke in a tight, whispery voice, "When you were meeting with Director Rodale, did you get any indication that he was being unduly influenced by Congressman Fischer?"

Her question came out of nowhere. The answer was yes, I had gotten that impression, but it didn't seem appropriate to say so. "Why would you ask me that, Margaret?"

She did not reply, seemed to be deep in thought.

"Does this have to do with Project Rukh?" I asked. "The research of Dr. Libet?"

Her gaze narrowed almost imperceptibly. "What do you know about that?" I'd posted the information from Rodale and Fischer on the online case files this morning, but I realized she might not have had a chance to review it yet.

"I know it's being utilized by the Gunderson Foundation, and I know Fischer supports their work and doesn't want word about his involvement to leak out."

"No," she mumbled. "He doesn't."

"What's going on here, Margaret?"

"Did you find any information about abortion?"

"Abortion? No, I . . ." That was even more out of left field. "What does that have to do with any of this?"

"The right to life," she said enigmatically.

"What?"

"That's what Vice President Fischer was going to speak on six years ago when he was shot at." She seemed to have disappeared into her own private world. "The changing views about the Fifth Amendment's guarantee that you cannot be deprived of life and liberty without due process."

"Changing views?"

"When does life begin? At birth? At conception? How do you define liberty?"

I was getting more and more lost here. "How is all of that connected to what's going on here this week?"

She shook her head. And when she spoke, she didn't answer my question. "There are some things I need to check into." Before I could get a word in, she added sharply, "If you have a problem with me, you talk to me. Not Rodale."

"If I have a problem with you, I'll make a point to let you know. Now tell me what—"

But, abruptly and without any further explanation, she excused herself and walked away.

All right. That was odd.

And a little unsettling.

After she was gone, Lien-hua approached me. "What was that all about?"

"Good question." I shook my head. "She started off by getting on my case, but when I mentioned Project Rukh, her whole attitude, her entire demeanor, changed."

"In what way?"

"She seemed uneasy."

No, she seemed scared.

Silence passed between us, then Lien-hua softly stated the obvious, but for some reason it felt reassuring to have it out in the open: "This case goes a lot deeper than just these four homicides."

Twana Summie, the college student.

Mollie Fischer, the congressman's daughter.

Rusty Mahan, the boyfriend.

Juarez Hernandez, the gas station attendant.

"Yes, it does," I said. "And Margaret knows something she's not sharing with the rest of the class."

What is obvious is not always what is true.

I gazed around the room. "Lien-hua, what are you going to work on right now?"

"Clearly, the killers had some grounds for choosing to use the same two Lincoln Towers rooms used by Hadron Brady. I think the key to solving this case will be zeroing in on the killers'—you're not going to like this—"

Motives, I thought.

"Reasons," I said.

A half smile. "Close enough. I'm looking into that. And there's one other thing: the lack of DNA and prints at each of the scenes, it really troubles me. All of these crimes? No physical evidence?"

"Hmm." I considered that. "The dog didn't bark."

"What?"

"Sherlock Holmes. It's . . . well, the idea is to avoid looking at what did happen and focus on what didn't happen that should have—and they should have left DNA."

"Yes."

"So by not leaving any, the killers have revealed something significant about themselves: they know how to avoid leaving even the most minute physical evidence at a crime scene."

"Someone in law enforcement?" she said softly, repeating her observation from the briefing.

"Or the military." I showed her the six names I'd pulled up during the briefing.

"Great minds." She jotted down the names. "What about you?"

"I'm going to review that video of Rusty Mahan's death," I said. "And then I think I'll spend a little time watching the news."

The baby kicked.

For the first time ever, she felt the child inside of her kick.

"I'm alive! Don't forget about me! Let me live! Let me live!"

The struggle to survive.

Always.

Always.

To live.

"Two for the price of one," her ex-lover had said just before rolling her into a shallow grave on top of a rotting corpse.

Her baby kicked again.

"I'm sorry I wasn't stronger," her father had written the night he gave up on life.

The night he let death win.

She heard a voice, nearly audible, "Don't let it win! Don't let it win!"

And as she felt the tiny life inside of her move again, despite her raw exhaustion, despite her broken hope, she promised her child that she would be stronger, that she would be strong enough to survive.

And she began to rage against her bonds.

87

Twenty minutes later

I pressed play.

It was my fourth time through the footage of Rusty Mahan's death. Each time I'd been trying to keep myself objective, focused not on his death itself but on what the video might tell us about his killers.

But I was finding that nearly impossible.

Watching him die was just too troubling.

This time, I did my best to keep my eye on the camera angles and the orientation in reference to the background images in the frame.

When I finished, I went to the WXTN website and reviewed the footage of the on-sites filed by Nick Trichek and Chelsea Traye, starting with the discovery of Mollie's body yesterday at the Lincoln Towers Hotel, and moving backward through the homicides this week to those they covered over the last two months, comparing the camera work to the footage of Mahan's death.

And came up empty.

Not surprisingly, almost all of the newsreels had been shot with stationary cameras rather than handheld ones, like Rusty's death had been.

In my searches I found that Chelsea had done a special in April on the Gunderson facility's primate research, but so had three other local stations over the last year. She covered most major crimes in the Metro area and had done a controversial piece recently on the movement to legalize prostitution in the District of Columbia. Other than that, nothing jumped out at me.

When I searched for any previous criminal offenses or misdemeanors, I didn't find anything for Chelsea and only a few speeding tickets and a marijuana possession charge against Nick from three years ago.

No red flags in the location of Nick and Chelsea's work or home addresses, nothing suspicious about the arrival times at the scenes.

In frustration, I slid my laptop aside.

Tunnel vision.

Try to disprove your theories, don't try to confirm them or you'll be blinded by your desire to prove yourself right!

I needed to clear my head.

I made a trip to the snack machine at the end of the hall, grabbed a three-course mini meal of Snickers, Cheetos, and a hermetically sealed cinnamon roll that might have been left over from the days of the Cold War, and returned to my work station.

C'mon, Pat, think this through.

How are this week's crimes connected to the assassination attempt on Vice President Fischer?

Why did the killers choose Mollie Fischer?

Brush off conjecture with the facts until only the truth remains.

Cheetos in hand, I pulled up the active screen for the case file updates and saw that Anderson, who'd been working the ViCAP linkage analysis, had posted a list of three homicides in the northeast that could potentially be linked to this week's crimes.

(1) A dismembered body in New York City three months ago. The body hadn't been found in suitcases but rather in three large boxes. Apparently, the killer had been planning to mail them to an ex-employer.

(2) In April a twenty-two-year-old male Baltimore native was found in his bathtub with his wrists slit, but there were lingering questions about whether or not it was homicide or suicide. His phone was beside the tub and had been used to record his death.

Hmm.

A possibility.

(3) A homicide in Vienna, Virginia, last month. The killers

had left a text message on the female victim's laptop, taunting the authorities.

Because of its proximity to DC, the Vienna crime had been covered by Chelsea Traye and the WXTN News team, and I'd seen the footage just a few minutes ago, but from what I could tell by glancing over the case files, there weren't any obvious links to the crimes this week.

As far as being related cases, none of the three looked especially promising, and none of them had anything to do with license plates—which might have just been a red herring anyhow.

A quick check of the time: 1:22.

I rubbed my head. I had less than forty minutes before I needed to pick up Tessa.

With a growing sense of apprehension about the 3:30 custody meeting and a tightening sense of disappointment from my lack of progress on the case, I turned my attention to the active screen and saw one more crime appear.

A triple homicide in Maryland last month. Two police officers had been killed as well as a female civilian, apparently as the result of a domestic dispute. Anderson seemed to think that the proximity to DC, a crime scene that appeared staged, and a possible discrepancy between the arrival time of the husband at the house and the time of death of the officers made it a crime to look into.

However, Philip Styles, the woman's husband, had pled guilty, presumably to avoid the death penalty, and was now in jail awaiting his sentencing trial. A connection seemed unlikely to me.

Still, we had four separate crimes that might be linked to the killings this week. And despite my initial impressions, I needed to have a closer look at them.

Taking a bite of my Snickers, I clicked to the first crime listed to try to eliminate, rather than corroborate, its relationship to this week's crime spree.

88

8 hours left . . .

1:29 p.m.

Brad used his fake ID to gain entrance to the police headquarters' parking garage.

"I'm a National Academy student," he explained to the officer by the gate. "I was asked to help with the Fischer case's task force."

The officer called Quantico and verified Mr. Collins's name and license plate against the NA student roster, and let him through.

As Brad searched for a parking place, he thought about his plan.

Q. How best to destroy someone?
A. Kill the person he loves the most.

And of course, where most killers get it wrong is that they assume there's only one kind of death.

Killing someone psychologically, slaughtering his reason for living, destroying his hope—these are at least as satisfying endeavors as just slitting his throat.

Q. What is a fate worse than death?
A. Wanting to die but not being able to.
Q. So, hell.
A. Yes. Or being buried alive.

And again, you could be buried alive in more ways than one. Some pain is even more suffocating than the lack of air.

He found a parking spot surprisingly near the car he was looking for. He left his vehicle, walked toward it.

After this week, the world would know who was behind these crimes.

And Bowers would come after him.

He had no doubt about that.

But the secret to defeating your enemy isn't by letting him focus all of his energies on you, it's by making sure that he can't.

Take the life of your subject's loved one, and you will indeed suffer the consequences; destroy her psychologically, and you make him spend time and energy taking care of her rather than searching for you.

Split his loyalties, his priorities, use his love to divert him.

Don't let him concentrate wholeheartedly on the hunt.

Brad picked the car's lock and left the surprise behind.

Ever since arriving at the Library of Congress three hours ago, Tessa had been trying to figure out what it means to be human.

And it was not as easy as it might seem to find the answer.

And that was really starting to annoy her.

She glanced at the pile of reference books around her and the notes she'd typed into her computer.

Okay, so first you had the religious party-line answer: created in the image of God.

But there was no real consensus, even among religious people, on what that meant—creativity, imagination, love, curiosity, dignity, freedom, responsibility . . . The list went on and on depending on which author you chose and on what he or she, a priori, seemed to feel was distinctive about *Homo sapiens*. So, circular reasoning.

Besides, it hadn't taken her long to find out that the Bible never says humans are the only animals with consciousness or intelligence or emotions or politics or self-awareness or even the only creatures with a spirit.

That last one had surprised her.

She pulled up the verse she'd stumbled across while reading a church treatise from the nineteenth century—Ecclesiastes 3:20–21: "All go unto one place; all are of the dust, and all turn to dust again. Who knoweth the spirit of man that goeth upward, and the spirit of the beast that goeth downward to the earth?"

The spirit of man.

The spirit of the beast.

She'd wondered if "the beast" was like Satan or something, so she'd checked a couple other translations; most rendered the phrases "the spirits of man" and "the spirits of animals" or something very close.

People could interpret those verses however they wanted, but she figured that for now she would just take them at face value.

Animals have spirits.

People have spirits.

So, putting the whole "who has a spirit/soul" question aside, from a naturalistic point of view, humans are simply highly evolved apes who, at some point, acquired abstract thinking that facilitated language use and the eventual development of the societal expectations and behaviors we have today. So humans would not be *essentially* different from animals at all.

Different only by degree.

Not kind.

In fact, over the last hour she'd discovered that a growing number of bioethicists were abandoning the whole idea of "human," arguing that it's an artifice based on anthropocentrism and our vanity as a species. But anyone could see that as soon as you erase the uniqueness of humanity, you take away the basis for moral responsibility.

After all, chimpanzees aren't held accountable for murdering their weak. Why should we be? Especially since, in the long run, it would only serve to help natural selection create a more vibrant and successful species?

But most of the atheists she was reading weren't advocating murdering the weak.

Most.

She looked at the notes she'd scribbled.

Through the years, evolutionist thinkers like Hobbes, Huxley, Freud, who all held unflinchingly to natural selection, had inexplicably encouraged people to rise above their natural instincts, a view shared by atheist proselytizer Richard Dawkins: "In our political and social life we are entitled to throw out Darwinism, to say we don't want to live in a Darwinian world."

Okay, but how, if we're the result of our genes, can we "throw out" being the result of our genes?

Talk about being illogical.

You can't have it both ways—either we're determined to be as we are by natural selection, or we're not. And only if we're *not* can we act in ways that are *contrary* to instinct. An animal constrained by instinct can't suddenly decide to become something that instinct doesn't allow it to be.

So, if natural selection really was natural and not somehow guided by God, the entire spectrum of human behavior would be natural. Instinctual. The good stuff and the bad stuff. All just part of being a highly evolved primate.

A species being true to itself.

People being true to their hearts.

To the fractures.

And the whole idea of "man's inhumanity to man" would be a logical contradiction, because it would be impossible for a human to act in a nonhuman, or inhuman, way.

Chilling.

Bestiality, infanticide—just part of human nature.

Greed, cowardice, slavery—well, they must have had a beneficial role in survival or reproduction, or else natural selection would have weeded them out.

And from there things just got worse.

The entire field of medicine—the practice of keeping the sick and genetically deficient (whatever that might mean) alive as long as possible, is actually counterproductive to natural selection and the advancement of the species—especially considering the earth's diminishing natural resources.

So why do it?

After all, natural selection requires the death of the weak for the good of the species, so why fight it?

What is good for the species is good.

What is bad for the species is bad.

Letting AIDS victims or starving children in Africa die would be moral. So would euthanizing the mentally or terminally ill. And since teenage girls are the most likely to reproduce, selective breeding and forced copulation with adolescent girls exhibiting genetically desirable traits would be acceptable, even desirable for the species.

Rape the gifted girls so the species might flourish.

It didn't take much of a leap at all to conclude with Nietzsche: "Whoever must be a creator in good and evil, verily, he must first be an annihilator and break values. Thus the highest evil belongs to the highest goodness: but this is creative."

Compulsory sterilization for mental patients, à la Woodrow Wilson's polices in 1907. Genocide. Aborting kids with Down syndrome or cystic fibrosis. Physician-assisted suicide. Eugenics.

Why not?

Given the assertions of naturalism, all of this was logical, of course, but even most of the ardent naturalistic evolutionists she came across were reticent to go all the way down the eugenics road.

In fact, most of them were, ironically, strong advocates for social justice and medical advances, which, considering their assumptions about human origins, didn't really make any sense.

But she actually gave those authors a lot of credit though, because even if they weren't intellectually honest to their premises about human nature, they were honest to their hearts.

To the shell of good.

Because they knew what all people know—what even Hobbes, Huxley, Freud, and Dawkins knew—that some things are right and some are wrong, regardless of how beneficial or detrimental those things might be to our evolution as a species. Compassion trumps torture because compassion is good and torture is bad. Period.

But not everyone would be courageous enough to be that honest.

Nietzsche for example.

Or Hitler.

And that was the thing.

All it would take was the right person wielding the argument to the right people—

She noticed the time.

1:56.

Dang.

Patrick was picking her up, like, any minute.

As much as she wanted to read more, she totally needed to get going.

She returned the books to the research librarian's desk and hurried outside.

89

Tessa was waiting for me when I pulled up to the steps of the Library of Congress.

"How was your day?" I asked as she climbed into the car.

"I didn't find what I was looking for. You?"

"No. Not yet."

"How about that? We actually have something in common."

Changing the subject, she told me she was starved, and since we still had a few minutes before we needed to be at Missy Schuel's office, I drove toward food.

Up until then I hadn't told Tessa about the meeting at 3:30, but now I explained that after we grabbed something to eat we were going to meet with the lawyer and then head over to a custody meeting with Paul Lansing's lawyers.

She listened with uncharacteristic silence. When I was done and she finally spoke, her voice was edged with anger. "Why didn't you tell me this earlier?"

I'd anticipated her question. "I knew that if I told you, you'd worry about it all morning. I couldn't come up with any good reason to ruin your day, so I waited. Trust me, I wasn't playing games with you, I was just trying to keep you from being upset."

She was quiet. "But you actually want me to come along?"

"Yes."

"Why?"

"You deserve to be present. It's your future we're talking about."

A pause. "It's yours too."

I wasn't sure how to reply to that. "Yes. It is."

It was a long time before she responded. "Thanks." After a

moment she sighed. "This whole thing with Paul, I gotta say, I'm kind of annoyed at you."

"Because I didn't tell you?"

"No, because you took me to see him in Wyoming in the first place."

"Hang on, you're the one who wanted to meet him. I just agreed that you had a right to know who—"

"I know. I changed my mind. That's why it's your fault."

"You changed your mind and that's why it's my fault."

"Yes. It's a woman's prerogative to change her mind and then blame someone else if things don't work out." She'd lent a lightness to her tone that told me she wasn't really angry after all.

"I don't think that's exactly how the saying goes."

"It's the twenty-first-century version."

"You just made that up."

"Maybe."

A moment passed, and her tone turned serious again. "You're a good dad, Patrick. Seriously. I mean that."

"Don't worry. Things will work out."

"No, I mean, whatever happens—" she began, but I didn't want to hear her say anything more.

"Don't worry," I repeated.

She didn't reply.

We grabbed a quick, very late lunch, and headed to Missy Schuel's office.

90

7 hours left . . .

2:29 p.m.

She had no idea how long she'd been straining
against her bonds, yanking, yanking, trying to get
free, but slowly, over time, more and more dirt had
tipped from her back and loosened around her limbs.

And now, as she wrenched her arm to the side as
hard as she could, Riah's arm nudged a little bit to
the left.

She yanked again.

It moved more.

Then she jerked her whole body as hard as she
could, back and forth, again and again, and all at
once, with a thick, solid squish, Riah Everson's
rotting left arm broke free from her body.

For a moment she lay in stunned disbelief. Maybe
God had given her an answer after all. Maybe.

Maybe.

Awkwardly, frantically, she smacked the corpse's
limb against the ground until the horrible thing
cracked at the wrist and fell from the leather
strap.

And her right arm was free.

Though the angle was working against her, she
grabbed the arm and tried to fling it to the side. It
took three tries, but at last she got it out of the
shallow grave, giving her own arm more room to move.

Then she got rid of the corpse's hand.

From the position her betrayer had left her in,
it wasn't easy to undo the gag, but at last she managed.

Immediately, she gulped in a mouthful of sour air.
The Dotracaine had worn off, and she vomited as she
gasped for breath, but still, with the gag gone, she
felt a rush of hope.

> She twisted her arm toward her head, reaching for
> the strap around her neck.

We arrived at Missy's office.

Considering her hesitancy to have me attend the custody meeting, I'd expected her to be reluctant to have Tessa there as well, but if she didn't like the idea, she hid it well. As soon as I introduced Tessa to her, Missy returned the diary. "I can only imagine how special this must be to you."

"Yes, it is," Tessa replied.

Missy took some time explaining that reading the diary had helped her better formulate the things she wanted to emphasize in the meeting today.

"I'll draw attention to the brief nature of Paul Lansing's relationship with Christie," she said. "It was a short-lived love affair that lasted less than a month." She nodded toward me. "During the last few months of your wife's life, and ever since then, you've been Tessa's caregiver—that's more than twenty times longer than Paul even knew her mother."

"That's a good point." Tessa let her eyes bounce from me to Missy as if she were looking for support. "That'll help."

"Yes, I think it will," Missy said. "Also, Paul corresponded with your mother long after their relationship ended, yet never mentioned you or tried to find out if you were alive, so I believe we can show that he—"

Tessa shook her head, the reassurance gone. "I already went through all this with him. He'll just say he thought Mom went ahead with the abortion."

"Perhaps, but we'll show that if he could find her, he could certainly have found you, or at least found out that Christie had delivered her baby. She never took any steps to keep it a secret from people, did she? That you were her daughter?"

"No. Never."

I felt a shot of optimism.

Missy was the real deal.

"All right." She looked at her watch, then promptly rose. "Their office is across town. Let's go. I don't want to be late."

———————————■———————————

Seated at her desk at the command post, Margaret Wellington clicked to Congressman Fischer's website to read his issue statements.

Last night she'd reviewed his voting record, but today, in light of what Agent Bowers had told her—or at least insinuated by his lack of an answer—about the congressman influencing Rodale, she'd decided to study the man's votes and platform more carefully.

From living in his district, she knew that he was for shrinking the military and FBI, decreasing the national debt, strengthening abortion rights, creating more green jobs, and expanding health care benefits to seniors, but she hadn't been aware of how strongly he felt about justice reform until she saw his record of cast votes.

Among other things, Fischer was adamantly against the death penalty.

That one brought her pause.

The man who'd tried to kill his brother had been a pro-death penalty advocate. After the assassination attempt, public opinion had pendulumed the other direction toward the congressman's position, and Director Rodale had been one of those swayed to change his mind.

During Richard Basque's retrial, Margaret had gotten into a discussion with Rodale about the justice (or lack of justice) of the death penalty—something he'd grown to oppose but she supported. And, knowing she was for reducing the number of abortions, he'd challenged her: "How can you claim to be pro-life when you're for the death penalty?"

"Greg, we're talking about the death penalty, not about—"

"I'm only saying, Margaret, that your view is inconsistent."

"Frankly, I'm not sure it's appropriate to compare—"

"See?" He looked satisfied. "Your position is untenable."

"I am for life," she said, "as well as for justice. With all due respect,

Greg, how can you claim to be for either when you support letting the guilty live and putting the innocent to death?"

Rodale had looked at her coldly. Had not replied.

Even at the time, the fact that he'd confronted her in such a way had seemed inexplicable to her. Why was he so emotionally invested in the issue as it pertained specifically to Basque's case?

The computer screen stared at her and her thoughts switched from Rodale to Fischer.

She turned back to his policy statements.

He supported ways to "enhance human potential and reduce unnecessary suffering," which included his endorsement, along with that of the National Science Foundation, of nanotechnology and transhumanism—the emerging field of genetically altering DNA to treat blindness, epilepsy, paralysis, cancer, and so on.

Margaret wasn't familiar with transhumanism, but it didn't take her long online to discover that it was controversial since much of it involved not just augmentation but species advancement—through neuro-implants and gene therapy—creating humans with better eyesight, strength, or mental capabilities than the human race had ever developed on its own.

Through genetic manipulation, scientists would soon be able to give people the reflexes of a panther or the strength of a gorilla or the eyesight of a falcon. And by implanting chips into their brains, provide them the ability to remember nearly everything they learned or experienced. Because of transhumanism's ultimate goal of improving the human race, transforming it even, into a superior species altogether, some people were calling it twenty-first-century eugenics.

Neuroscience. Nanotechnology.

Metacognition.

The primate research. *Could the Gunderson Foundation be doing transhumanism research? Gene splicing with animals?*

Hmm.

Perhaps approach this from a different angle.

She'd heard that Vice President Fischer wasn't exactly best

buddies with his brother—resentful of how the congressman had tapped into his political clout to promote his own standing in the House. She decided it might not be a bad idea to have a chat with the former vice president.

It took a few calls, but finally she found out he was at a climate change conference in Tokyo. His people said he'd return her call as soon as he could, but she knew how soon "as soon as possible" could be for a politician, so she wasn't about to hold her breath.

The congressman was pulling Rodale's strings. She didn't like—

Or maybe it's the other way around.

She paused.

Now that was an interesting thought.

Yes. Very interesting.

She found Doehring and told him she was heading to her office at FBI headquarters for a couple hours to catch up on a few things.

"Don't worry, I'll hold down the fort," he said.

"I know you will."

She left the command post with a realization that she was on a trajectory that would either end her career or just possibly land her in the job she'd been eyeing since she joined the Bureau.

91

6 hours left . . .

3:29 p.m.

Brad opened his laptop.

He knew that the task force had unwittingly found the bomb.

And he knew that ever since the anthrax scare nearly a decade ago, the FBI Headquarters and all of the field offices had been x-raying all incoming mail, packages, shipments, and deliveries as well as checking them for traces of biological or chemical compounds.

However, the Bureau did not x-ray or bio-scan evidence that was collected at crime scenes unless the specific nature of a crime warranted such action, such as evaluating evidence from an arsonist's or bomb maker's home.

And so.

Good.

Brad sent the email that would start the computer's internal timer.

An anonymous-looking Viagra ad.

In exactly six hours, the bomb he'd prepared on Wednesday morning, the one he'd left for the task force to find, would go off.

Now, he just needed to wait.

The explosion would set up everything for the perfect ending to the game.

He set his watch to vibrate at 9:29 p.m. so that whatever he was doing he would know.

Dr. Calvin Werjonic.

Gregory Rodale.

Annette Larotte.

A puzzle with so many interlocking pieces.

And Bowers would see all the pieces laid so neatly in place.

But only in retrospect.

Only after it was too late to save the girl.

The Law Offices of Wilby, Chase & Lombrowski
Suite 17
4:05 p.m.

"I'm sorry." Paul Lansing's lead lawyer, Keegan Wilby, shook his head. "We simply cannot allow her into the meeting."

Wilby had a squarish face and a Clark Kent curl of black hair on his forehead that only served to make him look like a middle-aged middle-schooler. His clothes told me he had wealth; his smug grin told me he knew it.

We'd arrived on time, over half an hour ago, but incomprehensibly, Wilby hadn't even shown up until 3:55 and had subsequently spent the last ten minutes arguing about letting Tessa attend the meeting. She was standing beside me, seething, but I had my hand on her shoulder to let her know she needed to keep quiet.

Missy said sternly, "Mr. Wilby, tell Mr. Lansing that this is not up for debate. She comes in or we are leaving."

He drew in a sigh. "All right. I'll go and speak with my client one last time." He spoke condescendingly, as if Missy were a child. "But I am not guaranteeing anything."

He left.

Tessa's teeth were clenched. "I feel like I'm a piece of furniture people are trying to shuffle around."

"I understand," Missy said. "However, Mr. Wilby does have a point. It would be highly unusual for the child—for you—to be present at a meeting like this."

"Yeah, well, unusual works for me."

Five minutes later Wilby returned shaking his head. "I'm sorry, my client said he does not want to upset her."

"Good." Tessa strode toward the hallway to the conference room.

"No, I mean by having you attend the meeting."

"*This* is upsetting me!"

"Tessa," I said. "Come here."

She didn't move.

I signaled for her to join me. "Please."

At last she came, staring at Wilby with blisteringly hot eyes the whole time.

"I'm sorry," he said to her in that tone of voice people use when they're not sorry at all. Then he directed his words to all of us. "I suppose if you insist that she be present, we will have to cancel this meeting."

"All right." Missy picked up her purse. "Good day, Mr. Wilby."

However, I wasn't so sure. I conferred with her for a moment and explained that I didn't like the idea of putting this off. I wanted to hear what Lansing had to say, to clear up my questions regarding his Secret Service involvement. After a short debate, she gave in. "As long as it's acceptable to Tessa."

I assured Tessa that she could sit in on future meetings, but for now to just let it be. "We need to get a feel for what's going on here. I promise I'll fill you in."

She was clearly not happy about it but finally complied. "When the meeting's over you'll tell me everything?"

"I will."

As Wilby invited me and Missy to follow him, he had a satisfied look on his face that made it clear he felt like round one belonged to him.

A wooden cabinet with a dozen cubby holes hung just outside the conference room door. Wilby unpocketed his iPhone. "I'm afraid I'm going to have to ask you to leave your mobile devices here. After far too many interruptions in meetings in the past, our law firm had to create a policy. I'm sure you understand."

That was definitely not going to happen and I was about to tell him so, but Missy beat me to the punch. "My client is a federal agent. His phone contains highly sensitive and confidential information, so quite obviously it cannot leave his person. And my phone contains his private number so I cannot leave mine either. I'm sure *you* understand."

I was really starting to like this lawyer of ours.

"I'm afraid she's right," I said.

Wilby looked like he might argue, decided against it and opened the door.

Round two: Missy Schuel.

As we entered the room, she said to me softly, "Now remember, let me do the talking."

I was switching my phone to vibrate.

She paused. "Will you let me do the talking?"

"I'll try."

"Succeed," she said, and we entered the conference room and I closed the door behind us.

92

Lansing and two additional lawyers were waiting for us at the far end of a sprawling steel and glass conference table. A south-facing window offered a spread of natural light to the otherwise institutional feel of the room. A pitcher of water sat on the table with seven glasses poised beside it. I assumed that the additional door on the other side of the room led to more offices.

Seven glasses on the table.

Perhaps they had been expecting Tessa.

Either that, or someone else.

Missy and I took seats facing Lansing and his lawyers. After introductions, Wilby thanked us for coming, which seemed a little disingenuous since he hadn't done so in the reception area when we first arrived, and we'd already been here for nearly forty-five minutes.

"All right." Missy gestured toward me. "Our agenda today is to find out what Mr. Lansing wants—"

"He wants custody of his biological daughter," one of Wilby's associates said tersely.

She looked at him with cool curiosity. "What was your name again?"

"Seth Breney."

"Well, Mr. Breney, please refrain from interrupting me and this will no doubt be a much more productive meeting for all of us." There was no question who was in control of this room.

Wilby cleared his throat. "Primarily, my client wants what is best for Tessa."

"That's good to hear." Missy was writing something on her legal pad in that scribbly shorthand of hers.

In the momentary silence following her statement, Lansing spoke up, "Patrick, before we begin here, I'd like to tell you how thankful I am for all you've done for Tessa ever since Christie passed away."

"It's kind of you to say that."

"Whatever the results of this custody case, I hope you will agree to stay involved in her life."

Oh man, did I want to respond to that one, but I rounded a conversational corner instead. "You didn't run for cover, did you, Paul?"

"Pardon me?"

"Six years ago. At the hotel."

I watched his reaction.

Despite what you might see on TV, when detecting deception it isn't so much what the subject does—looking into one corner of the room or the other, pushing up his glasses or peering over the top of them—but it's that he does *something* different than when he's telling the truth. There are always perceptible subconscious physiological changes that occur, even though they're different for different people.

Now, as Paul looked at me, I could see his Secret Service training in the coolness of his eyes, but he was lightly tapping his right thumb and forefinger together, which he had not been doing a few moments earlier. "We can discuss this later, Patrick."

"Yes," Wilby agreed emphatically.

"No time like the present." I shrugged. "We're all friends here."

Lansing said nothing.

"So, then . . ." Wilby said.

Lansing tapped his finger and thumb.

Thought so.

I jotted a note of my own on Missy's legal pad.

She glanced down, read it. Nodded.

"Back to the matter at hand." Wilby conferred with his stack of notes, although what he said afterwards didn't seem all that difficult to remember. "My client is Tessa's biological father. You do not dispute this, do you?"

"We'll want another DNA test to be done by an agency of our choosing," Missy said. "Just to make sure."

Wilby glanced at Breney, obviously his subordinate, who made a note of it. The third lawyer who was sitting beside them said nothing, simply sat there looking clueless.

Wilby said, "When Agent Bowers and his stepdaughter showed up last month at my client's home, they had a diary that contained a letter my client had written to Christie Ellis, the girl's mother."

"Tessa," I corrected him. "The girl's name is Tessa." The whole letting-Missy-speak-thing wasn't going so well.

"Yes," Wilby said. "In the letter, my client stated that he wanted to play an active role in the upbringing of the as-of-yet unnamed child Christie was carrying. From the very beginning, even before she was born, Mr. Lansing willingly offered to care for both mother and child, both relationally and fiscally."

"The letter only offers broad intention," Missy responded, "not specific design. And he never made any efforts to follow up on those vague promises."

"When Tessa's mother left him, he searched for her, but seventeen years ago, without the Internet, it wasn't easy to locate someone who didn't want to be found. My client didn't even know that the girl—Tessa—was alive."

Missy waited, one eyebrow raised, and I could tell that her silence was a way of controlling the conversation. "Anything else?"

Wilby flipped through a stack of papers. "I have here a copy of Dr. Bowers's work schedule for the first six months after his wife's death."

I felt a small quickening of my pulse.

How did he get that?

Then he addressed me directly, as if Missy were not in the room. "It looks like you spent quite a bit of time traveling, Dr. Bowers. Speaking at law enforcement and forensic science conferences."

"I spoke some. Yes."

"How many weekends did you leave Tessa with your parents while you went to consult on a case or speak at a conference?"

"This has nothing to do with—" Missy began.

"I traveled a couple weekends a month," I said.

"Fourteen weekends," Wilby pointed out. "Fourteen weekends in six months. That's more than two weekends a month."

"Which means," Missy countered, "Dr. Bowers was home nearly 80 percent of the time. And whenever my client was gone, Tessa was well cared for."

"I'm not here to argue about the competency of care that Dr. Bowers's relatives are able to provide. That's not the issue here."

Okay, this guy was really starting to get on my nerves.

"Tessa needs a more stable and secure home life than an active FBI field agent can provide." Wilby referred to his notes again. "According to police reports, last October she was almost killed by a serial killer whom Dr. Bowers was tracking in North Carolina."

Anger rising.

"She was inside an FBI safe house when he attacked her."

"And yet, this man, Sevren Adkins, was able to—"

"What is your point?" Missy said curtly.

"My client is concerned for the welfare of his daughter." He was looking directly at Missy. "Dr. Bowers has a history of breaking FBI protocol—"

"This is outrageous," she broke in. "At a press conference on Wednesday the FBI's Executive Assistant Director called him one of the Bureau's finest agents."

Wilby folded his hands in front of him on the table. "Let me cut to the chase. If this case ends up going to court, we have a man who is willing to testify that Agent Bowers threatened his life."

What?

"Agent Bowers would never threaten another person's life," Missy said.

Wilby wore that look again, the one that said he'd won a round, but it was Lansing who spoke up. "He's here right now. We can end this discussion. Perhaps come to a—"

"I haven't threatened anyone," I stated unequivocally.

Missy read my eyes, saw truth in them. "If he's here," she was looking around the room, "let's talk with him. Let's settle this."

Wilby rose and went to the door at the far end of the room. He swung it open and called, "Come on in." Then he stepped back, and a man emerged.

Richard Devin Basque.

93

5 hours left . . .

4:29 p.m.

Two twisting, serpentine caverns came together.

So, that's why Basque's in DC.

Because of you.

For a moment, the cannibalistic killer gazed around the room with his usual air of gentle confidence, the blue-green depths of his eyes reminding me of dark, arctic water. As he took a seat, I quickly ran through how Paul Lansing might have made the connection between me and Basque.

When Tessa and I visited Paul last month, Basque's retrial had only recently come to an end. At the time, the story of how I'd managed to thwart the attempt on his life was all over the news—as was my admission in court that I'd punched him—wait, technically, physically assaulted him—during his apprehension.

After Basque's release, Lansing could've easily contacted him and asked him to tell the family court judge that I had a violent streak. And considering our history, I could only imagine how glad Basque would've been to accept the invitation. What better way to repay me for sending him to prison for thirteen years than by destroying my family?

But what's this about threatening his life?

Missy recognized Basque. "This meeting is over." She stood.

"Just listen for a second," Wilby said.

"No." She was on her way to the door. "Come on, Dr. Bowers, we're leaving."

"Agent Bowers indicated to me," Basque called, his voice

remaining calm, resonant, "at Dr. Werjonic's funeral last month, that he was intent on—"

Missy spun around. "Intent on what? Last month Agent Bowers saved your life when a gunman tried to kill you during your trial. Now you're claiming he wants you dead?"

"Ask him." He turned his gaze to me. "He won't lie."

Oh.

The room went quiet.

Everyone's attention turned to me.

No, no, no.

Not good.

I hadn't told Basque I wanted to kill him, but I had thought it. Yes, I had.

Preemptive justice.

I took a moment to consider carefully what to say, but before I could respond, Missy exploded, "Did you say he won't lie? Well, you're absolutely right. Dr. Bowers is not the kind of man who would sit here and lie to you. However . . ."

She pointed to Paul. "Mr. Lansing lied to my clients about his previous job. He lied to Tessa about his reasons for coming to DC, lied about why he lives in Wyoming, lied about his friendship with a sculptor whose work appears in the Hirshhorn museum, and lied about his role in stopping the assassination attempt against Vice President Fischer six years ago. You are right, Dr. Bowers is not a liar. But in his dealings with my clients, Mr. Lansing has shown very little regard for the truth."

Nice.

Well played.

She eyed the people in the room one at a time. "If Mr. Lansing comes anywhere near my clients or continues to harass Tessa with his emails, we will get a restraining order—and considering the pattern of deception and intimidation he has already engaged in, I can guarantee you that no judge would deny that request. I suggest you drop this ridiculous custody suit and save yourself the embarrassment of having all of this made public." She swiveled on her heels, went for the door. "We're done here."

Wilby rose. "Agent Bowers is an angry, violent man who uses unnecessary force when arresting suspects—and he threatens innocent people's lives. Tessa needs a more emotionally balanced father than that."

I ignored him, looked at Basque. "Richard, where is Professor Renée Lebreau?"

He did not reply.

"Is she here in DC?"

Nothing.

"Did you harm—"

"This is not about Mr. Basque!" Wilby whined at me.

I glared at him, then at Lansing and Basque, and barely managed to hold back a rather pointed response, but I knew that if I said what I was thinking, it wouldn't be in Tessa's best interests; that it would only serve to reinforce Wilby's claims about my allegedly bad temper.

So instead, I followed Missy into the hallway, and although I was tempted to close the door rather decisively behind me, I let it drift softly shut instead.

In the hallway, before we reached Tessa, I told Missy, "Good job."

She was quiet.

"You did a good job in there, Missy."

"I heard you."

As we entered the reception area, Tessa approached us. "So? What happened?"

Missy did not reply but headed straight for the exit doors; I was punching a number into my cell phone. "I'll explain when we get outside," I told Tessa.

"What's going on?"

"Please, wait with Missy. I'll be right there."

She gave me a disparaging look: *I can't believe you! You're totally reneging on your promise to tell me everything that happened in there!*

I was waiting for Doehring to pick up.

"It's all good," I said to her. "I think Paul might drop this thing."

"Honestly?"

"Yes. Now, outside. I'll be right there."

Hesitantly, she obeyed.

Doehring answered, and I asked him to get an undercover officer over here ASAP to tail Basque as he left the meeting. "And call Ralph Hawkins." I gave him the number. "Tell him we know where Richard Basque is."

Then, I went outside and joined my stepdaughter and our lawyer on the sidewalk.

Missy was upset.

And I had a feeling that her anger wasn't just directed at the people who'd been sitting across the table from us.

94

Missy Schuel was stone quiet until we reached the car halfway down the block. "What happened at that funeral, Patrick, the one Basque made reference to? Did you threaten his life?"

"What?" Tessa exclaimed.

"I told him I would find enough evidence to send him back to prison. He said he didn't think I was capable of—well, at that point I cut him off and said that he had no idea what I was capable of."

"Which funeral?" Tessa asked. "You mean Dr. Werjonic's?"

"No idea what you were capable of?" Missy said, her eyes fastened squarely on me.

"Yes."

"That's all?"

"That's all."

"Nothing more specific?"

Tessa threw her hands to her hips. "Can somebody please tell me what's going on!"

"Richard Basque was in the meeting," I told her. "Paul is obviously looking for anything he can find to use against me." Then I replied to Missy, "No. Nothing more specific."

That seemed to at least partially satisfy her. "Anything else? Any more surprises I need to know about?"

"Probably." I saw an unmarked car with Officer Lee Anderson behind the wheel drive up and park across the street. "But none that I can think of right now."

It had to have been less than three minutes since I called Doehring. An amazingly fast response. Anderson must have already been in the area.

I averted my eyes so I wouldn't draw undue attention to him. "Let's go," I said to Missy. "I'll drop you off at your office."

———————————— ■ ————————————

She was free.

Free.

She scanned the woods as she crept through them, keeping an eye out for anyone, any movement at all.

It had taken her a long time to loosen the strap around her neck and even longer to get the other arm free. But after that the legs had been easy.

Free.

She arrived at the stream where she'd seen the corpse last night when she first entered the body farm with the man who had left her to die.

Stopping upstream from the body, she stripped off her reeking, insect-infested clothes and washed herself, scrubbing, scrubbing, scrubbing to get the stench and dirt and rot off her body.

Then she rinsed the clothes and wrung them out as much as possible, and she soaked her ankles in the cool water to relieve the pain of the ripped flesh where she'd been bitten by the scavenging animals.

The Academy's admin building wasn't far, less than a half mile from the trailhead. If she could just get to the parking lot she could steal a car, drive to a bank, drain the money from her betrayer's account, and be gone.

But be smart.

He had turned on her, yes, betrayed her, lied to her, tried to kill her. Yes, yes, yes. But—

A terrible chill ran through her as she was forced to admit that he was smarter than she was, smarter than any cop or FBI agent she'd ever run into. He would find her, yes, he would; it was inevitable. And considering what he'd done to her last night—strapping her to a rotting corpse—she couldn't even begin to imagine what he would do to her if he caught her now.

Or what he might do to her baby.

Even if he didn't come after her, he would certainly plant evidence that would lead the authorities to her.

He had the means to fake IDs.

He was good with disguises.

He could cover his tracks better than anyone she knew.

He would disappear and she would end up in prison for life.

And worst of all, they would take her baby away.

Foster care.

She'd gone down that road herself and she was not about to let her baby grow up that way.

She put on her wet clothes.

It was the end of her career, yes. The end of her old life, yes, okay, she knew that, but for the sake of her baby she needed to make sure she wasn't found. Ever.

Then it struck her.

There was one way to keep her baby with her and also stay free from both the one who had betrayed her and the FBI.

To live, she would have to die.

To the rest of the world.

But thankfully the one thing she was good at, the one skill she had, was setting people up for murder.

And this time, she would set her betrayer up for hers.

She headed to the parking lot, considering what it was going to take for her to make her death as believable as it would need to be.

Predator.

Prey.

This time she was going to have to be both.

After dropping off Missy at her office, I needed a minute to sort through my thoughts, figure out what to do next. Too many cables tugging at my attention.

Tessa was upset.

Basque was in town, apparently trying to help Lansing in this custody case.

Dr. Lebreau was still missing.

The killers were still at large.

My arm really hurt.

If there was ever a time for coffee, this was it.

I took Tessa to an indie coffeehouse in downtown DC. She

ordered a small soy milk latte; I went for a twenty-ounce Kenya AA and managed to down it and get a refill before she came out of the bathroom.

Now we were walking through a tourist-riddled park near the Capitol on our way back to the car, which I'd had to park about three blocks away.

Above us, the tangled branches of the trees lining the path seemed to snag the late afternoon sunlight, letting only jagged pieces of the day land around us.

Shadow and light, blinking at me every step of the way.

For no stated reason, Tessa and I both moved urgently toward the car.

So many thoughts corkscrewing through my mind.

I wanted to hear what Lien-hua might have discovered about the lack of DNA evidence, figure out what was going on with Margaret and her abstruse reference to abortion, go over my geo-profile again . . .

I'd had my phone's ringer off since the beginning of the custody meeting, and now I glanced at the screen and noticed I had a missed call from Cheyenne.

Great.

Just one more thing to work through.

Yesterday morning Tessa had told me I was being flirty with both of them, and I had to admit she was right.

So now, considering that I seemed to be patching things up with Lien-hua, I needed to make sure my flirtiness with Cheyenne came to an end. Feeling a narrow stab of guilt and not really wanting to go through my texts and perhaps find another message from her, I pocketed the phone.

Took a drink of coffee.

Tessa gestured toward a Metro station. "So, I guess I'll head home then."

"I'll take you. The car is just at the end of the block."

"You've been with me for like over three hours. You need to stay here, get back to this case."

"That can wait," I said. "I don't like it that Basque is here."

"I get that, but you've got an undercover cop following him, so—"

"What makes you say I have a cop following him?"

She looked annoyed at having to explain herself. "Basque shows up, then you make an urgent phone call before leaving the lawyer's office, then you stare at a guy with a mustache who pulls up outside the building in a sedan. Cops are easy to spot. Who else besides serial killers and cops have mustaches these days?"

"Pakistanis."

"Yeah, okay, and so do cowboys, but this guy was a cop."

I bowed out of the mustache debate. "I'm not leaving you alone. I don't trust Lansing."

"But in the meeting, Ms. Schuel said she'd get a restraining order if he showed up anywhere near me. He wouldn't dare follow me."

"And how do you know she said that?"

Tessa rolled her eyes. "She was yelling when she said it—look, Patrick, I'm fine. I have some stuff to do at home anyhow. I'll take the VRE. You need to stay here."

"I don't think so."

Our car still lay fifty meters away through the strangled sunlight.

She followed me grudgingly.

We walked.

Shadow to light.

"I'll make a deal with you," she said.

"What's that?"

"If you can look me in the eye and answer one question, then I'll shut up and I won't argue. You can bail on this case, come home, and babysit me."

I didn't like where this was going; I went for some coffee.

"Well?"

"Go on," I said.

"You have to be honest."

"I'll be honest. What's the question?"

"You have to promise."

"Tessa. All right. I promise."

Shadow to light.

"Look me in the eye."

Good grief.

We stopped walking, and I looked her in the eye.

"Now, tell me that the Bureau has a better chance of finding these killers, of saving people's lives if you're not helping. If you can tell me that, then I'll go home with you and I won't nag you."

"That's not fair. Besides, it wasn't even actually a question."

She stood in that slumpy-teenage-girl way and gave me a critical stare.

"Tessa, there are plenty of good people working this case. It's not like—"

"I can rephrase it if that would make it easier for you."

"You're more important to me than—"

"Don't do that."

My phone rang. Cheyenne's ringtone.

Unbelievable.

"Do what?"

"Use me as an excuse."

"I'm not using you as an excuse."

It rang again.

"I get it that you love me," she said. "But do they have a better chance of saving lives if you're at home babysitting me?"

"Why are you asking me this?"

Ring.

"Just answer it."

"I'll get it in a minute."

"No, I mean my question."

"The answer is no—"

"Okay." She sounded satisfied. "Now, get the phone."

Another ring.

Annoyed, I picked up. "Cheyenne. Hey."

"How are you doing? Just touching base. Seeing how the case was going. How your arm is."

"Listen, can I call you back?"

"Sure." But she sounded concerned. "Is everything okay?"

"Yeah."

Tessa said, "Ask her what she's doing tonight."

I shook my head at Tessa, spoke to Cheyenne, "Just give me a few minutes."

"Ask her," Tessa urged.

"Cheyenne, can you hang on a sec?" I held the phone against my chest. "What is it you want, Tessa?"

"It'd be stupid for her to drive into the city to help you out right now. With traffic on a Friday night? Give me a break. It'll take me like an hour and a half to get home on the VRE, she can work till then, hang with me for supper, and whenever you get back you can fill her in on the case. It'll give you a couple hours to work, I'll be safe, problem solved. Everybody's happy."

I tried to find a glitch in her plan.

"No," I said stubbornly.

"Can I see your phone for a sec?"

"Tessa—"

She held out her hand. "Here, just for a minute."

"I'm—"

She cocked her head and raised her eyebrows. A reprimand from an adolescent girl.

I resisted, but in the end I found myself giving in.

Tessa took the phone. "Detective Warren, hey, it's me. Um, listen, I'll be home at like 6:45 or so. Can you stop by until Patrick gets back? Yeah, he's getting all weird on me . . . I know. Yeah, no, we're okay . . . Whatever, you will *so* not beat me this time . . . Yeah, right. So, okay, do you want to talk to him again . . . ?"

She returned the phone to me. "She wants to say hey."

I said to Cheyenne, "I'm sorry about that."

"You don't have to be sorry about anything."

"Tessa's trying to flex her wings, and it's just not good timing."

"It's no big deal, really. I've been in class all day. I'll hit the firing range, get my rounds in, then head to your house and see you when you get there. You can bring me up to speed. Besides, this'll give me a chance to practice my new hobby."

"Your new hobby?"

"Remember? Coming to your rescue?"

Oh boy.

"Yeah."

Don't be flirty.

Don't be flirty.

Don't be flirty.

"Well," I said. "Thanks." I gave her Tessa's cell number so it'd be easier for them to connect, and we ended the call.

Tessa was finishing her latte. "So?"

"Are all teenagers like this?"

"It's possible that I'm gifted." She hitched her purse strap over her shoulder. "Don't worry, everything's cool. She doesn't have to stop being your friend just because you kissed Agent Jiang. Just remember—"

"Yeah, I know. Don't lead her on."

"Exactly."

I took a deep breath. "Here's what I want you to do: text me every fifteen minutes until Detective Warren arrives. To let me know you're all right."

"You've gotta be kidding me."

"I'm not kidding." I held up a cautionary finger to stem a comeback. It didn't work.

"You're not supposed to use mobile devices on the Metro," she countered.

"If you get arrested I'll make sure you don't serve hard time."

She sighed with her eyeballs. "Whatever."

"Call me if anything comes up, anything at all."

"I will."

I took her to the Metro stop, waited for her to board, then drove to police headquarters.

To map out this cave.

95

4 hours left . . .

5:29 p.m.

Margaret had stepped away, Doehring was at the reins, and it looked like the team had been making some progress.

He filled me in.

The big news: Agent Cassidy had found traces of military grade C-4 on some of the carpet fibers in the back of the van.

"I thought they cleared the van?" I said.

"After you linked last night's gas station explosion to the crime spree, they started going back over everything, start to finish."

The ATF has the best explosive and accelerant detection dogs in the business, so their teams had been sent to the Lincoln Towers Hotel as well as the congressman's office and the Gunderson facility.

The ATF.

One more agency added to the plate.

"Let's get them to the Capitol Police HQ as well."

"Right." He made a note of it. "Next: you know how Fischer has connections with the Gunderson Foundation? Well, a couple of my guys did a little looking into some of his biggest campaign supporters."

"Let me guess: the Gunderson Foundation?"

He shook his head. "No, but we did find two other organizations in the same neuroscience business, both trying to identify the parts of the brain that lead to psychopathology. And both have pretty deep pockets."

Hmm.

I recalled my trip to the primate center and Fischer's concern that his relationship to the Gunderson Foundation not become public.

"Is the info on the electronic case files?"

He nodded.

"All right," I said. "I'm following up on this. Stay on top of the bomb deal. Keep me informed."

He nodded, then crossed the room to speak with Officer Tielman, who had just arrived.

I checked my texts: only one—Tessa telling me she was fine. Good.

I positioned myself at a table near the wall, pulled out my laptop, and clicked to the online case files.

But after fifteen minutes of dead-ends I decided to try another angle and surfed to www.thomas.loc.gov to search through the list of pending legislation in the House of Representatives. It would take forever to read the bills, most of which were probably hundreds of pages long, but two topics could help narrow things down.

I had the first in mind already: justice reform.

And Margaret had given me the second.

Abortion.

She had drained his savings account and was in a hotel room cleaning up, thinking about the implications of her decision to disappear.

Everything she needed to fake her death was in their basement, in the room that the man she'd trusted had so carefully remodeled. All the tools. All the chemicals. But of course, since he might show up at the house at any time, she would be taking a huge chance going back there.

However, she needed to take care of this tonight, as soon as possible, and the basement was the most obvious place to do it. In fact, given the tight time frame, it might very well be the only place she could pull this off.

If she were a suspect in this crime spree, the

airports would likely flag her name, but being pre-
sumed dead she would be off the radar screen. She
would be free.

By leaving some of her own blood and tearing out
some of her own hair she would make it appear as if
she was the prey.

But a little blood and hair wouldn't be enough to
convince the FBI.

To make this work, she needed a body. One that
she could dissolve beyond recognition—put the body
in the tub, fill it with water, add a few gallons of
drain cleaner, turn the victim into soap. Even re-
combinant DNA becomes almost impossible to identify
when you use enough drain cleaner.

If she could leave just enough evidence that a
woman had been killed, and just enough evidence to
make it appear that the woman had been her, she
could at least buy enough time to get out of the
country.

To escape.

Disappear.

Start a new life and raise her baby.

So in the end she realized that even though returning to the house might be risky, it was a chance
she had to take.

However, she'd never killed anybody in NowLife,
just arranged things so that her lover could put her
ideas into action, and now, to her surprise, the
more she thought about taking another woman's life,
the more unsettling the idea became.

But there was no other choice. For the sake of
her own freedom, for the sake of her baby's future,
someone would need to die. One life for two.

And because of the research she had done for work,
she knew the perfect person to choose as her victim.

She changed into a new set of clothes, grabbed the
car keys, and left the hotel to go get her prey.

Margaret found what she was looking for.

She was in her office at FBI HQ and had just finished analyzing interoffice memos and electronic communication to track the
release of the Project Rukh files. She discovered that indeed it was
FBI Director Rodale who had approved the transfer of the Project

Rukh research to the Gunderson Foundation—just days before Congressman Fischer's contributions to the Foundation began.

Maybe the two men weren't at odds at all, maybe they were partners.

But then why would Fischer propose budget cuts to the Bureau?

Whatever Rodale's connection with Fischer, the next step seemed obvious to her.

Follow the money.

Margaret picked up the phone to make a few calls.

96

3 hours left . . .

6:29 p.m.

I didn't find anything specific on justice reform, but I did uncover two House bills with Fischer's name on them that were currently before Congress—either of which might relate to the case.

The first one, H.R. 597, would add restrictions to death penalty sentencing procedures. "In response to the burgeoning world sentiment on the human rights abuses often precipitated while carrying out lethal injections."

Second, a bill he was cosponsoring that would increase federal funding for the in-vitro testing of babies to identify genetic or neurological disorders: H.R. 617. The bill didn't appear to relate per se to abortion, as Margaret had intimated, but these types of in vitro tests were often used by parents who were considering abortion as a—

Tielman called my name and I looked up.

"We have another plate for you," he announced.

It took me a moment to mentally shift gears. "A plate? A license plate?"

"Yup." He crossed the room toward me. "A National Academy student going back to the dorm. Ends up, the plates on her car aren't hers. A sergeant at the front gate, guy named Hastings, noticed it. Just ten, fifteen, minutes ago."

"Which student?" I asked.

He glanced at the note he was carrying. "Detective Annette Larotte." He handed me the paper. "They're registered to her, but she says she never applied for them."

Her plates: SED-UAR.

Hmm.

I jotted the plates from Mahan's car beneath them:

SED-UAR
IPR-OMI

Or maybe,

IPR-OMI
SED-UAR

Ignoring the dashes and read together, the plates could be read "I promised you are—"

You are what? Who is it referring to?

While I was considering this, I noticed Lee Anderson step into the room.

"And get this," Tielman went on, "they're Colorado plates. From Denver."

"Denver?" I was only half-listening.

"Aren't you from Denver?"

"Yeah," I muttered, then I called to Anderson, "Who's tailing Basque?"

He looked annoyed. "I lost him."

"What? You lost him!" I left Tielman, strode toward Anderson.

"We were at a stoplight," he muttered, "I was three cars back— maybe he made me, I don't know. But he turned at the corner, and when I finally got past the light I found his car halfway down the block parked next to the curb. He was nowhere in sight."

"So someone's currently watching the vehicle, right? In case he returns?"

Anderson was quiet. "I didn't know this was that high of a priority."

I smacked the table beside us, and the chatter in the room immediately became silent. "Was there a woman with him? Anyone else in the car?"

"No." Anderson seemed defensive, resentful that I was making a big deal out of this. "He was alone in the car. He didn't meet anyone."

"Before you lost him."

He took a breath. "Yes, but he's not a suspect in this case, is he?" There was a subtle challenge in his words, an attempt to diminish his mistake and thereby excuse it.

I didn't want to get into this. Not here, not in front of everyone.

"He's of interest," I said and left it at that.

A door flew open, and Doehring stormed toward us. His eyes were knives. "Anderson!"

I decided to let Doehring deal with Anderson. As he approached I said, "We have someone monitoring the mass transit footage, right?"

"Angela Knight's on it." He was glaring at Anderson.

"Did she say if she's at HQ today or Quantico?"

"Quantico. With someone named Lacey."

Perfect. "All right, let's assign an officer to watch Basque's car." I shook my head. "Hopefully, it's still there."

Considering the killers' habit of leaving clues to future crimes, I asked Doehring to arrange protective custody for Annette Larotte until we could make some progress on the case. He agreed, then corralled Anderson to the other side of the room to get the location of the vehicle, and I phoned Angela, told her to keep looking for Basque's face to show up on the transit videos. "Dr. Lebreau too," I added.

"Anything else?" She sounded exhausted. "I'm sitting here with pretty much nothing to do, you know."

"You can look for Adkins."

"Who?"

I told her about Sevren, and she said, "I thought he was dead."

"He is."

What is obvious is not always what is true.

"I think."

I glanced at the slip of paper Tielman had given me with the plates. "Hey, can you do letter permutations for me? Or if you're too busy, transfer me to another analyst who can?"

A pause. "How many letters?"

"Twelve."

"Pat, do you have any idea how many combinations that would be?"

"A lot."

A few seconds later she said, "479,001,600."

"I'm not asking you to do it by hand. Lacey loves this kind of stuff."

Silence.

"Here they are—ready?"

A small sigh. "Go ahead."

"S-E-D-U-A-R I-P-R-O-M-I."

"You didn't tell me there were only ten different letters; that two letters were repeated."

This type of math was never my thing. "How much does that change things?"

"Now we're down to . . ." I heard a few keystrokes. "119,750,400."

"Great. 360,000,000 fewer to worry about. It should be a breeze. I just want to know what other actual words or phrases these letters might spell."

"Well, in that case," she said ambiguously.

"Thanks, Angela."

A pause. "Sure."

After she hung up I called Ralph, who answered after one ring. "Hey. I was gonna give you a holler," he said. "I'm on my way to the airport now. And I've got some news on the address book."

"You need to know something first, Ralph. The officer who was following Basque lost him."

"What!" He took the opportunity to utter some of the very same words I'd been thinking about sharing with Lee Anderson only a few minutes ago.

"You still think you should come back?" I asked Ralph.

"Yeah. If Basque is there somewhere, that's where I need to be. Now, listen, the address book: there's a person in the DC area whose address was deleted from her computer three days ago. We were able to do a data recovery."

"Who is it?"

A pause. "Gregory Rodale."

His words stunned me. "You're kidding."

"No. I just got off the phone with him. He said they met once at a jurisprudence conference years ago. Hasn't heard from her since."

That sounded weak to me. "Does Margaret know about this yet?"

"I just spoke with her."

I tried to sift through everything. "So do you think Professor Lebreau might have left Michigan of her own accord? Come to DC to see Rodale?"

"Man, I don't know what to think. I arrive at Reagan National at 9:02. We'll sort it out then."

"Call me as soon as you land."

We hung up.

Rodale?

I had no idea what to make of that. I pulled up the case files on Basque and started to look for anything that might connect him more closely not only to Renée Lebreau but also to FBI Director Gregory Rodale.

Margaret could hardly believe what she'd discovered.

The Gunderson Foundation was nonprofit, yes, but the two neuroscience research companies that supported Fischer's campaign were not. And Rodale held enough shares in each company, so that if their stock rose just 10 percent he would stand to make tens of thousands. If either stock doubled, he would make millions.

He'd purchased the stocks just after Project Rukh was terminated, just before he allowed the research to be acquired by the Gunderson Foundation.

While it was true that the Project Rukh files would have eventually ended up being released through a Freedom of Information Act request, he'd approved their release prematurely.

And now, considering his financial investments, Margaret could see why.

But then why did he tell Bowers about the Project Rukh connection yesterday? Why draw attention to it?

She didn't know. Maybe after the attack on Twana Summie at the Gunderson facility, Rodale realized it was too late to keep all of this under wraps; that the connections would eventually surface.

She paused.

She'd been the one to recover the Project Rukh files in February.

Rodale could tie them back to you.

Maybe he knew that everything was about to hit the fan and he was positioning someone else in front of him so he could walk away clean. That might be why he put her in charge of the case.

Time to have a little sit-down with her boss.

Margaret strode down the hall to Rodale's office but found that he'd already left for home.

She called his cell.

"Greg, it's Margaret."

"Yes?" There was a lot of noise in the background. Maybe he was in a restaurant.

"We need to talk."

"Was there a break in the Fischer case?"

"No. It might be better if we spoke in person. About this matter."

A pause. "What is this concerning?"

"Project Rukh."

Rodale said nothing. She went on, "I happened upon the memos. And I find your interest in nanotechnology fascinating. Would you like to wait until after my press conference to chat?"

A moment passed, then he gave her the name of a pub near his home. "Eight o'clock," he said.

"Eight o'clock," she echoed. "Semansky's Bar. On 4th."

As she hung up the phone, she took a deep breath of both anticipation and hesitation.

Things were about to get very, very sticky.

■

Tessa stepped into the house.

Locked the doors.

Gave Detective Warren a call.

"I'll be right over," she told Tessa. "Do you need me to bring dinner?"

There was still some of Lien-hua's leftover Chinese from last night, but Tessa decided not to suggest that. "Yeah, that'd be cool."

"No meat or meat by-products, right?"

"Right."

"I'll see you in a bit."

Tessa hung up.

And set up the chessboard.

Black versus white.

The two colors every piece, every person, travels across at some point during the game.

■

Brad parked across the street from EAD Wellington's house. From his research and prior excursions to the house, he knew the pass code to her security system.

No car in the driveway. The window to her garage revealed it was empty. But to be safe, he drew his gun and held it beneath his jacket while he crossed the street.

As he ascended the porch steps, he heard the jangle of Lewis's collar just inside the door. The golden retriever gave a friendly bark.

Brad picked the lock.

Entered the house, and as Lewis watched him, he located the security touchpad control on the wall.

"Good doggie," he said as he closed the door behind him.

97

2 hours left . . .

7:29 p.m.

I found no connections to Director Rodale in Basque's files.

Figuring that Ralph and Margaret would be looking more closely into that tunnel, I turned my attention back to the relationships we were aware of.

I typed:

> Vice President Fischer is tied to Lansing.
>
> Lansing is tied to Basque.
>
> Basque is tied to Lebreau.
>
> Lebreau is tied to Rodale.
>
> Rodale is tied to . . . ?

As I was puzzling over the list, I heard footsteps, light, quick. I looked up to see Lien-hua on her way toward me. She read the weariness, the frustration on my face. "You look whipped."

"Well, at least my looks aren't deceiving."

"Did the custody meeting go all right?"

I realized I hadn't spoken with her about it yet. "It was okay. I think things will work out. You heard about Basque? That he was there?"

"Yes." She seemed distracted. Something was on her mind. "And I heard that Anderson lost him."

I refrained from commenting, just nodded. "Ralph's on his way back. Should get in a little after 9:00. Oh, and Rodale knows Lebreau."

"I heard that too—listen, Pat." She lowered her voice until she was speaking to me almost in a whisper. "I may have found out why the dog didn't bark."

"Go on."

"Let me get my files. I'll meet you upstairs. Room 413."

Curious now.

Very curious.

"Why upstairs?"

"Trust me. Five minutes."

She left, I checked my text messages and confirmed that Tessa was all right. As I was collecting my things, one of the agents dialed up the volume of a television screen mounted near the ceiling at the far side of the room.

"Unnamed sources," the announcer was saying, "have confirmed that Congressman Fischer has made significant contributions to the Gunderson Foundation. In light of the Foundation's application for government funding for controversial nanotechnology research, Republican lawmakers are calling the news 'striking' and 'revealing.' We'll have more as things develop . . ."

Federal funding.

Nanotechnology research?

Interesting.

A cavern I hadn't thought of.

I jogged up the stairs to hear what Lien-hua had to say.

98

"Natasha Farraday," she told me.

"What?" We were in a vacant office on the fourth floor and she was spreading a stack of files across the table.

"I think we should take a closer look at her."

"You think she might be one of the killers?" I was shocked. "And what? Cassidy is her partner?"

"I'm only saying they warrant a closer look."

"Run it down."

"Remember how earlier today I was looking into law enforcement connections? I started with the six names you gave me, but that didn't take me anywhere."

"And then you were going to explore the lack of DNA evidence."

"Yes, but here was the problem: since we hadn't found evidentiary DNA at the scene, we'd been assuming the killers hadn't left any."

I considered her words. "That assumption seems pretty well-founded."

"I decided to assume the opposite."

"You assumed that the killers *did* leave their DNA."

Yes. Nice.

She pulled the lab analysis reports from the stack of papers.

"I had the lab rerun the samples, you know, in case the killers had tried to alter or fake the evidence, but it all came back with the same results, so I took a closer look at the evidence that we did have, the DNA that would naturally be present—"

"From those who worked the scenes."

"Yes."

"And that's what led you to Farraday and Cassidy."

As she spoke, she pointed to various notes she'd highlighted in the reports. "Take Natasha first. She's worked every crime in this series, was the first to arrive at the hotel the day you were shot. She was the one who found the wheelchair in room 809, the one who cleared Mahan's car and the handicapped van, and was even the agent who oversaw the evidence handling when the congressman went to identify Mollie's body at the hotel."

"The suitcases."

"Yes."

"So of course we would expect to find her DNA at every crime scene."

"Yes. And we do."

There had to be more. "What else?"

"The timing of her arrival at the primate center on Tuesday night would have given her just enough time to leave the facility in the guise of Aria Petic and then return with the emergency responders after Sandra Reynolds's 911 call."

Hmm.

An idea formed in my mind.

Some aspects of the Bureau's personnel files are confidential, but some are not. I flipped open my computer, set it on a desk. "Still all circumstantial."

"Her age fits, she has a build similar to Aria's, knows forensics, has a submissive personality, and arrived in the DC area shortly before the crime spree began."

Again, all circumstantial, but admittedly, each additional fact added weight to the possibility that Lien-hua was on to something.

Imagine it, Pat, the thrill of committing a crime, and then returning to process it. It would be overwhelming, the sense of power . . .

And it would be very difficult to build a case against you based on the presence of your DNA at the crime scene since your DNA would naturally be present.

"Cassidy found the luggage claim tag," I said, "but Farraday went through the car first."

"She could have planted it."

I shook my head. "But why take that chance if you were the killer? Why not just leave the claim tag when you left the laptop?"

"Hmm," she said. "Good point."

I tapped at my computer, brought up Natasha Farraday's files.

Lien-hua watched me. "I checked, Pat. She lives less than a quarter mile west of the hot zone."

One step ahead of me.

"So she fits both the psychological profile and the geoprofile."

"Yes."

"She's a new transfer . . ." I mumbled. Now I was scanning Cassidy's files. "And Cassidy is her superior, and his personality is more dominant . . ."

"I know it's nothing solid," she admitted. "Just a series of coincidences."

"But apparent coincidences—"

"Always warrant closer inspection."

"Very nice," I said, "word-for-word from my book."

"What can I say, I'm a fan."

I glanced over the evidence again. "What have you done so far to try and disprove Farraday and Cassidy's involvement?"

"Well, of course, that's the tricky part here. It's all a house of cards. Circumstantial, like you said. I can't just start showing pictures of my colleagues to the Rainey children or the taxi driver."

I considered that.

The Rainey boy had said that the man leaving the alley was scarred, but Cassidy had no scars on his face.

Scars can be faked.

"Could someone be setting them up?"

She shook her head. "I don't see how. The crime scene assignments came from either dispatch, Margaret, or Rodale. The killers would need to know the ERT's dispatch protocol and response time."

Who would know those times?

I'd first met Natasha Farraday at the primate center Tuesday night . . . then I saw her at the hotel on Wednesday . . . then—

Wait.

SED-UAR.

IPR-OMI.

Said you are . . .

I promised you are . . .

Natasha had mentioned she read my books . . .

She questioned you about Mahan's car, how you knew that one was the vehicle the killer had used . . .

I closed my computer. Stood.

"What are you thinking?"

"The lab at Quantico," I said.

Lien-hua shook her head. "We don't have enough here to justify talking to them. We barely have—"

"I don't want to talk to them. I want to look more closely at what they brought back from the scenes."

She quickly collected her things. "I've been in this building since 10:30. I'm coming with you."

I had no quarrel with that.

"We'll take my car," I said. "There are a few tunnels I want you to help me explore on the way."

———————————————◼———————————————

Tessa answered the door.

Detective Warren stood on the porch holding a grocery bag in one hand, her computer satchel in the other. "Hey," she said.

Tessa moved aside. "Come on in."

Cheyenne held up the groceries as she entered. "How does falafel burgers, humus, and tortilla chips sound? Oh, and some root beer?"

"Righteous." Tessa closed the door.

The detective's eyes flitted to the chessboard. "You're a glutton for punishment, Tessa."

"Not this time. Tonight you're the one who's going down."

A slight grin. "We'll see about who's going down. Come on, let's get something to eat, and then we'll get started with the game."

◼

Margaret stepped into Semansky's Bar.

A few pool tables. Air that reeked of stale beer. Slow, heavy country music drawled from the speakers hidden in the ceiling. A thin film of smoke creased the air. It was illegal to smoke in restaurants in DC, but it was pretty clear that the owners of Semansky's weren't too concerned about that ordinance.

She looked around.

A few sleepy businessmen sat in the shadows, caressing their drinks. Two of them looked up when she walked in but then disappeared into their own little worlds when she ignored them.

What a pit.

No sign of Rodale.

Over the loudspeakers, a country singer was hoping to get his wife back.

She scanned the room again, and this time saw Greg seated by himself in a corner booth, an empty beer glass on the table in front of him. She approached him, and he greeted her a little too warmly: "Margaret."

"Greg." She took a seat across from him in the booth. "Thank you for taking the time."

"Of course."

A wispy waitress with frenzied hair and too much makeup appeared out of nowhere. "Refill?" she asked him.

"Give me another Strasman Dark." He looked toward Margaret. "Want a drink?" She wondered how many he'd had already.

"No thanks."

"You sure?" the waitress asked her.

"I'm sure. But thank you."

"Thank you," she replied in that tone of voice that means "Then why are you taking up my table space?"

"Bring us a basket of fries too," Greg added.

Their server sloughed off into the darkness. Music throbbed.

"So," he said.

"So."

"You wanted to discuss some memos." Obviously he wasn't interested in wasting any time.

"Greg, you passed along Defense Department files to the private sector before they'd been carefully reviewed, vetted, and cleared."

"There was nothing top secret in the research, Margaret. Project Rukh had been terminated. Besides, the program had originally been subcontracted to a private firm."

"Under the oversight committee's supervision."

He let a moment pass. Didn't reply.

"The decision was ill-advised and premature."

He dismissed her concerns. "So we have a difference of opinion concerning the matter. What else?"

"Tell me about Dr. Renée Lebreau."

"You've been talking to Ralph Hawkins."

"How do you know her?"

He gazed into the shadowy confines of the room. Ran his finger gently across the tabletop. "Renée and I met at a conference years ago, before I was appointed FBI Director, before she was a professor." He said the words as if they were a prepared statement.

"Before your divorce."

He eyed Margaret coolly. Stilled his hand. "Yes. Before my divorce."

"Did you suggest that she look into Richard Basque's case two years ago? Is that how she became involved?"

"Why are you bringing this up, Margaret?"

"Because she disappeared and Basque is here in DC and I don't believe in coincidences."

"Now you sound like Bowers."

The waitress reappeared, deposited the basket of fries, Rodale's beer, and a glass of cloudy water for Margaret, then vanished into the shadows again.

Greg took a sip of the beer. "Considering all the media hype and Basque's claims over the years that he was innocent—and the fact that the case involved Bowers, one of our highest profile agents—yes. I reviewed Basque's files."

"And?"

"And I felt there were enough inconsistencies to justify a lawyer giving his case a fresh look."

"Not just a lawyer, a law *professor*. He had plenty of lawyers. She's one of the nation's most outspoken anti-death penalty—"

"I knew Lebreau." His words had turned hard. "I gave her a call. That's it. There's nothing unethical about that. On the phone you mentioned nanotechnology."

Now for the big one. "You stand to benefit if the Gunderson Foundation has any breakthroughs."

"How's that?"

"Stock."

"The Gunderson Foundation is a nonprofit organization. What are you talking about?"

"It was clever," she said. "If they make any breakthroughs, it'll catapult the whole industry forward, sending stock prices at the other firms in the business skyrocketing. But through it all, you stay one step removed. Still, with the purchase of those stocks, we have breach of trust, conflict of interest, possibly insider trading."

He took a long sip of his drink. "Did you come here to blackmail me, Margaret?"

"By no means, but there are too many holes in all this. It's going to come to light eventually. I'm giving you the opportunity to bypass all that, to come clean before it happens."

"Before you make it happen."

She didn't reply.

He set down his beer and gave her a look that seemed to contain both derision and defeat. "You just want my job, Margaret."

He was right about that, and they both knew it. The FBI Director was appointed by the President of the United States with the Senate's approval, but an executive AD would almost certainly make the short list if the Director resigned or was asked to step down. "That's what this is all about," he said, then repeated, "You want my job."

"That's not all I want."

He nodded as if he'd been expecting that. He slid the beer aside. "What else?"

"I want what's best for the Bureau, Greg."

He waited as if expecting her to go on, but when she didn't he said, "You can't prove any of this."

"Give me time. I'm pretty good at connecting the dots."

He poured ketchup on the fries. "So you want me to resign, is that it?"

"I want you to give a press conference. Explain your reasons. Clear the air."

"And then resign?"

"Do what you feel is right."

He left the fries alone but drank some more beer, and it seemed to bring him new resolve. "You quoted a bogus regulation to keep Bowers off this case for forty-eight hours."

"He was shot. I was doing it for the good of the Bureau. For his own good."

"That might not be how the Office of Professional Responsibility will see it. We all know your history with Bowers; you've been gunning for him for years. I assigned him to the case, and even though he was willing to continue working it, and physically able to, you lied to him, pulled him from it, and hampered the investigation. It might have put innocent people's lives at risk."

"That's absurd."

His voice grew softer, but colder. "You didn't follow up to make sure the ME positively identified the body found at the primate center Tuesday evening. If you had, Mollie might still be alive. Two hours ago the Summie family filed a lawsuit against the Bureau. Now that's on your shoulders. Something you're going to have to answer for."

Margaret hadn't heard about the lawsuit and wasn't sure what to say.

"If you want to play hardball, Margaret, I can play hardball."

"With all due respect, sir. Bring it on."

A stiff silence.

"Do you know where she is?" Margaret asked. "Renée Lebreau?"

"No."

"Do you know why she might have disappeared this week?"

A deep sadness swept across his face, and Margaret was shocked to see how quickly his demeanor changed. "Basque," he said. The strain in the word told Margaret that Greg had not just known Renée casually. "I was wrong about him."

"So now you believe he's guilty?"

No reply.

"Is she dead, Greg?"

He shook his head. "I don't know. I haven't seen her in over a year." Margaret wasn't sure if she believed that. She waited for him to go on.

Rodale cradled his beer in his hands, and she realized that he looked small and frightened. But she was wary. She'd learned long ago that when people get scared they become desperate. And desperate people take desperate measures.

He took a breath, met her gaze. "Think about what I said concerning you and Bowers. Your last run-in with OPR ended up with you stuck at a satellite office in North Carolina for what? Almost five years? Think about your future, Margaret."

"Oh, I am, Greg." She stood. "That's why I came here tonight."

Then she paced out the door and left for home to prepare the statement she was going to give to the press tomorrow morning.

99

Lien-hua and I were on I-95 heading toward Quantico.

I checked my texts again. Tessa was home and she was fine and I was starting to feel like an overprotective parent—not a bad feeling. I had Lien-hua text Tessa for me, asking what she was doing, and she replied: "nmjc c/dw."

I knew that nmjc was teen texting lingo for "nothing much just chillin'."

With a little deduction I realized c/ is short for the Latin word "cum," which means "with," and dw would be Detective Warren.

I only wished it was that easy to decipher this case.

As Lien-hua set down the phone, she said, "So what are these tunnels you'd like to explore?"

"Psychopathology and justice reform."

A moment. "Go on."

"Here's what I've been thinking. The congressman is financially in bed with this whole neuroscience research industry."

"That's Washington, Pat. Special favors, lobbyists. Politics as usual."

"Except that because of the location of Twana's murder, it ties in with this case. Besides, people only lobby when they have an agenda. And it's almost always either money or morals—to make a buck or to make a point."

"That sounds like profiling."

"Just an observation."

"No, definitely profiling. I must be wearing off on you."

"Well, I won't argue with that, but here's the thing: the Gunderson Foundation is researching primate metacognition, neuroscience, and aggression—the neurology of violence. Meanwhile, Fischer is cosponsoring a bill that'll provide federal funding for the in-vitro testing of babies for neurological or genetic disorders."

She listened quietly. "I didn't know that."

"And two of his biggest campaign supporters are firms that provide this service."

"They stand to benefit a lot if the bill passes."

"And if they benefit, so does he."

Silence. "How do you see this relating to the murders?"

"I'm not sure, but in the context of the Project Rukh files and Gunderson Foundation research, what if scientists could do that?"

As a profiler, Lien-hua was one of the Bureau's top experts on criminal psychology. I was anxious to hear her take on this. I continued, "What if it *were* possible to definitively identify the specific neurological or genetic conditions that cause violent behavior or psychopathology?"

"We already know some of the neurological factors," she said, "but behavior could never be pinned down that narrowly, that conclusively. There are just too many things that influence our decisions and condition and affect our behavior. You know that as well as I do."

"Upbringing, socialization, environmental cues, neurological differences, genetic makeup, chemical imbalances—some people even think spiritual forces are at play—"

"Yes, but we can't blame bad genes or our parents or the devil for our crimes. We're each accountable for our own choices."

"Not if we don't have free will."

A slight pause. "Dr. Libet's experiments."

"Yes."

She shook her head. "This afternoon I looked over the articles you posted in the electronic files. There are any number of precipitating factors that could have produced the precognitive neural activity that he found: participant expectation, mental rehearsal, goal orientation to either impress the researcher or confound the experiment. Besides, there's a burgeoning field of research that seems to indicate that there's no such thing as the unconscious."

"But, Lien-hua, there *are* actions we do that we're not consciously aware of."

"Yes, but rather than a duality between the conscious and unconsciousness, it's likely the brain processes information along a continuum, and that intentionality occurs at differing points depending on the stimuli involved and the complexity of the decisions being made."

That made sense to me, seemed almost self-evident. "Okay, but consider how some people are interpreting Libet's findings. What if you believed that free will really was an illusion? That instinct trumps conscious intention? That we're hardwired to unequivocally act certain ways when exposed to certain stimuli at certain times? Courts have already ruled in favor of this defense."

She was quiet.

"You read about those rulings? In the files?"

She took an uncertain breath. "I did."

"So," I said, "assuming we interpreted the findings as some people are—that behavior is directly and fixedly caused by genetic and neurological factors—then, if we understood enough about the brain, we could tell by genetic or neurological testing who would be a psychopath." I glanced at her. "For argument's sake."

"Putting epigenetics aside, the fact that behavior and environment can alter epigenomes, all right, I'll go along with that."

"Tie that in with the in-vitro testing . . ." Margaret's words about society's changing views on the right to life came to mind.

Justice reform.

Congressman Fischer's policy: a more progressive approach to curbing criminal behavior.

And the pieces slid into place.

"Lien-hua, here it is. Test the unborn, find out who's going to grow up to exhibit psychopathic behavior—"

"And abort them," she said softly, echoing my conclusion.

Motives.

That can change everything.

"Get rid of serial killers," she said, "before they ever kill. Cut down on crime by eliminating potential criminals."

"Preemptive justice."

The death penalty. For crimes that had never been committed.

"If you agree that abortion is morally tenable," Lien-hua said sensitively, knowing how tender a subject it was because of how close Christie had come to aborting Tessa, "and assuming you concur with the verdict that the courts have started giving—that in some cases we're not morally responsible for our behavior because it is, for lack of a better term, instinctual, then the reasoning makes perfect sense. Tell a mother her child is going to grow up to be another Jeffery Dahmer or Sevren Adkins and who wouldn't terminate the pregnancy?"

"But it wouldn't stop at psychopathology," I said.

"No." Her voice was soft, strained. "It would not. Pedophiles. Rapists. Where do you draw the line? Maybe people who'll grow up to be manic depressive or inclined to drug addiction—"

"But if there is no free will, there is no line." I thought of the countries that pressure women to abort their baby girls—the most lethal kind of sex discrimination in the world. "Get rid of anyone whom those in power don't feel would be good for society."

"No." Lien-hua shook her head. "This is crazy. You can't determine what someone will do, only what they might be prone to do. We're free to choose, to act or not to act."

"Not if you interpret Dr. Libet's findings as some people are."

"The neurological tests could never be that conclusive."

"They've already been conclusive enough to get people off for first-degree murder. I don't think this is much of a jump. It's just social engineering in the name of justice reform. And as the house minority leader, Fischer is powerful enough to actually push something like this through Congress."

A pause.

Then she said, "Aren't people supposed to have a right to life, liberty, and the pursuit of happiness? We have a right to make our own choices. To determine our own future."

"But what if we can't? If free will and moral responsibility are only illusions?"

"Then pursuing happiness would be an illusion too."

"And so would liberty," I said.

The comment brought a stretch of palpable silence.

I took the exit to the Academy.

Earlier, when I was at the command post, I'd tracked the relationships forward in time. Now with a renewed sense of urgency, I mentally did so backward.

Rodale to Lebreau.

Lebreau to Basque.

Basque to Lansing.

Lansing to Vice President Fischer.

Vice President Fischer to . . .

"During the assassination attempt," I said, "there were two rooms on the eighth floor that were used—do we know if they were both paid for by Hadron Brady?"

"Remember? The hotel didn't keep the records that far back."

Who would?

Who would keep the—

"No," I breathed, thinking aloud. "We don't have records of the rooms, but there are records of the payments."

"No, Pat, they're all gone. They—"

"But yet they exist."

She looked at me curiously. "What are you thinking?"

"At six hundred dollars per room most people wouldn't have paid for their stay in cash."

Then it hit her. "Credit cards."

"Yes."

"Aha." A slight smile. "Since 9/11 the government has required all credit card companies to keep records of all transactions for ten years to help track terrorism suspects."

"Exactly. We won't be able to tell who stayed in which room, but we can find out the names of people who charged a room at the Lincoln Towers Hotel on March 15 or 16th six years ago."

"And we can see if a person from the suspect list used a card to pay for a room," she finished my train of thought.

"Yes. Or someone named Patricia E."

She tugged out her phone. "Pat, I have to say, the way you string things together sometimes . . . I don't know, you remind me of Sherlock Holmes."

"Don't tell that to Tessa. She might just agree with you."

"There you go."

"Trust me. From her it would not be a compliment."

"We'll need warrants."

"Then we'll need Margaret," I replied.

100

1 hour left . . .

8:29 p.m.

Margaret came through for us.

It'd taken her less than five minutes to call a judge and get the warrants needed to contact the four largest credit card companies and begin the process of pulling up the credit card charges on the dates we were looking at.

I turned onto the road that led to the Academy. The security checkpoint lay a quarter mile ahead.

Lien-hua phoned Angela to get her team started on the project and found out she was in the middle of reanalyzing Mollie Fischer's laptop—apparently, another technician had failed to follow up on the emails sent and received, and Angela was left picking up the pieces.

When Lien-hua hung up, she said to me, "She sounded a little overwhelmed."

"Imagine that."

I drove up to the gate, only one car in front of me.

Sergeant Eric Hastings, the young Marine who'd been working Tuesday evening when I'd arrived with Tessa for the panel discussion, and had also noted the discrepancy with Annette Larotte's plates, was finishing checking the driver's license of a man in the Toyota minivan just in front of us.

As he waved them through, I eased forward.

"Evening, sir," he said as he approached my window.

"How are you, Sergeant." It was more of a greeting than a question.

"I'm good, sir."

He finished verifying our creds, and as Lien-hua and I were putting them away, I realized Hastings looked slightly disappointed as he inspected the inside of the car. I wondered if it was because my cute stepdaughter wasn't with me. The father in me didn't like that possibility, but for the moment I held back from commenting. Now wasn't the time.

Not now, but later. Eric's gotta be at least three years older than she is . . .

He opened the gate, told us good-bye, and I drove through.

"I'm concerned," Lien-hua said. "About Angela."

I was still caught up in my thoughts about Hastings. "I'm sure she's okay."

"Her office is just down the hall from the evidence rooms."

It was an obvious hint, and I took it. "All right. We'll swing by and check on her on the way."

I parked near the FBI Lab's east wing, and we headed inside.

Brad parked the car.

In one sense, Bowers was right about motives—the offender in this case had more than one. The game wasn't just about revenge, it was about revealing the bigger picture.

About stopping people from playing God, stopping them from tampering with the fabric of human nature he had designed.

He stepped out of the car.

Brad figured it would be about a fifteen minute walk through the woods to the house, which meant he'd get there just as dusk was deepening into night.

Good. Because he needed it to be dark for the climax.

He sent the text message that would put everything into play, and, carrying the third and final license plate, he entered the forest.

Angela has a big heart but usually wears a slightly concerned expression. Late thirties. Slightly overweight. Thick glasses. Big loopy earrings. Kind but anxious eyes.

Three computer screens sat on the desk in front of her. The one on the left was scrolling through hundreds of names, presumably from the credit card search. The right screen was filled with tiny icons of live video feeds from the mass transit system, scanning faces.

The center screen showed a spam email ad.

I wondered about the letter permutations, but for the moment, I didn't ask.

Angela glanced at us only momentarily. She looked more worried than normal.

"Are you all right?" Lien-hua asked.

"Take a look at this." She directed our attention to the middle screen, then slid the ad to the left to more clearly reveal a timer I hadn't noticed when we first walked in.

A countdown.

Endgame: 49 minutes 15 seconds
Endgame: 49 minutes 14 seconds
Endgame: 49 minutes 13 seconds

Immediately, I thought of the traces of military grade C-4 found in the back of the van the killers had used.

"A bomb?" I said.

"I don't know," Angela replied. "The timer was embedded in the email I pulled up."

"When did the countdown start?" Lien-hua asked.

"The message arrived earlier this afternoon, at 3:29."

Endgame: 48 minutes 53 seconds

Lien-hua looked at the computer's clock, did a quick calculation. "So 9:29. But what happens then?"

"It might be nothing," Angela said.

"No," Lien-hua replied. "It's something."

An explosion?

Another murder?

What's the endgame?

Taking into consideration the C-4 and the explosion that occurred at the gas station last night—

Endgame: 48 minutes 22 seconds

"Could this laptop itself be an explosive device?" I said.

Angela shook her head. "I inspected it inside and out this morning. It's just a laptop, nothing more."

"Is it possible it's a detonator though?" Lien-hua asked. "Or could it be used to initiate a detonation sequence?"

A slight hesitation. "It did send an auto reply to the ad."

I was a bit surprised she hadn't already looked into it. "Pull it up."

The reply appeared, mostly techno-jargon, but the subject line included a "return to sender" notice. That was all.

"Return to sender," Lien-hua said reflectively. "If there is a bomb, it could be a message: 'return to sender,' i.e. 'return to God.'"

That seemed to be on track with the way these killers thought.

"Can you back trace this?" I asked Angela. "Find out where the ad was sent from, or who received the reply?"

Endgame: 47 minutes 4 seconds

She typed, then said, "The ad was sent to this computer from a Motorola Droid." She pointed to the longitude and latitude coordinates on the screen.

Lien-hua drew out her phone and called the command post to have them send a car to the downtown DC location.

I leaned over Angela's desk. "Can you tell where the reply went? Who received it?"

Angela explained something about a mail server host and a Cybrous 17 cellular modem relay sending out bits of code that could have been accessed from anywhere. "We might be able to trace it, but it'll take time. An hour, maybe more." She tapped at her keyboard. "I'll get a team on it."

An hour.

That's too long . . .

"You're sure there's nothing explosive in this laptop?" I asked her.

"Yes." But she sounded more uncertain this time. "I guess you can have the bomb squad check it out though, just in case."

Lien-hua nodded, ended one call, made the other. My attention went back to the computer monitors. "Do we have anything on Basque or Adkins?"

"No. But I did finish those permutations for you." Angela tapped at her keyboard, and the middle screen switched to a seemingly endless display of letter combinations.

"I think you should stick with interpreting it, 'I promised you are,'" she said. "Lacey analyzed the other letter combinations that contain actual words, but she thinks that the letters in their original order make the most . . ." She paused for a long time and stared at the screen, at a small portion of the list that contained nearly 120,000,000 sets of letters.

"What is it?"

"Patricia E.," she muttered. "How could I have been so stupid."

"You know who Patricia E. is? Who is she?"

Angela pulled up Lacey's permutations calculator and typed in the name PATRICIAE.

Instantly, thousands of nine-letter combinations began scrolling down the screen.

Angela tapped the keyboard, paused the list. Scrolled up a few dozen lines. Then pointed.

ARIAPETIC.

"An anagram," I whispered. "Angela, you're a genius." I tried to process the implications. Calvin had uncovered the clue about Patricia E. three weeks ago, which meant that somehow he knew about these crimes.

Or the killers knew about his note.

But how . . . ?

"The bomb squad's on the way," Lien-hua said, pocketing her phone.

"Angela found Aria Petic," I told her.

"Where?"

"Not where, who," Angela said. "It's Patricia E." She explained the connection but was eyeing Mollie's laptop computer uneasily the whole time. "Listen, if this is a bomb I don't want it anywhere near Lacey."

She had a good point. If the laptop was an explosive device, it didn't make sense to leave it in the building. "I'll take it to the parking lot," I said.

"No, Pat. Just leave it," Lien-hua objected. "The bomb squad will be here any minute."

"Angela already checked the laptop this morning," I said. "There's no indication that it's a bomb; all we have is this timer. Besides, it's been shuffled around all day and there's still over forty minutes before the countdown ends. I'll be fine."

I donned latex gloves to avoid leaving yet another set of prints on the laptop. "Call Cassidy and Farraday," I told Lien-hua, "and find out where they are. It might be good to . . . touch base."

She was quiet, then pulled out her phone. "Be careful."

"I will."

"Please don't blow yourself up."

"I won't."

Day folded in on itself across the bottom of the sky. A sliver of sunlight fingered out from beneath the clouds and then it was gone.

And then it was night.

Brad was surprised that Detective Warren was here; he'd expected Tessa to be alone, but really, it was perfect. He couldn't have planned a more fitting ending to the game.

He knelt beside the rear bumper of Cheyenne's car, unscrewed the plates.

He could see the two of them through a slit in the living room curtains and was tempted to smile, to gloat, but held back, stayed attentive. What he had in mind was so elegant, so devastating, no one would see it coming.

The rematch he'd challenged Bowers to.

Eight months in the making.

And now Detective Cheyenne Warren would play one of the most important roles.

He finished with the plates, returned to the woods. Pulled out his Walther P99.

And sent the final text message to the next victim.

101

34 minutes left . . .

8:55 p.m.

While I waited for the bomb squad, I phoned the command post and told them to check for a bomb in the handicapped-accessible van, the Honda Accord that had been left in front of police head-quarters, all related crime scenes, the congressman's home, and to notify every agency working even peripherally on the task force to put them on alert.

Despite all of these steps, however, considering the way these killers worked, if they truly had left a bomb somewhere, I didn't expect it to be someplace obvious.

No.

Misdirection all the way.

I thought of what I'd told Annette on Wednesday morning about the fourth premise of environmental criminology—progression.

With each additional crime, offenders become more efficient, learn from their mistakes, develop preferences for specific activities and behavior—

Endgame: 31 minutes 9 seconds

The bomb squad arrived, and after I'd passed off Mollie's laptop I jogged inside to find out if Lien-hua had been able to locate Agents Cassidy and Farraday.

Tessa and Detective Warren faced each other, the chessboard between them

"You're playing better tonight," Detective Warren said.

"I'm trying to think like you."

"Aha."

Tessa took her time evaluating the position of the pieces on the board. "I wanted to ask you something."

"Sure. What's that?"

Tessa moved her queen. "You're Catholic, right?"

Detective Warren scrutinized the board. "I am."

"And Catholics believe people are born evil, don't they?"

"It's not that simple, but—"

"Well, in sin, or whatever. Original sin."

Detective Warren looked up from the chessboard. "We believe that people are born with a fallen nature, that all of us are in need of a Savior." She didn't sound defensive or preachy, but she did seem surprised by the direction the conversation was taking. "Just watch the news for ten minutes and you can see how true that is."

Tessa was silent. Patrick's words from last night came to mind: "*Fractures . . . I don't think we can seal them . . . I don't think anyone ever has . . .*"

Detective Warren gave her attention back to the chess pieces. Slid one of her rooks to block the square Tessa had been eyeing for her queen.

"A fallen nature," Tessa said.

"Yes."

"So is that the difference, then, between us and other animals? That we're fallen and they're not? That we need a Savior and they don't?"

Detective Warren eyed Tessa somewhat suspiciously. "This conversation isn't some kind of ploy to make me lose my concentration on the game, is it?"

"Maybe."

"Aha. Well . . . That's one thing that makes us different, yes." She seemed like she was going to say more, but held back.

Human beings, being human.
Following their hearts.
Tessa made her move.
Detective Warren countered.

"What about you, Tessa? What do you think makes us different?"

Her thoughts cycled back to her recent reading and research. "Did you ever read *The Strange Case of Dr. Jekyll and Mr. Hyde* by Robert Louis Stevenson?"

"I've heard of it, of course, but no, I don't believe I've ever read it."

"Well, it's not like Dr. Jekyll is the mad scientist or something, like he's usually portrayed. He wasn't trying to create a monster but to isolate one."

"To isolate one?"

"He wanted to separate his good nature from his bad. But it didn't go so well."

"The bad took over?"

"Pretty much. And after it got loose there was no stopping it." Tessa moved one of her pawns. "Anyway, last night Patrick and I got talking about being true to your heart and about these guys—like the ones the Bureau is tracking this week—how, when they do these things, they're being true to their hearts."

"To the fallen nature. But—"

"To the fractures."

"Fractures?"

"It's Patrick's thing. Anyway, if it's true we evolved from primates, maybe we're not different from animals at all—"

Detective Warren's ringing cell phone interrupted her, so Tessa quickly finished her thought. "I mean, how can we not be true to who we are? How can anything act in a way that's incongruent with its nature?"

"Incongruent with its nature." Detective Warren tugged out her phone, looked at the screen. "Hold that thought. It's your dad."

102

25 minutes left . . .

9:04 p.m.

"Cheyenne." I was on my way to Evidence Room 3a. "Something came up just a few minutes ago. We're looking into the possibility that there might be a bomb set to explode at 9:29."

"A bomb? Where?"

"We don't know. Is everything all right there?"

"We're just sitting around talking about good and evil, Jekyll and Hyde, original sin. Nothing heavy. Tell me about the bomb."

Angela flagged me down. I stepped into her office and saw that Lacey had finished her analysis of the credit card charges at the Lincoln Towers Hotel on the night Hadron Brady tried to shoot the vice president.

No Patricia E.

No Aria Petic.

No one from the suspect list.

"Pat?" Cheyenne said.

"Sorry. Listen, there were traces of C-4 found in the van. We have a timer, a countdown that was emailed to Mollie's laptop. That's all."

"Were they there when the van was first checked?"

"What?"

"The traces of C-4. I read the files, Pat. That van was processed on Wednesday. Maybe the ERT didn't find the traces the first time because they weren't there. Then."

Now there was an interesting thought.

Cassidy and Farraday cleared it, then rechecked it.

Plant the traces of explosives after the gas station explosion? Another clue to a future crime?

I scribbled a note for Angela to look for the names Cassidy and Farraday in the credit card list. She stared at me incredulously but tapped at her keyboard.

Cheyenne said, "Is there anything I can do from here?"

"I'll call you if there is, and I'll get there as soon as I can, but things are a little up in the air right now."

No one by the name of either Cassidy or Farraday had paid for a room at the hotel on either the night before the shooting or the day of it. I pointed to the printer to let Angela know I wanted her to print a copy of the names that she did have.

"Okay," Cheyenne said. "Be careful." The same thing Lien-hua had told me just minutes ago.

"I will. Keep a close eye on Tessa, all right? Tonight, I don't know, everything feels off balance."

"Don't worry. She's safe with me." She hung up, the printout finished, and I grabbed the pages. Studied the names.

The As . . . Bs . . . Cs . . .

I wasn't even sure what I was looking for.

D . . . E . . . F . . .

Just a name I might recognize. Anyone.

G . . . H . . . I . . .

Anything out of the ordinary.

J . . . K . . . L—

I stopped.

Stared.

At the name: *Lebreau, Renée.*

103

The entire cave system I'd thought I was looking at collapsed.

Lebreau disappeared at 11:00 on Tuesday, that would've given her enough time to get to DC before Twana's murder Tuesday night . . .

Renée Lebreau had connections with Basque.

Lien-hua appeared at the door. I told her, "Professor Lebreau's credit card was used to pay for a room at the Lincoln Towers on the day of the assassination attempt."

"What?" She sounded stunned.

"I know. I'm not sure what it means. Were you able to reach Cassidy and Farraday?"

"I spoke with Natasha. They'd both already gone home for the night. I asked if she could come back in to evaluate some evidence with me. She's on her way. So Lebreau was at the hotel?"

"At least her credit card was. What about Cassidy?"

"I couldn't reach him. Natasha should be here in about fifteen minutes."

I checked the time.

9:10.

Nineteen minutes before the endgame.

Whatever that was.

"We came here to review the evidence in the lab," I said, heading for the hall. "Let's go do it before she arrives."

Brad positioned himself in the trees.

All right.

There were a number of ways things might play out tonight, but the result would be the same. He would make sure two people died and Bowers ended up scarred in the way that never heals.

There are many kinds of death. Physical, spiritual, emotional, psychological.

Yes.

And this would be the most fitting kind of all.

For both Agent Bowers.

And his stepdaughter.

———————————————■———————————————

Evidence Room 3a.

All of the evidence collected from the scenes lay before us, sealed and numbered in plastic evidence bags: straw from the primate center, the leather restraints the killers had used, the contents of Mollie Fischer's purse, the cartridge case of the bullet that had gone through my arm, the two cryptic license plates. Beside them lay the blood-soaked suitcases, the wheelchair, carpeting from the van.

C'mon, Pat, what are you missing?

"We need to start at the beginning," I told Lien-hua, but I knew we didn't have time, and by the look on her face, she was thinking the same thing. Six lab techs worked quietly on the other side of the room, giving us some space.

"All right." Lien-hua slid the bags with bloodied straw aside to focus our attention on them. "Tuesday: Twana Summie is abducted and murdered, but the killers make it look like it's Mollie Fischer's body."

"No, let's go back before that, to the note."

"The note?"

"Calvin's note that mentioned Patricia E., the anagram for Aria Petic. There's no way that's a coincidence. He died last month. How did Calvin find that out?"

"Or, on the flip side, how did the killers find out about the note?"

"Exactly."

"How many people know about that note?"

"I'm not sure. Angela. Ralph. Me. A few other people. Cheyenne. I haven't exactly advertised it."

"And how'd you find it again?"

"Calvin started to suspect that Giovanni was responsible for the murders Basque was on trial for. He was looking into it when he was attacked. Then while he was in the coma, I found the note in his things."

"And we have no idea how he discovered the information?"

I scanned the piles of evidence and had a thought. *Maybe he didn't.*

H814b Patricia E.

Yes.

Of course!

"What if this clue about Patricia," I said, "has nothing to do with Giovanni or Basque?"

"But because of the name Aria Petic, the mention of Patricia E. is clearly related to this case."

"No, no, listen." I jotted the clue down on a slip of paper, pointed at the name: Patricia E. "Since the killers left an anagram for Patricia E. at the primate center, we have a connection with the second part of the note. And here. H814b. They killed Mollie in room 814, to connect the hotel to Hadron Brady—"

She hit the table. "His initials—H.B."

"Which means that somehow the killers put all this together last month."

But why write an anagram? Why a code?

"No. Hang on." I shook my head. "Calvin was a man of science. To him, everything was about clarity, specificity. Why isn't the *b* capitalized? And why add another layer of obscurity to a case by creating this cipher—"

"Unless he didn't discover it; unless it was given to him."

My head was spinning. "In either case, the genesis of everything seems to be that assassination attempt. Lebreau was there, Brady was there. Vice President Fischer and . . ."

I waited, unsure I wanted to say his name.

"Paul Lansing," she said.

"Yes." I nodded. "Exactly."

I looked at her, let my silence speak for me.

"Pat, that's insane," Lien-hua said incredulously. "There's no way he had anything to do with this."

I didn't know Lansing's phone number, but I figured Lacey could find it for me. "I need to talk to Angela."

As I hurried toward her office, Lien-hua kept up with me. "Pat, you don't actually think Lansing is involved?"

"No."

"But then—"

"Just a sec." I was at Angela's door. "Can you pull up all the phone numbers for any Paul Remmer Lansing from Wyoming?" I asked her.

She typed. "Nope. Nothing."

His lawyers will have the number.

"Get me the number for Keegan Wilby in DC."

"Pat, this is crazy," Lien-hua said.

"I know."

Angela found Wilby's cell number, I called, he didn't answer. *Come on!*

I left him a message to call me as soon as he could with Lansing's number.

The scars.

Endgame.

The plates left on Larrote's car were registered in Denver, where you live.

Lien-hua put a hand on my shoulder. "Pat. What are you think-ing?"

"Tessa. I need to check on her. You stay here, wait for Natasha."

"Call me."

"I will."

Then I remembered that Paul had emailed Tessa on Wednesday, asked her to call him.

She'll have his number.

I speed-dialed my stepdaughter as I burst out the door and raced to my car.

104

10 minutes left . . .
9:19 p.m.

"Do you know your father's number?" I was pulling out of my parking spot. "His phone number?"

"No."

"How could you not—"

"He never gave it to me. Patrick, what's going on?" Her voice had a crack of fear inside it. "Is there a bomb somewhere?" She must have overheard me talking with Cheyenne a little while ago.

"I don't know. Listen, if Paul contacts you, emails you, anything, I want you to call me immediately. Stay in the house, make sure the doors are locked."

"You're scaring me."

"No, don't be scared, just stay with Detective Warren. I'll be home in a few minutes."

"Did Paul do something?"

"No. But he might know who did. Don't worry," I said. "I'll be there by 9:30."

End call. I punched the gas and left the Academy.

■

Margaret Wellington was deep in thought about Rodale's connection with Lebreau as she entered her house, set down her purse, and dropped her keys into the dish on the counter, but even as she did those things, a small uncomfortable chill began to crawl through her.

Her dog had not run up to greet her. "C'mere, Lewis." Her voice sounded lonely, muted by the empty house.

Nothing.

"Come here, boy."

He didn't come.

"Lewis?"

Stillness.

A vacant, silent house.

He would have come if he could.

Margaret kicked off her shoes so that she could move through the house without making a sound.

Unholstered her weapon.

And started down the hallway.

———————————◼———————————

Eight minutes from home.

Who could have found out about Lansing's past? Someone in law enforcement? The NSA? Who would know about the congressman's financial records and his connection with the Gunderson Foundation?

Who was Aria Petic?

It would need to be a woman who knew inside information about the Gunderson facility as well as the assassination attempt against the vice president, someone who'd been at every crime scene, who'd built her mental map of DC from her workplace, who had almost unlimited resources for research at her fingertips, who would know the response time of the ERT—

Oh yes.

She knew about the basement at the hotel, that you were shot there. She knew!

I had it.

But I needed to be sure.

Ralph's flying in to Reagan National. Perfect.

I punched in his number.

"Hey, man," he began, "we just land—"

"Ralph," I interrupted him. "There are two 911 calls from a triple homicide in Maryland last month. I need you to have the lab do a voice analysis. Now. Fast, before 9:29."

"What are you talking about?"

I explained whose voice match we were looking at here, and he told me I had to be joking. "I'm not joking," I said. "Listen, her house is near you. Get some backup and a bomb squad and get over there. If the voice print matches—"

"You sure about this?"

"No, but I don't want to take the chance that I might be wrong." I cornered the county road at seventy. "Get to the house, get the analysis, and move on it if it's confirmed."

"What about you?"

"I need to talk to an eyewitness."

Then I looked up Mrs. Rainey's number and got her on the line. "Do you have a computer?"

"Yes."

"Turn it on. Go to YouTube. And I'd like to speak to your son."

Margaret finished an initial sweep of her house.

Found no sign of her dog. No sign of an intruder. Nothing was out of place.

Someone took him!

Which meant they'd been in her house.

And that meant they would have likely left evidence of their presence somewhere.

Still carrying her Glock, she began a more detailed search.

Pay attention, Margaret.

For Lewis's sake.

Pay attention.

The female killer was Chelsea Tray, the investigative reporter for WXTN news.

Danny Rainey recognized her on the online WXTN coverage. "But her hair's different," he said. That didn't surprise me—it was different when she was caught for a second on video as Aria Petic as well. I called Ralph and found out the voice print matched as well, confirming my suspicions. "Get to the house!" I told him.

End call.

But who was her partner? Nick?

The killers left clues to future crimes: they left the gas station receipt, then killed the attendant . . . left Mahan's car, then killed him . . . left Mollie's purse, then killed her . . . left the plates on Annette's car . . .

Who thinks that far ahead?

My thoughts went once again to Sevren Adkins.

But he was dead—

They never found his body, Pat.

What is obvious is not always what is true.

You can never be sure you've eliminated the impossible, remember?

Okay, eliminate this possibility.

I speed-dialed Cheyenne.

IPR-OMI.

SED-UAR.

The body size of the male suspect matched Sevren's, the scars made sense, both men were left-handed, the male suspect favored his right leg—*Remember, Tessa stabbed a scissors into Sevren Adkins's leg after he attacked her.*

Sevren knew explosives . . . he liked to watch . . .

I waited for Cheyenne to pick up. *What's taking her so long?*

The plates: IPR-OMI.

SED-UAR.

Six letters.

Each plate has six letters.

Denver plates.

Cheyenne lives in Denver too.

Six letters—

She picked up.

"Cheyenne," I began—

It's either you or her. Your car or hers.

But I wasn't about to stop and check my plates.

"Pat? What's up?"

"Is your car in the driveway?"

"What?"

"Outside. Your car!"

He leaves clues that point to the next victim.

"Can you see the plates without going outside?" I punched the gas.

A moment passed as she crossed the room. "No, I'd have to go outside."

"Don't, it's—"

"Pat, what's going on?"

"Tessa's room. Try from Tessa's room. The sight-line will be more direct."

Only one killer had ever challenged me to a rematch. The same one who left clues to future crimes. Sevren Adkins.

"Pat—"

"Go, Cheyenne! Take her with you."

I heard her call for Tessa and then there was a pause and a door banged open.

It's going to say EMA-TCH.

And if it does—

"Okay." Then shock. "What the—?"

I spelled it out before she could tell me what it was: "E-M-A-T-C-H."

Exasperation in her voice. "How did you know?"

"Get away from the window!"

IPR-OMI   SED-UAR   EMA-TCH.

I-PROMISED-U-A-REMATCH.

"He's there!" I whipped around a curve in the road and nearly skidded out of control. *A bomb. A car bomb?* "Don't go near your car!"

"Who's here?"

"Sevren Adkins. Get to the center of the house, away from—"

"Pat, he's dead."

I heard Tessa in the background. "Who's dead?"

What is obvious is not always—

"I think he's alive. I think he's back."

"But he fell to the bottom of a gorge."

"He promised me a rematch, Cheyenne. No one else knows about that."

As I was finishing my sentence she gasped; I heard Tessa cry out.

A jolt of fear. "What is it?"

"The lights," Cheyenne said. "They just went out. All of them."

The clock in the car: 9:26.

Three minutes.

I floored it.

Call dispatch, you have to call dispatch!

"I'm going to have a look around," Cheyenne said.

"Be careful. Don't go outside. And don't leave Tessa alone."

I was still nearly four minutes from the house, but because it was in the country, the response time for the sheriff's department would probably be at least that long, I called them anyway.

This time I definitely wanted backup.

───────────────■───────────────

"What's going on?" Tessa asked Detective Warren.

A moment ago she'd drawn her gun. "Get down on the floor, Tessa."

"What is it?"

"Please."

"Tell me."

A pause. "It's Sevren Adkins."

"What!"

"Pat thinks he's back."

Tessa felt a terrible shiver slide through her. "It can't be."

The man who kidnapped you. The man who cut you. The man who tried to kill you. He's here. He came back. He came back for you. "But I don't understand—"

With one hand, Detective Warren gently but firmly guided Tessa to the floor. "Stay low," she whispered and then headed toward the front door. "And follow me."

Margaret noticed something.

The rolling chair in front of the computer desk was not positioned as it should have been, as she always left it, directly facing her keyboard.

Rather, it was swiveled to the right about forty degrees, as if someone had been sitting in it, then turned from the desk to get up, forgetting to straighten the chair again.

She surveyed the room. Everything else was in place.

But not the chair.

To avoid disturbing any prints that might be on her keyboard, she tapped her fingernail on the space bar to wake up the computer screen.

A document appeared.

Someone had left her a message. Just four words: "Check your trunk, Margaret."

Tessa glanced out the dark windows. With the lights out and the moon full, she could see part of the backyard, but only faintly. The inside of the house was even darker. "Detective Warren, where are you?"

A voice came from a shadow eight feet from her. "I'm here. Quiet now. Shh. Just stay down. Your dad's on the way."

Cautiously, still in stocking feet, Margaret left the house.

Her thoughts flashed back to Sevren Adkins, the man who'd left the torso of one of his victims in her trunk in North Carolina.

But she was sure Adkins was dead. *A copycat?*

She studied the neighborhood. Saw nothing unusual.

Her Lexus was less than a dozen paces away. She pressed the keyless unlock button twice, and the car made two soft blips as the four-way flashers blinked on and then off.

Weapon out, she approached the driver's side.

Made sure no one was under the vehicle.

Clear.

Checked the front and back seats. Clear.

She surveyed the area one last time, steadied her gun. Then pressed the trunk release button: the trunk clicked open slightly, but not high enough yet for her to see inside.

Margaret steeled herself and reached for the handle.

105

2 minutes left . . .

9:27 p.m.

A DVD was in the trunk, a note beside it: "I hope you enjoy watching this as much as I did filming it." She felt a surge of dread, gazed around the neighborhood one last time, then took the DVD inside to watch it, thinking only of what Adkins, or his copycat, might have done to Lewis.

◼

Out the back window, Tessa saw someone in the backyard.

Just a glimpse of shadowy movement along the edge of the rock wall.

"Detective Warren! He's in the yard!" Even though she couldn't see his face, she knew.

It's him. It's him. It's Adkins!

Cheyenne leveled her gun, slid to the back door, opened it a crack, yelled, "Stop and put your hands to the side!"

The figure fired a shot toward the house and dove for cover.

◼

We still didn't know what would happen at 9:29.

An attack on Cheyenne? On Tessa? On me?

A bomb?

So far we only had evidence of C-4 found in the back of the van that the killers had used to transport their victims.

That was all. Nothing else.

But they transported more than their victims back there, Pat. They transported—

What is obvious is not always what is true.

No, it's not.

But sometimes it is.

They'd also transported the wheelchair in the back of the van.

And now it was in the FBI Lab. I whipped out my phone.

Punched in Angela's number.

A second gunshot, and the doorframe just inches from Detective Warren's face shattered. Tessa cried out, but Cheyenne hardly flinched, just crouched to a shooting stance. Studied the yard.

Tessa noticed a smear of movement in the deep shadows, a figure edging carefully toward the house. "There!" she cried. "By the wall!"

"Stop!" Detective Warren aimed.

The man flicked his hand up, fired. The window above Tessa blistered apart, showering glass onto her.

And then, time froze.

Ice covered everything, stilled everything.

For a fraction of a second, Tessa saw Detective Warren's body tense.

And then she took a shot.

Another. A third.

The ice of the moment shattered, and Tessa felt as if fragments of time and sound and fear were falling all around.

Then silence.

The night was still.

Her heart was hammering, hammering. She peered out the window.

"Stay low," Detective Warren warned.

But before she ducked down, Tessa saw a man sprawled near the rock wall skirting the woods. He was on his back, his gun a few feet from his right hand. His face turned the other direction.

"You got him?" Tessa said. Dry, airless words.

"Yes." Detective Warren still had her gun aimed at him.

"You sure?"

"Yes." To Tessa she seemed unbelievably calm. "You stay here."

"You're not going out there!"

"I have to see if he's still alive."

"So you might have missed?"

"I didn't miss." Detective Warren opened the door and, gun ready, arms taut, stepped onto the back deck. "I'll be right back."

Brad thought of the murders at the Styles house last month. Thought of the woman and the two cops. Thought of how he had laid so still on the carpet, waiting for one of them to approach him, the shotgun just within his reach.

He thought of those things now. Everything coming full circle.

But this time with a little twist.

His watch vibrated on his wrist.

Time's up.

106

It happens now . . .
9:29 p.m.

The bomb at the FBI Lab exploded.

———————————■———————————

Chelsea positioned the unconscious woman in the tub and opened a second bottle of drain cleaner.

———————————■———————————

Tessa stared out the window, watching Detective Warren step careful and catlike toward the body.

———————————■———————————

Margaret Wellington popped the DVD into her computer.

———————————■———————————

I swung the car to a stop.

Only seconds ago I'd heard gunshots from behind the house.

I leaped out. Unholstered my weapon.

Sprinted around the corner of the house and saw a woman.

"Stop!" I yelled.

"It's me!" Cheyenne's voice. "I got him. Over here."

"How many shooters?"

"Unknown."

I eyed the tree line, looking for movement. Covered Cheyenne. She was approaching the rock wall that fringed the lawn. A body lay on the ground. "Is that Adkins?"

"I didn't see his face." She was less than five meters from the body.

"Where's Tessa?"

"In the house."

"I'm going in." But I'd only made it two steps when Cheyenne gasped. "Hurry, Pat! It's—"

A gunshot erupted from the shadows near the back deck. I heard a deep, solid *slap!* behind me, and knew instantly what it was—a bullet hitting a human target.

Out of the corner of my eye I saw Cheyenne crumple against the stone wall.

No, no, no, no!

Darkness seemed to breathe on me.

Inhaling.

Exhaling. Shadows panting all around me. I sprinted to her.

Scanned the woods. The deck. Still no movement.

She'd been shot in the right side and was gasping for breath. She had her left hand over the wound, but bright, frothy blood was oozing between her fingers. *Her lung. She's hit in the lung.*

I heard sirens, but they were too far away to get here in time.

No visual on the shooter.

She'll bleed out!

As quickly and carefully as I could, I moved her three meters to the opening in the wall so she wouldn't be exposed in the field. Then I called 911.

Darkness.

Breathing.

Get to the house, Pat. You have to find Tessa!

In a handful of seconds I told the dispatcher what I knew about Cheyenne's GSW and explained exactly where she was.

"Go," Cheyenne coughed. "I'll be all right . . . just . . ." Her voice trailed off.

She was still pressing against the wound, but when I put my hand on hers I realized she wasn't applying enough pressure to stop the bleeding. *She's too weak.* "You need to press harder," I told her urgently.

Get to Tessa, you have to get to Tessa!

Cheyenne's eyes fluttered, then closed. She went limp, unconscious. "Cheyenne!" I slapped her cheek, but it didn't rouse her.

You can't stay. You have to go!

I saw a glimmer of light in the house. A flashlight moving through the living room.

No!

Tessa would lay low, wouldn't use a flashlight.

I tilted Cheyenne to her side, wound against the ground, so her body weight would at least provide a little pressure, maybe slow the bleeding, keep it from pooling, flooding the other lung. Maybe it would buy her a few extra minutes until the EMTs arrived.

I rose to sprint to the house and finally saw the face of the person Cheyenne had shot.

Paul Lansing.

No!

Hastily, I knelt beside him, felt for a pulse. Nothing. No pulse. No breathing. Cheyenne had put three shots center mass, and his chest was shredded, blood-drenched.

He was gone.

Tight, hot anger shot through me.

Sevren set this up! He lured him here!

Sirens, blaring sirens. Distant but growing stronger.

I bolted toward the house.

MagLite out, gun level, I entered from the back deck. Moved slowly through the doorway. "Tessa?"

No reply.

I tried the living room lights. Nothing. "Tessa!"

I don't pray often, but I did now, and it was as raw and real as they come. *Please, please let her be okay. Both her and Cheyenne. Please!*

Then I heard it. Muffled sounds coming from the hallway.

Flashlight in my left hand, SIG in my right, I flared around the corner.

Tessa was standing, gagged, at the far end of the hall, just outside her bedroom. A man was hiding in the room, clenching a handful of her hair with his right hand, holding a Walther P99 pressed to the side of her head with his left. She had a welt on her forehead, blood trailing down her cheek; he must have hit her with something when he overpowered her.

Anger. Prowling. Roaring.

She tried to cry out. The gag stopped her.

"That's far enough, Bowers." His voice was a hiss. Though I couldn't see him, I pictured him: dark hair. Medium build. Stained, primal eyes.

"Drop the gun, Sevren!"

I stepped forward lightly, but he jerked Tessa's head backward and she cringed.

"I said that's far enough!" he shouted.

I froze. Somehow he was watching me.

"Here's what's going to happen," he said. "You're going to throw your gun to Tessa. She's going to pick it up. And then you're going to watch your stepdaughter die."

———————————◼———————————

There are many kinds of death, Sevren thought. *Physical, spiritual, emotional, psychological.*

And this would be the most fitting kind of all.

107

Sirens outside. "You hear that?" I called. "It's over. There's no way out of this. Let her go."

"Throw her your gun."

I eased forward slightly, but he yelled, "Take another step and she dies!"

How does he see me?

I studied the hallway. No mirrors. No windows.

Tessa had her teeth clenched. Eyes squeezed shut.

"I'll give you three seconds," he said.

"Sevren—"

"One."

Do not relinquish your weapon, Pat. He will kill you both!

I scrutinized the hallway, in front of me, behind me. And saw a cell phone on the floor of the living room, behind me, propped against the wall, taking video.

He's got another phone in the bedroom. He's watching—

"Two."

I flicked off my flashlight so he couldn't see my movement, then sprinted toward Tessa, but Sevren yanked her backward into the room. Slammed the heavy oak door shut.

I grabbed the doorknob, tried it. Locked. Behind the door, I heard Tessa struggling, trying to get free. I backed up, raised my heel, smashed it against the door, but it held.

Sevren's voice: "Kick that door again and I'll start playing with your stepdaughter."

My hands squeezed into fists, one tight around the grip of my SIG, the other around my MagLite. Inside of me, a terrible fire roared to life, one I did not want to put out.

There's no other door to the room—

"Sevren," I called through the door. I could hear movement, then a swishing sound that was probably the curtains being pulled shut. A small, gentle light flicked on, shimmered through the crack beneath the door. *He set his flashlight down.* "There's no way out of this," I yelled. "It's over. It's done."

"I want you to tell her," he said. "Who that is. Outside. Who Detective Warren shot."

No.

Stall.

"We found the bomb, Sevren. We found your partner."

"You're bluffing."

"No I'm not."

"Prove it."

"You used the metal tubes of the wheelchair. It was smart. Even if the lab guys had x-rayed it, the explosives wouldn't have been visible. But we got to it in time." I wasn't sure about that last part.

A pause. "And my partner?"

"Chelsea Traye."

Silence.

"She did specials on both the assassination attempt and the Gunderson facility. Then at the hotel on Wednesday she announced that the shooting was in the basement, but that was before Margaret revealed the location during the press conference. No one else knew where I'd been shot. Making the 911 calls in Maryland at the Styles's house was sloppy. We matched her voice. It's all over."

No reply.

Keep stalling, keep stalling.

"It was Tessa's email, wasn't it?" I said. "You hacked in. Found out about her father. Then had Chelsea look into Lansing's past. She had access to the archived footage of the assassination attempt's coverage. You sent Calvin the note. You set this all up weeks ago."

Silence from the room.

Long and dark.

Then he spoke, "I didn't come here to kill your stepdaughter,

Patrick. But I will if you don't tell her who Detective Warren shot."

But he just said you are going to watch her die—

"Tell her!"

Time. Buy more time.

"Take off her gag so I can talk to her."

A slight pause.

"Patrick!" she cried.

"I'm here, Tessa."

"He's just to my left! Shoot at my voice through the wall— Ow!"

I banged the door. "Don't touch her!"

"Tell her now or the gag goes back on."

The red-blue, red-blue of the approaching squads' overhead lights flicked through the living room windows, washed through the hall.

"Tessa," I said, "listen to me—"

She loves Paul. She wanted to hate him today, but she loves him.

I had an idea. One chance at this, that would be all. I backed away from the door. "That man outside . . ." I aimed my weapon at the wood beside the doorknob.

One chance.

One chance.

We give platitudes to soften the blow, to dull the pain, but that's not what I was about to do. To help her I had to hurt her. I couldn't think of any other viable option. I had to stop Sevren. I had to take him down.

"The man Cheyenne shot is . . ."

I would kick this door harder than I'd ever kicked anything in my life. Right next to the lock. *Drive your heel in. Locate Sevren. Drop him.*

I eyed down the barrel. "Tessa, it's your father." I waited. Waited.

C'mon, Tessa. Please.

"Paul?" A fragile, broken word.

"He's dead. He was shot three times in the chest."

"No."

"Yes, Tessa."

Louder. "No!"

"He's dead. Your father Paul Lansing is lying dead in the back—"

This time she shrieked, "No!"

The word cut through the night like a terrible, terrible knife. The instant she screamed I fired into the wood beside the lock, even as I rushed forward and drove my heel against the door. It splintered, flew open.

In a fraction of a second I swept the room and saw Sevren in the corner, standing behind Tessa. His flashlight sat on the floor to my left.

Tessa stood between us. Sevren had the gun pressed against her temple, her hand beneath his around the grip, her finger against the trigger.

Oh no. Please no.

The curling red and blue lights outside seeped into the room through the closed curtains.

Backup.

I eyed down the barrel but I had no shot. Sevren held her head steady in front of his by squeezing a tight fistful of her hair with his right hand. What little I could see of his face was covered with brutal scars.

"Tessa," I said softly, trying to sound calm. "Do not move your finger. No pressure at all."

"That's good advice," Sevren said.

She had her jaw set, trying to be strong, but a tear was squeezing from her right eye. "Shoot him," she whispered.

But he was squarely behind her; I couldn't get off a shot. I edged forward—

"That's far enough," he said.

I paused. Still no shot. If I fired I'd either miss him or hit Tessa. I heard officers pounding toward us down the hall. "Get back!"

I yelled. "He's got my daughter." They paused. "There's a woman outside, by the stone wall, she was shot. Get to her now!"

No movement.

"Go on!" I called. "Do it!"

"Tell them to clear the house," Sevren said.

"You heard him, clear the premises!" At last their footsteps retreated. Sevren glanced at a phone propped on the bed, and my eyes followed his. The house lights were off, but in the flicker of police lights from outside, the screen showed the outline of one officer still crouched in the hall.

"Go," I yelled to him. "You, in the hall. Now."

Finally, he left.

"Detective Warren?" Tessa said, defeat and fear in her voice. "Is she okay?"

"I doubt it," Sevren said. "I'm a pretty good shot." Then to me, "I said set down the gun."

I ignored him, told Tessa, "She'll be all right."

Rather than demand again that I set down my gun, he took a small breath. "So here we are." The words seemed to writhe from his mouth. "Just the three of us. Just like in North Carolina."

"No," Tessa said with tight resolve. "That time you had a scissors sticking out of your leg."

No, Tessa! Don't provoke him!

"Tessa," I said. "Shh."

"You should be thankful, Patrick," Sevren said. "I hear custody cases can be expensive. Detective Warren saved you a lot of time and money tonight."

"Kill him!" Tessa yelled.

He tightened his grip on her hair. She winced but refused to cry out, denying him the satisfaction of hurting her.

"Now, put down your gun," he said to me. "Slowly."

Sight-lines.

Angles.

If I could edge forward, drop to one knee as if I were setting down my SIG, I might be able to make the shot.

Do it.

"Okay." I eased my finger from the trigger guard, held the gun loosely. "I am. Don't hurt her. We can talk about this, but just let her—"

"Don't insult me!" he roared.

He would either die tonight or go to prison for the rest of his life. He had to know this. He had nothing to lose by killing her. And if his goal was to make me suffer, he had everything to gain by squeezing the trigger.

Nothing to lose.

He has nothing to lose.

I paused. Tried another idea. "Stop hiding behind my stepdaughter. If you were half as brave as she is, you'd step out here and face me like a—"

"It's not going to be that easy, Bowers."

"It's over. Let her go. Take me, if that's what this is about."

"No!" Tessa screamed.

He spoke to her then, softly, but I heard the words: "It would have saved us all a lot of trouble if your mother had just gone ahead with the abortion."

"No!" She squeezed her eyes shut, crossed her right arm over her chest, hugged herself.

"Well, Patrick." Sevren smiled. "Looks like I win."

And everything that happened next happened all at once.

He jerked the gun from the side of Tessa's head, angled it backward toward his own face; I swung my SIG into position and fired just as his gun went off.

Tessa's finger still on the trigger.

108

Sevren's body slumped to the ground.

I rushed to Tessa.

She was breathing heavily. Adrenaline. Fear.

The gun was still in her hand; I eased it from her grip, set it on the bed.

Unlike in the movies, people who are shot in real life don't fly backward, they crumple; and Sevren's body lay just behind Tessa. One entry wound was through his chin; my bullet had hit his forehead. Both bullets had exited the back of his skull, leaving a fist-sized hole behind. Gray matter and blood were splayed gruesomely across the wall. As I holstered my SIG and took Tessa in my arms I found that the blowback had left her hair damp with a spray of Sevren's warm blood.

"Don't turn around." As I took her in my arms I gently wiped my hand against the back of her head, then onto my other sleeve. "It's okay. I'm here."

She stood stone-still. Said nothing.

An officer rushed through the doorway, weapon leveled at us.

"It's over!" I hollered. "It's over."

He saw the wall behind us. The form on the floor. He lowered his gun and edged uneasily toward the body.

In a horror film Sevren might have somehow risen again to attack, to kill, but not here, not now; he was never going to rise again. Not ever.

I wanted to get Tessa out of the house, as far away from this room as possible. I hurried her down the hallway.

"My dad is dead." The words came out like shards of glass.

"I'm so sorry, Tessa." All other words escaped me.

We were halfway through the living room when she called to

one of the officers entering through the front door. "The woman who was shot. Is she alive?"

He glanced at another officer who'd just arrived. The man shook his head. "I don't know her condition, ma'am. They have her, though." He pointed toward the window. "On an ambulance."

We stepped outside.

One ambulance was pulling away from the house. I guided Tessa toward the other.

I expected her to start trembling, crying, but she did not.

"My ear," she mumbled. She was shaking her head as if to get water out of her left ear, the one that had been only inches from the gun when it went off. "I can't hear out of my ear."

The fact that she was focusing on something relatively insignificant compared to what had just happened told me she was going into shock.

"It'll be all right," I said, promising something that was out of my control. A pause, then I went on, "The way I told you about your father. I needed to make you cry out, to distract Sevren. I'm sorry I was so blunt. Will you forgive me?"

She remained silent but nodded.

"Thank you," I said.

The ambulance was just ahead. I still didn't know if Ralph had found Chelsea Traye or if the bomb had gone off.

"I killed him." Tessa's voice was distant and chilled. It didn't sound at all like the girl I knew. "I killed Sevren."

"No. That's what he wanted you to think. He was trying to shoot himself and make you think you did it, but I shot him. Muscle contraction in his hand made his finger squeeze. That's what made the gun go off."

"I killed him."

"No."

She shook her head. "I did it." I wasn't sure if I heard regret or a dark sense of satisfaction in her words and I didn't know what to say, but this was clearly not the time to argue. "What matters now is that you're safe."

We made it to the ambulance, and two paramedics wheeled a gurney to Tessa for her to sit on. One of the men looked at the welt on her forehead. "We need to get you to the hospital."

She was quiet as she took a seat, then lay down on her side.

"I'm riding with her," I said.

He nodded, and as he and his partner rolled Tessa's gurney into the back of the ambulance, I quietly asked him about Cheyenne. He told me that he'd heard she was in serious condition, but that was all he knew. "As soon as I hear more, I'll let you know."

"Quantico? The bomb?"

"It went off. Evidence Room 3a is gone. A few people didn't quite make it out of that wing. Minor injuries, but I think everyone's okay."

I was thankful no one was killed or seriously injured, but if Evidence Room 3a was destroyed, it could negatively affect dozens of cases.

I wondered how Lacey had fared, hoped for Angela's sake that she was okay.

"Oh," he said, "they got to Chelsea Traye; she's in custody. She was about to kill a woman, a prostitute. Agent Hawkins stopped her."

Well, it was nice to at least hear a little good news.

In the ambulance now, I knelt beside Tessa. The police sirens outside had stopped, but the flashing lights hadn't, and they twirled and flickered in the window beside me, blurring the night with colors it was never meant to contain.

I held her hand. "You're going to be okay."

She said nothing, just stared blankly at the side wall of the ambulance. A single tragic tear fell from her left eye. "My dad is dead."

And when I saw the brokenness and rage in her eyes, I had a chilling thought.

Maybe Sevren had been right.

Maybe he had won after all.

109

Tessa and I were staying in the spare bedroom in Ralph and Brineesha's basement so we wouldn't have to be near the house where
Sevren Adkins and Paul Lansing had died.

Right now Ralph was following up on a lead that Lebreau might
be in the DC area, and Brineesha was shopping with their son Tony,
so Tessa and I had the house to ourselves.

I checked my watch: 1:22 p.m.

Cheyenne had come home from the hospital at 1:00 and we were
leaving in ten minutes to see her.

Tessa was downstairs getting ready.

This would be the first time they were going to see each other
since the shooting.

I'd visited Cheyenne every day except for the two days Tessa and
I were in Wyoming. Even though Cheyenne had invited Tessa to the
hospital and had sent half a dozen notes telling her how sorry she
was about her father, my stepdaughter had declined to see her and
instead simply requested that I ask Cheyenne to read *The Strange
Case of Dr. Jekyll and Mr. Hyde.*

I assumed it was Tessa's way of telling Cheyenne that she was
some kind of monster, a female Hyde, and it seemed vindictive to
me, but Cheyenne readily agreed to read it. "Anything I can do to
help," she'd said. So, two days ago, after I'd read the story myself to
understand the context of what was going on with Tessa, I delivered
the book to Cheyenne.

It'd taken some time to piece together what happened that night,
and there were still some gaps, but here's what we knew: after

hacking into Lansing's lawyers' website and getting Paul's phone number, Sevren had lured him to the scene by sending a number of distress text messages that supposedly came from Tessa's phone claiming she was in danger, that the killers from this week had her, and NOT to call the cops or her dad, but to please come help her!

It's not easy to mask the origin of text messages but Sevren was smart and had done it well.

Considering that Paul was an ex–Secret Service agent, it wasn't surprising to me that he'd come armed and ready to save his daughter.

It still wasn't exactly clear who'd fired the first shot—Sevren or Paul, but Sevren had orchestrated the shootout, no doubt knowing that it was likely either Paul would kill Cheyenne or she would kill him—or Sevren might have planned to kill them both. Either way, it would have devastated both me and Tessa. And I couldn't help but think that if Cheyenne had not been there, the shootout would have been between Tessa's father and me.

After Paul's death, Vice President Fischer sent Tessa a personal note expressing his condolences and explaining that indeed Paul had been the one to save him six years ago. For security reasons Paul had been told never to share that information, and the VP asked Tessa not to blame her dad for misleading her, and from what I could see, she had taken that to heart.

Despite my early suspicions, Paul had only wanted what was best for his daughter and had fought to protect her every chance he had—first when she was a baby, and now when she was a young woman. Knowing that he really had cared for her seemed, more than anything else, to be helping Tessa deal with his death.

Lien-hua, in her evaluative profile, postulated that Sevren had been telling the truth when he claimed that he hadn't come to the house to kill Tessa. "He wanted you to tell her that Paul was dead as a way of controlling you, of hurting you both," Lien-hua explained. "Killing Tessa would have only ended her suffering. Even though in the end you cornered him and it looks like he resorted to suicide, I don't think that was his original plan."

"What was his original plan?" I asked, though I anticipated her answer.

"We'll probably never know."

If it had been to end his life, as it turned out, my bullet had helped him along.

So.

Now.

Tessa still hadn't come up from the basement. I decided to give her five more minutes.

While I waited, I spent my time trying to think of specific things I could say that might encourage her, that might help quiet some of the malice she was harboring toward Cheyenne.

◼

Margaret Wellington hadn't gotten over what she'd seen in the DVD that had been left in the trunk of her car eight days ago.

It wasn't footage of her dog Lewis being slaughtered as she'd feared, in fact, after Sevren's death, the task force had found Lewis in the backseat of Sevren's car, drugged but okay.

Thankfully.

Thankfully.

Lewis was okay.

But still, the videotaped images had been ghastly and disturbing.

The DVD had contained videos of seven of Sevren's victims: Twana Summie screaming as the two chimpanzees attacked her, Mollie Fischer lying unconscious in the back of the van, Chelsea Traye struggling to escape a shallow grave in the body farm. And four other victims who still remained unidentified.

But to Margaret, some of the most unsettling footage was at the end of the DVD. It wasn't video of another victim but of her lying asleep in her own bed. The video had been recorded from inside her bedroom.

He'd been there, in her room, watching her. Standing over her as she slept.

He'd even leaned close, filming only inches from her face, and she'd never known, never even suspected a thing.

It shook her deeply. The man had violated the one place she felt most safe and he had stained it with his presence, leaving her feeling powerless and vulnerable—most likely exactly what he'd wanted.

She parked in the underground garage across the street from the Capitol building, picked up her briefcase containing the documents she was going to give to Congressman Fischer, and left the car.

But she couldn't shake her thoughts of the DVD.

Why her?

Why had he snuck into her house?

She could only guess that it was because they had a history together—she'd been the agent in charge of the task force in North Carolina that had been tracking him when he drove off the cliff. He'd left a body in her trunk then, and now, through the DVD videos, had left a trunk full of figurative bodies.

All an elaborate, twisted way of showing off.

How many nights was he there? Standing by your bed, watching you sleep?

She strode down the hallway of the Capitol toward House Minority Leader Fischer's office and assured herself that Sevren was dead and he was not coming back. It was over.

But as she walked, she tried not to think about the one remaining fact that no one was talking about: there was no actual proof Sevren was the one who'd taken the video of her lying asleep in her bed.

Tessa was finishing with her eyeliner and thinking about what she was going to say to Detective Warren, when Patrick tapped on the bathroom door.

"Raven, it's me," he called. "Almost ready?"

She could tell he was speaking loudly and she was thankful. She still had hearing loss in her left ear. The doctors weren't sure whether or not it would be permanent.

But that was the least of her worries.

"Just a sec," she said.

Too much had happened in the last two weeks, just way too much to deal with—the crime spree, the custody case, her dad's death.

The day after Paul was killed, Patrick had tried contacting people who might have known him, but not even his lawyers had a list of his relatives or emergency contacts. In the end, Patrick had arranged for Paul's body to be flown back to Wyoming and he and Tessa had flown out as well. They buried her dad in a small cemetery near his cabin in the mountains with only a few local townspeople in attendance.

"Tessa?" Patrick urged from outside the bathroom door. "I told her we'd be there by 2:00."

"Yeah, I'll be right out."

Paul had been flawed, yes, but he had loved her and he had come to save her. The vice president's letter had meant a lot to her.

Her dad was a hero. Just like Patrick was—two men who were both willing to die for her. And one of them had.

Because of that, Paul's death held at least a little meaning.

However, there was the other matter.

Since last Friday Patrick had reassured her a hundred times that Sevren's death was not her fault. "He knew there was no way out and he wanted you to think that you killed him just to make you suffer. I'm the one who shot him. You didn't kill anyone. Do you understand?"

She appreciated what Patrick was trying to do, and after a while she'd told him that she understood, but she knew something that he did not.

She was the one who'd tilted the gun backward, not Sevren Adkins.

She was the one who'd pulled the trigger.

She'd wrapped her right arm across her chest, grabbed her left elbow and shoved the gun back toward Adkins's face, squeezing the trigger as she did.

Yes.

She had.

She'd stepped into the fracture and been true to her heart and killed the man who'd set her father up to die. She'd taken the life of the man who was about to kill her.

And she was glad.

She set the eyeliner down, glanced in the mirror and it reminded her of Belle and the mirror self-recognition test at the primate research center.

Tessa stared at her reflection. Self-recognition, huh?

You took a man's life.

She didn't recognize herself at all anymore.

For a few more moments she stared at her reflection, then she took a deep breath, and joined Patrick to go see the woman who'd shot her dad.

110

"So, it's all here?" Congressman Fischer asked Margaret.

"Yes, sir."

He flipped through the files she'd given him. "Unbelievable. All documented?"

"Yes."

He gave a small sigh. "When I present this to Congress I'm sure we'll have Rodale's resignation within a week." He shook his head. "He was with that Lebreau woman the night Brady tried to kill my brother?"

"Yes."

"And she helped Brady set it up?"

"To sway public opinion, yes. Have a pro-death penalty supporter assassinate a popular vice president and you guarantee public opinion will swing your direction, against the death penalty."

Which is what happened, actually.

"Was Rodale involved?" Fischer's tone had turned dark.

"I couldn't find any evidence that he was, and Lebreau is still missing so we can't ask her."

He set down the files, looked at her quizzically. "And how did you find all this out?"

"I did some checking. I'm pretty good at connecting the dots."

He waited.

"I can't reveal my sources at the moment, sir, but if need be, I will. I'm sure you can respect that. One question—do you know why Chelsea Traye and Sevren Adkins targeted your family in this crime spree?"

He shook his head. "The two bills I'm sponsoring, I'd guess. The killers were trying to make a statement."

It wasn't clear to Margaret what that statement might be. "So, are you going to pull support for the in-vitro testing bill?" In her research over the last week she hadn't found any evidence that Fischer had acted unethically. It was all Rodale. From the start he'd been using Fischer to promote the legislation and the research that would lead to breakthroughs that would make him rich.

"No." He shook his head. "In fact, I'm more committed to it now than ever."

"Because of your daughter's death."

"Yes. Anything we can do to stop other psychopaths before they slaughter more innocent girls like Mollie. We're going to pass this legislation and get the Gunderson Foundation their funding. I don't care anymore if people find out I've been contributing to them. It's time this issue reached the public forum. From the start I've just wanted less crime, fewer people suffering. And you can be sure that now I'm going to see that happen."

"But cutting down on the number of criminals by aborting more babies?"

"If that's what it takes."

"Terminate a life because someday the person might turn violent?" She could tell her tone had turned curt. "That doesn't make any sense, Congressman. Let them be born. Teach them. Help them. We have the ability to rise above our instincts. To choose."

"The jury's still out on that. Let's see where the research leads." It was clear he was done discussing the matter. "I'll put in a good word for you in the Senate. They'll need someone sharp to fill Rodale's post. You'd be a good Director, Ms. Wellington."

But she was still thinking about the social implications of the policies he was promoting, still troubled by them.

He led her to the door. "By the way, have you ever thought about running for Congress?"

"The thought has crossed my mind."

"I won't be holding this office forever, you know."

"No, you won't."

"Well, good day, Ms. Wellington."

"Good day, Congressman."

───────────■───────────

```
    Chelsea was in prison, but to avoid the death sen-
tence she had told the authorities about all the
goldfish in the freezer. Even now, their cases were
being reviewed, their sentences revoked.
    But she was not concerned about that. She was
thinking about her baby.
    Once born, the child would be allowed to stay with
her in prison for perhaps the first year. And all
that while, she would be planning her escape so that
she would be free to raise her baby by herself.
    Free.
    Free.
    Free.
    Just the two of them.
    No one was going to take her baby away from her.
    She patted her stomach as she stared out the bars
of her cell. "I will be strong enough," she whis-
pered. "I promise."
```

───────────■───────────

Tessa still hadn't indicated to me what she was going to say to Cheyenne, and now that we were on our way up the front steps of her apartment I felt I needed to bring up the issue. Before I rang the doorbell I said, "She feels really badly."

"I know."

"What are you going to say to her?"

"It depends."

"On?"

Tessa looked at me. "On what she says to me."

"Tessa—"

"She killed my dad, Patrick. I know it was an accident, but that doesn't make him any less dead."

"I know you're feeling angry, okay? Hurt. But you can't give in to all that. This is one time you need to be true to something bigger than your heart. Whatever else might make us different from animals—we can acknowledge people's mistakes and we can forgive. We can learn to love again."

She stared at me. "Did you just make that up or did you prepare it beforehand?"

I was quiet for a moment. "Okay, I worked on it for a while, but that doesn't make it any less true. Sevren is gone. He only wins if we let anger swallow us up."

"Anger, huh?" She paused. "What about the promise you made to Grant Sikora? That you wouldn't let Basque kill again?"

Time to listen to your own advice, Pat.

"I'm starting to think that it isn't our job to punish people for things they haven't done. Justice shouldn't try to predict the future, just judge the past."

But he's guilty, Pat. He's—

Tessa looked at me with surprise.

"What?"

"It's just, I don't know, for a minute there you sounded wise."

"I won't let it happen again."

"It wasn't that bad."

The door opened and Cheyenne greeted us. She looked well-rested and in good health, certainly not like someone who'd been in intensive care just four days ago.

However, as she took a step aside so we could enter, she winced.

"You can sit back down," Tessa told her. "Seriously."

"Maybe that's a good idea," I said.

But Cheyenne shook her head, said to Tessa, "Come here."

For a moment no one moved, then Tessa walked toward her slowly.

Cheyenne took her in her arms and held her and told her in a heartbreaking way how sorry, so sorry, she was. From where I stood I couldn't see Tessa's face, but her shoulders began to tremble slightly and I heard her start to cry.

For a moment I hesitated, wondering if there was something I should say, but finally, I joined them and held them both and didn't say anything at all.

And that was much better.

EPILOGUE

After a few minutes, Tessa stepped back, wiped away a smudge of tears, and said to her stepdad, "It'd be nice if we could maybe be alone for awhile. Detective Warren and I."

"Sure."

"I'll bring her home," Detective Warren offered.

"You're good to drive?"

"I drove home from the hospital. I'm fine."

"Okay." He looked at them awkwardly for a moment. "Have a good talk. I'll see you both soon."

"Yeah," Tessa replied, and at last he made his way outside. Detective Warren invited Tessa on a walk to the Potomac. "It's only about a half mile away," she said.

Tessa noticed her copy of *Jekyll and Hyde* on the end table. Above it hung a crucifix. "You probably shouldn't be walking around."

"I'm fine." Detective Warren gestured toward a table where a chessboard and a small leather bag that presumably held chess pieces lay. "We can talk while we play." She picked up the book and chess set. "I've been lying on my back for a week; I need to move. We're going on a walk."

I was almost to my house when my phone rang. I answered. Ralph.

"Hey," I said.

"How did the meeting go with Cheyenne and Tessa?"

"There's a lot of healing that needs to happen. But I think things will work out."

"You still at Cheyenne's place?"

"No. They wanted some privacy."

"Good, because I've got some bad news. Renée Lebreau is dead. I need you to get over here, right away."

Tessa could tell that Detective Warren was still in pain so she slowed her stride.

"You don't know how many times I've gone over that night in my mind," Cheyenne said with deep regret in every word. "Playing through everything, wishing I could make things turn out differently."

"Me too."

It was a long time before either of them spoke again. They'd almost made it to the river. Detective Warren held up the book. "I think I know why you wanted me to read this story."

"Why?"

She flipped to a bookmarked page and then read the words of Dr. Jekyll:

I learned to recognise the thorough and primitive duality of man; I saw that, of the two natures that contended in the field of my consciousness, even if I could rightly be said to be either, it was only because I was radically both . . . .

It was the curse of mankind that these incongruous faggots were thus bound together—that in the agonised womb of consciousness, these polar twins should be continuously struggling. How then were they dissociated?

"They're not," Detective Warren said. "Not dissociated. That's the difference between us and animals. The incongruities. The 'thorough and primitive duality.'"

Tessa thought about that.

The shell of good . . . the fractures . . .

They walked in silence for a few moments until they made it

to the trail along the Potomac. Detective Warren motioned to a picnic table.

As they were setting up the board, Tessa was thinking about the last ten days, and when she picked up her bishop she said softly, "I forgot."

"What do you mean?"

"The way it moves."

Detective Warren looked at her curiously.

"Back when everything happened, on that night, I was thinking about how we shift from black to white just like chess pieces do." She gestured toward her pieces. "But I forgot about the bishop."

It took Detective Warren only a few seconds to make the connection. "It's the only piece that stays on its color the whole game. No incongruities."

Tessa set the bishop on the black square beside her queen. Remembering Sevren Adkins, how dark, how evil, how stained his soul was, Tessa asked, "Did you ever meet one? I mean a person who never changed colors at all? Who had no duality?"

Detective Warren reflected on the question for a moment. "Just one."

Tessa figured she was talking about the killer in Denver, Giovanni, who'd been the reason EAD Wellington had allowed her into the National Academy program—to help give her some distance from Denver, from the case. "Giovanni?" Tessa said.

But Cheyenne shook her head. "No. A carpenter. From Nazareth." Considering the detective's faith, the answer didn't really surprise Tessa. She was quiet. "Yeah," she said at last. "My mom met him too. Before she died."

Darkness and light.

Back and forth.

Every move of the game.

You killed a man.

The thorough and primitive duality.

Tessa stared at the board. The white pieces in front of her, the black pieces in front of Detective Warren.

"White starts," Cheyenne said, stating what they both already knew. "It's your move."

Yes, it is.

It's your move.

Trying to turn from the fractures she'd seen all too clearly in herself, Tessa reached for her king's pawn to begin the game.

◼

Ralph met me at the door to the condo where, apparently, Professor Lebreau had been staying. His words were tight with anger. "It was Basque."

"Confirmed?" I stepped inside.

"Oh, yeah, it's confirmed." He turned his head to the side, revealing a massive contusion. Most people would have been flat on their backs in a hospital bed.

"Are you all right?" *No one beats Ralph in a fight!*

"They had baseball bats."

"They?" I thought again of the unidentified DNA at the crime scenes thirteen years ago.

An accomplice?

"I recognized Basque," Ralph said, "but it was too dark to see the other guy's face." He shook his head, obviously frustrated with himself for not taking out both baseball bat-wielding assailants. "The second guy got me from behind. At least I managed to break Basque's arm. Fast and clean. But they both got away."

So Basque was back and he had a partner.

Perfect.

I was observing the evidence of the fight in the living room. Overturned furniture. Blood spatter. Broken lamps.

Dozens of handwritten letters were scattered across the floor, each signed "Love, Richard" and I remembered what Ralph had told me about how quickly Renée went through boyfriends. The pieces began to fall into place. "He seduced her?" I said. "From prison? Is that it?"

"Yeah." Ralph motioned toward the letters. "He wrote to her for over a year. She found the evidence to help get him free. Then he turned on her." Apparently Basque's conveniently timed conversion in prison hadn't changed his true nature one bit.

"Do we know if she faked the DNA evidence to get him released?"

"Believe me, we're looking into it."

I wondered how Rodale fit in with all of this—if he did at all.

Ralph gestured toward the kitchen. "Renée's in there. Or at least most of her is."

Lien-hua emerged from the doorway and I was glad when Ralph went on ahead to let us talk for a second. She'd spent a lot of time with Cheyenne over the last week, helping her recover, and we'd put our relationship on hold for the time being. "Cheyenne likes you," Lien-hua had told me. "It's obvious. But she has enough to recover from right now. I don't want to hurt her any worse."

I couldn't argue with that, even though distance from Lien-hua was not what I wanted.

It'll work out, I'd told myself. *We just need to get past this. Settle in. It's going to be okay.*

Now Lien-hua walked toward me, and behind her I saw four members of the Evidence Response Team, including Cassidy and Farraday, moving around the kitchen.

I couldn't see much, but the refrigerator door was open, and Cassidy and two agents I didn't know were gathered around it. He held up a jar. From where I stood it was impossible to make out what was inside, but the woman next to him grew pale, hurried out of my line of sight. I heard vomiting.

Splayed across the linoleum floor I saw a frenzy of blood.

Lien-hua must have seen the look of anger on my face. "Pat, I know you vowed to stop him, but this wasn't your fault."

"I know."

"You couldn't have prevented this."

Not unless I'd killed him in Chicago last month.

The road to the unthinkable is not paved by slight departures from your heart but by tentative forays into it.

I was reminded of my somber thoughts at Calvin's funeral: we're born, we struggle, we endure, we die, and there's hardly anything left to show we were ever here.

Dust to dust.

Ashes to ashes.

The grim poetry of existence.

But life is more than that.

We foray into our hearts and look for ways to rise above them.

We ache and we love, we hurt and we heal.

Human beings, being human.

The sunlight was playing strangely across the linoleum.

Death matters because life matters, and the day I stop believing that is the day I'll no longer be any good at my job.

But for now, I still am.

I approached the refrigerator.

And peered inside.

To be continued in
The Queen
Summer 2011

ACKNOWLEDGMENTS

Thanks to my military and law enforcement consultants, Lt. Col. Todd Huhn, Lt. Col. Greg Hebert, and Special Agent Scott Francis; my editors and first readers, Shawn Scullin, Trinity Huhn, Pam Johnson, Wayne Smith, Jen Leep, Kristin Kornoelje, and Liesl Huhn; my agent, Pamela Harty; my firearms consultants, Jim Huhn and George Hill; my ethics consultants, Dr. Bob Wetzel, Jim Kevin, and Dr. Marc Roberts.

Thanks to Congressman Dr. Phil Roe for taking the time to meet with me and giving me the inside scoop on Capitol Hill, and to Randy Vernon for his hospitality.

Thanks also to John and Lisa Bunn at the Coffee Company and Lee and Tricia Smith at the Adobe Garden Bed & Breakfast for giving me a place to work, to my students at the Blue Ridge Christian Novelist's Retreat for introducing me to transhumanism, to Becky Malinsky and Dr. Suda-King at the National Zoo for helping me fathom primates, and to Wayne Smith and Agent Curt Crawford for arranging my tour of the FBI Academy at the Quantico Marine Corps Base.

A special thanks to J.P., Todd, Pam, Liesl, and Chris for being my faithful sounding boards.

I'm indebted to Dr. Kim Rossmo's book *Geographic Profiling* and Paul and Patricia Brantingham's *Environmental Criminology* for the theoretical information on the underpinnings of geospatial investigation.

I found the following resources useful in my research on primate metacognition, as well as the differing perspectives on and implications of theories regarding the evolution of morality.

The Think Tank exhibit at the Smithsonian National Zoological Park.

Primates and Philosophers: How Morality Evolved by Frans De Waal, edited by Stephen Macedo and Josiah Ober (Princeton: Princeton University Press, 2006). Specifically, see pages 9–10 for the references to, and inferences from, Richard Dawkins's writings.

Hardwired Behavior: What Neuroscience Reveals about Morality by Laurence Tancredi (Cambridge: Cambridge University Press, 2007).

A Reason for God by Timothy Keller (New York: Dutton, 2008).

There Is A God by Antony Flew (New York: HarperCollins, 2007).

Steven James is the bestselling, award-winning author of four thrillers, including *The Knight*, which *Suspense Magazine* named one of the top ten books of the year. Armed with a master's degree in storytelling, James is a popular conference speaker and has taught writing and storytelling throughout North America, as well as in India, Kazakhstan, and South Africa.

SEE WHERE IT ALL BEGAN . . .THE FIRST PATRICK BOWERS THRILLER.

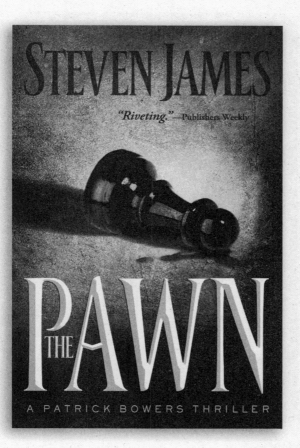

"A must read."
— *TCM Reviews*

MORE ADRENALINE-LACED SUSPENSE TO KEEP YOU UP ALL NIGHT!

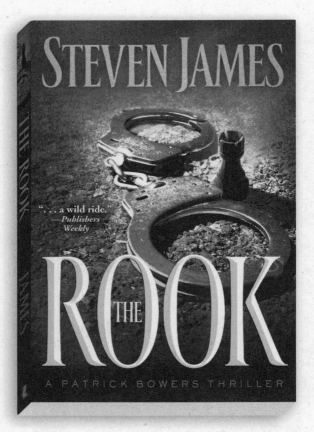

"Best story of the year—
perfectly executed."
—*The Suspense Zone*

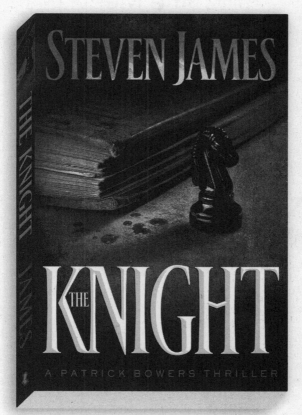

Come Meet

STEVEN
JAMES at

www.stevenjames.net

Learn fun facts about the
Patrick Bowers Thrillers,
sign up to receive
updates, and more.